SAFE HAVENS: PRIMED CHARGE

SAFE HAVENS: PRIMED CHARGE

A SEAN HAVENS BLACK OPS NOVEL

J.T. PATTEN

To Ben ~
Your books are
as entertaining as they
are the bar to achieve.
Hope you enjoy my version
of "the black."
Best,
J.T. Patten
7/30/16

Escape Your Reality Press

J.T. Patten and J.T. Patten Books
Published by Escape Your Reality Press,
A Donovan Black Holdings USA LLC
Naperville, IL 60540

Please visit our website at **www.jtpattenbooks.com** or follow us on Twitter @jtpattenbooks

ISBN-13: 978-0692664292
ISBN-10: 0692664297

This manuscript has been submitted to the Central Intelligence Agency (CIA) Publications Review Board and Department of Defense Office of Prepublication Security Review (DOPSR).

To my children. Sorry, you can't read this one either.

Author's Note

I write fictional stories that exist in the world of characters who work the **shadows of black operations**. That story contains a mix of espionage, some conspiracy. It's a fantasy blend of a lot of things, including military and war. Some liberties have been taken with historical events and personalities. Great strides have been taken to avoid sensitive disclosure.

A lot of readers probably won't know what black ops really entail. After all, it's classified, it's compartmentalized, or it's disavowed. Fewer than one percent of the population has such access. I'm not sharing that access, but do share the reality that the cloaked world isn't a cool fun place with rainbows and unicorns, with happy endings and where things fit nicely into "correctness." It can be soulless, violent, cruel, vulgar, frightening, and have an element of moral ambiguity. Just like my book. It is what it is.

However, if you look deep enough, which I encourage you to do, you will see into the heart, soul, comradery, and trust of these shadow warriors and their families who sacrifice everything for a duty, a belief—and a hope—that they are doing the right thing in their silent service jobs. For themselves. For you.

So, if you want to take a peek into the world of the "black" and the often vulnerable everyday heroes within, follow me and let me show you a seemingly realistic place that rings with authenticity and that few will ever travel to. Those who have simply can't share the actual details but can share a sense of the emotion and conflicts of values.

We live in a dangerous world. Sometimes in order for a nation to thrive or survive, unspeakable things must happen. If you understand that … welcome inside. If not, no worries, take a pass and find a novel that is less dark. Don't dip a toe in the morass hoping for a white towel to clean yourself. Because someone, somewhere, in some shadow is walking into the black so you can have such luxuries of keeping clean far and away.

Sean Havens is such a man. I just tell his tale.

Enjoy!
-JTP

"If an injury has to be done to a man it should be so severe that his vengeance need not be feared."

—Niccolo Machiavelli

"I remembered my many years in Afghanistan and Iraq [fighting insurgents]. We kept decapitating the leadership of these groups, and more leaders would just appear from the ranks to take their place. That's when I realized that decapitation alone was a failed strategy."

—Lt. General Michael T. Flynn (USA-Ret)

Chapter 1

Sean Havens had knocked on the devil's door enough to know that when Old Scratch returned the calling, there'd be hell to pay. And such a price he paid. Incessantly.

Sean lay awake on the basement sofa for the third night in a row. He refused to sleep in the master bedroom, alone. *'Til death do us part* had come to the Havens household too soon. His daughter was recovering far away, adding to the eerie silence of the house.

Cougar, his Belgian K-9, sprawled and pushed to absorb every inch of free couch. Havens' lean six-foot frame was an unlikely contest, both wrestling for comfort atop the leather-upholstered real estate.

An indigo glow from the cable box clock revealed that it was still early. Too early to get up, too early to go for a run, too early to deal with shit.

Havens was supposed to be mission support—intelligence. More brain than brawn. Lately, he was the tip of the spear carrying iron and doling fire. *Murderer.* Innocent lives were lost, and they could be pinned on him. He had been played.

Cougar grunted and was soon snoring again.

Glad you can sleep, old girl. It'll be one of your last nights.

Sean stared at nothing in the darkness above. His muscles still ached from the bruising, adding to his discomfort. Fitful nights eroded his clarity. Sleep was a struggle, reminding him of themes symbolic of War and Death: two of the Four Horsemen of the Apocalypse. Were they seeking atonement or retaliation?

They're going to know I designed those attacks. It's just a matter of time.

Cougar sprung to all fours without warning. She was battle ready. The war dog barked, and the abrupt call to attention startled Havens.

Shit. Now?

Havens fished as fast as he could for his .45 semi-automatic, wedging his hand between the sofa cushions.

Cougar leapt from the furniture and jetted up the stairs in a beeline toward the front door, barking all the way.

Here we go.

Sean was sprinting toward the wall safe for more artillery when the doorbell rang.

Whew. He stopped for a moment and calmed his raging fight or flight instinct. His wild heart rate slowed. Someone was actually requesting permission to enter.

Okay, you're not here to kill me if you ring the damn doorbell at five in the morning. Just wait a minute so I can get myself together. Doubt it's Girl Scouts with cookies.

The bell tone was subtle and melodic; Christina's last purchase while he was overseas. She installed it herself, not wanting to wait a month for his return. Christina Havens. His wife of nearly fifteen years, a speech therapist with Nordic blonde hair. He adored her not just for her captivating beauty but for her wit. And her laugh. Her giggle calmed a warrior's soul, turning a tempest into warm seas. And now she was gone. As was his safe haven.

Havens heard a light rapping knock follow the chime. It was faint and barely audible from the basement with the dog on full volume alert.

Dammit, you wanna come this early, be patient. Or bring donuts. And Starbucks.

Havens rustled through a heap of clothes, groping for his Chicago Blackhawks sweatshirt. He had last seen it on top of the bar, the widower's closet of choice, with his other laundry.

Havens headed toward the staircase, slipped the Glock in the back of his pants, and pulled the black hoodie over his head, the tail end covering the weapon.

The bell rang again.

Jesus, enough already.

The dog barked nonstop.

"Cougar, shut up!" He shifted his attention to the door. "I'm coming. Dammit. Who the hell is even up this early on a weekend?" he interrogated the entrance.

Just outside of Chicago, Death was awake and mounted its steed. The black stallion bore a 5.3L V8 engine and was shod with Goodyear All-Season tires.

A hand covered in a black leather Camelback tactical glove keyed the address into the GPS system—13 South Mockingbird. It was the home of black ops intel asset Sean Havens. Twenty-six miles. ETA forty-three minutes.

Another dark passenger joined in the vehicle and made two. "Kits all in."

The assassins pursued a prize, and Sean Havens was their prey. Yesterday, he was declared a target in the far reaches of the shadowy Internet world. A single notation was made under Havens' name—*Enemy of the people.* What it failed to note was just how many enemies of the people Sean Havens had sent to the grave. Fewer than twenty hours had passed since the notice was posted, vetted, and contracted to the current on-site kill team. Bitcoins paid upon proof of kill or capture.

Death's hot breath warmed the pistons with a turn of the key. The beastly truck roared to life with a deep, guttural awakening.

"Let's do this, man!" The driver threw the truck in gear."

"Roger that, mu-tha-fuck-ah. Gonna get ... me ... some!" the second assassin hooted from the passenger seat. He slapped the dashboard giddily, adding fingertip drum rolls on the molded plastic console, crashing an air cymbal beneath the sun visor.

The driver cranked up the radio. Sirius XM was playing Motorhead's "Ace of Spades."

Both men took long pulls of Wild Tiger "liquid cocaine" energy drink. They fist bumped and nodded, accelerating toward their target's Beverly neighborhood.

Miles away, Havens offered an early morning glass of Dalwhinnie Scotch to the man at his front door, his former CIA recruiter. The two old spies were reacquainting after handshakes and a morning toast. His boss shared the available intel about the hit and expressed concern. Yet Sean Havens, a man fully prepared to die at any time, decided not to run. He'd sooner give Death the middle finger and ready himself to cheat fate.

The burning question for Havens was, simply, *For the devils I know, which weapons are best?*

The assassins wanted blood. More than a decade of war had created opportunities and honed the skills of thousands. For some American operators, the taste of battle was now an addiction—especially the young whose thirst was forged on the battlefields of sand and rough mountains.

Others tried in vain to put combat behind them and retched at the thought of more exposure to direct action—until a time that the warrior beast re-awakened in the mind, coursed through the veins, enveloped the heart, and howled for the longing sights, smells, and sensations attributed to the game of death.

Drew Grace and Ryan Kuhn were the tactical operators preparing to strike the Havens' home. As college graduates, they'd seized the opportunity to enlist in the Army's Special Forces 18-X Recruitment Program, better known as "X-rays" for those who made it in. They fast-tracked in the elite special mission world, and just as quickly, developed their combat experience in Iraq and Afghanistan—eventually moving to Tier One special mission units and finally pulling duty as contractors with OGA's special activities division.

But these young men were not created by the military to be future leaders. They lacked the foundational special operations forces' mindset and big picture vision. Yet they were readily enticed by the promises of adventure and sold on the duty of patriotism to vanquish the world of those who dared attack the United States on that fateful day in September.

As highly trained war fodder, Drew and Ryan traded in dorm room video games for live runners. They counted their man kills now like they had previously tallied sexual conquests.

While the metropolis slept, the unsuspected SUV trolled its final yards to the Havens' address; music killed. Belted rubber treads cracked the iced curbside gutter.

Another set of heavy black vehicles were parked at the residence.

The two young assaulters validated the situation with an exchanged look of mutual indifference. They didn't discuss turning back or driving by for a feasibility recce. It was guns on, safeties off.

Their hearts pounded. Chemicals from the Wild Tiger energy drinks surged through their veins. They tossed questions under their breath: Why were the other black vehicles there? Did the target have armed protection? Were there others inside the home? Children? Drew huffed, "It doesn't matter." One thing the two-man hit team knew for sure—there weren't hundreds of armed Taliban surrounding their position. Anything short of that shit would be Groundhog Day-level routine.

The CIA security detail relaxed in their war wagons while their boss remained inside the house for a closed meeting.

The rushed pre-dawn flight left a slight haze that affected the sharpness of their minds, their eyes splintering pink. Despite Dunkin' Donuts coffees all around, the pasty taste of morning lingered in their mouths.

"Cream and sugar?"

"Nope. Or do you mean those two strippers in Miami?"

"Smartass."

"I'm actually going back down there for the primary debates in March."

"I hate Florida. We just got back from Disney over Christmas. I'm so over hotels. After the election, it'll be interesting to see if this gig gets any better between the chick or the dick."

"We need a Paris or Belgium attack *here* to get things going again."

The men all raised eyebrows at the unsavory but career-beneficial prospects.

One of the more quiet of the team added, "I think we could all benefit from moving up pay grades and 'fighting the good fight' again."

His buddy toasted him with the coffee. "True. Those Paris attacks clearly weren't painful enough for the politicians."

"None of the bureaucrats are taking the risks seriously. Meanwhile, this country has a huge sight target on it."

Few discerned that, in addition to the recent acts of terror across Europe and the United States, some had been a series of events orchestrated by a shadow organization—the Pond—that set up attacks to look like global terror groups, contrived front covers to hide their involvement with proxy pawns, and fractured lives to bolster government spending and political favor. Havens was the latest patsy.

White vapor emitted from the tailpipes. Rear tailgate windows were layered with jabber-made frost over the tempered glass.

The war boys dismounted and positioned themselves on opposite sides of the security vehicles. Through a segment of unfrozen passenger glass, the assassins could see the security detail sipping coffee, reading sports pages, and sending text messages.

The two-man kill team counted down with gloved finger signals. *Three, two, one!*

They rushed forward with an unspoken harmony of movement built from years of operating and training together. Weapons on full-automatic fire shattered glass and slumped men with the first squeeze of triggers.

The rounds were unstoppable, like a sonic metal-clad killer bee swarm engulfing everything in its path. The cone of fire spread a wave of death as the assaulters advanced, killing everything in the zone.

With speed, shock, and violence, the young combat veterans mercilessly decimated the agents.

The federal security element died sloth in complacency, hands in reach of their firearms but a life away from the efficiency, preparedness, and situational awareness that their younger adversaries displayed to the point of easy victory and fierce operational dominance.

With dead govies in the rear, the pair advanced to the home's entrance unscathed. Breath fully intact. Their GTX Salomon tactical boots supported their rapid movement up the icy walkway to the next objective.

Ejecting their magazines, both men reloaded fresh and full.

With another slight nod, the Heckler & Koch G36C tactical rifles' NATO rounds made short work of the Havens family's wooden artisan front door and the forged metal fixtures that secured both its lock and frame.

Empty cartridges discharged and rained to the ground, dancing off the concrete; their bouncing pings inaudible until the competing gunfire ceased for but a moment.

Drew kicked in the ammo-fractured entrance, now a frayed panel of stained and bare wood splinters, pockmarks and holes throughout.

Ryan came up and leapt through the doorway.

The assaulters executed a short sequence leapfrog clear and cover, scanning the Havens' hall and living room, weapons drawn.

Ryan discharged a burst of rounds into the nearby couch, just in case Havens had stolen away for cover waiting to pounce in counterattack.

The point man quick-stepped to his right in harmony with his breach bubba. He covered down on what he hoped would be a dead target. Too easy, but one always held out hope for the good fortune and opportunity of a quick and easy kill who couldn't shoot back.

Drew panned the room. He sprayed another burst at a thin separating wall that divided the entryway and den from the kitchen.

Just as there are skilled warriors, other honed gamesmen exist in the death system. The shadow masters of the intelligence domain were prepared to receive the intruders. They waited patiently; nevertheless, their hearts fluttered as fast as their foes'.

Steady yourself, old boy. It's like riding a bike. What good are you if you can't still do field work from time to time? Jerry, a CIA Cold War relic, remained secretly cached in Havens' hallway closet while quietly spreading the thin oak louvers to steady and rest the borrowed Glock 30 with his aged and frail hands.

The blue gemstone adorning the old man's Yale class ring knocked against the wood door panel as he repositioned himself. Jerry gasped. The dull tap seemed to echo in the silence while the gun rapport paused, if for only a moment. *This is not coming back to me fast enough! Not with this blasted vacuum cleaner poking my ass. Hurry, Sean.*

Jerry was forced to play the hand he was dealt. He prayed for an ace in the hole while he bought Sean Havens time for a basement escape. Jerry was steadfast in his resolve that he would at least die trying to accomplish the feat. The last man Jerry shot was in Russia nearly thirty years ago. Back of a KGB intelligence officer's head, thus breaking Moscow Rules. He had used a much smaller .22 pistol, but Jerry recalled now that it was on a similarly insignificant and frigid winter day.

As the young fighters motioned to spread out, the venerable CIA spymaster steadied his bony, liver-spotted hands with iron will. He held his breath and fired the .45 semi-auto at the intruders.

Crack!

The bullet impact blew Ryan's skull and brain matter into his concealing face mask. Blood sprayed on a family picture of Sean, his wife, Christina, and their daughter, Maggie. Shades of red speckled the canvas like a Jackson Pollock painting. Ryan dropped to the floor like a marionette whose strings had been snipped.

Drew shifted toward the shot's sonic bang origin, willing his eyes from his war mate.

Who the fuck would hide in a closet? Drew was freaking.

Surprise lost.

Drew peripherally saw the muzzle fire come from the thin closet door slat now fractured from the .45's heavy recoil. But it was too late. A tactical error dropped his partner and now threatened Drew's life.

Time froze for both men. Each movement slowed in the mind's eye as the brain processed for muscle memory and trained response.

Jerry was in the winter of his own life and secretly hoped that this would be his good death, one that would carry on the secret legacy he had created as a career intelligence case officer now in his eighties. Few Americans would ever know what he had sacrificed so that they could be safe and free and oblivious to the way the world was really run.

In the split second of his mind's eye, he convinced himself that today was, indeed, not a good day to die for the Agency's covert clandestine service director. And as the oldest serving spy leader, failure would sully his family reputation. Worse, it would smudge his legacy with the Yale society men of Skull and Bones. And that would just not do.

Jerry fired another round.

The gunshot met its target but hit the metal lower of the H&K in the assaulter's grip. It missed vital flesh.

Drew dropped his weapon upon impact.

The recoil jolted Jerry's weak grip. The Glock, like his adversary's, dropped from his hands and thudded in the closet's greyed darkness.

Drew held enough presence of mind to quickly employ a side arm strapped on his thigh in a low-draw holster.

Jerry bent and floundered for his weapon.

What sounded like thunder, then an explosion, came just beyond the closet enclave.

Chapter 2

God bless the Chicago mafia. From a chambered basement room, Sean Havens ripped at the control box wires powering the former homeowner's motorized hidden staircase overhead. He wrenched a ten-inch metal wall lever connected to the emergency release gear. The nitrogen-charged gas springs abruptly heaved a large section of the stairs above like a beastly mouth opening. The monstrous jaws exposed a dark shadowed cavern from within.

Drew held position, dumbfounded, his mouth agape. His grip on the firing hand softened around the side-arm. The muzzle dropped down under the gravity of sheer fear and alarm.

Sean bounded from the black, ascending armed with a Jackhammer combat shotgun.

The Mk3A1 weapon was loaded with all-copper slugs designed to fan upon impact and expand to three-inch warheads. They had been described by the manufacturer as creating holes "big enough to throw a cat through."

Havens nearly stopped when he saw the young armed man before him. *You stupid bounty-hunting kid. You came to the wrong house.*

Sean fired repeatedly at the armed home invader, sending flame and death from the matte black barrel.

The booming jettison of metal punched fist-sized chasms into the young assaulter.

Training be damned, Havens slap fingered the trigger aggressively as he neared his target. The twenty-round ammunition drum fed the custom kill-candy as its wielder commanded.

Blasted shell impacts pitched Drew farther and farther away from Jerry's closet position.

Blood sprayed up, out, and from behind as bone and limbs were ripped and cast from Drew's body by the hot metal's devastating power.

Enraged by a year of violent and emotional turmoil, Havens bellowed, "THIS … HAS … GOT … TO … STOP!"

Within moments he stood over the lifeless intruder's wasted body pulp.

Sean scanned the room for other danger. As he towered over the bloody and broken heap to regard his foe, his lower lip was resolute. *Are there more?* He sensed no.

His heart felt like an incensed caged creature trying to escape by smashing out of the breastbone confines.

Sean Havens squinted his eyes and lowered the still-smoking barrel. His grip was steady under the weight, and he fired another shot where Jerry's .45 mm round had struck the man's weapon. *Yep, big enough for a cat. Meow.* Sean fired again. *Meow, meow.* Havens intended to leave only one weapon as viewable home security evidence. *Just business, boy.*

Police could log the shotgun as self-defense and document the scene as a reasonable means to protect the Havens' household from intruders—again.

More importantly, it would clear Jerry, and thus the CIA, from any blowback of involvement.

"Jerry, you still in there?" Sean called out.

A muffled "Yes," from the closet gave Havens a trifling measure of relief.

"Jerry?"

"Yes, Sean, I'm all right," Jerry said as he opened the battered closet door.

"I heard you, Jerry. Just wanted to say thanks for coming over for breakfast. This is exactly what I had in mind when you came to the door after all these years. Maybe the hordes of Gung Adin can come storming in on horseback before lunch and liven the party up a bit. Famine and Plague have yet to visit me in my nightmares."

Sean cast an eye of dread over the household, assessing the damage. It added to the enormity of his burdens, shame, and disrespect to his late wife's sanctuary. His feet were sticky on the bloodied floor.

It was all because of Havens' operational baggage that the two worlds had collided. It was his domestic world that was destroyed.

Sean sighed, resolving himself to a perpetual life on the razor's edge. He failed at keeping his distinct lives separate. "So it starts again, Jerry. Belay that," he paused. "It never stopped."

"I'm afraid so, Sean. My son, Rick, will be here soon. Anything else on your mind?" inquired his mentor in empathy.

Sean scrunched his face, not quite understanding the question or the timing. "Damn, you're still an awkward dude."

The expression morphed to over-accentuated bewilderment.

"Hmm. What's on my mind?" Havens laughed a mad-man's cackle. "Gee, I don't know, I could go for some pancakes. Hey, was just thinking maybe a nice warm bubble bath." *On the other hand, an interior decorator would be nice.* "Then there's the bloody goopy shit sprayed all over my dead wife's picture. What the hell kind of question is that?" he stormed, wide-eyed.

Like a tank turret, Havens mechanically revolved to the other dead assaulter. Rotating, processing, ready to unleash more hell. He became transfixed by the sprayed mist, the bright red and dark trauma borne by Jerry's shot. The dark blood creep was slowed beneath the head by the cracks in the hardwood floor. *Christina would definitely not approve.*

Havens turned again. "Yep. I want pancakes."

Without compunction, Sean squeezed the shotgun's trigger once more and destroyed further evidence of his mentor's involvement. *That one might have been too close. Trajectory review will show point blank.* He glowered in unmitigated thought. *Whatever. Meow, eff-in' meow.*

"Sean, he's dead," mumbled Jerry.

"Oh, yeah, Jer?" He said sarcastically. "Okay. My bad. Thought I saw him move for a sec. Just a security round." *Kicked your ass, took your gas, punk.* A sardonic smirk broke Havens' clenched jaw. *Haven't heard that in a while.*

"Ah, just cleaning up. You're a real pro," Jerry reinforced through a lie, hoping that Havens hadn't fully transformed to a broken sadist through a career wrought with extreme trauma and violence. Jerry looked at the mix of impact wounds in morbid astonishment. He said nothing more.

"These guys were experienced." The words were dry and Havens seemed lost in myriad thoughts as his eyes flicked and his head revolved around. A radar picking up everything in range. In search of another warning signal.

Jerry tried to bring Havens back to attention and agreed with the obvious statement but added, "Their over-confidence omitted the possibility of when overzealous students might actually face off in combat against their masters."

Havens returned his cognizance and gave Jerry a quizzical look. The statement was profound. True. Contextually, highly accurate. "That's a pretty fancy way of calling them shitheads, Jerry."

"Indeed, Sean. Veritable ... shit ... heads."

"They were war punks. Stupid shooter kids playing high-speed games with the wrong people."

With sorrowful eyes, Jerry observed his former recruit thoughtfully. Jerry considered how the next months would all play out in the game. He was taking a risk on Sean Havens again. Taking a risk on a lot of things. High risks often paid off in dividends. If they didn't wipe you out.

As two generations of intelligence professionals stood together in silence over two of the next generation's warriors, thin white smoke and the aromas of heated metal, gunpowder, plastic, vaporized bullet lubricant, and death, hung in the air.

Old Scratch left appeased, until it was time to knock again.

The former family home was Hell incarnate.

Sean Havens presiding.

Chapter 3

Blessed be the pain, love be the pain.

A harbinger of danger, Paulo Violardo coolly surveyed his surroundings. He stroked his chin's three-day-old greyed whiskers with dissatisfaction. Paulo favored a clean shave routine that also accentuated his Mediterranean olive skin for operational utility worldwide. The beard's texture felt like the coarse goat-hair shirt that he wore while fasting. *Penitence is purity.* Paulo kept his wry smile to himself and muttered inaudibly within the Bangkok club. "You will command, and I will obey. My flesh, my bone, is merely a vessel."

Sitting amidst the crowd with slight alterations of demeanor and disguised as a disheveled tourist, Paulo's role in the reformed Servizio per le Informazioni e la Sicurezza Militare (SISMI) was similarly undetectable. Likewise, no peer of his within the Italian Military Intelligence and Security Service would ever presume that Paulo had yet another secret membership as a Freemason Propaganda Due knight of the ancient underground Sovereign Military Order of Malta.

Paulo thumbed a silent text in the auto-encrypted mobile phone using off-network communication. AMERICANS ARE HERE.

He pushed the burn prompt function on the device display. The message disappeared, destroyed from sight, record, and forensic discovery. Paulo rested the phone on the faux-teak cocktail table. And waited.

The tabletop was barren save for his sweating drink on a condensation-soaked napkin. No books, no souvenirs, nothing that could spur innocuous conversation and the reaches of Murphy's Law. Fate tempted fools to engage strangers—and fought against men trying to remain estranged. Paulo taught this rule to his students of the intelligence craft. Craftsmanship and contingencies saved missions and kept covers in tow.

Paulo awaited the pending message response on his device while sipping a native Thai Beer Chang. He pursed his lips. His tongue licked the backs of his teeth and swam in the effervescence of the bitter lager. He enjoyed the vice drink and savored another lingering taste that hitched a ride on his budding salt and pepper moustache. *Non nobis Domine, non nobis, sed nomini tuo da glorium*, he prayed. Not unto us, O Lord, not unto us, but unto thy Name give glory. Paulo took another sip, relishing what was to come.

The Order enjoyed a legacy of power throughout Europe and the Holy Land vested centuries ago by the Knights Templar and of the Temple of Solomon. This fact was as equally shrouded as the members themselves and their secret society sub-entities that fed to the master organization.

The public enjoyed it as conspiracy theory folklore.

The Order's Propaganda Due cell, or P2, also claimed roots to the Crusades. It was an historic secret society splinter faction of the Freemason Monte Carlo Lodge that initially resided in Italy before spreading worldwide.

The group's alleged misdeeds ranged from gun and drug running to assassinations of politicians and popes. No one could prove it. No one would dare investigate the dark tales. Those who did met suspicious untimely demises. Freemason lodges had autonomy. Most chapters were driven by good deeds and God-fearing honest men. Other lodges had guidance from invisible hands and hidden agendas. P2 had all of that, including active links to the mafia, the U.S. Central Intelligence Agency, foreign militaries, and global intelligence community elites. And today, P2 had Paulo doing its bidding.

The music in the Baccara Go-Go thumped loudly through the sub-woofers. Red and blue strobes pulsed rhythmically to the beat. A hip-hop techno time-warp remix of DJ Rob Base's "Joy and Pain" blared loud enough to seduce prospects walking in the open air market red light district.

The awaited reply appeared on Paulo's Blackphone screen. THAI SURVEILLANCE?

Paulo's thumbs danced on the mobile device keys. YES. AND PERSIANS. NO TO RUSSIANS. He burned the message traffic again.

The bar's patrons ogled the stage dancers, who gyrated to the music mashup.

The girls wore scant naughty-schoolgirl outfits and stiletto high heels. As professional seductresses, they teased the crowd by tugging and lowering their immodest getups to coax interest and to stimulate a release of cash from the deep pockets of lusting men.

Paulo remained transfixed on the slate-colored phone. He pushed down hard on his thigh and gasped in pain, which was quickly assuaged by a surge of adrenaline.

Invisible under the cloth of his pants, and covered with a light gauze wrap to collect trickling blood, a self-made spike chain cilis was tied to Paulo's leg. With more than fifty diminutive barbed hooks twisted in the wire wrap, each push upon the adornment achieved further religious penitence. Unlike Opus Dei, the secretive wannabe religious organization whose members used tiny barbs that produced a low level of discomfort, Paulo's hurt. The medieval-looking metal chain delivered corporal mortification to cause physical pain to a man trained at length to withstand physical discomfort—and torture.

He spoke to himself under breath, "Sanctified be the pain. Glorified be the pain."

Nearly a minute later the text response appeared. STATUS YELLOW. AFTER RUSSIANS SHOW. GREEN. YOU ARE CLEAR. WE ARE THE WAY.

Paulo typed onto the ebony glass screen, NOTHING WITHOUT SACRIFICE. I WILL SEND THEM IN. *It has been good doing business with you, Mr. Passport.*

Devoid of even a curious glance at the strippers on stage, the celibate whispered an invocation to a new world order before leaving the bar, "Novus ordo seclorum." *May the blood of a few spare the blood of many.*

Chapter 4

Neighbors snapped photos from their frosty window panes. Some braved the cold to extend their devices out the door cracks to capture a better image. These would be fantastic Instagram, Facebook, and Twitter contributions, random acts of violence that would surely garner thumbs-up "Likes" and comments galore. *Surely someone else has called 9-1-1,* they rationalized as the lure of social media approvals charmed their egos.

Jerry's son, Rick, slowed his vehicle on approach to the residence. The driveway carnage had to mean it was Havens' place.

He was cautious in the approach.

Neighborhood faces pulled away from the glass to hide from sight. They were safe in their homes if no one saw them. This was Havens' problem, not theirs. The neighbors' thumbs deftly moved from photo to video settings on iPhones and Galaxies. They hoped to capture the action digitally this time, not just the aftermath.

The car's tires crunched tread by tread on the ridged ice below until it ground to a final stop, save for a slight frozen slide to the curb.

A seasoned intelligence case officer with the Agency for more than thirty years, Rick kept a level head. Having survived multiple tours in nasty places with nastier inhabitants, not much surprised him. Still, he knew his dad was at the Havens' house. And that was not good.

Father and son were not bosom buddy tight, but they were blood. That should count for, well, everything. Rick's dad was supposed to be inside with a man who was a target to an indiscernible number of suitor assassins.

He surveyed the scene, probing his own body for a firearm. It wasn't there before. It wasn't there now.

Dad, if you are still alive in there, I'm sure you won't mind waiting a few more secs so I roll in a bit heavier.

Rick did a quick assessment and brief site exploitation of the dead, hoping to find not signs of life but an automatic weapon to borrow.

Blood was frozen on the dash and within the spider web of the cracked window from the gusting bite of sub-zero wind-chill that ripped across the Windy City.

Rick heard distant sirens. *Hope you have your Homeland Security ID, Dad, whether you're dead or alive.* It wouldn't be good to try pulling off the old CIA relic excuse. That caused phone calls and phone calls got people involved who should not be involved in anything other than upscale DC lunches and ineffective inter-agency saber rattling.

No. Certainly no one would want to know that the covered old man, Director of Operations, was running domestic ops today. In Illinois, no less. Slightly out of authority and jurisdiction by a mere country. Rick had chastised his dad before, despite being outranked by a senior CIA official, for wanting to alert Havens in person to potential danger. "You owe that guy nothing, and you're clearly walking straight into danger," Rick had cautioned. *And here we are. Shit show central.*

Rick crouched low as he moved tactically up the walkway to the front door. Rationale had told him coming to Chicago was a stupid idea. Last minute. No plan. No clear picture of the threats. The dead proved his instincts.

Jerry and Havens exited the ruptured doorway to assess casualties out front. Both knew the scene would be grim.

Rick whistled an exhale of relief that his head told him to stand fast while his gut had said, "FIRE, FIRE, FIRE," at anyone who exited the home from the winter shadow-draped entryway.

"You all right, Pop? Everything okay?" Rick asked with his gun trained on Havens. Rick's finger was directly touching the trigger. Safety was not a protocol in this situation.

"Oh, yes, I'm … well, we're okay. How's about these poor lads? We suspected the worst."

"Smoked, Pops. All gone. Not a shot fired on their end. Sitting ducks. Useless as tits on toast. How many did you guys take out inside?"

Jerry bowed his head solemnly with a slight wobble for remorse. "Poor boys here were protecting me."

"Yeah, well they didn't do much and lost their lives because of *him*." Stone-faced, Rick's eyes bore into Havens with utter disdain. "You need to get inside, Pop. The peanut gallery surrounding us is taking a lot of pictures. You don't want to end up tagged."

Jerry said nothing but sunk his head some to avoid direct visibility for a facial capture.

"Long time, Rick."

"Sean-fuckin'-Havens. Here we are again. Still a disaster spun by ego and recklessness, huh? And my dad and I are here to bail you out."

Looks like you didn't bring donuts either.

"Rick, that'll be about enough. You know the situation here. Be fair," Jerry scolded the grown man as if he were still a boy.

Jerry added, in the tension of the silence, "You've had your share of losses over the years, Rick. I think it's best if we go in before the authorities arrive so we can have a quick chat. There were two men who came in the home and who been dispatched accordingly by myself and Sean."

"Dispatched. Huh. You can say 'killed,' Dad. Yale might say dispatched, but the rest of the world, which includes your flesh and blood, calls it like it is."

Jerry ignored his son's comment. His son had always dismissed upper-crust refinery. And the Ivy League opportunities that could have come with it. "Come inside, Rick. I've seen enough out here. Sean, is there anything you need to see?"

Havens remained silent, attentive, and waited for Rick to ease his finger off the trigger. *Quit with the trigger on the finger act, tough guy. Between me or you getting shot, that's a no brainer, on my end.*

"I'm afraid I must go in." The old man turned, seeking warmer refuge in the war-ravaged house.

"Put down the gun, Rick. You might *kill* somebody," Jerry feebly uttered without turning back around.

Rick brushed it off, "We don't all have to be shooters, Jerry." *Asshole.*

Havens stood his ground.

Rick similarly remained ready to engage, ignoring the recommendation.

Some neighbors came outside but didn't stray from their sanctuary. They gawked at Sean and the gunman. More pandemonium at the Havens' house. Disaster of the year.

When would the police arrive? the residents wondered.

Havens ignored the neighbors—as usual. He tried to calm Rick, who he knew was all bravado. But bravado with a finger on the trigger nonetheless. "Rick, Jerry has a point about that thing staring at me. I'm no threat to you."

"Is it making you uncomfortable?"

"You're just in the middle of a long line of people who have been pointing guns at me, Rick. Not the first, not the last. Thing is, they have the balls to pull the trigger if they're going to point it at me. What kind of balls do you have?"

"Is that what you want me to do? You think it's wise to challenge my authority here and now?"

"I really don't give a shit," Havens answered matter-of-factly. He lacked even a hint of concern.

For the first time, Rick noticed that Havens had a hand in the pocket of his Blackhawks hoodie.

"Guessing a mini hockey stick isn't what's pressed out on your sweatshirt."

"Nope. But *my* finger is off the trigger."

It had been more than twenty years since Rick ran Sean through an initial mini-selection process for the CIA while Jerry deliberated Havens' ongoing selection and recruitment.

Sean sized up Rick, who had aged well over the years.

Rick, now in his mid-fifties, maintained the chiseled jawline. His age only showed in the grey in his short, wavy hair and wrinkles near his ears. The spook wore grey chinos and shined leather shoes with rubber Vibram soles for traction. Rick's black car coat met both style and tactical requirements. He was squared away for an intel guy; a playboy operator who fancied himself as a modern-day James Bond "Double O." He liked guns and looking tough, but had never been in a scrape, much less a gun battle of any kind. Still, Rick trained to fit the impression he had of himself.

Sean aspired to be as squared away at some point in his career—even though he too was nearly twenty years in.

Havens relieved his weapon in the confines of the pocket and extended his hand to Rick. The younger Sean Havens harbored a mutual degree of ill will. In reality, sour grapes had led to Havens not being more embraced and nurtured by Rick in the early years, as some of Sean's earlier law enforcement mentors did for him. But Rick practiced government-style arm's length leadership. Don't get too close to the guy who could replace you.

"Rick. I get it," Sean acknowledged. "This shit all around you here is just aftermath of something that is beyond me. I could really use your help. I'm not saying I'm a different guy, but I'm more experienced, more seasoned, and this shit is beyond any man. At least, it's beyond me. I've got nowhere else to go."

Rick directly gave Havens a last hard look. What he was looking for, he didn't know. He knew the situation and knew Havens had been a pawn in a game that was destined to have big-time losers.

The man standing before him now looked like absolute shit but certainly carried himself a lot differently than he had than during the collegiate years when Sean was a young recruit being evaluated by Rick. Rick passed him on to the next steps, but that didn't mean he wanted to work with him.

Back then, Rick saw Havens as a potential career threat down the line. Now, however, he saw the man that Jerry knew he was to become. A hard-edged intel asset. Rick no longer felt a competitive threat. Havens brought success. Those working with him brought body bags for the casualties that came with his work.

Rick recognized that his dad was spot-on regarding recruits. This could work after all. If Havens could withstand all that he had endured without being a crazed whack-job, he could be the perfect man for the job. The question was, what level of crazy was Havens clocking in at? There was a big difference between stories told within the text of a Top Secret compartmentalized file and the man who stood before Rick now.

Rick extended his hand in forced solidarity. "This isn't a parole board hearing, Havens. I hate Chicago winters. Freezing my nuts off. Don't want to catch our death out here."

Havens forced a smile.

"Jeez, I sound like my dad. Let's move it in."

Havens wasn't sure if he could put his life, and, more importantly, his daughter's protection, in the hands of this man. But what choice did he have?

"You're eyes look like you've drunk every last drop of booze in Chicago," Rick tested.

"I don't sleep much. The scotch on the table inside was at your dad's request this morning. So don't ask me again. I'm clean. I'm no cliché of whatever I may look like to you."

Earlier that day, Jerry had stated that Rick would take Havens into the CIA again, but more formally this time. The job would provide healthcare to Sean's convalescing daughter. Patriotism was pay for soldiers, healthcare benefits were the reality requirements of a single dad.

Havens had few choices and had to give it a shot. Meeting halfway, at least initially, worked for his daughter's sake. "Come on in, Rick. Sorry, but the cleaner stepped out. And watch your step. Your dad made some spills."

Dismissing the morbid humor, Rick right-steered the conversation. "Whole thing's a mess, Sean. I think we need to call in some favors quick and get you cleared from this debacle. You need exoneration, pronto, especially if we're bringing you in from the cold. So to speak. I've already used up all the shoulders I have looking behind me for bad shit. I'm too old for your baggage too. Hell, I'm too *young* for your baggage. I'd like to live through the year at least. Someone must really hate you."

"Yeah, lately it seems that way."

Cougar heard Sean and came back upstairs with a series of small whimpers. The Malinois flopped down by her master's feet, ignoring the horror show around her. First shots had sent her to the basement cowering. Sean gave his Belgian veteran K-9 a pat of reassurance, knowing the dog's prior war trauma.

Sean saw Rick admiring the dog. "My only friend is a rescued PTSD dog. Two fucked-up traumatic stress disorder peas in a pod. Pretty soon, I won't even have the dog." Havens groaned. "Cougar was retired and passed around but her ex-handler tracked her down to me. I gotta give her up. I'm sure the soldier has seen his share of shit too. Seemed best not to fight giving her up if it would help someone else." Havens stroked the dog and scratched around her ears. "Never wanted her in the first place. Now it feels like I'm giving up my own child."

"Well, pretty much sucks to be you," said Rick, moving on and examining the raised staircase. "Yeah, friggin' pathetic story, but I like your decorator. This thing is right out of *The Munsters*. Just need Smog the dragon." Rick took a closer look at the spring lever, nodding with approval. Sean Havens was resourceful. And a fifty-pound head. Just what they needed. If they could break him of some habits. Others they would count on being unbreakable.

Havens shrugged. "Got the place in a bank bid. My cop brother-in-law turned us on to the auction. Owner was a former mob heavy man. I upgraded the hardware. First time I ever used it aside from showing it off to some friends. Wife thought it was stupid and wanted me to take it out. I held ground saying it could be good for an emergency."

"Hmm," Rick approved. "Well, glad to hear you wore the pants. Good news is I think whoever stuck this bounty on you did it as an afterthought. Probably to buy time. Maybe personal. Maybe cleaning up loose ends. We pretty much know who did it, based on our intel. Dad picked up on it with his channels, but the rest of the community probably isn't buying that you really committed terrorist acts. Or they haven't heard anything. Don't think you'll be on the news as some stereotypical rogue operator, so your aspirations of being as cool as Mitch Rapp or Bourne are dashed.

Should be pretty easy to put to rumor or accusation to rest, but you might have a few of these freelancers still on your ass." Rick continued with hardly a breath. "But we need to get you out of here so we don't all end up dead."

Shit. Shit. Maggie! Abruptly, Havens started scurrying around. "Rick, I need to make a call right away. I need to reach my brother-in-law."

Rick watched, completely entertained. He knew. "If it's about your daughter, I already have someone on it in Arizona."

Still rummaging around the room, Havens remained focused on finding a phone. "Yeah, been through that before." He stopped. "How would you know where …?"

Rick raised his hand to deflect the question. "*Puleeze*, Havens. You're back with the big boys. We always know where you are. And in this situation, we know where your daughter is too. It's what we do. Even on home turf." Rick strolled into the kitchen, stepping over a body. "Hey, you got any fresh coffee?"

"Sounds to me like you should already know if I do, and where it is."

"This is going to be really testy until I can keep you beat down to your rightful place, Havens."

"If I was in my rightful place, Rick, we wouldn't be having this conversation. Would we?"

Chapter 5

As Paulo exited the club, a Thai hostess meandered grudgingly to the secluded back alcove of the nightclub. No doubt the stoic, burly bearded patrons sitting at a rear table would want another round of drinks.

Tips were normally bountiful in the posterior shadows of the building. Waitresses were not opposed to the touching and groping that seemed permitted where scant light annulled house rules. These five Westerners did not appear to be interested in the women. They wanted drinks, and they wanted their drinks fast— and frequent.

The waitress sensed that these men were the dark, silent soldiers of America. Such warriors had no interest in her. Three types of Americans drank at the Thai club: loud and grabby tourists, loud and grabby soldiers, and the quiet ones who wanted to be left alone.

Before the Americans at the rear table reached for the swill, one man pushed a lone sacred bottle into the middle of the circle of guarded beers. After the bottle was revered with a moment of reflection and mumbled words, each man grabbed his own beer. They hoisted the drinks to the center with a curt nod of heads and bottles.

The silence was broken only by the somber tone of the soldier who pushed the lone bottle. "To Eric," he toasted.

They all responded "To Eric," in deep, solemn unison. Less than twenty feet away, but closer to the open club floor, two members of the country's nearly dozen Thai intelligence agencies intermittently lost focus of their surveillance targets amidst the near-naked wiggling distractions.

The Thai spook's "marks" at the backroom table were foreign to Thailand and considered U.S. friendlies, but still required vigilant observation. Thai superiors wanted to ensure that no American covert source ops were transpiring on Thailand's sovereign soil without proper political coordination—and due respect to this host nation.

Everyone affiliated knew it was a game. A game played 'round the world between spy agencies and their allies. It was assumed by the Thais that the American's were running assets in the country, but the factual answers were locked down by yet another Thai intel group that wasn't sharing what they knew. So much for coordination and respect. But if it were coordinated and overt, it wouldn't be called spying.

The tier one American joint special operations teams that came in country to train and advise often gave their surveillance watchers the slip before settling in to an establishment for food, drink, or sleep. Today, hired street paver eyes informed on the U.S. ops team. These soldiers were not easy to miss, nor were they trying to be discreet. They had no interest in the cloak and dagger game at this time, nor did they care about counter surveillance in this semi-permissive operating environment.

Two young raven-haired Thai strippers approached the street clothed soldiers' table when the waitress left. If the girls were even seventeen years old, it would be a stretch. They slinked over to the table pushing their boobs out to some men and their butts out to the others. The young women rubbed their hands on the men's shoulders and necks, hoping to join the party and solicit business for later.

"You won company, boys? Some party, party?" one underage dancer purred. She tried to force her hand through the shirt buttons of the man closest to her but was rejected. "Boom, boom?"

"No thanks, toots. Private party. No 'won'!" He shook his head. He remained in disbelief at the girl's young age, despite it being so believable here in Soi Cowboy, and in so many other foreign lands that the men had traveled before.

"Hey sweetie, try the table over there." The soldier pointed to the Thai spooks and gave the girl a handful of local Baht monies.

"Go sit on their laps." It could be fun to watch Thai intelligence react to the solicitation.

The small, playful act gave a little levity and broke the table's gloomy mood.

The soldier who had placed the lone beer bottle in the center now retrieved it with his left hand. He took a pull and passed the honor drink to his right. Each man took a swig and passed the bottle around until it returned back home drained empty.

"Danny-boy. You go next."

"Roger that. Glad to be away from the Zamboanga station. Screw the jamma-lamma ding-dong mission," he said, referring to the designated terrorist group Jemaah Islamiyah, or JI.

"JI targeting is shit." The soldier slouched down a bit in his chair as he took a pull. With a hard swallow he forced, "You just know those guys we smoked were Abu bandits. I don't know who's saying they're guerillas or AQ affiliates. They're all just working for cash. Al Qaeda, ISIS, my ass."

"Doesn't matter, man. Not our play. Filipino 15th Strike Wing can take all the credit they want. We lay low. I sleep fine at night. Silent service, baby."

The team nodded and drank their beer in the relative silence of their circle; the music played on as they anticipated two more rounds in tribute before moving on for the night.

"It's what we signed up for," a teammate validated.

"Not me," groaned another, who was clearly among the disenfranchised of the Unit's saber squadron troop.

The team had lost the absent comrade, Eric, only a month before this short deployment and their hearts still hung heavy from his death and departure from Delta.

"Pat, don't tell me you're checking one of those chicks out. You've been trance-like for the past few minutes." He pressed further to elicit some response. "Which one'r you scoping?"

Before he could answer, another added, "They're too damn young, man."

Still no response.

Silence elicited more convincing. "Patty, you know better. It's been three weeks in the sticks, but you probably have a kid somewhere that age. Just shake one off in the rack instead. Or find one at Tilac's club." He paused for a sec and contemplated. "And, if you strike out there, we can head to the other districts. Get a sweet Russian or Uzbek in Soi 3 or 4 neighborhoods. All good if you just keep your mouth shut so they don't know you're a Yankee and go reporting to their bosses on us." He would have kept babbling, but saw he was now getting the start of a reaction.

Pat responded to the badgering but retained focus. "Shut-the-fuck-up," he hissed. "I'm checking out those dudes. And no one calls us Yankees except you and your hillbilly inbred cousins."

"Dudes? Oh, perfect," he said, leaning in to Pat, and whispered, "Who's the lucky guy you're gunna ask to dance? Hot lady-boy?"

Still fixated, Pat replied, "We may ask 'em all to dance. Check 'em out. Table five over my '3.' Front corner, kinda tucked away like us. Whaddya you see?"

"The Thai spooks?"

"Nooo." He gestured his head slightly and, with only his eyes, directed his teammate just a bit further. "My '3.' Just past the spooks."

"I marked 'em," confirmed another man on the team. Danny, the youngest of the group, could do a Where's Waldo? anomaly search in a second, and was now discreetly checking out the possible bogey. Danny was the team's natural Intel guy, even though it was not his primary Military Occupational Specialty or team role. "They Iranian?"

"I'm guessing yeah."

Pat leaned in a bit and hissed, "Al, you dumbass, don't stare right at 'em."

"Chill. I'm not. I'm looking over my bottle when I drink," responded Al, the team's Neanderthal breacher.

"That's your fourth pull in about half a minute. Little better FTC, if you please," scolded Danny.

"Don't bust on my field tradecraft, bro, I'm total stealth. Ninja mode. Go, go gadget beer. They can't make us out anyway back here." Then he popped. "Shadows," he trilled effeminately while making a jazz hands gesture.

"Bro, you did not just do that."

Al then moved the hoisted bottle in front of his eye and peered through the obscured glass jokingly, thus demonstrating on yet another evening his lower alcohol tolerance than the rest of the team.

Needing the adrenaline downtime, Al tried to sway his mates from thinking there was danger present. He wanted to party and switch off for the night. "I think they're just videotaping the girls and having drinks. Smuggle it back to Tehran and put it on a VHS tape for the mullahs to spank off to. Dude, there's lots of Iranians near our hotel. Who gives a shit? Let's just drink. We earned it."

Dave sucked his cheek in, thought, then nodded his head in disagreement. "No, they've been taping the crowd. And taping the room. I watched the bartender fill their glasses. I'm guessing with apple juice or something similar. It's not booze. They want it to look like scotch."

"Dude, maybe they don't drink," Al persisted.

"Duh. They're Muslim," said Danny rolling his eyes like a sassy teenager.

With similar exaggeration, Al, rebutted, "Duh, then why try to blend in? Why tape the crowd?"

Danny recognized the futility of argument. He was still subtly scanning the Iranians. "I hear ya, bro, but military type wristwatches, nice clothes, and a wad of cash on the table. Guys with the short hair, slick duds, and all the other things that don't look right, isn't working for me. A regular unemployed Iranian twenty-something isn't going to have that look or that kind of money to be rolling on the town in Bangkok unless, maybe, it was Nawruz. That's their version of New Year. Gross departure rate for that demographic is too low. Someone is bankrolling them. Watch them scan. They're military, too."

"You're friggin' Intellipedia," smirked Al. "Dork."

"I see it, dude," said Dave. "IRGC. I'll bet Qods force. Think they're live ops or just tradecraft field training?"

Pat shifted his chair slowly to get a better scan. "I copy what Danny is saying. We did some advance work on the hotels before you guys came in. Iranians that are at the Marriott, Hyatt, and the other biggie hotels are more affluent than these boys. The less-affluent Iranians in this age range stick to the northern half of the city. Soi Nana or Soi Arab between Sukhumvit 3 and 5 roads. North Nana area if they were buying or doing drugs or hanging out with Russians."

"Right," said Danny. "Around that area they'd be staying at the Grace Hotel or Galaxy. These guys are more squared away. Fit the middle profile, which is government and military. But these guys are definitely NOT govies."

Pat's eyes widened. He addressed the team under his breath but audibly as he competed with the club noise. "Dudes, did you just see who else entered the picture? Slowly to your right, off my ear."

"Yep, I did. Damn Ivans." Danny was now swiveled a bit to the right looking at two new patrons who entered the club. These characters were quite different from their former spots.

"Let's kill these beers and slip out the back. Nothing good can come of this," warned Pat, wiping his palms on his jeans. "We don't need exposure."

The two new customers now seating themselves had shaved heads, tattooed hands and neck tattoos that were just visible above their black leather jacket collars. Based on the bar's current occupants, they appeared to be of Slavik origin.

"Hold one, Pat," Danny countered. "Guys, those are the two mugs we saw over by Pattaya Beach. We saw them the other day when we were doin' surveillance runs by Club Tony and the Marina Club."

The Eastern European thugs appeared on edge. Restless. They scanned their surroundings with both scrutiny and heavy stink eye. First the Iranians were spotted. Next, the Thai intelligence men.

"Aaand now everyone is looking at each other. Awesome," Dave said coolly to keep high-speed boys in low-speed gear. "Thais see what's going on too. Chill, everyone. They seem a little freaked. They're going to bounce and bolt."

"Uh, guys, we've been marked," Pat interrupted. The men looked at Pat and then over at the Iranians, who were looking at the team, who were now being looked at by the Russians. The four-way exchange of glares made all parties very uncomfortable.

The Iranians were the first to blink and made a call on a handset.

The Russians were next.

The Thais remained frozen in fear and looked to the Americans for direction.

Two Caucasian men entered the club. They both sported linen sport coats and carried backpacks. They separated.

Pat watched them with curiosity, but only for a moment. The men moved with resolve. Together, but not. To Pat, they looked more like New York City bouncers than … well, than anything that he was currently seeing in the club. He caught Dave repositioning himself and Danny made a movement. *Chill.*

Danny pushed the empty bottle to the middle of the table and tapped it on the lip with his beer bottle in final tribute. The team did the same and finished their beers.

The four groups continued to assess the situation and chatter amongst themselves.

Pat found it odd that they had all converged on the same bar. His team was given the local recommendation casually from a local Special Operations Command Pacific Navy SEAL whom they bumped into earlier in the day, as chance as that was. Given the situation now, perhaps it wasn't so random. Pat glimpsed the two white men who last entered the go-go. They rejoined one another and left the club with the same air of purpose. No communication between them. Americans? *Focus. One situation at a time. No threat.*

"Eric, we'll catch up with you later," toasted Danny to memory of his mate. "We've got some business to attend to. Just hope we don't get PNG'd from the country when this goes down. I assume none of you guys are carrying?" he lied faking responsibility. Declared persona non grata, or unwelcomed, due to international incidents would not fare well in their personnel files.

"Well, I've got a biscuit in my boot. Shorty .38," said Pat.

"Blackjack sap and CQC for me," stated Al, finally convinced of the threat. Plus, getting in a fight was as good as getting drunk or laid. He'd love to try out his new Emerson CQC knife.

"Got my Emerson Horseman and a coil baton," said Mike, who had been sitting silently, soaking it all in. He now toyed in his pocket the knife's opening feature.

"Same for me, I got some toys," replied Danny, checking his body for assurance.

"Ah, shit. Here we go. Time to lift and shift. Our first aim is to just get out. These are not targets. Talk first, kill last."

"Uh, yeah. Sure," smirked Al, eyeing the prize.

Like wild cats ready to pounce, the men prepared themselves for conflict.

Pat leapt from his chair in a moment of clarity. "The bags!" He beheld his brothers in horror. "Get down!" he screamed.

A split second of surprise and alarm prefaced three detonations overtaking the club and its entryway.

The carbon and nitrogen atom-based explosions were simultaneously time chained for detonation. Within milliseconds, flashes of light and fiery gases emanated into and out of the club. The paramount eruption began in the center, popping the go-go's ceiling with an immense force that blasted from the sides of the structure, then drew in the night's air from smashed and now exposed partitions of the club and its rooftop.

The blaze of high-velocity oxygenated flame walls engulfed the club while projectiles and the effective energy in the reaction zone tore apart everything in their path. The concussion and force of the detonation collapsed the remainder of the beam and the gable covering on top of the patrons, adding to the burnable material that consumed all from within.

Billows of black smoke arose from the blast wreckage below, an amalgamation with the night sky.

Two men walked casually on the crowded street nearly three blocks from the destruction. They hesitated upon hearing the explosion and looked back in the bearing of the sound as a tapering concussion wave embraced them. Both feigned astonishment for any cameras that might be capturing surveillance footage. Their eyes met Paulo's.

Twenty feet away, with the break of a grin, Paulo Violardo gave a slight affirmation to the contracted men of the Pond, another mutually interested discrete affiliate group. An operational marriage of convenience. Paulo drew up his hands, steepling his fingers and extending his thumbs to a meeting point that constructed a triangle.

"No ideal becomes reality without sacrifice. It is so beautiful to become a victim," he muttered to himself.

Paulo let fall his hands to pant sides and pressed the cilis barbs deeper into his skin, sucking air to bear the pain before spiritual ecstasy followed his act of devotion.

The blood oozed under the light gauze wrap.

J.T. PATTEN

Chapter 6

Lars Bjorklund sped away from his new Arizona dream retirement house off Camelback Mountain. Hitting eighty miles an hour, he raced to the Scottsdale Mayo Clinic to secure his recovering niece, Maggie, from any threats.

Who was he kidding? With family like Sean Havens, retirement from the Chicago Police Department was going to be too stressful and too dangerous to remain idle. Lars had learned this quickly over the past month and most recently as sniper bullets whizzed past his head in the comforts of his own kitchen.

Fortunately, the kill shot ammunition was discharged by Sean feigning the assassination. It was an attempt to draw out and validate another accomplice in Christina Havens' death. Red Peterson. And now Red was dead.

When the phone rang this morning, Lars knew it was going to be another unpredictable day of unsafe Havens. He was thankful that Maggie was safe from any current harm while recovering from brain trauma. She had survived the attack that killed Christina, Lars' only sister and Sean's wife. Maggie remained a moral compass and symbol of hope for both men to hold on to as they coped with the loss of their loved one.

Lars punched number four on the CD counsel. Buddy Guy's guitar riffs would get him to Mayo even faster.

Crap, it's Sunday. A creature of habit, Lars Bjorklund hit number three on the display. Sunday is for Lonnie Brooks. *We mustn't jinx the day.*

By the time Lars arrived, there were covertly armed heavies near his niece's hospital room. Looking around the ward, Lars noticed that another goon was in the darkness of a room proximate to the elevators.

What now, Sean? These guys aren't cops, Feds, or secret service. You aaare trouble.

Despite Lars' hulking Nordic physique, the man at Maggie's door demanded ID with firm resolve and assertive posture. It meant stretching up a bit.

A nurse left Maggie's room and, in passing, acknowledged knowing Lars as she continued to her station, annoyed with the inconvenient presence of these rough men.

Lars peeked his head into the room. "Hi, Sunshine!"

"Hi, Uncle Lars."

"How ya doing today, little lady?"

"Mmm. It's still bright, and my eyes still hurt in the back. I did good on my tests today, but the doctor says he wants to talk to Dad about something he says is 'interesting,' but nothing I should worry about."

Maggie was starting to gain a little bit of weight back and had decided to shave her head fully until everything came back evenly. She wore a Northwestern University Lacrosse hat that made her gaunt and frail body look like a boy undergoing chemotherapy. "Uncle Lars, is everything okay? Is my dad okay?"

"Yeah, kiddo. You and your dad are okay. Boy, you sure are talking better." Lars hesitated a moment. He was concerned about the news he had and debated whether sharing it would cause Maggie more emotional distress. She was having a good day, from what he could tell.

Maggie read him like a book. "Spill it. I'm good."

"I just didn't want to upset you. Someone came back to your Chicago house and there was a break-in of sorts. Your dad is going to pack up your things. You guys need to move where you can still get better and see specialists, and your dad can get some work."

"We have to move?" Maggie shook her head in disbelief. "What about Mom? We can't just leave her. Her grave." Maggie curled her lip and tightened it as she struggled not to cry. She winced from the head and eye pressure pain. The pain increased in intensity from the gunshot trauma that left her comatose months before. Complications and additional surgeries to repair neurologically damaged areas left her tender and numb in other areas of her body.

"Kiddo, if I thought your mom was anywhere but with us, I wouldn't have moved here to Arizona, would I?"

The young teen wiped her nose and eyes with the backs of her hands and forearms. Lars got up to find a tissue.

"Hey, so what did the doctor think was so interesting? Did he tell you?" Lars inquired, bringing a handful of rough hospital tissues to his niece.

Maggie smiled and gave an impish shrug as if withholding a deeply guarded secret. She took the tissue as a gesture of appreciation. "They think I am kind of a freak with learning now. Hippo ... hippocampus ..."

"Acceleration."

"Yeah." She cocked her head, wondering how her uncle pulled that word out of nowhere.

"I would have gotten that. But yeah, hippocampus acceleration is what one of them said. Can't believe I remembered that, but guess they have been saying it enough."

Lars grinned to affirm her good news. "I think the hippo part is all that I would remember.

Lars, who was a forensic investigator with education in pathology and his own knack for learning, nodded in understanding. "Heightened short- and long-term learning." He had done his own research on the powers of the mind and had begged his brother-in-law to allow him a small indulgence while his niece was recovering in an unconscious state.

Maggie disagreed. "They say I know the basics of some stuff I never learned, like a language. They quizzed me on Russian and I knew a little bit of what they were saying. It was so cool. I couldn't speak it but I understood what I heard, and could repeat it. I've been getting some math problems right too."

Lars tapped his fingertips and pursed his lips, looking to his left and right with raised eyebrows. He shrugged his shoulders and nodded. *Sean, guess you and I were right about stimulating the brain while she was in her coma.* "Well, that's pretty great news, kid. You sit tight here while I talk to the doctors a bit about transport paperwork. You're going on a plane, and I'm gonna see if I can come with and help you out some more."

"Okay."

"You really all right? I know it's a lot of change lately. That's hard."

As Lars moved towards the door, Maggie pulled him back. "Uncle Lars?"

"Yeah, kid?" He looked back.

"I know you were a cop, and Mom said Dad did global risk consulting stuff."

"Detective, but right. What gives?" *Don't go there. Please don't go there.*

"What does my dad really do? He isn't like some assassin or something bad, is he? I'm just trying to figure this all out."

You went there.

"That's a conversation for the two of you. I can say that he's pretty much just a guy trying to keep people like us safe. I'll be back in a bit, and we can talk more."

Maggie wrapped her arms around her tiny body. Her hunch was confirmed. The travel, the stuff she found in the no-go area of the basement. All the secrets and his toy staircase. The paperwork for an updated background check and a letterhead request for a periodic polygraph. Dad was in the CIA. And it got her mom killed.

"Uncle Lars, one more thing." Her tone had changed. This was something deeper.

I gotta get out of here. Lars regarded his niece and held her eyes in a stare-off.

Maggie winced.

Lars was unsure if she was experiencing physical discomfort or if she was really troubled. He waited patiently for her to continue.

Maggie wrapped the bed sheet around her finger. She had done that since she was a toddler. It could be with her shirt, a blankie, or a string, whenever something was bothering her. When she started speaking, she kept her head down, looking at the sheet as it tightened around her finger.

"Did my mom have an open casket at the funeral or were things just ... I mean, could they, like, *fix* her so she was pretty and peaceful?"

A mental picture of Lars' kid sister dead in a coffin all but took the air from his lungs. He inhaled into his nostrils and gave an enduring exhale. "Sweetie, it was a closed casket. I never saw her. I'll be frank. I've seen a lot of bad things and I can put that somewhere in my brain all tucked away, but I couldn't bring myself to see your mom."

He paused to make sure she didn't have anything else to say, and remained attuned to her reactions. It was safe. She was handling it well. "I couldn't view her for no other reason than her being my little sister. Your dad's FBI friend, Red, identified her while your dad was away." Lars knew Red was now dead. A traitor. Killed by Sean a few hundred meters from Lars' home. "Anyway, we decided that a closed casket was best for everyone to remember her. I know that right now, she is as beautiful as ever. I think we all said goodbye to her in our own way."

Maggie sniffed loudly. She looked up at her uncle with welled tears that cascaded in rivers down her cheek. Neither attempted to wipe them. Instead, Lars sat down on the hospital bed, making a big creaking sound. He wrapped his long arms around his only niece. He nestled her gaunt body, bringing her in close to him.

"If this bed breaks, we might both end up in a coma," Maggie joked.

The two chuckled, forcing a bit more of a laugh than the situation warranted. The alternative was more reflection and resurfacing the silent pain.

"Know what else I miss?"

"Huh?"

"Milwaukee. National Bakery and Deli éclairs. Wouldn't that taste good?"

"Oh my gosh. Uncle Lars. Ham on rolls from there, too. Mom loved ..." Maggie stopped.

Lars' arms already engulfed his niece with his massive frame. He squeezed her tight. Secure. "Your mom sure did love them. She could eat three of them in one sitting. I miss her tons."

"Me too."

Silence filled the room with memories of Christina Havens running through their hearts and minds. Silence also brought up the repeat question of late. Where was Sean Havens when his family needed him?

Chapter 7

Sean Havens tossed the last firearm into his tucked-away basement vault. He'd see what else needed to be cached before closing it up while the cops checked out the place. He slid the wall panel behind a cable-suspended etched mirror that hung over the bar and regarded himself in the mirror for a moment before running back upstairs. His face was haggard. His eyes sunken and red.

You look like shit. You look like you feel.

If it wasn't for the routine high body count coming from the Havens' house, it would almost be a joke for police to be dispatched to the location yet again. With increased rumor of Sean Havens being a person of interest in national terrorist events, tension was high as the officers converged on the scene.

To most of them, Havens was a decent guy who was on the receiving end of the violence in his home. If he was guilty of planning the acts of terror, surely someone would have brought him in. From their perspective, Havens was just a traveling business guy and no threat to society unless, of course, you lived next door to him. The past months saw a lot of activity in this otherwise quiet neighborhood. That house was bad news.

Each call to the residence revealed a serious crime and often a body or two. Only a select couple of trustworthy Chicago detectives knew the truth about Havens. They were friends who wouldn't say a thing.

The 9-1-1 call had reported multiple gunshots heard by a neighbor and a description of black SUVs in the driveway. Some officers assumed that Havens had put up resistance and there was a shootout or a standoff. Havens sent a quick text to his new buddy, Detective Neil, in hopes that the stage could be set to avoid any further issues or casualties.

HVNZ HERE. HOSTILE ARMD FRCE CAME TO HOME. MLTPL KIA. BLUE AND RED. WE SAFE INSID. HAVE 2 GSTS. GOVIES. PLS PASS TO CPD. I DID NOT ENGAGE BLUE. JST RED.

Neil texted back, RGR. WHAT DID YOU DO NOW?

Havens did not reply.

Neil continued, THEY WILL SET UP A PERIMETER. BEST JUST COME OUT WITH HANDS UP. UNARMED.

Before Havens had to address the situation with the officers, Rick also stashed his unused firearms in Sean's safe and the three men had a quick discussion.

"Sean, you should go to Arizona and secure your daughter for travel to North Carolina. Use a Company plane. It'll be readied for your use," Jerry promised.

Rick added, "The jet will transport you and Maggie to a lesser-known Duke medical facility for further treatment. She'll have a trusted asset personal attendant for therapy, medical advocacy, and guardianship. She'll take care of your daughter while you're away … periodically."

"Where will I be away?"

"Since you will be working within both CIA and the Joint Special Operations Command, I need you to go to a few weeks of training."

JSOC. Meat eaters. "So I'll be away from Maggie more?"

"Initially. We'll try to keep it as short as possible, but our clandestine wars are blending partnerships more and more with a bunch of the military secret squirrels. SEAL Team Six, Delta, TFO (Task Force Orange)—the Activity's Belvoir boys, and our Ground Branch Agency guys."

"So where do I fit in with that as a local intel guy?"

Rick cast a glance toward Jerry.

"Rick, tell him. He has a daughter and has to consider everything."

Sean ping-ponged his head following the verbal and non-verbal communications between father and son.

"Havens, there might be some mission sets where you need to know how each one operates separately, and also how they operate jointly. In truth, you might just sit on a tarmac with them for a few hours like we did for a while in Somalia recruiting warlords. You'll more likely work with TFO—the Activity—more than the others. You'll be backup and reach-back support, installing technical intelligence devices and other electronic intercept equipment. Advance force stuff. You're good as a singleton, but you need to work on a team."

"I see," Havens replied, seeing where this was going. *I won't be home. You're buying me a nanny.*

"You'll live within a secured Unit-shared compound just outside Range 19 when you're not away training and working. When Maggie is released from the facility, we'll set you up within a secured hide site at Fort Bragg. You'll be together. In a couple weeks you'll meet the team. I'm Chief."

"So where are you sending me initially?"

"You start with Special Training School 304. Advanced Operational Clandestine Warfare."

"Detailed planning, violent execution," Havens stated the training school's mantra with a sigh.

"That's the one. I think you'll like it. Something new, building off skills you've developed. We just have to get the team thing down."

"Sure. Hopefully sometime folks will realize that the conditions have changed for this type of warfare. It's not about remote bases and sabotage. It's about mediated message manipulation, civil ideology resistance, and provoking responses globally. This is just sending me off to summer camp."

Jerry cleared his throat. "Sean, when you and I first met, you were in college Reserve Officer Training Corps struggling with the reality that you had to learn conventional warfare before you could learn unconventional. That friction is why you were passed to me. Here we are again at a crossroads. You must learn the mentality and tactics of the men you will be working with so you can influence change. Your change. Until that time, you will simply be looked at as a dissenter."

"Exactly," Rick confirmed.

"Look, I'll shut up. I know that both of you are blowing smoke up my ass until it's too late for me to change my mind. I'll be quiet. Just give it to me."

The rest of the conversation was a one-way dialogue from Rick and Jerry to Sean. There was little argument on Sean's part, as he had no options.

Rick arranged for a staffer to have a precious cargo moving truck arrive at Havens' home the next day and literally load everything up.

Unknown to Havens, his home was immediately sold to a building contractor and leveled, with the Agency picking up the difference in value for the quick sale and demolition.

No trails, no trace.

Given the killings of the Federal security officers, Jerry was able to drum up immediate support to cover up and clear Havens at National and State levels for any implications in the prior terror attacks.

Sean Havens slipped away for a moment and made a call to one of his few remaining trusted friends.

"Hey X, Havens here."

"Hey buddy, it's the Sabbath, my day of rest. What's up?" the tech ops support wizard inquired.

"One, I know you're at some office working, so spare me. Two, you're Jewish, so spare me again. This has to be quick. I need you to do some cyber digging. I have a hit out on me."

"That's nothing new," X interrupted.

"Ha ... ha," Sean dragged out, then switched back to all business. "They just visited. Cops are coming but it's all clean kills on my end. If you can, I need you to find out how many more visits I might have and if there's anything that mentions my brother-in-law, Lars, or Maggie. I'll call you in a few hours. This'll take a while. Not sure if the police'll hold me for my use of *extreeeme* home protection force."

"I assume you laced them up?" X asked.

"With everything I had."

"*Noice*. And Sean?"

"Yeah?"

"I'm half Jewish, a quarter Irish Catholic, and a quarter Methodist from the Danish side of the house. So … I really have the whole weekend for prayer and reflection."

"Good. Pray for me and I'll give you something to reflect on. Hey, sorry to cut this short, but I need to check on my kid and give her a call. Can we chat later?"

"Roger, buddy. Out."

X spun around in his chair and went downstairs to the corporate IT department. It was a cold and damp Sunday morning in Arlington, Virginia, and no one would be in the downtown consulting firm's office. If he bumped into a wayward techie or two who had braved the miserable weather, most employees would assume, mistakenly, that Terry Donaldson, or "X," as he was known in the special operations community, still worked there.

In fact, X had joined a few firms over the past few years as a systems analyst while still working covertly for the government. He had selected large companies where an employee could literally get lost, provide false Social Security numbers from his own sources, attain access to the computer systems and change his administrative settings so he had neither a department, a boss, or, for that matter, a record. However, payroll had his information as a retained consultant for a three-year renewable term.

With a company ID code, X keyed in access across the firms and would simply move from open office to open office to conduct his government special activities while lost in the noise of millions of communications being sent over the companies' networks. As such, Terry Donaldson, Michael Bloom, and David Alexander, his other pseudonyms, existed simply on his badge, payroll direct deposit, W-2, and postal box. Not even his closest friends were one hundred percent sure of his real name.

X had come up with the idea years back when he realized that he and all of his fellow DoD coworkers all entered and left the same government facility, where surveillance detection routes could be employed along the way but ultimately didn't work if someone knew where he lived or saw where he worked.

By having a mixed bag of companies, and his own design of supplemental income, he could remain safe and never had to worry about static surveillance.

The only routine X had after leaving his home and catching the Metro was taking his on-schedule 7:30 AM bowel movement, which he always unloaded in a clean, upscale hotel toilet of his choosing. From there, he would meander the streets, cutting through various buildings until he found one of the offices he decided to work at for the day.

Now on the fourteenth floor, when the elevator door opened, X swiped his key to the IT department entryway. The office was dead. He situated himself at a table with three large-screen monitors, each connected to a separate CPU, and went to work. While the computers were searching, X strolled over to the break area, found a dark roast blend K-Cup and brewed a cup of coffee.

The employee mail cabinets were within steps. X took a quick look overhead, looking for any new surveillance cameras. Clear, he rifled through a number of employee bins until he had two American Express corporate card bills. The credit and personal information came in handy when ordering more technical equipment, satellite phones, and throw-aways, which he would have sent to a mailbox upstairs whose owner was on a long-term project in Singapore.

Coffee and bills in hand, X returned to the work stations and finished his searches. It was a good Sunday morning.

Outside the office location, five men in multiple layers of drab street clothes discreetly confirmed the next day's stakeout sites around local hotels. Through their throat microphones, they relayed the same routine to the static and mobile technical crews in the area.

The target's pattern of life was now apparent after just a week of man-hunting.

X was marked.

Satisfied with the answers that both Jerry and Rick gave, the police excused them from the crime scene.

Rick passed Havens his personal mobile number, whereas Jerry simply gave Sean a double-handed hand shake and wished him the best.

With so many distractions and priorities, Sean simply acknowledged Jerry and hoped that they would have another time to talk about many things that went unsaid over the years.

"Rick, you won't mind dropping me off at Marjorie's, will you?" Jerry asked his son. "I know she will be expecting me and I need a few things from her. She may be able to get things cleaned up for our friend here. You know she'll have a pot roast and Yorkshire pudding. I could use a sherry once my hands calm down."

Rick was happy to oblige.

Aunt Marjorie was a wonderful woman now in her mid-nineties. A former Office of Strategic Services (OSS) propaganda specialist who served in India and Asia during WWII as a covert operative, she was one of "Wild" Bill Donovan's favorite warriors within the sisterhood of spies.

Now retired from the CIA, she had made the North Shore of Chicago her home for the past thirty years. There, she maintained powerful philanthropic contacts, key political relationships, and a heavily secured armory in the basement for her family who was still in the business. She stayed connected to others through the Association of Former Intelligence Officers. At annual meetings and special events, she and "the girls," hailing from the OSS and CIA, would stay up for hours like they had over sixty years ago.

With her own financial support to the president's prior election campaign and her historical clout, she could make direct calls to make things either happen or go away.

Jerry had made her abusive, now ex-husband disappear half of a lifetime ago. Though not required, Marjorie felt a lifetime of debt to her brother. She would help make the allegations against Havens disappear.

Sean and Rick could then make the CIA's rival sister agency, the Pond, disappear.

A bonus would be eliminating Sean's former friend and operational field partner, Prescott Draeger. The man who created this mess.

Prescott Draeger, for his part, was creating another problem.

Chapter 8

"Ah, damn, that feels good." The heat from the water burned Prescott Draeger's body beyond pain to the point of heightened delight.

He revered the red heat streaks on his bare skin as he dried himself off from the hot shower nearly a half a world away from Sean Havens. The operational puppet master had fled the U.S. to Albania after orchestrating a series of terror acts that were to be blamed on his former colleague and "friend."

Still, the near-scalding cleanse failed to wash the past year's toxic memories from his mind. Memories that chained themselves to other operational nightmares. They plagued him with paranoia and sleeplessness. The hellish stress trauma he had endured for years, with no end in sight.

Draeger briefly contemplated going back in to the searing shower to relax a bit more. Then he would go another round.

Solar panels, generators, and a stream hydro-pump provided all the necessary power for basic amenities, technology, and his unique therapy requirements.

The Albanian safe house remained secure under the paid protection of one of the most powerful crime clans in the northern region. Payments ranged from light money laundering services, drugs, and weapons to relationship brokerage from the covert U.S. government intelligence agency, the Pond, to its enabler, P2.

The stone farmhouse that Draeger temporarily called home was surrounded by dense forest with a mountainous backdrop and sheer limestone cliffs dropping hundreds of feet down to the lush valleys below.

With two nights of decent sleep while on the run, Prescott hoped at first that he was rid of the night terrors, flashbacks, and headaches, but he found that his endorphins from escaping the U.S.

borders were likely affording the PTSD reprieve. He wasn't pleased with the thought of taking the neuro-toxin pills for relief, yet he couldn't think of any other way to survive.

In short time, upon arriving in Albania, Prescott Draeger was able to re-establish some local contacts that benefited him with pills, a business opportunity, and the naked whore now lying on his bed.

Prescott grabbed a small handful of a personal drug cocktail consisting of Zoloft, Paxil, and three ibuprofen. He returned to the bedroom, where he remembered seeing a near-full glass of wine on the nightstand, a remnant from the foggy night of passion before. Taking the glass and shoving the handful of pills into his mouth, Draeger let the towel fall as he climbed back onto the bed. He swallowed hard, forcing the straggler pills that resisted the wine flush down his throat.

"Mnom, mnom, mnom," he exaggerated, chewing out loud in the young woman's ear.

Irena stirred from her sleep as she heard and felt Draeger's presence behind her.

She was a beautiful gift brought to him days before by the local "kryetar" underboss who wished to "Ensure that Mr. Black's stay was enjoyable for however long that may be."

A local of Vlore, Albania, Irena had planned to finish her education and study in France before a jealous brother arranged for the sale of his two sisters.

"Not more, please. I begging you," she pleaded to Draeger. "Give me a little time. You said you like me, yes?"

"Yes, Irena, I did say that," said Draeger, emotionless, as he refamiliarized himself with the room he had been in for the past few days.

"Then please, just let me sleep little time more. I can be stronger and have maybe something to eat?"

"I don't think so." Draeger reached over her shoulder for the other glass of wine sitting on the high wooden night stand. He guzzled half and licked at the wine that dripped down the sides of his mouth. He poured the rest of the deep red liquid on Irena's skin.

She arched as the wine burned the long, fresh cuts on her back.

Draeger admired her still-raw scratches. They resembled fingernail clawing.

Mine? Draeger examined his nails. Clean, but then he did just come from a long shower that brought back faint mental clarity.

"Irena, I realized while showering that I don't want full-time company." Draeger pulled the bedsheets over, trailing his glossy eyes over a thin, darkened stain track of blood on the down comforter. "I like to be alone." He resumed attention to Irena's body.

"Where will I go? You can't send me back or they will be very angry with me. Kristoque, he will hurt me." She tried to roll to her side and thwart his intentions and physical advances but was pushed back over. She squeezed her legs tight together.

"Oh, honey, I'm not going to send you back to him. That would be insulting to my new business partner. I have already found a nice place for you to go. You will have some money, be able to travel, and sleep in a different place for as long as you choose to live that way."

"That sounds very … "

"Stop talking!" Draeger fumbled his sexual maneuvering.

"Why are you so … changed? Last night you were so sweet. Then you become angry again and then get peaceful again."

Draeger fought with her legs. Anger rose as she continued to speak. He wilted.

"I held you to me as you cried on my breasts? Are you okay? Do you want me to be Christina again?"

"What did you say?" Draeger erupted. "What did you say, you little whore?" He pulled Irena's arm, wrenching it over to force the young woman onto her back. He gripped her throat as she braced to stop whatever might come next. "Where did you hear that name?" Draeger catechized.

Irena struggled to breathe. She fought against his strength out of fear and desperation. Sparkles and blackness clouded her vision. She was used to this type of abuse, but never knew which man would see that abuse through to her eventual death.

As Irena gasped to talk, Draeger released the viselike grasp but maintained his grip while allowing her to speak.

"Pres ... cott, you called it to me last night when we made the sex. You don't remember?"

"No, I don't fucking remember," said Draeger in a childlike, whiney voice. Then shifting to a tone of bafflement, he softened his tone. "I said *my* fucking name to you, too?"

Prescott Draeger's face reddened and he wiped the dripping sweat from his forehead. Steamed corners of glass on the window panes signaled to Draeger that the room was much hotter than the cold relief outdoors. He craved fresh, cool air.

Irena half nodded while compressed on the mattress. "You said you were Prescott Draeger and you kissed me very passionately and loved me and called me Christina, you do not remember this? You were so kind and gentle. So loving. You wept for long after the sex and I held you. I think maybe you are not well, Prescott." Irena reached up to touch Draeger's face. She rubbed his cheek and reached up to run her fingers through his hair.

He smashed away her hand with the open knife edge of his palm.

Irena shrieked from the shock and the pain.

"Of course I'm not well, you stupid little bitch! I'm all fucked up in the head!" he hissed through clenched teeth while rapping his knuckles at his temple.

Draeger removed his hand from Irena's neck and rolled over on the bedside, staring at the beamed ceiling above him. The heavy wood was cut straight and lined uniformly but the grain waves made an illusion of movement in his re-intoxicated state. He laughed.

"I can't believe I told you my name. You have no idea what this means," he said, amused at his complete lack of discretion in pillow talk.

"Do I still get to go away?" Irena negotiated in despair.

"Yes, darling, you get to go away," he appeased. "Oh, yes. Far away." Draeger closed his eyes. "Do tell, sweet thing, what else did I say about Christina?"

"You said you were sorry, and that you missed me, I mean … her? And you were sorry to hurt her and her daughter and it was wrong. And you apologize to make Sean do the bad things but you had to for job. How did she go away? Did you love her? Who is Sean, Prescott? Is he your friend?" Irena bit her knuckle as she waited for answers that could calm her anxiety and fears.

"Irena? It is Irena, right? Your name? For real?"

"Yes, I thought you knew this?"

"Whatever. Besides Kristoque, who else knew you were dropped off here?"

"Just Kristoque, Prescott. And his driver. Why do you ask?" Irena started to sit up and moved her legs off the bed.

"Don't call me Prescott."

"What should I call you?"

"Don't call me anything. I need to think," he spat. Draeger fought the drug and alcohol euphoria clouding his mind.

Irena looked down to the floor in search of clothing.

"Irena?"

"Yes?" she whispered.

"Are you happy with your life?"

"It is no longer my choice. I have no freedom since I was taken. It is sad and I meet very difficult men who have like to hurt me." Her face tightened as she reflected on being sold from one man to another since she was seventeen. "I have no family now and my sisters I do not know where they have been taken. My father he is dead and my brother made some men very mad and tries to fix this when they came for us."

"Yeah, yeah, I know the story, probably killed your dad, raped and killed your mom, raped you and your sisters then took you into the trade. Boo hoo. Not my problem," dismissed Draeger as he flipped his hand in the air. His hand movement was mesmerizing. He repeated the action and watched its slow flow in the air. He snickered. He was high again.

Irena sensed grave danger and fought to buy time. "This is very bad hurting what you say. It has happened this way. I think you are good man inside, Prescott." Immediately regretting saying his name, she feared a backlash reprisal that didn't immediately come. She winced, "I'm sorry, I should not have said the name."

Irena inched back to Draeger's position, finding no clothing nearby to soften her naked vulnerability. Fighting a yet unspoken combat for her life, she returned to the learned trade of satisfying men for survival. "Please, let me stay with you. I will take care of you. I will love you and make you feel good." Her hand moved down his chest to his loins.

"Irena?"

"Yes, my dear?" She kissed his neck and lifted her leg and shifted her body to straddle Draeger and take him inside.

"Are there still wolves in the woods of this area?" inquired Prescott while he ignored her seduction. His hands danced in the air like a musical conductor.

"Yes, of course? I will protect you though," she whispered sensually. She licked his ear and started moving her hips rhythmically.

As Irena moved from his ears to his lips Draeger pulled back one of his dancing arms and shot a balled fist at her mouth.

Irena doubled over the bedside from the smashing force. She lost teeth.

They cut Prescott's hand.

He pounced over and barraged her with punches until her arms resisted no further and they dropped still.

Draeger regarded his knuckles, not sure whose blood stained his skin. He spoke to his spanned fingers bemused. "Well then, my dear, I think that tonight you will be dining with the wolves. And I will have to do better with my pillow talk." Prescott licked the blood, then wiped his fists on the hanging sheets.

Draeger's veins surged with adrenaline, speeding the drug and alcohol absorption and flow to his mind.

Enchantment kicked in as another rush, followed by a primal lust that flowed and tingled all over his body.

He licked Irena's bloodied lips and kissed her neck. "I've missed you, Christina, will you have me?"

J.T. PATTEN

Chapter 9

Being a good investigator also requires the mind of an adversary, and X could be both simultaneously.

The three computer screens glowed and reflected their content off X's glasses. With a few leads coming in, he started querying databases using artificial intelligence parallel processing systems, geek speak for a bad-ass computer hunting capability, until he scored hits on the search parameters.

Once he found a lead, he input the numbers for currency transaction reports within yet another database that was linked to the Currency and Banking Retrieval System.

X typed in another query string while searching the dark web for any other indicators of Havens' family as targets.

Nothing.

He paused and slurped more coffee. Hammering on the keys of the third laptop, he ensured that his access was not monitored and that no one was tracking his movements.

X was clean. With the exception of the watchers outside.

Government credentials that provided a secure handshake with the systems enabled X full rites of passage.

He continued searching, selecting accounts, relating transactions, and adding the findings to his Analyst Notebook social network analysis tool.

The financial intelligence capability that X was accessing was designed for anti-money laundering and tracking terrorist funding, but for X and the work of Sean Havens, the systems enabled blackmail, bribery, and extortion of their targets. Today it was a hunting tool.

X selected another string of transactions then tapped more commercial and government databases, broadening the search. Eight reports popped up. The connection between names, accounts, and property ownership materialized. He logged into the Deposit Tracking System.

"Bingo!"

Outside, a watcher received a call.

"Yo."

"Any movement? We're tracking his system access. Don't know what he's doing exactly, but he's using a ton of bandwidth. We can't keep up, so we're just measuring keystrokes and processing. This guy's a wizard."

"Fine. You stick to booger-eater stuff, we'll mind our lane. No movement. I hung back with a couple other guys so we don't miss anything tomorrow."

"If he moves, don't engage. We're just keeping tabs on him until we get the order."

"I'm on it and my team is on it. Just make sure your guys pay the invoices on time. No more of this 90-day shit."

"Suck it up. It's not a sole source contract, you were a low bidder and the terms remain the same. Think of it this way, the pay isn't great, but you'll get it for three years unless they recompete or terminate the DoD contract."

"Beautiful."

"Call if you need anything. Out."

It was just about two hours on the nose when Havens called X back.

"Anything?"

"Holy shit, Sean, I totally forgot!" X smiled to himself and the screens.

"Not now, bro. I'm too wiped for screwing around."

"All right, all right. So here's what I've got. On the assassination hit, there isn't that much. Looks like a light user was able to pull some strings to get you posted. Can't tell, but there might have been maybe a surrogate who had some link and clout, but can't tell. Good backstopping."

"Is that bad?"

"Nah, pretty benign. I'm also seeing that based on IP hits on the sites that the feds are all over this shit now, shutting down links, access points, and shit like that. You've got some clout on your side, that's for sure. Has to be the Fibbies."

"So it might have been stopped already?"

"Yeaah," X dragged the word out, uncertain. "But what I don't like is that if feds shut it down now, why couldn't they have done it beforehand? I saw three trails of users who hit on the targeting post. All three had been notified. Not by the poster, but by someone else."

"So the guys who happened by my house were actually turned on to the post or even recruited or tasked?"

"I think so. That was the beauty of the site. You could have anonymous creds and your boss could task you for a gig like a cut out. Shit, I wish we would have thought more about a tool like that for our own ops."

Havens was silent for a moment then replied, "Unless maybe we are."

Miles away, X nodded in agreement. "True. But anyway, here's what else I found. There were enough bread crumbs that I could see the accounts that funded the hit. Even though it was Bitcoin, I could trace the registers and peel back other accounts. Bottom line is I found the kitty."

"Do you know whose it is?"

"I don't exactly. Well, maybe one. There were a few backstops but they ultimately linked back to the Silver Star program office in like a slush fund. There were two custodians and the links to those accounts went offshore and back again. One is in Eastern Europe, and I can't get much info on that one, although I might have pinpointed a geo-coordinate. The other one is linked back to a retired general officer and his east coast personal account. Pretty fucking stupid, but without an XO, the general must have thought he was slick enough." X laughed at his own joke that Havens didn't quite get. *I thought it was funny.*

"Thanks. Can you map more trails of funds for those two account streams?"

"Already on it." X slurped more coffee. He licked the side of the cup, where some dripped.

"This shit always comes full circle, doesn't it?"

"Yip. We're overseas fighting bad guys that someone up top tells us to hit. Meanwhile, we're the ones caught in the cross hairs."

"Okay, well, thanks for the insights. I owe you one."

"One? Havens, you owe me like a bajillion."

"Just know I'll be there if you ever need me."

"I know. What are you going to do now?"

"Packing up. We're heading toward Fort Bragg. Gotta pay the bills and not many employers are looking for my skills other than Uncle Sam."

"Have you considered Israel? Iran? Russia? China, even. They could use a guy like you," X joked.

"Maybe after I retire and get a pension. I can freelance there."

"Shit, you haven't stayed in one place long enough to get a pension."

"Then I guess I'll just have to remain a loyal American and slug it out defending democracy."

"What an idealist. Keep me posted if you need anything. Enjoy your new home."

"Home will always be Chicago, buddy. Where ever I may roam. And you call me too, if I can help you in any way."

"Will do. Guess it's my turn to be in a jam," he joked as his name was sent to the targeting team.

Chapter 10

Havens snapped right, two more punches, lower left. He raised a knee that buried deep into the heavy bag, leaving a wide smear of sweat on the leather. His drenched shirt hung on his body like the draped weight of guilt clinging to his heart.

Three months back from training and he realized that working the heavy bag each morning in North Carolina was doing little for his emotional baggage. His shadow boxing punches barely touched the bag. He worked high to low, freestyle, and shifted his slips and simulated head dodges.

The gym was a sauna and steamed the windows despite the increasing heat of the morning sun outside.

The tucked-away boxing facility, in the tougher part of Fayetteville, North Carolina, was frequented mostly by military men.

Havens jabbed more. Threw a right cross. The stay-away Advanced training was bullshit. Warrior MBA school of tactics, joint exercises, and communication. It was one of the reasons he failed to stay interested in Army ROTC so many years ago and was handed off by the military cadre to the local CIA recruiter. Havens preferred to do things alone. Teaming was not his thing. And in a team of two, as father and daughter, he wasn't doing so well either. Working on his own was a strength and weakness. He never realized until now how much Christina kept things together.

What do I know about being a good dad? I have ... Havens punched ... *to* ... upper cut, upper cut ... *figure this* ... cross, cross, faster, another, cross ... *out* ... right cross ... *soon.* He sped up the volley of punches. *She doesn't* ... *even look* ... *at me the same... as* ... *she used* ... *to. She knows. She blames* ... *me.* Havens pummeled the bag as he wrestled with what he needed to do for his daughter as a single dad.

The routine was the same. Dropped pounds, stronger shoulders, adaptable warrior, but still no answers on how to live his life like the man he wanted to be.

A heavily tattooed soldier was running his mouth, taunting guys into taking the ring for a friendly spar. Havens found himself in his crosshairs and was distracted enough to quit feeling sorry for himself for a second.

"Hey old man, wanna go for a round if your heart won't stop?"

"I'm just packing up. Sorry. You'd probably knock me out anyway. Just getting some aerobics in so I can get off Lipitor and my prostate medicine. Maybe one of the younger guys will take you up." Sean wanted to keep the soldier moving. The guy didn't get Havens' self-deprecation. "Maybe next time."

"Yeah, you're right. I'd fucking knock you into tomorrow." He stood close to Havens, trying to intimidate and bully the older man.

"I'm sure you're right," said Sean, not moving or breaking eye contact. "So probably no need to ever fight, huh? You win." Havens held out his glove for a friendly bump. The Marine batted it down.

The soldier, sporting red shorts with golden piping and a Marine crest silk screen on the thigh, waved off Havens and moved to the next man. A younger, slighter boxer. Sean recognized him from back at the JSOC intel shop.

"What the fuck is this?" The Marine punched a quick shot to the smaller man's arm tattoo. "Airborne? You gotta be shitting me. I bet you can't even heft a ruck with that teeny bony body you got. Shit. Put a tick on your back and your legs would give out. You some 'Don't Ask Don't Tell' slip-in? Get your ass in the ring. C'mon. That a dick in your shorts or is your maxi pad full? No combat for women, pussy."

The fledgling Airborne Ranger broke eye contact and moved to the side of the heavy bag. He tried to create distance and obstruction—and time. "I don't want to fight you. Ask someone else."

"I asked you, you turd!"

"Hey, bullet sponge. I'll fight you. I think my prunes and oatmeal just kicked in."

The Marine turned to see Havens directly behind him. Sean stood there with a fourteen-inch metal bar.

The Marine smiled a full-on shit-eating grin. "Well, well. Your grandpa just came to the rescue, Ranger stranger. I see you need a crutch."

"Yep. I don't think I can beat you in a fair fight. But I'm not going to listen to this shit anymore. Move on, kid."

The Marine smacked the Ranger hard across the head. "Wimps," he taunted as he walked away.

Sean gave the Ranger a wink. "I know you had him, sorry I jumped in."

"Yeah, thanks."

"Thank me later, you haven't seen the end of this if you come back. Better figure out now how you're going to deal with it."

The Ranger nodded. "Maybe I'll eat a barrel of creatine for lunch," the young soldier joked. "If it comes down to it, I'm fine fighting him. I've just had enough of the real shit downrange to deal with an asshole in the gym. Detached retina, too. IED. You know how it is."

"Yeah, I do. Catch'a round." Havens collected his gear casting an eye down the gym. The Marine returned a hard stare.

Score one, Havens, keeping your cool. Sean's heart beat strongly. *Let's get to the range and see how I shoot with a little morning adrenaline.*

Sean drove ten miles out of Fayetteville to a range run by a few old local acquaintances. At the complex, he went down to the six hundred yard Range Three. It was early and no one was at the site. After checking in, he walked down the trail and unloaded his three cases, then did a series of burpees and jumping jacks.

First up was a Heckler and Koch 416 carbine. Standing, he sent four sets of three rounds downrange in succession, hitting the gongs and iron silhouettes at 100, 200, 300, and 400 yards, respectively.

He returned the long-rifle to the table, kicked his feet out and pressed out fifty push-ups.

He snatched his next piece, a mid-range MK 14 Mod O Enhanced Battle Rifle. Havens lay prone and extended the bi-pod. He exhaled and mentally started to slow his heart. Sean flutter-kicked his feet nearly twenty times while looking through the sight and tried to slow his heart again. He aimed at the top right corners of each target and sent one round down to the 300- and 400-yard targets, hitting them both. He adjusted and went for the bottom left corners. Hits.

Still seeing no one around, Havens sprinted down the range to the 100-yard marker and pushed himself, running back faster, faster, and faster to his full-out maximum dash.

Breathing heavy and seeing pale stars in front of his eyes, he next loaded an M40A5 sniper rifle. Heart pounding and hands a bit jittery, he peered through the Schmidt & Bender scope. At six hundred yards, he nailed the target effortlessly. Not perfectly where he wanted it, but who gives a shit. He was intel.

Still looking through the optic, he caught movement at about three hundred yards. It was a cat bounding after field mice in the light brush and grass.

The cat sat rotating its head left and right like a pendulum. It pounced. Then jumped again. The cat reared its head, a prize rodent in its mouth.

The mouse kicked and wiggled but the feline's mouth held firm. The cat gave its meal a few swats.

Havens made a slight adjustment on the scope. He let out a breath and counted. *1, 2, 3.* Sean squeezed the trigger.

Retribution? Or redemption?

The cat launched straight up in the air, surprised as the mouse was effectively vaporized. The cat took off in a run.

Bingo. Mercy kill.

Havens kept the cross hairs on the running cat as he followed it through the grass. Sean put his finger on the trigger and took in a low breath.

Bam. Havens smiled as he got up, watching the cat frolic a bit more in the grass. *You're lucky my daughter likes cats.*

Sean felt better about the day and his accomplishments as he hiked the small distance to his car. *Good workout. Good range morning. Stayed out of a fight, which is more than I can say about yesterday in training. Baby steps, buddy. Baby steps.*

As Havens walked around his new-to-him used Jeep Grand Cherokee, he noticed a black pickup at the end of the lot. Short of a couple of the owner and range cadre's vehicles, the idling truck was out of place. Maybe someone waiting for the range to open. Sean couldn't make out the driver. No biggie. He reached for the door latch and saw the etching keyed into the paint.

Semper Fi.

The truck sped off, raising dust and gravel as it tore around the corner to the roadway.

Seriously? Keying my car? Thought we were done with this. You wanna play, let's play. Back to a shit day, after all. Piece of shit war punk.

Chapter 11

It was official. Sean and Maggie Havens had settled in as poorly as they could to new routines around Fort Bragg. Neither of them were happy—Maggie with being in the hospital, Sean with the state of mind in which he felt equally trapped.

Sean was slowly easing into a new job, a Title 50 CIA sub-command of what was previously known as OMEGA-50, a joint program between the CIA and the Joint Special Operations Command. The blended CIA/JSOC team nested under OMEGA was an In-Extremis joint program office Task Force "Operational Detachment Foxtrot," code-word "Ice Snap." Known by the rank and file as Ghost Hunter. It basically meant that when the military wasn't allowed to do something nasty, they could hide under the CIA's authorities.

Sean was, for the umpteenth time in his career, buried under confounded terms, codes, and secrets that kept even those in the know confused about what they were doing, who they were doing it for, and whether the program name they were read on to was still relevant. As a result, no one really used the terms. Someone up top was pushing the buttons and the lower echelon just went through the motions.

With Maggie living at the hospital for the time being, Sean started his own physical training regimen, one designed to punish him. In theory, physical pain from PT would overcome the mental pain, one workout at a time. Resentment of his situation was building. He felt like a prisoner waiting for penitentiary staff to let their guard down so he could attempt an escape.

For survival and to buy time, Havens tried to integrate himself into the odd mélange of defense and intelligence community personnel who resided within a compartmentalized spook-run Joint Special Operations Command support group, which made it difficult to understand who was actually on "the team" and who was working for someone else. He found it hard to start conversations. He fell back into his old introversion and preferred to be alone. Reprieve for Sean was temporary as he received additional training at advanced capabilities schools at Harvey Point, Bragg, and Camp Perry while his daughter continued recovery and rehabilitation.

While riding a desk one day, Sean was briefed by Rick on the Pond's global activities. The Pond, according to Rick, was like an octopus.

Rick observed, "It has tentacles composed of human asset networks and corporate fronts supporting operations to even the most remote locations. The same agile muscle moves each tentacle. That muscle is made of discipline, fortitude described in underground relationship-based services, logistics, and operational execution."

"But it sounds like it isn't a leaderless movement. There is still hierarchy, right?" Sean could see weakness already.

"Exactly. It appears that they are pretty standard, like traditional military, corporate, and criminal enterprises. Should be classic 'cut-the-head-off-the-snake' mission sets. We don't know who is funding them, though, so there is probably a criminal element or some other deep pockets supporting the activities. They have huge amounts of money at their disposal. My guess is that some pretty powerful people are at the top and they wouldn't want exposure. Think political and social elites."

"I'm guessing finding this out is easier said than done."

"Correct. Jerry has had me on this for years, both officially and unofficially. As you know, this program office receives some analytical support from Langley, but it flows directly to me through Dad."

"I'm guessing that's because the issue is so sensitive, or are there concerns of broader Agency infiltration?"

"Both. With a high-scrutiny process for selection and recruitment, the Pond establishment has a predictable amount of cut-outs and compartmented layers, but as an unstructured organization, no one agent or asset's actions can hinder the achievements for the greater entity. Tentacles can be severed, and another regenerates from the strongest trunk. But as you saw, there were ties to DoD. Jerry guesses the same. If it's got political and social ties, then their individual recruits could come from anywhere. In that case, it isn't an organization, but rather a movement or ideological bond. He has some of his more trusted contacts working on it too, but he had to go to Israel to get that kind of old loyalty."

Havens looked quizzically at Rick. "You guys neglected to tell me that your dad is a bit more than a CIA relic. After I was recruited in school, I never knew much of what he was involved with. Sounds like he's still pretty active with a lot of program clout," Sean fished.

Rick dodged the question. "To improve upon the CIA's agent inducements with money and weak threats, the Pond has typically targeted potential recruits based on ideology or violently demonstrated repercussions for disloyalty. This eliminated layers of bureaucracy, accounting parameters, and flipped loyalties. The Pond's case officer's authorities were incontestable, and additional linkages were at the sole discretion of the free spymaster. It's our assumption that old Agency Bay of Pigs Cuban program officers, some old OSS, and old Viet Nam Phoenix intel program guys got the ball rolling."

"So they were still inside."

Rick nodded. "And still are, I'm afraid. While the CIA attempted to identify a purity of motive for their agent recruits, cemented with promises and pay or a flutter test on the polygraph, the Pond started enduring relationships with brutal interrogation and investigations to detail the newcomer's family, personal and professional relationships, strengths, weaknesses, and breaking point levers. This was coupled with a series of tests designed to break the boundaries of ethics, morals, and limits of the soul. There could even be some ritualistic aspects. The CIA has old history with Yale's Skull and Bones society. The Pond has similar links closer to Freemasons."

Havens started playing with the wood laminate on the edge of the table. It was pulling away from the particle board base.

"Sean," Rick launched another monologue, his hands clasped behind his back, pacing the perimeter of the twelve- by-twelve-foot room. "You will be mapping this hydra by envisioning the roles that an actor would have to play in this organization. We have a baseline of suspected individuals in a fairly crude order of battle, but their cover takes on a variety of methods outside of the cocktail party circuit that our elders were used to."

Sean nodded in appreciation of the Cold War veteran references. A war was starting. *Would Moscow Rules apply once again?* Sean wondered. "Rick." Sean paused a moment to mirror Rick's thinking and communication style. "Do you have any reporting that identifies some observed cover stories that they use, or anything that depicts visible evidence of clandestine activities? I mean, if this has been a seconded element of the CIA, there should be staffers with a lot of this knowledge if they worked with the Pond."

"The short answer is 'yes,' but their cover is more of a durable long-stay role than our traditional short-term exploits. There is no temporary assignment. Most Pond members become fixtures in their environments. Lone agents and officers are cloaked by legitimate organizational covers. They aren't NOCs who are written off by a CEO of some big company with some bullshit stipulation as to why the ..." Rick emphasized with finger quotations, "'employeeee' doesn't have to show up to quarterly company meetings and corporate golf outings or ever make a fuckin' sale on the biz dev charts. They have no indications of skullduggery on their part, aside from one tell ... " Rick paused again.

Sean waited wondering if Rick was holding out for dramatic effect or if the guy was just a bit weird.

"Dun, dun, dunnn." Sean harassed with dramatic widened eyes.

His comment made Rick whirl around like a teacher catching a disruptive student.

"You think this is fucking funny, Sean? You're in your forties. I swear, you act like a child. Clearly it isn't a game since they likely had a part in your big fucking Chicago mess. You're just lucky that that stupid contract on your life ended with our cleanup. Hell, Havens, we had to involve DOJ on your behalf to raid the Bitcoin execs and shut down Silk Road. These guys literally had to forgo the administrative platform access of the Silk Road site. That's big shit, Sean. They had commandeered accounts and had the capacity to change PIN numbers and other aspects of the site. They were on the inside of the dark network. We all took a hit since the government's knowledge of what was being done with that access was limited."

"I had no idea." Sean slumped down a bit, embarrassed about what it took to clean up the mess around him. He had to remind himself that he didn't bring it on. The failures of the system did.

"A lot of people had to call in personal favors so books got scrubbed, paperwork went missing, and people were encouraged to shut the hell up if they ever wanted a corner office. It's being done because one, you've had some pretty amazing successes over the years for your country and kept things low profile. You're the breed they want--having Ph.D.'s and still able to win a bar fight.   More importantly, for some reason, my dad takes his recruits all very personally.   Even though he never interacted with you after you were brought into the community, he kept tabs on you, and in some cases guided your career. You were one of the chosen ones. So, he feels some responsibility. Shit, he cares more for his hand-picked cadre than he does for me."

Havens took it all in and held the snarky comment that was percolating.

"We were using those illicit websites as listening posts for bigger issues and it gave us opportunity to siphon off Bitcoins to help fund ops. We had to pull the plug for you."

"Sorry, Rick. I appreciate what you all did, but I'm not taking all the blame on that. When your bus runs into a preschool and I give you the repair bill, it isn't because I was driving the bus."

Still not able to resist pushing Rick's buttons, he added, "You have my permission to continue. Are there any Agency resources or dudes who worked in the field and might have Pond insights? I mean, shit, you could debrief someone like me if I was working with them and had some travel patterns that could be assessed."

Rick heard nothing after the initial flippant comment. "You haven't changed, Havens. Twenty years later and you are still a snarky know-it-all asshole. You think that cavalier attitude is going to work with me? I'm doing you a favor. You have nothing. Nothing left. Laugh away, funny boy. Laugh away your dead wife, vegetable kid, and all ... "

In an instant, Sean was out of his chair, lunging for Rick. The bait worked, and Rick stepped back with his right leg, pivoting his hips quickly and opening up space. Sean had miscalculated and could see where this was going. He couldn't stop the momentum.

Shit.

Rick reached a right arm forward to the jettisoned Havens, grabbing hair and twisting Sean's head. Rick's left arm pushed Sean's shoulder and the combination move sent Sean crashing into the small room's wall. The impact punched a hole through the drywall and left Havens flat on his back.

"So much for the hundreds of thousands of dollars we put into your training."

"That was pretty good, Rick, for your first time in a fight."

"You are completely out of control. I've been getting reports from the instructors that you are a pain in the ass to work with and have been too aggressive with anything physical. I can't keep you chained to a desk if you're going to attack anyone who pisses you off. Face it Havens, you've tasted blood and have been emotionally wrung through the ringer. You're fucked in the head like all the other broken misfit toys. You need to get right in the mind and refined in your physical abilities. This brings me to my next briefing, which I knew you would resist. This afternoon, you are running over to Tier One. I've managed to get you in with the Unit's latest crew so you can take part of OTC."

Sean knew that Tier One was code, in this case, for Delta.

74

"What?" Havens protested. "I did the Operator Training Course years ago. Rick, I don't want to be in the field. I need to stay right here with my daughter. And Tier One? No way. Those guys won't want me around anymore. I haven't been there in years. All the old guys I worked with have moved on."

"You don't have a choice."

"Bullshit. Running me through OTC feels kinda cheap. I never went through any formal Delta selection when they ran me through post 9/11. It's a new breed over there, and I'm an old man. And more importantly, *I am not military.* No one cared when we were getting fast tracked after the towers fell. Shit, we were all purple and hunting terrorists together under overnight contracts and special program offices."

"Sean, like I said, they don't have a choice and neither do you. Show me one intel or targeting ops job description that doesn't call for employees needing to maintain global readiness and be available to deploy on a non-notice basis to hazardous duty or combat zones. They all say the same thing—permissive, uncertain, or hostile environments that can be austere conditions for unknown durations. I can't justify you and all your associated expenses to be just a desk targeting analyst. Take advantage of it. You never did selection because you were proven to be able to endure most anything on your own. Now it's team time. That needs to be your focus, along with consistency and tempered action. Team. One is none, two is one. Team is all. Embrace it."

Havens paused a moment in contemplation. *It would be good to reconnect with the Unit if they'll have me, but I know I'll get sucked back into field ops. I'm done shooting at people with them shooting back.* "Rick, Maggie has to come first over deployments, but if there is some balance and lower risk short temporary duty taskings, I'm okay if they're cool with it. I'd rather be a reach back advisor to them when possible, so I can stay local."

"You want fries with that order?" Rick didn't enjoy being tested.

"C'mon. You know the situation."

"We have an aide for your daughter, Sean."

"She needs a dad, Rick. Shit, she needs a mom, but I don't have that now, do I? Thank you very little, Uncle Sam."

"Look, Sean, I wouldn't say the Unit's cool with it, but you've got backers there who think you don't need to be tested for your resolve or willingness to endure. Commanding Officer knows who you are."

Havens nodded in understanding. "If the new Pope said its okay, I'll do it. So what will I be doing? Last week you sent me up to the crash and bang course. I've got a lot of these T-shirts already."

"Just checking the boxes to ensure you have trainings our way and their way. We know you know *your way*. The old you was admittedly less conventional, but conventional will have you in less austere situations solo. It's another brush up for you on the Delta side of tactical HETC, CQB, room clearing, marksmanship. Somewhat like what I've been sending out at the Point and Farm with our special skills boys. You'll forgo hostage management and forced entry, skip the fast cars, intel, and commo too. You've pretty well mastered instinctive fire but you need to build some muscle memory for shooting."

"Hang on. Aside from the deployment details, why has the value of me being less conventional and spotable changed? And I thought I was going to be behind a desk when I signed up for this. When did that change, too?"

"You go where I say and when I say. Mostly you'll be behind a desk. Sometimes you will be in the field. I'm not going to keep repeating myself. Sometimes you might be accompanied, or not. It might set you up nicely to get back into the Delta NOC program. Get you out of my hair."

Havens liked the idea of non-official cover work for the Unit. Still, he held the grimace on his face.

"What aren't you getting? Sometimes you'll be seconded to Green, sometimes Brown, Orange, or Grey," Rick informed using the old color code references to the elite military units. "No matter what, you need to get yourself right to know more of our ways and their ways and be more seamless in everyone's TPPs. If I need to send you out, you need a regular refresher on contact management, physical tactics, and pre-threat recognition. I'm not planning on having you with ST6, so don't worry about too much take-down choreography. But with Delta's OTC, that means you will also learn when someone like me is drawing you in, identifying possible responses and scenarios. You'll still have that routine for the next few weeks. And, I need to personally see how you work with team guys. You aren't a singleton anymore and you need to be mainstreamed a bit more so we can be more agile with your duties. Last time we discuss this."

"Not what I was signing up for," Havens repeated, still lying on the floor.

"You're exhausting. It is what it is. Truth be told, I think you could adapt to any situation, but your attitude sucks. If you can learn to adapt to them again, you will be a better joint team member. Don't you see the value in this? We value you enough to say 'join us.' Before, it was about you doing stuff *for* us. Just remember, if it wasn't for us, you would be dead in your house killed by bounty hunters."

"If it wasn't for this whole screwed-up black ops shit, I'd still have my family intact."

"Sean, I get it. Just jump through the hoops for me. Go throw some punches, fit in, and learn what they teach you. There's only a handful of guys who get cross-bred like you."

"The Unit's Gracie Jiu-Jitsu is pretty old-school, though. Krav and Systema pretty much nullified their moves every time."

"Always an argument from you, Havens. Big whiney bitch. Always a comment."

"Actually, that time I was joking."

"Make it more obvious. Or better yet, cut it out. Reinforces your asshole-ness, if that's even a word. Tuesday and Thursday mornings, you are at the stress range with the regular snake eaters. I'm turning you into a team-playing controlled predator, Havens. Like it or not. Get your brother-in-law to stay longer to help look in on your girl. I have some stuff he can get involved with to keep himself busy so he doesn't whine about missing Arizona retirement. Worst case, he can have full access to my golf club. If he says no, tell him your boss knows about the Bahamas account of his that ends with a number seven. Fight me if you want, Sean. But I might be the closest thing you have to a friend right now."

"I don't need friends anymore."

"Then you don't need to call this a friendship and you don't need to trust me, but you will respect me and you can be friendly. You've got three hours before you need to get over there to the compound. There is an old African saying, Sean, 'If you want to go fast, go alone. If you want to go far, go together.' Go see Maggie, and remind yourself of what you have to work for and what you need to do it right."

"Good thing this is nothing like the Pond recruitment methods. I'd hate to be sucked in to something that I have no control over."

"Thin ice, Havens. Thin ice."

"Anything else?"

"You mean like jump school?" Rick walked around the table opposite Havens and opened the door. "That's next week. Hope you aren't too sore from PT to pull the lollipop. Be a shame for all this investment in you to splat."

"You're kidding me."

"This time I am," Rick grinned. "Get the fuck out."

"Can't. I'm stuck."

"Then *I'll* leave."

When the door closed, Havens slowly elevated himself. He brushed off the white drywall dust and decided to leave his ego on the floor. *Rick's right. I'm carrying my baggage on my shoulder. Not healthy, not professional. Not me. Not the old me.*

As he started collecting his belongings from the table, another thought occurred to him.

Why do I need more combatives and ops training if I'm not going back into the field unless it happens to "come up"? Clearly, it will come up. I'm going to be Advance Force Operations hunting the Pond's links and trying to tie back to them, hunting and interrogating along the way in more shitholes. Clearly, I'll be running around the world.

The answer was clear. Trust no one.

Wish I would have interviewed with a few more companies before accepting this job. Screwed again, Sean.

Christina, I'm holding on to strings. I sure could use a friend. God, I miss you.

Chapter 12

It was springtime, and the rains were plentiful in the National Capital Region.

Jerry, the old spymaster, waded through the mud in his garden boots. He surveyed the community planting plot, which would open in the coming month. He concluded that the postseason tilling did not change the terrain much. Drainage looked to be about the same. His plot at the edge of the tree line would afford mid-afternoon shade just as it had for the past fifteen years.

He scraped the mud off his black rubber boots with the trunk of a small sapling. As he dragged the thinly treaded sole across the bark, he peered into the wooded edge. The two rocks at the base of the maple were unchanged. The sister rock one tree over showed dimplings. Its underside was smooth, but with all signals clear, the dead-drop remained embedded in the earth. No word from his asset. It had been months. He still needed to identify PASSPORT. The Israelis thought they may be able to assist.

Jerry heard the familiar sound of the Chevy pickup sploshing through puddles on the near-flooded gravel access road. He moved back to the field.

When the truck neared, the passenger side window slowly cranked down as the old driver struggled to reach across the seats from the driver's side.

Jerry stood his ground. *Robert, don't you have better things to do than personally following and harassing me all the time?*

"It's a little early for gardening. Someone might wonder what you're doing here. Might mistake you for being up to no good."

"I'm the damned Master Gardener here, Robert. No one would give it a second thought. They pay more attention to you driving around here with no business at the plots."

Robert seemed to give that some thought. "You should worry less about me." The man in the 1970s light blue pickup adjusted his black-rimmed spectacles. He rubbed his red, bulbous nose and gave a quick glance to his knuckle. He inhaled deeply from his nose and let it exit his mouth. His nostrils remained flared.

Jerry understood why Robert was miffed. He was the competition, competition since days at Yale a half century ago. Like a childhood bully, Robert would never let that go. It was his lifelong monkey on the back.

"These aren't old games Robert. You broke the rules."

"What rules, you damn dinosaur?"

"Our Company sections were a checks and balance so the overlap would ensure coverage across the global playing field. For intelligence collection, not for the crimes you're orchestrating."

"Bullshit, Jerry." Robert hacked and spit out the window. "You used us to do the dirty work that you embassy cocktail pussies were afraid to do. You wanted us with the Mafia. You wanted us to partner with the black markets. You needed us when you had no access. *We* didn't need *you*. Damn your rules."

"Leave me. I detest you. And your means. You help fund orphanages in war zones so you can skim off the kids you want. It's barbaric! That was never a request of ours!"

Robert pursed his lips. Nonchalantly, he replied, "Fetches a pretty penny and, as you know, it's good for blackmail and international relations. Those Saudi princes pay us a million bucks a kid. Easier to send them a useless war-torn kid and curry some favor than give 'em another gold-plated pistol. They can buy anything. They want the kids. Ain't *my* business. Just my *business*."

"You've made it Company business, Robert."

"Shit, Jerry. It's good business. Builds rapport, builds leverage, builds war chests. That builds a strong nation."

"Its sexual humiliation, torment, and eventual death."

"To whom? Those rug rats we dump off would have just been a burden to the global system. Shit. Most of them would be shooting at us or someone else in a few years."

"How dare you?"

"Jerry, even if I did give two shits about those street urchins, it's above my pay grade. Ain't me buying up land and property to house and farm those kids. That's executive level decisions. Presidential. D-i-c-k-l-o-m-a-t-i-c 'relations.' But hey, if you're wanting to paint me up, don't forget our ritualistic offerings category. That fetches a dime too," Robert winked.

"Monsters!"

"Don't blame me, Jerry, blame the Finders. Blame the buyers. Their intel runs through your departments. If it's good intel, why does it matter if it costs drugs, kids, weapons? Right? It's intel. And it's political leverage for policy. That's our job. That's *your* job. You still think you can get intel by pouring martinis and serving bacon-wrapped dates and shit like that to diplomats. Fuck that! That's fairytale shit. It doesn't work with rag heads. Tell me the last time you were introduced to a Taliban warlord or ISIS hatchet man while spooning caviar at an embassy party."

"We were in the same class, lest I remind you *again* of our mutual tenure in both school and tradecraft," Jerry scolded.

Robert snorted. He wiped his nose again, and rechecked his hand, indifferent to Jerry's remarks.

Jerry continued, "You needed our financing and you needed our political and foreign dignitary assistance so they would look the other way."

"Squawk away, Jerry. Are you really shitting me? You think his holiness and the Freemasons of the world need your assistance? Shit. Pope reaches a billion people with his policies. Priests hear confessions of half the world. With our alliance, we don't need CIA assets or your money networks. We mint money. His priests tip the Vatican, the Vatican tips us off for a fee. While you guys were sleeping, we grabbed the upper hand with regulators too. So fuck your Rothschilds and Rockefellers. We could pay off the national debt tomorrow. Finance is all locked up for us and our needs. We're strengthening America. You all are strengthening yourselves."

Jerry knew the Pond had nowhere near national debt amounts, but he was sure they had billions at their disposal. Cash, gold, diamonds, other securities. Jerry had initially noticed some of the patterns in the Pond's travels and recruitment activities in and around the globe's financial and tax centers. Sean Havens had been a part of this for a time, unwittingly. The directorate running the Pond activities had done an admirable job cloaking the continued use of the degenerate Freemasonry lodges, Mafia circles, and those intertwined. "Don't say it's about this country. It's about power just the same."

"Don't be so sure about that, Jer-itol."

Indeed, Jerry was not certain. He knew the operational placement and control that the key Pond leaders had within the financial sector. For the right price or favors, they could have anyone. That's how the greater shadow world of the Illuminati's affiliates worked. Jerry's smaller network controlled the banks and old money, but the Pond acted in the blind spot and captured the upper hand through a network of financial regulators and global corporations.

"See, Jer, we learned from your opium business that drugs, women, and guns were always in high demand and had to be routed away from the law or through the law. We just kept nudging it along. If we owned it, we could control it. And if we could control it, we could reap profits all along the lines. And if you controlled it, we could police you to give us our cut. Them is sweet apples. Thing is, we continued to evolve. Agility is key. Guess you Templar boys had something to teach us good Catholics after all, but then we saw a new light."

"Catholics. Bosh. True Jesuits would burn you and your masses at the stake if they were privy to your treachery. You still possess Neanderthal polish, Robert. I know history. And indeed it is our lineage that roots to the true watchers."

"I'm not so sure you do know history then, Buttercup. Or, oh, my apologies, 'Odin' as you boner robe pullers call you under your woobies. I call you 'Pussy.' I don't personally think you can pull off a god's name." Robert pretended to whisper. "I seen you piss your pants at Yale."

"You are a swine."

"Sticks and stones, skull and bones, you old bitch. You're pissed that we beat you at your game. Subject the American electorate to cycles of propaganda, let them choose from pre-selected candidates and winners who have come up the ranks of secret societies and old money. Then mix in some more psy ops to rip the population from the teat of Constitutional establishments that were made to serve them. Tsk, tsk, naughty boys. You aren't the only ones now with private donor steering committees and Super Patriots footin' the bills for business nods. And with our godly men, we are insulated against your Langley Center for Creative Leadership brainwashing."

"Robert, your venom comes from not being tapped by the Order as a knight to be a moral leader."

"Listen to you. You and your small band of godless cronies. Lest you forget, both of our organizations trickle from St. John and both benefit from the Order. Difference being mine remains of faith while yours remains a fraternity of pagan butt-bangers sleeping in coffins, hoarding with Assassins, and looking for fuckin' dust artifacts. I dare say our hundreds of thousands of intel assets have greater power and reach than your mere five or six hundred. Even if you include your sand monkey Arab Assassins. There ain't a true intelligence entity today that can hold a candle to ours."

"I'll say it again. That is not national intelligence collection."

"Fuck your intelligence, Jer. Your perception of intelligence is a myth. With the shitty sources that you have, you don't know what's a goose chase or not. Information changes on a button. This is about power, influence, and the real New Order. It's all about leverage. Business continuity. Two ops boys talking to one another, knowing that if we can influence, we can control. And if we can control the Pope as the illuminated ones, we control the weak masses and reinvigorate our Nation. I'm done here, Jerry. I told you your son Rick was getting too close and that I had no problem killing him if you didn't get him to back off."

"You know my boy is off limits."

"No one is off limits, Jerry, not even you. And then you go testing me with that Havens boy. I know you put him in only so you can serve him up instead of Rick if push came to shove. Who's the whore now?"

"Sean Havens has served this nation as a true patriot and warrior on my team and yours. Certainly even you can appreciate that."

"Bullshit words, Jerry. Save it for your Bonersmen and Tea Party pals. Another day, another time. Your era of spycraft is done. We've ushered in a new breed, and you can't tell who they are, you old pompous fart. It is how it was supposed to be. No rules, no Yale, no diplomatic protection. It's back to the days of Joshua when our spies lay with prostitutes and sleep with the shadows. And we masters can eliminate the weak ones and reward the strong ones. No tenure, no family contacts, no old boy's network. Good old-fashioned performance metrics and men who can keep secrets without leaking them to the press. No piece of paper to keep a secret, we take oaths to conceal the secrets and crimes of our brothers. We vow to shield them. It's an obligation and blood oath. Pay is simple, you build good assets you get better assignments. You make money, you earn money. You sell guns you win wars. You fail, you get caught, you die in silence like a man, execution style. *Your* best unconventional approaches are now conventional in the eyes of the rest of the world. And Jerry..."

"Yes, Robert?"

"You need to offer me up another strategic win. You owe me a concession offering of some sort. I'm blacking out the Agency until you do. And it might be too late for me to stop things that are already in motion. You never walked away from our game. You cheated. Soon, you'll be blind."

"We are mere pawns. And *you* threatened my sister's life. You had her thrown from the Agency on her ass. For what, for politics? Travesty."

"Oh, fuck-all Jerry, that ol' bird was bouncin' on Donovan's lap with her skirt up while we wuz in school. But I will say, I appreciate the OSS days even though we were just cuttin' our teeth. She still has chops. Didn't see her clearing Havens by calling her last chit on top. Smart play, but foolish on your part. You owe me, and I intend to collect. It was my turn to pick. You rosined up that bow to play the fiddle fer a pot of gold and lost. Now I get your soul or your blood. Hell, that Havens boy isn't even your blood. You should have served him up earlier so I could release my insurance policy. Don't try to back off now, and I'll say, you best keep your head on a swivel, old boy."

"Well, Robert, then I suppose you'll have to come find us. This is just a game to you. Not one of their lives or mine matters to your needs."

Robert laughed. "True. But what fun would life be if we didn't raise the stakes while we played with the big pawns? Election's coming. Appointments will be made. Who will near the finish line? Wanna bet that both are in our pocket? That we already know who the winner will be?"

Robert reached out to the air with a limp finger, creating the illusion of breaking the finish line with ease. "And find you? You are in your fucking garden plot playing with your pansy every time I turn around. It's amazing to me how you could still run clandestine services. Your security assistant Roland was found dead in the brush last season. How do you think we knew he would be there keeping a watch on you so no big bad wolves happened your way?"

"I'm untouchable. There are still cross points for checks and balances. It would be all-out war if you touched anything within the National Clandestine Service. But if you did infect me with your treachery, then I'll see you in Hell. Don't forget to say hello to Maury today at the airport."

"Don't you play that Jew shit with me. There is no Mossad asset network that you are handling in the airports. We would know. Even if you did, you don't know what PASSPORT looks like and have no way of identifying him."

"Good day, Robert. It has been a splendid game."

Robert sat motionless with his hands on the steering wheel. He watched a crow fly across the wet garden plots. A hawk followed swiftly, silently. He wanted to follow its path but doing so would meet Jerry's eye contact.

"I think you're bluffing on the Jew."

"Take your chances, Robert. And what makes you think it's only one? You know we have the whole of the Mossad."

"We've got the Russians and the Vatican. We would know. But you be careful, old boy. I'll take your sister's life and the two boys tonight if I so much as get a whisper that you aren't pulling back."

"Someday those threats won't hold up."

"They will while you still care. Pick one, Jerry, or I will. And back off the Pond. The Pond is nothing but a little toe and our foot will crush the Agency and bleed your rich allies dry. Mark my words. One series of market shifts and I could have it all."

"I won't back off, Robert. We might not be as strong as we were, but we still have a place. I know what the Pond is doing in South East Asia, too. I think I know what you'll use Prescott Draeger for now, as well."

"You don't know the half of it. Black smoke, white smoke. It's never by our hands and never what you think. You should be keeping an eye on the Ruskies and Chinks. They have a new bedfellow too. Think *Maskirovka*, the hallmark of Russian battle strategy to mask intent and activities. Russians expanding West, Chinese moving their fleets toward their desired territories, Iranians putting their chess pieces in Syria and around Israel. They're making their play here, and you're more worried about old club rivalries and summer turnips. Pathetic!" he spat. "I guarantee, Jerry, you all are going to be calling on us soon, and you will've used up your value for partnership. Taa taa. Lights out soon, Jer-bear, to you and all your Boners."

The truck jerkily rolled through the water-filled potholes and turned onto the main road. Jerry watched as it drove out of sight. He wondered where it was that both Robert and the truck transformed each day from hillbilly Virginian into a suit and Mercedes in Foggy Bottom.

Jerry walked over to the water spigot, washed his hands, and took a long drink from his cupped palms. As he wiped his mouth with the back of his hand, he watched two crows in counterattack mode against the hawk that sped just over the fields. The hawk was in retreat, and the crows continued their pursuit.

Jerry concluded that it would be an interesting spring.

Let the next round of games begin.

Chapter 13

Within the tight apartment, Paulo watched the two Pond operators insert the time pencil detonator.

"Now we shall add one more," he instructed patiently.

The men looked up at their advisor-client, questioning the odd command.

Paulo informed the men, like an easygoing school teacher to adolescent students, "We have a very special target. A very high-value target, as you say. It is recommended best way to use the two detonators from different families so if the one pencil breaks, the other one comes to the rescue to make the charge. You see?" Paulo smiled and raised his brow with a nod to affirm understanding. Paulo pointed to the next box so the men would select another chemically activated time fuse from a different batch.

Once connected to a silver azide detonator and to the charge, it was a near certainty to detonate.

Paulo started to mix two components together.

"What's that? I've never seen it." an operative questioned.

"This is God's kiss. It is made in your country, no? You do not know?"

Both men shook their heads, admitting ignorance of the blend.

"I actually meant your hands. Is that a burn?"

"The explosives business is not so good for beautiful hands. Now, please stay your attention to the lesson. This is Paulo's favorite. It is the HELIX. The high energy liquid explosive. It's one part the Yin, and one part the Yang. Completely field mixable. It's a phoenix. More powerful than other binary explosives."

"This is what we used on the go-go?"

"Yesss," Paulo hissed with another broad smile. "You see the phoenix rise to the sky to be blessed by God? Twenty-thousand feet per second. The gas. The energy. And the parts? Nothing. This liquid not make explosive. This liquid, nitromethane, not make explosive. Keep it. Carry it. Shake it."

Paulo added an activator component of blended aluminum powder and other agents to a plastic bottle and shook it vigorously, much to the discomfort of the other two men. "But you make love together and it is then a sensitive mixture. Blessed is the one most divine. Blessed is our purpose. Blessed is our reward. Blessed is the new world."

Knowing the power of the last explosion, the men watched in reverence as Paulo continued to gently blend the mixture until it created a new compound.

"We are almost ready to go."

The Thai national security agent followed the Russians discreetly into the small hotel, all unaware of the two male tourists further down the chain tailing their every move for blocks.

The Russian diplomats greeted the Chinese special interest group while the Thai security agent continued up to the hotel front desk.

Having placed a leather duffel on the bellman's cart in exchange for a room number and a handful of cash, the tourists exited the hotel while keying in a phone number. They pressed the final button once around the corner as the luggage cart made its way through the center of the entryway.

The explosion shook the ground and shattered windows a block away. Hemispherical shock waves vaporized those closest to the blast. The center of the burst exploded front doors and those along the entryway with an overpressure drag that sucked in loosened objects.

White smoke followed the blast that incinerated the small hotel lobby and those congregating within.

Nearly a quarter mile away, Paulo watched from the Thai Freemason Lodge window. The dark plume rose and hovered above the district buildings. Paulo pressed another button. A parked vehicle to the side of the hotel erupted in a violent explosion. The explosive, composed of triacetone triperoxide, or TATP, engulfed the two Pond operators in shock and heat, incinerating them instantly.

"Obedience is the sure Way. Obedience to the Superior is the way of sanctity. In the work of God, one is to obey. There is beauty in the victim, in the sacrifice. Thank you for your sacrifice. Your silence was needed. No one must see Paulo. It is now in order to begin."

Paulo sent an encrypted text message. MY BROTHER, I HAVE COMPLETED YOUR TASK. IT IS UNFORTUNATE TO REPORT DEMISE OF YOUR AGENTS.

Back in the U.S., on the seventh floor of the Central Intelligence Agency, Robert was meeting with the Director. He received a secure text transmission confirming an explosion in Thailand.

"Robert, do you need a moment?"

"Uh, yes, sir, one moment. It appears there has been another explosion in Thailand. I'm requesting more details. Robert responded to the text. START BLINDING.

Regina Hobson sprinted down the slick Georgetown neighborhood driveway as rain drops pelted her back and splashed up, soaking her nylons and the soft foam insoles of her black flats. As the wife of the current deputy director of the Directorate of Intelligence to the CIA, surely there had to be people who could get mail from the box a couple hundred feet away from the house. Her husband insisted on keeping things the same. Their lifestyle didn't reflect his promotion. They were academics, not dignitaries.

Nearly slipping as she tried to stop at the wooden mailbox, Regina regained her balance and pulled the latched door open.

The attached wire pulled the small rubber plug from the clamp, which closed and made a connection, igniting the Research Department Formula X charge and propelling the ball bearings and nails in a calculated 90-degree trajectory of primary and secondary fragmentation. The RDX military grade explosion tore Mrs.

Hobson's head from her frail body, which fell to splash and briefly hiss in the curbside puddles below.

George Yackley, Agency Directorate of Intelligence's So. East Asia Chief, turned the ignition key in the Audi A6 and immediately felt a slack in the motion, the engine failing to start. The combined HMX and CL-20 high-energy, high-density explosion erupted from the vehicle, setting the car aflame with the black smoke billows pouring from the shattered windows.

Two senior CIA Palantir targeting analyst contractors assigned to the Iranian Persia House suffered a similar fate while ride-sharing as they left the Booz Allen Hamilton parking lot.

A twofer, the Pond operative said to himself from across the highway. *Bingo, right on schedule.*

Robert received the new reports from the rear of the chauffeured town car and was briefly pleased. He continued to pick at his teeth. A small shred of the Ruth's Chris filet crust was stuck between his teeth. He sucked at it to no avail. How annoying. He needed a mirror. He wondered if the Director had noticed it. *Guess the Director is going to have his own shit in his teeth soon.*

Chapter 14

Rick was filling up his car with premium unleaded gas when his phone buzzed. He looked at the sign above the pumps warning of cell phone use. *Mythbusters disproved that,* he rationalized.

"Hey, what's up?"

His face froze in surprise, then quickly turned to anger.

"Wait, do we know who the Russians and Chinese were meeting in Thailand?"

His mind raced while he listened.

"Did we have anyone reporting this beforehand?"

Rick closed his eyes and shook his head in disbelief.

"Pond assets were killed?"

He waited a moment.

"Wait, how do you know they were Pond? Were they also at the meeting with them? That may rule out them planting these bombs. Shit! We need eyes on."

Rick listened while watching the gas gauge. Fifty dollars and counting.

"Our Agency people were also attacked there?"

He began to pace.

"Wait, so a different bomb? On our soil? Multiple? Is it public yet?"

Rick looked up to the sky and again shook his head in disbelief.

"Thanks for getting the girl transferred down to me. She will be an asset if we're going to do this right. Changes our approach a bit with these bombs, but I'll see what I can do."

Rick paused for a response and nodded, affirming something finally going according to his vision and plans.

He pressed his luck further. "Wait, it's my op. And what will you do about this situation once you have what you want?" He added, "I know when you are up to something and there has to be a reason you wanted Havens. It would be nice if you could share it with me."

Rick topped off the tank and returned to the car to continue the conversation in the relative privacy of a makeshift SCIF, a Sensitive Compartmented Information Facility, designed to keep those not in the know—with listening ears—out.

It took Sean about twenty minutes to drive to the private Duke medical facility. The atmosphere of the therapeutic research center reminded Sean of an upscale country club or resort. If you had to be in a place to recover, this place was it. He greeted the security staff as he passed by and then continued down the east wing to Maggie's suite.

The heavy door was slightly ajar, but Sean chose to give a gentle knuckle rap.

"Maggs?"

Sean could hear a flapping noise come and go from within. The light knock and well-oiled hinges eased the door open.

The room was still dark, save for the hallway entry and the sun's infrequent penetrating rays that shone from an open window over an empty bed and abandoned laptop. Each time a breeze caught the closed drapes, the bright light hopped in only to retreat back as the fabric slapped back against the window frame.

"Maggie? Hey. Maggs?"

He peered at the computer screen to see if the Kali Linux dragon screen saver was playing. The logo was a symbol of his wanna-be hacker daughter's more cerebral side. Mock cyber-attacks and script kiddie writing was good for her neuro re-development. She had already messed with Sean's IP address to demonstrate her growing technical prowess.

Havens caught a glimpse of the light switch as the next gust illuminated the room. He was reaching for the switch when a hand stopped his movement.

"Keep it off," an older female voice ordered.

As he turned, the silver honor bracelets on her wrists gave a tinny clank. Another hand touched his back.

"Aimee, where's Maggie?"

The nurse, who had lost two sons in overseas wars, wore her cuff memorials as a badge of honor. She had another son still abroad and a husband at home who was medically discharged from duty due to floating shrapnel. Sean had never seen husband or wife without an ear-to-ear smile despite their losses.

"Oh, hon, hope you didn't have a scare there." Aimee was fully aware of the Havens' situation. She patted his shoulder with heartfelt sorrow, knowing that this man would immediately jump to a conclusion with anything out of the ordinary. Aimee knew her patients' families and knew her local military community. Her senses were attuned to the stress, grief, and fears of "Fayettenam" that accompanied the patriotism, honor, and pride. The Havens family of two was new to the area, but they were now part of the greater Fayetteville–Fort Bragg family.

"Where is she?" Sean pressed.

"Well c'mon, I'll show you. She's in therapy right now. Had a bit of a headache earlier and she's sensitive to the light, so we're just keeping it dim for her. I keep the window open so she gets some fresh air and a tease of light. It's good for the soul. I think the laptop she's on all the time is also causing some pain, but she insists. Between trying to become a hacker and her PT, she's busy. Won't be long, I suppose, and she'll give those Chinese a run for their money on the Internet. Did you hear about their latest attacks on Personnel Management files?"

"Yeah, I was a bit concerned … and, yes, I was concerned when I didn't see her. You're loading me up on info, Aimee. I'm still dealing with a lot with the …" Sean stopped mid statement and realized Aimee had lost even more than he had. He continued, "Uh, her progress and would like to see what she's been doing."

"Oh, Sean, she's a fighter. Bet she was like her mom. Was she?"

"I suppose." *What could you know about her mom?*

Havens looked uncomfortable. Aimee saw a strong man not doing so well at holding it together.

"Sean, she might be gone, but the way we keep them alive is by talking about them. Keeping them at the forefront of our minds and lips. The world just forgets about 'em and moves on. It's up to us to keep their memories alive. Why, I make sure I say James Jr. and Jeffrey's name at least five times a day. Can't say the same for James Senior. He still has a time with it all if he isn't doing something active. Shame he couldn't stay in the military. Doctors should have stayed out. He's perfectly fine. You should see the chairs he's crafting out back in the yard when he isn't playin' in the woods. Heck, I don't know what he's going to do with all of 'em, but its keepin' his mind straight far as I can tell. I half expect he might build silhouettes out of wood and get to target practice."

Sean nodded as Aimee laughed out loud to herself.

"Ya know, Sean, I keep tellin' him to grow one of them Amish beards since he's doing all that woodwork. I even bought him a black Amish hat off the Amazon store." Aimee beamed at the recollection. "I thought it was a hoot. James Senior didn't like it one bit."

"What'd he do with it, pitch it?"

"Well, that is the funniest part. He put it down and walked just away. I should've known he was having a bad day either thinking about the our boys or his work boys. I felt so darn awful, but I was just teasin', ya know? Next thing, I go finish off some pulled pork I was making in the crocker...oh, you should try that some time. I make it with a bit of ginger ale at the bottom. James Senior puts in a little Knob Creek bourbon, to cut the sweetness he says. But we all know that makes it even sweeter. But I don't say nothin'. Had the pastor over one night for the pulled pork, and I was thinkin' good thing he ain't Baptist. James Senior cut a lot of the sweetness from that batch, if you know what I mean. Anyway, I peek out to see if he's still sore at me, and he's out in the yard wearing that crazy hat heading out for the woods."

"That's funny. Did he shave his moustache and trim down to an Amish beard?"

"Oh, no. He won't touch that. Pineland needles never get cut, just trimmed. What with all these boys running around here now with beards from the teams, I think he has to remind everyone that he should be running around Afghanistan and wherever else they're going that I don't know. I know he misses it, but 1st group gets him out there in the woods for Q course, so that keeps him happy to help with qualification screening. I put a little special forces 10th group flash pin on that Amish hat just the other day. Bought if off the eBay. I suspect he may wear it to church on Sunday."

Sean laughed out loud. It was the first belly laugh he could remember in quite some time. He had met Aimee's husband once and could play the whole scene in his head. James Senior was a long-tabber with a career in Special Forces as an enlisted. Despite some work in Africa and Europe, based in Stuttgart, Germany, his passion was jungle warfare until the desert wars started. His wish came true when he went into Colombia with Special Operations Command-South (SOCSOUTH), which was as close to being back in Vietnam as he could get. An explosion while hunting FARC rebels took him out of the game after only a few months in the country. It was suspected to be a way to put a battle-hardened lieutenant colonel (LTC) out to pasture. Truth be told, it was killing him. The depression from the loss of his job let the heaviness of his son's losses get to him. Aimee didn't mention it, but James Senior's deteriorating health was becoming a concern.

"There she is." Aimee opened the door and waved an arm toward Maggie in dramatic presentation.

"She shaved her head into a Mohawk?"

"Yep, I did. 'Cuz I can walk!"

Maggie Havens lifted her hands off of the parallel bars and took two steps toward her dad.

Sean Havens didn't even try to hold back the tears as he walked to his daughter with outstretched arms.

All he could do was shake his head as the words couldn't quite come. Overwhelmed with joy, relief, and awe, Sean could only hold his daughter.

And that was all she wanted.

"Havens, you don't get the money. You only took two steps."

Maggie and Sean looked to a young man sitting on a therapy table and sporting artificial legs. Sean assumed by the gold-lettered Ranger tab silk-screened on his black T-shirt and his various scars and skin grafts that the soldier had lost his legs in combat. Likely one of the many miraculous survival stories coming from the Middle East theater.

"Easy, Megatron. My dad got in the way."

"Did you just call me a Transformer?"

"You called me April O'Neil."

"That's flattering cause you're a computer whiz and all smart like the Teenage Mutant Ninja chick. You called me a robot."

"At ease, Perkins, I called you that cause you're badass with those metal legs," Maggie rebuked with a grin.

Sean looked back to Aimee. "Did I miss something here?"

Aimee smiled. "We have some friendly competition going on here between Miss Maggie and Staff Sergeant Perkins."

"Friendly nothing," said Maggie. "Outta my way, Dad. I've got a buck to win."

"She did this for a buck?" Sean raised his eyebrows, looking quizzically at Staff Sergeant Perkins.

By the time Sean looked back, Maggie had made it to the end of the rails.

"And now…" she started.

"Oh, no you don't. Hang tight. You need a rest, sister. Let me get over there to you." Aimee hustled alongside the apparatus over to Maggie and helped her back to the mats. "Let me help you down here, and I want you to try and do some lifts. But only a few. Let me get over to Staff Sergeant here."

"Nuh uh, I'm getting my buck back." Staff Sergeant Perkins pushed himself up for the first time without assistance.

"Mike, that's far enough. I'm coming over," ordered Aimee as she maneuvered around the apparatuses. "Good grief gravy-train. You two are giving me a fit of a workout."

Aimee saw the pain in Perkins' face. She knew the pain wouldn't stop him. He wouldn't be bested for a dollar or by a teenage girl. "Sean," she called, "you get on the other side of Mike here, but don't touch him. He doesn't need your help or mine. But we are going to be there in case the floor reaches up and pulls at his leg."

Sean nodded in understanding. "Okay, Mike, you can do this," he assured the young man quietly.

Mike was slightly distracted and turned to Aimee for guidance.

"Don't look at him, Ranger. Focus on me. One step at a time. Ready. Hup!" Aimee barked. "Give me another! Two. Girlfriend, you just lost your dollar," Aimee called out without unlocking her eyes from Mike's. "One more."

"C'mon, Mike, do it," encouraged Maggie from across the floor.

Mike looked over and became unsteady.

"Hold your arms out, Mike. Don't look at her. She's pretty, but she's too young," Aimee redirected. "Rangers lead the way."

"All the way!" echoed Mike as he reached the bars, grimacing. "All the friggin' way! And I didn't even need my Percocet."

"That's my boy. Getting off those painkillers is as fantastic as you walking," said Aimee. She gave him a round of applause. *Now if we could just get Mr. Havens to recover,* Aimee thought to herself.

Chapter 15

Havens' cell phone rang while he was enjoying some alone time with Maggie. Even though the conversation was kept light, he hesitated for a moment, wanting to give his daughter uninterrupted quality time.

"Are you going to take it?" she inquired with a slight testing attitude.

"I should. It's my boss."

"Well, then you better. Boss comes first. Right?"

"That's not fair, Maggie."

The phone kept ringing.

"Life's not fair, Dad." She turned away, pretending to tighten her shoes.

Sean took a deep breath and exhaled before answering.

"Sean, I need you in a briefing today. You need to get back over here a bit sooner," Rick said in his typical dry and curt way.

"What's up?"

"Just get back. Come see me when you get in."

Sean bounced his phone on his knee, searching for words. *How do I communicate with a teenage girl who has lost everything, and who, for all practical purposes, is imprisoned alone here with strangers? Not the best route for emotional recovery. For either of us.*

"Hey, kiddo, you know that was a call for me to get back to the shop. We should probably talk."

"Sure, how about now?"

Sean knew he had left himself open for that remark, and was certainly willing to letting his daughter get it out. His number one loyalty was to his daughter, and while he felt an obligation to work, he would stay by her side however long it took. Or so he told himself.

"Great. I don't mind being late."

"I don't want to talk, and you have to go. So just go."

"Maggs, what's bothering you? I know we've been through the wringer. But if you tell me, maybe I can help."

"Well Dad, do we start with you getting Mom killed, you working for the people who cause people to want to kill us, or hmm … how you have completely changed and could care less about your own family, or, hey, how about how you can't even go see your own wife in the morgue and send a friend instead?"

The words stung like a swarm of bees. Defensively, Sean protested her last accusation. "I didn't send a friend, Uncle Lars was there. You know I was overseas."

"Uh, yeah, wrong. Uncle Lars didn't. He said he couldn't and that your Red friend did. He said pretty much everyone did everything for you for Mom. It's like you didn't even care about her."

Red? "Hang on. I had help, yes, but that doesn't take away from how I feel about your mom," Sean objected. He felt eerily like he was debating with Christina.

Maggie wasn't having it. "I can't even imagine her lying there in some freezer and some stranger looking at her. She deserved better! You left us! They tried to kill us! And you weren't there, and you keep leaving me! And I'm all alone! I pretty much hate you right now. I hate you for what you've done. You killed Mom 'cuz you failed! You totally failed us. And now you are failing me *again*." Maggie sobbed uncontrollably. "I should just sign up for the military, maybe then you would care."

Sean put his arm around his daughter, but she tried to shrug it off. She then knocked his arm away with hers and scratched it on his rugged PVD coated Smith and Bradley Atlantis Rogue edition watch.

First she looked at her arm. Then the source. "Oh my God. You are even wearing the watch. Oh. My. God." She bawled harder.

"Maggie, please. Don't."

Maggie thwarted his attempt again to calm his daughter. "She gave you that 'cuz you promised. You promised to stop. And when you couldn't stop she made you put it away, and now you are wearing the watch. You are such a *liar!* Go!"

Sean tried reaching out again and this time she didn't resist. She turned toward him and rested her head on his chest, still bawling.

"I just miss her so much. I miss her," she cried.

"I know, sweetheart, so do I. Every moment of every day. I never wanted this to ever happen to you. I never thought it was possible."

"Then why are you still doing it?" she asked while drawing infinite circles on Sean's leg. "Can't you see that I miss you most of all? That's the worst of it. Mom's gone, you're here, and I feel closer to her. You come here at dinner and then just sit with me watching TV, and you don't say anything except dumb stuff that doesn't even matter. I can totally even tell that you don't want to be with me. It's like you can't wait to get back to work. And then you leave again and say you need to go for training. Training for what? To leave again? Why can't you just quit?"

Where do I start? "It's all I know how to do. It's the only way I can pay for you to get better. It's the only way to keep you safe right now while I'm working and away from time to time. I'd quit right now if I thought I could get another job or one that would give us what we need while protecting us. We could still be in danger. We just don't know. I can't let anything happen to you."

"You're always away now."

"I know. I don't want to be. Once I can get you better and know that we aren't at risk any more, we can see about some changes. I just need you to hang in there a bit longer. I know that's hard to ask of you. And I'm not asking you to trust me, I'm asking you to believe in me and to hold on to our future."

"Do you even like your job?"

"I like helping people, but somewhere things have gotten a bit cloudy. When I can see that I'm doing something to help someone else, I love it. When it isn't so clear, I hate it. It's getting harder for me to make some of my work choices. Too many things and too many people I care about get all crossed up in the lines.

105

What happened to our family was something that I have never heard of happening. I would never put you and Mom in harm's way."

"Are you kidding me? I was raped dad. I got a phone call from you. A phone call. Next thing, people are in our house shooting at us. And you were still gone. You were helping someone else god knows where. Mom wouldn't even tell me. You have no idea. No idea what that was like. I'm glad I was shot in the head, since I can't remember it all. I mean, if you're so important why couldn't those people fly you home with like on the President's plane or something to save your own family?" Maggie started sobbing again.

"Hey, I did. I own that, and I deal with that. It won't bring your mom back and for that I can never forgive myself, and I will never ask you to forgive me."

Maggie stopped the circles and Sean could tell that she was either processing what he said or thinking about something else. He felt ashamed that he checked his watch outside of her view. The watch was a symbolic compromise that he would stop deployments and spend more time with his family. Christina had bought it for him from a rural Illinois ex-SWAT craftsman who could give men the tactical functionality with the look that didn't shout "military." She gave him a rubber diver's strap for travel and a metal band for home. The watch was a success in the field but a failure as a family anchor.

Sean sighed. He would stay here as long as he could, but he couldn't jeopardize their precarious situation by losing the only job he could land that could give them what they needed.

"Do you miss your dog?"

Havens could tell that his daughter's mind was all over the place today. "Yeah. I miss that dumb dog a ton, too. Cougar was a great dog, but it was right to give her back to the soldier who worked with her in Afghanistan. It'll help them both. I talked to him. Real nice guy. He's having a pretty hard time adjusting from war. He was pretty close to wanting to end it all. He needed someone. He needed Cougar."

"I think she was helping you, too, though. You've been even madder since you gave her back to that guy."

Havens gave a small laugh of admission. "Probably right. But, I think maybe he needed her more than I did. Sometimes people need something or someone to take care of. Sometimes a soldier like that who was young and saw a lot of bad stuff just needs to feel responsible for someone else so they hang on."

"Like to not kill themselves. I know. There are pamphlets all over here about that."

"Then you get it."

"I miss home. I mean, the people are nice here, but it doesn't feel like our world. It's not Chicago."

It's my world, but I've kept it from you.

"You know, you're my Cougar. I can't forget about that."

"Gross, Dad. Do you even know what a cougar is? It's like a horny single mom."

"Enough." He poked her ribs. "Is there anything else you want to know or talk about right now?"

"No. I know you have to go."

"Are you sure?"

"Yeah." His teen looked up at her father with red puffy eyes. Her nose was still running. She looked like his little girl again. And he was going to walk away again. "Dad?"

"Yes?" He took a hard swallow.

"Have you killed people?" she asked like it was an everyday question, which it was for the Havens family.

Sean wasn't as surprised as he thought he would be if the question ever came up. He still didn't have the answer. *Don't lie, she knows you have. You're already a liar.* "Yes."

Not missing a beat, she probed further. "A lot?"

"Even one person is a lot."

"So you have."

"Yes."

"Do you think about those people? And their families?"

"Always." *Sometimes. Their faces come to me, I don't seek out the ghosts. Images of the moment. Scenes of battle in my dreams. But different.*

"Are you some kind of weird killer that they send out to assassinate people who won't listen to our government?"

"Is that what you think I do?"

"No. I know you work for the CIA. I know that's spy stuff."

"If you think you know, then why do you ask?"

"I want you to kill the people who killed Mom," she said flatly with command in her tone.

"Honey, those people *were* killed."

"All of them?" Maggie looked up at her father, wiped her eyes and nose, and rubbed it off on her pants. She looked him directly in the eyes, holding his gaze.

"I'm not sure. It's complicated. We don't know who everyone was."

Maggie lowered her voice to a near whisper. "I want you to kill them all. That's what I want you to do. If you're going away. Go away to kill those men."

What teen has a conversation like this? How can I fix this? And to his little princess, as if she were asking for a puppy, Sean Havens replied, "Okay, honey. I promise."

"What the hell took you so long?" Risk asked wanting an answer but not really looking to put much thought into it.

"Got here as soon as I could. I got stopped at the gatehouse for a while. Something about them not accessing my security tickets. Thought I was perm-certed here and good with my badge. They had to look me back up at the gatehouse. It was fine this morning."

"Not sure, what did they have to do?"

"Look in JPAS, but I wasn't in that system, and then they had to go to the SMO to get it from Scattered Castles, but there was some error there too. A few Deltas that I had bumped into at the Point who knew I was here pushed it through. I came in with them."

The DoD system of record, Joint Personnel Adjudication System, was notorious for not interfacing well to the Intelligence

Community's Scattered Castles database to validate eligibility and accesses to Sensitive Compartmented Information and other caveated programs. Often the Security Management Offices had to intervene just to let someone in the door. Most errors were due to failures of proper inputting by management.

Rick deflected any blame, "Strange. Anyway. There've been a growing series of bombings. You're going to hear in the next minutes about Intelligence community attacks CONUS."

"Holy shit. Terror groups?"

"We're not sure. Yet. There have been a series of IED attacks in Southeast Asia over the past days. You've no doubt heard of them here in the JOC and on the news."

"Sure. Took out a team of ours. They said car bomb."

"That's what they said, but the images tell me a different story. I requested a country team to check things out. SOG SAD (Special Operations Group / Special Activities Division). They just flew in. You'll be reach back and providing insights and Courses of Action designed to identify and understand the insurgents, violent extremists, or terrorists. Since it started there, that's where I want us to focus. Could also be Pond related given their MO of starting fires to fuel sentiment. They may have their own version of our Xbox IEDs that we use in the Middle East when we want it to look like someone else. We won't be able to do anything about these attacks on home turf, but maybe in Asia we can look at scenes with a different lens. Question the questionable."

"So I'll research and design something for the special activities ops group to attack weaknesses, vulnerabilities, or chokepoints in the VEO or FTO value chain?" Violent Extremist Organizations and Foreign Terrorist Organizations were known to collaborate when there were benefits in logistics, relationships, or profit.

"Exactly. Our A-team will go in to better detect, map, and analyze whatever is going on. Then you can simultaneously figure out logical supply routes, relationships, logistical networks, and whatever else that would facilitate their IED ops. It's pretty conventional, but those funding us can relate to that approach better. If you need to go outside the lines a bit in your thinking, weave in your own sauce but make sure there is enough grey beard shit so the powers that be don't reject it. No mention specifically of the Pond. Reference it as an unknown adversarial group or something."

"Sounds good. That would be a welcome little change and help on the home front. Not to pass the buck, but why isn't this a JIEDDO lead or a SOC forward group?" Havens probed, citing the responsibility of the Joint Improvised Explosive Device Defeat Organization, the DOD's lead dog in the fight against IEDs.

"It is a JIEDDO gig. But they didn't get very far. They lost a lot of funding. Plus most other decent military resources are out of the area on a joint-funded counterterrorism exercise in West Java. I can't have JSOC or SOCOM scramble folks back to the AOR without raising eyebrows and making it look like we're poking our noses in their shit."

"Okay, and you don't already have Ground Branch or a Global Response Staff to look into this?"

"Not for this. Our ground guys are sniffing out something else. I don't have anyone else in the area I can use. Fingers are in too many dykes."

"And did JIEDDO pull all their people from the area?"

"Yep. They took stuff back to their labs and whatnot. Each layer that they look at is going to have its own data types and data sets. They'll look for unwitting and witting participants and monitor them. There will be FBI, DEA, SOCOM threat finance guys, a whole shit-load of players looking at their analysis, but we won't get it in time to see how it relates to other events. Especially if the Pond is involved."

"So where do we come in?"

"While they have their head up Palantir's ass doing data analytics, and figuring out max explosives capacity and lethal air blast range, I want boots on the ground doing old-fashioned collection."

"Have you done any analytics? Not challenging, just wondering." Sean put his hands up, testing Rick's response in an attempt to improve his outward attitude towards the boss.

"I have a group that was doing social media intel. They looked at the events prior, during, and after. The algorithms were calibrated across text and semantic analysis and then mapped across the GEOINT to see what we could find on key influencers and any chatter."

"What'd you find?"

"Nothing."

"So it's a Brown HUMINT team, or are you using mostly guys from another Tier One element seconded to us?"

"You'll know when you see them. These guys have had some recurring access and placement. Pretty much full recurring freedom of movement and access with some cover for action. Status is good. They also run some surrogates. We had been working with a Delta team that was more visible in Thailand. I hate to say bait, but those guys were wrong place, wrong time in one of the explosions."

"You sure it was an accident?"

"No. We intercepted some traffic that Thai intel was there and picked up some buzz from sources on the ground there that an Iranian and Russian team were also caught up in the blast. The latest explosion involved Russians and Chinese. Something must be going on with those three, but aside from the Five Eyes community, I don't know who else would want to disrupt it."

"Three intel teams taken out and no one's raising an eyebrow?"

"We haven't exactly shared all of that with everyone. The badged operators that we had were your basic Advanced Force Operations task force made up from Delta. The guys were also seconded to the Activity for HUMINT and discrete action. They were listed as SOF training advisors in the Philippines and they hopped back and forth to Thailand."

"Were they working with the Joint Special Operations Task Force?"

"Yes. They and the JSOTF guys were hunting Khair Mundos, an Abu Sayyaf leader who we suspected was helping launder money from Al Qaeda to Khadaffy Janjalani on Mindanao Island."

"And you all thought the Thai bombings could be linked to the bombings on the island and in the Philippines?"

"Exactly. Thais said their guys were diplomatic officers as liaison to our crew. That was easy to bluff out. The other explosions had nothing related. Could be coincidence. Just not sure. Heard chatter that some Russians and Chinese were killed to send a message to their in-country intel assets. Others think they were negotiating resources in Thailand and Burma. It varies."

"So who is in this team I am going to meet today? They ST6 or CAG types?"

It always seemed to be SEAL Team 6 or the Combat Applications Group, otherwise referred to as Delta, by many.

"You'll see. Usual Tier One. Mostly old Delta crew. No SEALs. But they said to tell 'Fritter' they said 'hi.'"

"Said, 'Fritter,' huh?"

"That's what they said," Rick smirked.

"Oh, hell. The Clandestine Support Survey cell?"

"Nope. Not anymore. Moved on from some of the stuff you were doing. Was it called Grey Fox at that time?"

"I dunno. Task Force something. Still Activity work. Different day, different names." Sean showed concern about the crew with a twisted expression on his face. He was processing who all may remain on the team.

"Well, anyway. It's a mix of green badge contractors and military now retired or semi-retired, but pretty much Delta and Agency folks. They're contractors now for us. Couple blue badge paras through Agency, one through DynCorp, few through MVM or Academi, maybe Triple Canopy. Not sure. Don't care. It's just a contract vehicle. We pretty much okay who we want on the team. Speaking of which, I still need to read you in to the program—Rapid Frost. They know it as Primed Charge."

"Shit. These guys hate me, except for the general."

"Pretty much. The medic likes you. General will be coming soon. He's checking out a new obstacle course. Looks to me like they outsourced it to the Tough Mudder race guys so the military can save a few bucks and change things up a bit without investing in structures. But that's their business."

"Is the general overseeing it?"

"Nope, he's running through the course right now to make sure it's hard enough."

"That sounds like the Danger 6 I know."

Chapter 16

General Bain, AKA Danger 6, ran through the twenty-five-yard path of burning hay.

Smoke was thick.

He leaped over the low flames burning the four-foot-long wood obstacle, still holding his breath. The landing gave his sixty-four-year-old deteriorating hip a jolt. His mouth agape in unacknowledged pain, the general took advantage of the fresh air filling his lungs.

Most of Danger 6's pain was in his knees and shrapnel-damaged shoulder, so another shocking bump wasn't worth the distraction. The fresh wind he caught oxygenated his blood, reinvigorating his limbs.

Danger 6 focused on the next obstacle, which was a thirty-year-old Delta operator whom the general had been pursuing for the past six miles.

The young operator knew the old man was closing the distance.

The dangling electrical charges were just up ahead.

The operator smiled at the thought of shocks setting off the general's pacemaker, if he had one, which he didn't. The younger soldier would take any advantage over the "old man." As he heard the nearing footfalls, the younger Delta warrior was reminded that Danger 6 wouldn't have a pacemaker, a pacemaker would have a Danger 6.

"Hurry your ass up, kid, you don't want an old man to beat you," the general taunted.

"No sir, I think I've got this one," he shouted back, trying to keep his breath.

"That's what the other boys said, and they're all behind us now."

"Yes, sir, but I'm in front of you and intend to keep it that way."

"Hoo-ah."

"Sir," the young soldier puffed, "the electrical wires are up ahead. Don't suppose you have any undetonated charges lodged somewhere in your body, do you?"

"I hope so, I've got an itch on my right shoulder and I don't want to take the time to scratch it!"

The operator snorted and willed his body faster as he entered the electrical field. He viewed the nearly 100 dangling wires that charged with electricity every few seconds. The 10,000-volt shock could easily bring even the fittest men to their knees. It appeared that the wires to the left were more spaced out. The operator shifted his gait slightly and veered toward the seemingly weaker area.

The stings of current were initially tolerable despite the discomfort of the searing, white-hot live wires. Then a loud, cracking shock dropped the young soldier to his knees.

"Don't move your hand, I'm coming through!" Danger 6 warned.

The soldier looked up to see the general breezing through the wires by holding up a rubber tire to part the dangling current lines.

"Shit!" The younger man struggled to get up as he received additional jolts.

"Unconventional warfare! Don't give up until you're dead, kid!" the general called out as he sprinted to the finish, tossing the car tire.

"Screw you, Dad. Tough old fart."

"Hoo-ah!" Danger 6 called back while grabbing a water for himself and his son.

Chapter 17

"Get him today," the voice said over the phone.

"We'll put a team in place around his route and rendition him when the opportunity presents itself."

X continued to weave through the streets of Arlington, Virginia, in an effort to evade whoever was on his tail.

Early in the morning, as he targeted a hotel for the daily deuce drop, he sensed something was off. It started with a heightened awareness of flows. At first it was a weird feeling. A few passersby seemed more coordinated. Linear walking patterns. Cars flowed in and out of streets without the normal challenges with entering traffic from a parallel parking job. It didn't seem like life. It seemed structured. Like surveillance or a hit.

On foot for hours, X maintained circuitous routes. He was careful not to let on that he knew he was being followed and he never looked back. Nor did he try to pull any traditional schoolhouse countersurveillance tradecraft.

And he still had to shit something awful.

From Rosslyn, X continued down Wilson Boulevard. He considered the Metro but was afraid that he might get boxed into a situation and lose the feel of the street. He turned down Courthouse Road and grabbed a quick coffee at the Bayou Bakery, then continued on his way.

Yes. Same Nissan Altima. Same white Kia Sedona.

He walked down 15th Street toward Clarendon Boulevard and saw a blue Ford Focus slow after Adams Street. Quickly, but not too reactively, X turned into the Residence Inn Arlington Courthouse.

There was only one thing to do in a time like this. Enter an elevator, get off on a floor with other guests, find a room that was being cleaned, and take that shit. The rest would be sorted out.

The courthouse. Get to the courthouse. Anyone pursuing me with electronics or weapons will have to go through metal detectors. I can go in, make a phone call, and stay safe. I need a safe haven. Shit. I need Sean Havens.

When Havens walked into the large briefing room, he recognized a number of faces that he had assumed would be present. Including one he hoped would be absent.

"Well bless my soul, Casper the spook wasn't bluffing us. We really are getting a shit-weasel that we've met before. If it isn't Sean Fuckin' Havens, dicksmack extraordinaire," Cooter harassed. Cooter was a legendary breacher and an even more legendary asshole.

"Fritter!" a more affectionate acknowledgement resounded from the group in unison.

"Fritter?" Rick inquired, casting Havens a curious glance.

"Never mind."

The team busted out laughing.

"Let's just get down to the meeting, guys," Sean deflected. He scanned the room and recognized almost all of the team members.

In the far corner, he could make out Danger 6, still splattered with mud in a T-shirt and shorts. The general had two banana peels and two crushed Monster energy drink cans in front of him.

Sean nodded in acknowledgement to the revered man to whom he had provided intel support over the years. "Hello, Sir."

"Hello Sean. Good to see you. You know, I kinda like how Fritter came about. Go ahead. Tell your boss."

Rick smiled in anticipation, "That's probably an order, coming from a general officer." He crossed his arms, awaiting the explanation.

"Retired general officer," Havens corrected. Then he drew a coy glance to the general. "With all due respect, Chief, as a contractor he might not have the clout," Havens responded with a smile.

"Havens, if you don't tell him the fucking story, I will." Havens recognized the voice but hadn't seen the man in his initial scan of the room. "Doc" Chang. Former team medic with at least five times as many confirmed kills as field saves.

"It's not worth this bullshit," Sean said, knowing it was just a matter of moments before he would cave.

"Weenie."

"Fine. But it's stupid. Everyone gets a dumb nickname that ends up sticking."

"I don't," Rick smirked.

"Not that you know of .... Anyway, I was working the south of France and running some soft assets around the Mediterranean. These guys needed to target a Tunisian ship coming in to Marseilles."

"Skip that bullshit," called another team member.

"Fine. I was going to provide countersurveillance and they wanted to scramble up some new call signs."

"Oh, my sweet baby Jesus, Havens, you are putting me to sleep," said the monstrous breacher, now putting his head down on a table in mocked boredom.

"Shut up, Cooter," a team member scolded the former Alabama Green Beret.

"So anyway, Chuckles, well, Chuck, decides we will use bear names. They start off, Kodiak, Grizzly, Black Bear, Brown Bear, and as they were getting to me, Cooter shouts out..."

"Fuckin' Bear Claw!" Popped Cooter, springing his head from the desk. "Like a donut 'cuz he's an intel donut eater. But then Doc said he never heard of a bear claw donut."

"Then Scottie says, 'Like an apple fritter.'"

"Then I yell out 'Fritter,'" cackled Cooter.

Doc Chang giggled, "If you ever see anyone up at Fort Belvoir, they only know him by that name. Fuckin' Draeger was the only guy who ever called him by his name."

"Shit, how's he doing, Sean?" Cooter inquired with a look of sympathy that was anything but genuine.

"Hey! Over the line, Cooter," warned the general. "Your shit is getting a little thick."

In an act of intelligence community solidarity against the operators, Rick addressed the team. "Well, that was a pretty lackluster story. If you guys need to name each other teddy bears, do it on your own time. Havens will be reach back and acting ops planner for this op. Sir, you will have Sean as your resource for whatever you need. I know he knows your style and preferences, so it should give good continuity."

"Roger that, Rick. Thanks. Usual package will do, Sean."

"Roger that, Sir."

Cooter threw up his arms and addressed the faded and stained drop ceiling panels. "W-T-F-O. Sir, with all due respect, Havens is going to give us an over-complicated, over-detailed goat rope, CGSC SAMSter PowerPoint, Ranger soup sandwich that ain't going to mean shit in the field. He ain't no trigger puller, he's just a fucking sick call ninja. I could step away for a ten-minute pump and dump and come back with a better operationalized intel report than he's going to give us. Then we have to deal about his whining about needing more time to do it right. Needing more time to get the answers. Needing time to think."

Cooter started bobbing his head obnoxiously while continuing on, "Come up with a contingency plan. Run through the scenarios. Then I'm going to get in trouble for telling him to shut his dick-trap even though everyone else is thinking the same thing. Am I right?"

The team averted their eyes regardless of their opinions.

Rick justified, "Havens has been through more training that is directly applicable..."

Cooter dragged on his rant, "I'd say it's not real training. Havens isn't dead. You're pussyfooting him through. I've seen his file. Boy Scout here doesn't have the stones that we have. You guys drop him into trainings like he's a foreign operator getting an international love tour. Everyone goes soft on him whether you want to believe it or not."

Rick countered, "I don't believe you are cleared to see what he has done and can do."

"Couldn't hardly save that group in Kenya."

"Cooter," the general addressed firmly. "I'd be careful." The general nodded to Havens approvingly and then to another one of his men sitting just behind Cooter.

"Sean, be cool," Rick said in a lowered voice. He hadn't thought there would be an actual problem, but clearly there was bad blood lingering. "Okay, guys, enough is enough," he said in an attempt to gain some control of the room. He looked to General Bain as a fellow senior leader, but saw the general blessing Havens to respond with simply a look. Rick sensed a prison fight brewing and guards being told to let it go.

They're baiting you, Sean, just chill, thought Rick.

Meanwhile, Sean recognized that he was being instructed to step up as an Alpha dog to regain his place with the pack. To back down would mean slaughter and banishment. Rage was overcoming him. He had to find a balanced response where he wouldn't lose control. *Keep cool dude, you're bigger than this. Walk away.*

"Cooter, you're probably right. The roast is over, and I just hope to be able to support you guys in a way that best aligns to your mission." Sean extended his hand. *Now you take the bait, fucker, while I go on record for standing down.*

Cooter received a look of encouragement from one of his teammates to keep pushing the envelope. Cooter was back on the playground trying to make the new kid cry. Final blow. "What a pussy. Sir, you have got to be shitting me. If Havens had skills, his family wouldn't be all …"

Chill's over. Havens pushed a notepad off the table just to the left of Cooter. Quickly, he grabbed another notebook from the next table and rolled it tightly. Cooter turned his head to follow the papers and missed the upcoming paper baton by Havens that connected with Cooter's upper lip and nose. Blood splattered in a spray through the air, misting the desk.

"Fuck, Cooter, you sprayed me," laughed Scottie, wiping his own face. "I'm gonna get AIDS," he spit.

Still in the fight, Sean cranked back his torso and right arm. He swung the makeshift weapon and met Cooter's swinging head, solidly connecting to the agape jaw and contorting the big man's face. Rebounding in momentum, Havens slapped Cooter's left ear with an open hand, then the right side of his head with the rolled tablet before his opponent fell off the chair to the ground, stunned.

The general started moving. He needed Cooter for the mission and couldn't afford having him in the infirmary before they set off.

Havens flashed back to his attack on Harrison Mann, who had kidnapped Maggie from the hospital not five months ago. The surprise attack. The barrage of punches.

Why is everyone messing with me?

Havens snarled his teeth and lips and moved to stomp Cooter but was pulled back by Rick.

The general moved to shield Cooter.

Havens at first resisted, yanking an arm free from Rick but caught the old man's gaze.

Danger 6 lifted his chin and shook his head, signaling the time had passed and Sean had done just enough to prove himself and take his place again with these men.

Havens panted like a wild dog. "Sir, would you like that briefing printed in PowerPoint or a Word doc?" Sean flipped the bloodied notepad back on the desk.

"Shit, Havens, whatever you think is best," the general snickered.

"You go, Fritter," said Doc, who had moved into the melee to sit on a table with a better view.

"Doc, help clean up Cooter," Danger 6 ordered.

"He looks okay to me, Sir," replied Doc Chang, not budging and leaning back on his elbows. "Havens just hit him with a piece of paper and then slapped him a little."

"Doc!" Bain commanded.

"Fine. Fine. Hope you have a concussion, Cooter." Doc winked at Sean, who was still trance-like.

Havens turned around to Rick, slowly snapping out of his state of fury. "Am I in trouble, Chief? I tried doing it your way. Made sure I didn't punch anyone and cause a lawsuit."

"Get started on what the general needs." Rick turned to the general. "Sir, anyone you'd like to work with Havens to ensure your tactical needs are directly in sync?"

"Let him take a chop first. Shea, brief Havens on the platform we're using to get in and out. Doc, you put in your two cents, too, after Cooter's squared away."

"Cooter's fine. I took a look at him. I'll get with Sean now."

"Doc!"

"Fine, fine, fine." The Asian, a former young hot-shit back surgeon turned enlisted special operations medic, tended to have more interest in doling out pain and death to his enemies than in caring for the team's wounded. In a hot environment, he could do both with equal precision and passion.

Doc Chang looked at Cooter with contempt. "You say that kinda shit to me ever, I'll cut your throat, white trash piece of shit. Big chicken dinnered you out of the military for a reason. Bad conduct never stops. You shake hands with Havens."

Cooter said nothing and didn't move.

"Let them be, Doc," said the general, walking out the door with his back to the men. "I know what you're doing, Doc, and there will be no more fights."

Chang fired a stiff locked thumb between Cooter's ribs. "Shake!" he whispered in a last act of defiance.

"I'm good if you're good, Cooter. We don't need to shake." Havens said, also not moving to make amends.

"I'm good, Sean. You can sucker punch, but you'll never be one of us."

"Never said I was."

123

X tried Havens again. "Pick up, Sean. Pick up. It's my turn now."

Chapter 18

"Contact Draeger," PASSPORT ordered his regional intel chief. "I need to meet with him. I need to see him again for myself. Get him to Turkey and then have him book a ticket to Greece. I'll give you more details later."

"Kristoque continues to watch him and support his vices. He reports Draeger's not well."

"'Not well' in the sense that his is ill, or 'not well,' as in he is an utter demon?"

"The girls they give him end up missing. Kristoque supplies Draeger with enough pills and liquor for a dozen high-tolerance addicts."

"But he's functional, correct?"

"I don't know how, but yes. But functional is relative. The man is a powder keg and, it appears, a murderer as well."

PASSPORT tried to appease him. "You know I'm smiling at that statement. Who among us will cast the first stone? Give it time. We'll clean him up. I want to further assess him in person. He's just a tool. Broken works for him. Broken will work for us."

"He's moving money on his own. He has assistance, but they are good at covering their trails."

"I'm sure he's trying to hide his personal and stolen funds. I do need him to follow protocol for wire transfers and money movement. Langley is going to have their schnoz up our asses for a while until we can cut off their noses. You will need to send him that message directly. Kristoque can't be trusted with this. I don't want Kristoque to have much power, either."

"How much autonomy do we want to give Draeger?"

"As much as he wants for now. Let him feel empowered and let him get creative. I want to see what he can do. Then we'll reel him in."

"I think he's a huge liability."

"We're all pawns to someone. If he screws up, he disappears. Make sure he doesn't screw up. We might need to clean him up and give him some small sense of purpose for now. Prescott Draeger is a man who needs to belong to something bigger than himself, but it must be elite. Exclusive. And, moreover, worthy of the image he has of himself and his capabilities. Give him that and he will rise to meet the challenge. I have a plan for him."

"Understood. I'll wait for your orders before I deploy the others for his indoctrination."

"Not a moment before then. I have to be certain. Security and reputation are everything."

Prescott Draeger was making friends quickly.

"I'll have another woman for you tonight, Mr. Black. You'd better take more care with this one. I say this to you with the utmost respect, I owe your people much, but not this much. This is business for us. Not favors. These girls are to make money. More girls is more problems."

"Just get me the woman. Not a young one. I will not accept another offer for a nubile."

"What is this 'nubile'?"

"Children. No children. Those little teens you try to pawn off on me. It's disgusting."

"It is interesting hearing *you* speak of disgusting. You have morals somewhere in there, that head of yours?"

"I asked you last time. Someone with blond hair, over thirty."

"This will be very hard to find. I may have to charge you. These woman for this age are old for the business. They are dirty. Diseased. For fresh high-quality, they have families and they would be reported missing. The young girls we can find. They are very nice. You have curious appetite. People pay millions for the young ones I present to you."

"Just do it," Prescott barked at Kristoque. Lowering his voice, Prescott asked of his host, "So who are we meeting here?"

"These are business men. They are local power men. They control the gambling, some drugs, women. They have cash but need to move the money without nose picking in their business."

Draeger chuckled out loud. "Nose sticking, you mean? People sticking their noses in their money flows?"

"This is what I said," Kristoque punched back defensively.

"You said nose pick." Draeger stuck his gloved finger to his nostril.

"Maybe mister funny man would prefer my language then. You will be cautious to not make mockery of these men, Mr. Black, they will cut your throat."

"Just helping you out," Prescott patted Kristoque as they wound through the deteriorated neighborhood. Pale, washed-out brick buildings with random splintered wood and masonry scattered over patchy grass, cobblestone, and gravel. "General, start calling me Mr. Kordova when we get close. Are we far?"

"We are nearing. You can hear the men now."

Prescott Draeger cocked his head and strained to hear voices. Instead, he heard cheers. As Draeger had been walking into the village, he assumed the noise was from white waters that ran along the town borders in rushing streams. Waters that reminded him of fly fishing in Montana with his grandfather.

He wiped those memories and tucked them back into their corner. As Draeger neared the village, the shouts and cheers became more discernable as men grew excited about something. Happiness. Anger. He could not yet tell.

"What are they shouting at?" Draeger inquired with a puzzled look as he tried to make out context without more details.

"You will see, turn here. Keep near me, say nothing. I will make introduction to the powerful ones when it is time."

"I'll follow your lead, but don't make me look like an underling. We get one shot at first impressions. I need to gain respect immediately."

"Turn here, Mr. ... Kordova."

Prescott counted about twenty men. They were circled around something to which the shouts and cheers were directed.

A dog barked aggressively to the right of Draeger as they entered the clearing. Prescott whipped his head and jumped to his left. A chained dog gnashed his teeth aggressively.

Good lord. Pit bulls.

"Come, Kristoque!"

The men parted as the general ordered them to move. They shoved others back to clear a path and gave Draeger the stink eye. The men ranged in ages from teens to twenties and thirties. They were unshaven, smelled of body odor, and wore workmen's clothes. Blue-collar thugs, it appeared.

As Draeger deduced, they were betting and howling at the dogs fighting in the makeshift ring composed of three foot plywood walls draped with blankets and rugs. The ground was similarly adorned with a patchwork of bloodstained cloth that was constantly being readjusted by the spectators, who would lean over and straighten the coverings when the canine gladiators untidied them.

Two brown pit bulls rolled in a death grip. One dog had the other's full muzzle clamped in its viselike jaws. The dogs thrashed and clawed one another, trying to gain leverage to reposition a fatal bite.

Draeger scanned the crowd. Rough hands held wads of paper money. Each of these hooligans were probably carrying twenty thousand dollars or more, Prescott estimated. Back in the U.S., Draeger would have expected these men to be fifteen-dollar-an-hour laborers. He further presumed that these guys must be involved in ephedrine manufacturing or marijuana cultivation and trafficking to Montenegro. Probably some traffickers and henchmen. Maybe some had their hands in the Afghani heroin trade. Either way, a good source of funds for Draeger.

Their expressions also told Draeger that this was not a big bet. There was likely a winner or loser in this match, but all the men were smiling, laughing, and cheering. No one seemed stressed. No one was panicking at the thought of financial loss. This was a nickel, dime, quarter Saturday-night poker game for these men. A really good source of funds for Draeger.

He leaned toward the general. "How often do these matches happen?"

The general turned around with a scowl, annoyed that his warning of silence was not followed. He snapped under his breath, "Every day. Five, maybe ten matches."

Holy shit, Draeger thought. Draeger had witnessed cultures like this before. It could be misconstrued that the men had blood lust. However, in truth, it was an accustomed indifference to violence. The dogs were a means to an end. Entertainment.

The cheers became thunderous.

Draeger turned his eyes back to the pen, where a clear victor fully straddled a twitching loser.

The handlers entered the ring to claim their dogs.

The losing owner laughed and took in the taunting of the onlookers, who exchanged the fistfuls of currency.

With less time than the span of a breath, a new melee ensued as two more dogs were thrown into the ring.

The cheers started again as the two beasts charged one another in a Greco-Roman wrestling hold. Jaws snapping and ripping.

Draeger resumed a scan of the crowd.

On the outskirts, he saw a number of older men who received occasional handshakes. The power brokers' henchmen, to their rear, received what Draeger assumed to be tribute monies. Handfuls were stuffed into black leather duffel bags. More cash. Nowhere to enter the conventional monetary system without tripping alerts for money laundering.

How long was this going to take? Prescott wondered. He was disgusted by the Neanderthal behavior. He gave two shits about the dogs, but detested the spectators. Put two men in the ring and let them fight it out. That would be a show.

Draeger was getting itchy. He wanted a drink. He felt like a nail was being slowly pushed through his eye socket to his brain. The headaches were coming back. The blood on the blue-and-green-flowered blanket in the ring was curious. Did the spatter from Christina and Maggie Havens look like that in the room where they were shot? *Christina.* Draeger fantasized about seeing her again. Her reaching a soft palm to his face and saying his name.

A man jolted Draeger back to the situation at hand when he threw a shoulder to crane a better look while a dog repositioned for a reversal, losing half an ear in the process.

"Enough!"

Prescott barreled through the remaining crowd to the pen, pulling out his firearm. Draeger pointed and fired at the two dogs, killing them instantly.

The crowd was shocked into silence, not taking their eyes off the dogs for a moment while Prescott Draeger stepped into the ring.

Nearly in unison, most of the men drew arms and pointed them at the dog-killing stranger.

"Thank you for your attention! I am Mr. Kordova!"

"You killed my dog! You will pay with your life!" the enraged owner hopped over the wooden pen gate while reaching for something covered by a well-worn leather jacket.

Draeger fired two rounds to the man's knee and he crumbled. Still no one fired on Draeger.

"I am here to make you an offer. All of you. And for you redneck Albanians, you will be able to buy millions of dogs if that's what gets your rocks off."

A voice from the crowd shouted, "I like this guy," and started to laugh. The crowd laughed as well.

"Yes, millions of dogs!"

Kristoque folded his arms and watched the spectacle. *Mr. Black, you must go.*

With a bank account full of operational funds liberated from the Department of Defense, Prescott Draeger knew it would be only a matter of time before his money was found and frozen.

As a matter of utility and business value to the locals, he received cash monies in exchange for his access to vetted bank accounts that were used for large and frequent international wire transfers and financial conversion.

With a finite window for activity that would flow under the noses of DoD and bank compliance controls, Draeger facilitated the placement and layering function to launder illicit funds for the local Albanian crime families.

His former communications expert, Jason, at the helm from a remote location in Europe, ensured that the accounts remained clear of red flags and suspicious activity filings.

"Jason, we're going to be running low on time and account equities. I need you to convert what we have and put funds into unaffiliated accounts. Also, check the slush account that Silver Star had for us. I had an account only General Frye and I knew about. I should be able to message it to you in three bursts, numbers will be in reverse order. I'll discuss with our organization their go-forward protocols and preferences. I'll send you a secure file with his personal information."

"Will do, Prescott. You sure that I'm safe out here in Luxembourg? I'd rather be somewhere like Dubai. DoD could pull of a snatch and grab pretty easily here."

"If they want you, they'll get you wherever, Jason."

"Thanks. Reassuring."

"I'll talk it over with the boss. I just got word that I'll be meeting with him soon and can discuss your role and usefulness to me."

"I'd appreciate it."

"Are you still laying low, Jason, no outside communications to the community, friends, or family?"

"… No."

"You paused."

"My kid sis, Judy, is on the inside at JSOC somewhere, but we've had a couple benign exchanges on secure chats. I ensured that there was no way our commo was compromised. It gives us an ear down at Bragg."

"Loose lips, Jason. I'll make you an example before they make me one," Prescott warned. "I swear to god if we get hunted because you called a baby sister …"

"Roger that."

"Roger what?"

"I understand."

"You understand you can never have contact? That you no longer have a family to go back to?"

Silence filled the airspace. "I understand," Jason lied.

"Good, then we have no more problems," Prescott Draeger lied back. *Sorry pal, but I need to remove you as soon as all finances are confirmed. I won't have you running a sibling asset at Bragg. Counterintelligence will be up your ass in a matter of a month.*

Chapter 19

After hours of trying to reach Havens, X contemplated his next move. He was a lone sheep amongst wolves. And worse, his cell phone was almost dead.

The watchers were overt and had bypassed security, discreetly handing weapons to their colleagues waiting in the wings.

Shit! X paced. He needed to flee but was concerned about losing a signal in the marble-lined halls.

It was a punt or pass decision, and X decided to pass. He logged into a secure cloud account and started moving files.

The battery level went red.

X logged into his secure email and sent the cloud account and password information. The application hiccupped, signaling power failure.

Two men mounted the stairs and ascended at a rapid pace.

X started to move farther from the area and watched his signal diminish. He doubled back to recapture strong connectivity to the cellular tower and hit send.

His phone blackened. It was time to run.

During the next few days, Prescott Draeger's patience was tested as he traveled to an unknown destination to meet PASSPORT at an unknown time.

He was instructed to sit in the terminal between American Airlines and British Airways at Athens International Airport. And he was specifically told to remain in the second row of leather seats, where they would meet each other like business partners.

"Mister Ludwin. How good of you to see me during your connection. I trust your travels have been good?"

Prescott turned to see PASSPORT with another man. Draeger vaguely recognized the aide from the National Capital Region in years past.

"Indeed, Frederick," Draeger replied, using a false name provided to him to address PASSPORT. "It was fortunate to be in the same place." The two men shook hands and Prescott tried in vain to place the other man.

"I'd like to introduce you to my colleague, Steven. We have been traveling together these past weeks."

Steven, a medium-sized man fit with a viselike grip, was clearly security. He never made eye contact with Prescott and continued to discreetly survey the area.

Curious, Prescott, pried. "I didn't know there would be others, are we still free to discuss the account?"

PASSPORT waved off Prescott. "Just a precaution. There is rumor of increased, shall we say, nuisances who might be lurking. Nosy little Jews, as it were," he whispered.

"'Nuisances,' huh?" Draeger leaned in. "The Mossad kind that can burn us or the Sayeret Matkal kind that can kill us?"

"Let's let Steven worry about that. On to other matters. I understand that you are making friends?"

"I'm making some progress rekindling old contacts and making some new ones."

"From what I have heard through our dear general, you are doing less kindling and more fuel-fed burning. What of this stunt you pulled with the locals, their dog hobby, and their monetary policies?"

"Just leveraging some operational autonomy to let them know who was in charge. They're fine now that they have a place to put their money. It was a gamble. But it paid off."

"Hmm. A gamble with other people's reputations and money. And speaking of money, this money, Prescott, that you are exchanging. I don't believe it is all yours. Wouldn't you agree?"

Prescott Draeger had thought that his personal financial activities were far enough from Pond oversight and secure enough that they would go unnoticed. Either someone was talking or the

Pond was even better connected to the financial world than he realized.

"Mr. Ludwin, I am waiting for an answer. You know that it is in your best interest to tell the truth and ensure that I find you to be trustworthy. Stealing from the government is untrustworthy. Stealing from us ensures a very assured and unpleasant demise."

"I'm only pausing while trying to think of what you know. These are my personal affairs as well."

"When your 'personal affairs,' as you say, involve you propping up assets and individuals who will be assisting with our work, it is of my concern. When it is about your appetite for fucking then killing whores, swallowing endless pills, and whatever other vices you might feed behind closed doors, it is also of my concern. When you need to buy a toothbrush or a pair of socks, then and only then is it not of my concern, nor my interest. That, sir, is your own money."

"Understood."

"In truth, you don't understand. You can rationalize, but it is eating at you and I know it. This is our honeymoon period. We're building the foundation of our new relationship and trust is everything. We have big plans for you. You are a potential candidate for something very special, which will give you continued benefits of privilege."

Draeger perked up. "I'm listening. What do you need me to do?"

"Your money exchange is in direct correlation with activities that we, as God's bankers, are involved with. We seek to increase drug trade and illicit funding exchanges to destabilize areas so others can become more stable—or so that we may restabilize them in a more appropriate, shall we say, *vision* befitting us. This means you will cease your activities to liquidate monies that you have stolen, clean up your affairs of that matter, and start your work on our priorities. It is my error that you were less informed. See, I too am fallible." PASSPORT grinned cheesily. "Make note, because you will likely not see me fail again."

"It's clear to me, and I will follow your request."

135

"Splendid. And quid pro quo, did you really kill the little missing whores that you were given by one of our business associates? He has voiced, shall we say, his *inconvenience* in delivering additional little trollops to you since they tend to run away in the forest."

"I'm working out some personal issues."

"Well, you have two choices. You can continue in this manner, and we will readjust your job description to be more like Steven's, dealing with security and the vices of the world. Or, and this is what I would prefer, you will assist in our business activities and we can count on you at a higher level."

"What exactly are your business activities? Clearly, my former participation has been more in operational capacity."

"That was a bit of our old model. Drugs, armament, political influence, typical clandestine service work but a bit edgier. All in an effort to retain political power so we can keep our nation and world safe. We are a state within a state of sorts. Now, we have money in banks with global financial reach and understandings, just as you did, at fleas' spit level. We buy cash and get rid of cash. We move markets, shift markets and influence markets through our global, shall we say, like-minded brethren. Our specialty has been buying legitimate businesses that are foundering and using those businesses for legitimate transactions that fit the profiles of the financial institutions' due diligence and monitoring of activity."

"Just like mafia using a restaurant then burning it to the ground."

PASSPORT winced. "So pedestrian. No. We flood it with parallel legitimate transaction flow patterns. We control major aspects of electronic funding globally. Have you heard of the SWIFT financial messaging mechanisms?"

Not waiting for a reply, PASSPORT waved a dismissive hand in the air and continued.

"At low levels, to keep things interesting, we don't use those pizza-eating, Monster-drinking, hoodie-wearing hackers to get into the banks that are less cooperative. We find and hire the best. Most banks are securing wire transfers. We are at a level of sophistication where we can leverage individuals to go into shared drive servers to access the risk management anti-money laundering standards. We can gain access to AML protocols, risk system tuning metrics, and thresholds of all major banks. It's cheaper to secure those resources than it is to recruit and induce a bank executive when all the alarms will go off if we go outside of typical transactional patterns."

"That's a little deep in the weeds for me. I took a pass on that summer internship as a bank teller and went into the Army. So you are money launderers now? What does this do for national power and intelligence?"

"Don't disappoint me. I had hoped you would catch on better. I know you are a smart man. Act like it. If I wanted a knuckle dragger, I'd have Steven doing your work."

Prescott turned to Steven, who appeared to be more attuned to potential threats than off-the-cuff insults.

"Since we know the amounts, frequency, locations, tagged correspondence banks, and historical monitoring of institutions, we can navigate and control the global financial system. Our clientele are world leaders, military junta, criminal cartel leaders, you name it. We no longer have to recruit them. They beg us for our services. Further, if we can penetrate a bank, we can inform the regulatory enforcement agencies who is being naughty or nice. Then we have the banks by the balls."

"Seems a bit ... inflated. No disrespect."

"My boy, you have no idea of our reach or how we manipulate the markets and global exchanges without a single alert going off in the international banking community."

"Where do I come in? I'm no MBA, as you well know."

"I want to keep flooding funds in at low-risk institutions first. Burn them and we go to next tier and up to high-risk as last resort. Take all the high-risk countries, identify the major banks that we conduct transactions within. Ensure that all money transfers only go to low mid-risk countries. Those in turn will go to low. We will continue to focus on correspondence banks or their affiliates around the world that are not Five Eyes of the U.S. Your route will be to use Albania, Hong Kong, and a few others that we will provide information on."

Draeger yawned. "If we do a surge, we'll get additional financial analysts on our tail, I suspect."

"That's where your other skills come in. We have started a global purge of financial intelligence analysts, key regulators, Bank Secrecy Act and OFAC officers. Hits that look like crime groups."

"I would think the CIA will start to put that together, though, wouldn't you?" Draeger found the tasks menial. Anyone could do this. Jason could do it in his sleep with his deep technical and business savvy.

"You must think we are different than the CIA. We are but one in the same. Holds true with other agencies, political parties and organizations. We are everywhere. And therein lies our other plan. Kill the key analysts. Make them not go to work. Hit them coming from the Pentagon, Crystal City conferences, Maryland's eateries, taxis, buses, trains. Kill special project and country managers, leads, chiefs. Find them on LinkedIn, Facebook, whatever. They post their profiles, pictures, hometowns, and write white papers with their emails all over the place these days. Get their names and cities and then use databases to see where they live."

"Shit, how am I supposed to accomplish all of this, and in what time frame? Don't tell me you really need me to plan out how to kill a bunch of intelligence dorks."

"We have nearly a hundred men like you internationally. Each is his own cell that flows up to our...lodge relationship. Nothing coordinated, so to speak, more of a charter. Your own planning. Your own resources. Your own MO and flavor of dispatching. Targeting is done. You know what we are looking for, and you will stay in your lane and execute. Your regional touchpoint will add additional clarity."

"When does it start?"

"You don't think all of those investment bankers around the world are killing themselves because they are depressed about putting on a tie in the morning? We hit Wall Street's biggest banks and groups from New York, London, to Hong Kong. Fifteen 'suicides' in total so far. They helped us get started. Now it adds to the mystique."

"But you don't want the mystique for the intel analysts. That's thousands of targets."

"We will get the top ones directly and try to get the others all in one place. We will wipe them out and make a show of it for psychological effects. Blind the intelligence community, blind the world. Let things happen. Put egg on their faces. Change administrations and appointees. Once we establish more of our people across the power structures, as true patriots, then we will really have some fun."

"I'm not sold. This analyst killing seems a bit much. It's hokey. Pretty much a waste of time. It's like JSOC spending time whacking low-level IED targets with raids all day and all night. If you are so powerful, why not emplace the people you need within the CIA or wherever else? I don't give a shit whom you whack, but seems like that's going to draw attention. Also opens you up for getting guys caught or changing their minds. Your organization is turning into James Bond villains or Chaos. That's pretty old school. I always thought the Pond was a hidden program or organization that could put people on the inside and orchestrate things clandestinely. Not sure I'm up for this type of circus act."

PASSPORT was speechless. In a moment, he replied, "It is— and it isn't." He paused again. "It is when we need it to be, it isn't when we need to be more of an apparition. You don't see fundamentalist groups carrying membership cards, do you? They are a movement and assemblage based on belief. So, too, are we. As sons of liberty, we are an ideology, a belief, a promise, a truth. But our reach is vast. It was constructed hundreds of years ago."

"That's unbelievable."

"It's believable. That's why we hire a nut job sadist like you to help put our house in order."

"Excuse me?"

Prescott waited a moment. PASSPORT touched his ear for about the third time and briefly turned away. "Yes, that was a bit droll of me. You have the ability to destabilize things in a covert manner. We require secrecy to keep outsiders from knowing our involvement globally ..."

PASSPORT paused again.

Prescott sensed something was off.

Steven continued to look in the same direction. *What is he looking at?*

PASSPORT continued. "We need to protect our cousins in Italy, Austria, Germany, and Switzerland."

"Hold the phone, Freddie. You're not PASSPORT," Draeger accused. He started backing up.

Steven closed in on Prescott's position.

Prescott looked for an out.

The man claiming to be PASSPORT pulled a transmission device from his ear and offered it to Draeger.

"Put it in," he ordered.

Prescott made an exaggerated wipe of the plastic before inserting the device within his ear.

"Very observant of you, Mr. Draeger. Well done."

"What the fuck is this? Cyrano de Bergerac? And I quote, 'What if she turns out to be prude or an intellectual? I wouldn't dare speak to her. I haven't the brains.' I'm not in the mood to play some faggot spy game, if you don't have brains to talk to me direct. And if you're too afraid to come out and talk to me, you're going to make a shitty patriot."

"Manners, Mister Draeger. You know neither my values nor my orientation. Not very P.C."

"Fuck you. And fuck this goon who's closing on me." Draeger turned to Steven. "Back the fuck up, dude. This isn't how I do meetings."

"Settle down, Prescott. This is how I do meetings until trust has been established."

"This is either a group as fucked up as I am, or it might just be the vision of what this world needs."

"I assure you, it is more than you can imagine and, at this point, yours to lose."

Draeger smiled. He somewhat liked the test. These guys were pretty good. Question was, how much of what they said was true?

"Do you wish to continue, Prescott? You've got one strike."

"That makes us even."

"No turning back now." PASSPORT held Draeger's eye contact.

Draeger didn't blink. "I'm not planning on it, but I don't think the role you have for me is right."

"That is good to hear. We can discuss your role further. But if you are committed, you won't miss the funds that have been converted to cash, nor your spirited accounts managed by your colleague, mmm, Jason, I believe. Well, actually, it *is* Jason, and you know that I know that."

"What the fuck did you do? That was my money!"

"Your money? Oh, I think not. Having a multitude of inspectors general in our grasp has certainly verified that the monies you siphoned from Silver Star were not yours. Those are operational funds that are now our operational funds. You will be provided what you need, nothing more, nothing less. We will see you again soon. Now run along back home so we can actually get started."

"What about Jason?"

"That will be our onboarding gift to you. He is no longer going to be a problem for you or anyone else."

X was frantic, but kept his outward appearance cool. He knew there was only one exit available for civilian use. If he could get down to the basement garage, he might have a chance to slip out of the building using one of his current Federal ID cards. X selected an Air Force CAC-card from his wallet and slipped it into the plastic casing of a neck lanyard.

Beyond X's view, the watchers split up.

X located an elevator bank and a car going down. He slipped in behind two U.S. Marshalls and pressed the garage button. A Marshall looked X up and down, keying in on the neck lanyard. X gave a smile and faced the stainless steel elevator

Phew. Too easy.

As the door opened, X saw a watcher standing with another man not previously spotted.

X froze, contemplating fight, flight, or other, which had not yet come to mind.

"Mister Donahoo."

How do they know my name?

"Excuse me," a Marshall begged while maneuvering around X, still frozen with indecision. The two Marshalls exited and a watcher stepped forward, stopping the elevator door.

"Xavier Donahoo, I'm with the Inspector General's office. No need to run. We'd just like to ask you a few questions."

On the one hand, X was relieved. On the other, he was even more afraid.

The man held out a badge and ID in a worn brown billfold. "I'm with the Office of the Deputy Inspector General for Intelligence and Special Program Assessments. I have a car coming down here so we can speak privately."

X turned his head toward the watcher, who had one hand on the elevator door, one hand in a jacket pocket.

"Sure. Caught me by surprise there for a moment. Not many people know my full name."

The two men escorted X down the basement walkway to the garage opening, where a black SUV waited.

The investigator waved his badge at the guard, proceeding with the nod of approval. He leaned in to X and whispered, "We also know the names of your two young nephews. So get in the fucking car and shut up."

"You're not with the IG," X accused.

"I am. But that's not what I'm here for."

The watcher forced X into the vehicle.

As X struggled, fear turned to anger. *Havens, you shit. You owed me.*

Chapter 20

Paulo raised himself from the bed boards. His mattress was tossed to the side.

He prayed in the cold shower and then performed a series of pushups, planks, squats, and sit-ups.

Still in prayer, he retrieved the cattail whip from the small table. Unclothed, he whipped his back and buttocks repeatedly.

Within minutes, blood speckled the walls. The braided rope cut through the air with a whoosh as eight tightly knotted tentacles deeply stained with blood dug deeper into his skin. He continued to flagellate himself until his phone rang.

"Si?" he answered the unknown number.

Paulo paused for a moment, raising an eyebrow in amazement. He responded, "Thank you, Luciani, it has been my honor. Yes, I will stay here as long as needed. Can someone arrange for a replacement to my post? I will need orders sent."

"Thank you," he responded after a long pause, listening to the arrangements being made. "It is God's work. It is my privilege to assist. I will await further instructions to coordinate my travels and review the sites."

Thank you, Father. Blessed am I. You have answered my call. I am your servant. I am your chosen; your new Gabriel with my own flaming sword. Keep my family safe as I do your bidding.

Chapter 21

Sean Havens sat with the ops team, hashing through their mission plan and the supporting intel reports.

"Doc, shoot me over your documents and files, and I'll take a look at what you all have done so far."

"Can't, Sean."

"Why?"

"Access. I'm on a DoD system."

"I'm still fully cleared. Rick said they've plugged in all my updated certificates."

"It's our systems. Our stuff is all JWICS and SIPR. SIPRNet Inteldocs file size limit is 1GB, and half the logistical docs we need are on the low side. Can't get it up to high-side terminal on JWICS. Tried file transfer through DOTS, but I also couldn't find your account address. Even though we're contracted to the intelligence community, our access mixed high and low side DOD systems since we are working with JSOC, too."

"What's DOTS?"

"DoDIIS One-Way Transfer Service but that has a lower file transfer threshold. Nothing changed, Fritter. Same old shit."

"Wonder why my address can't be found on the system, though?"

"Probably some half-assed contractor has it in a stack of work orders."

"Okay, screw it, what's your cover platform when you get there? Rick said you all travel back and forth as part of a pattern."

"We have a stupid computer consulting company that we say is doing risk assessments in the region for emergency response."

"Do you run it like a business?"

"Nah, we just have a little shop and pay off whomever sniffs too close."

"You don't think that could be a problem, not knowing the international tax laws and regulatory stuff? Acting like a real business?"

"Sean, we don't have time to set 'em up like real businesses. I don't think anyone notices."

"It's a matter of time before you're rolled up. Platforms that don't go through the hoops to show they care about sanctions, trade forms, Foreign Corrupt Practices Act, third-party due diligence ..."

Cooter rolled his eyes but kept his mouth shut.

"Preaching to the choir, buddy. They even ship our computers in from the U.S. brand new. It's not a true business pattern from where we're working in Asia. A total tell."

"Shit. If you pay off locals in the area, and they know you don't worry about anti-corruption regs, they'll keep coming back for more. You keep it up, and pay cash all the time for a small business, someone will have you pegged as intel or ops."

Scotty inserted himself to the exchange. "Buddy, I know you're real smart and all, but let us just do our jobs and you do yours. Half of these guys were Rangers. They just think we can power through it and adapt if something comes up. Not worth the fight. Let's just stick to the task, and if I need you in the field I'll send you an email."

The rest of the team was rummaging through a number of boxes that had been brought into their space. "Doc, here's a few more clotting packs," one of the contractors said as he tossed them to Chang.

Chang shook his head. "I don't need these. Where do you put a bayonet?"

"Shit, Doc, take 'em. We may need 'em. We shoot, you patch.

"Patch yourself." Doc chuckled to himself as he stowed the supplies.

"Leave it," said Rick.
"Huh?"

The former squadron sergeant major admired his 7.62mm H&K G3 assault rifle dressed for scope, laser, and CQB light. "I can take this, right?"

"You guys won't be needing any of that. We have to go in clean. Nothing different from what we would need as risk analysts and area surveyors. Not an assault team. Play the part. If we need hardware on the ground, we'll use the normal network. The rotary wings will have first aid kits if we need anything in flight. Sean, that's the right play, correct?" General Bain asked.

Havens understood that the general didn't need validation, he needed Sean as a deflection.

"Roger that, sir. Sorry, guys. When are you dudes heading out?"

"Three days. Have to arrange flights and some coordinated efforts between third parties."

"That's a pretty tight time frame."

"Thanks, Havens. We'll manage, but let me note your dissention on a whiteboard," snipped Cooter in a mocked proper business tone. His face showed the bruises.

"We need to keep it loose. Danger 6 has a theory and wants to check out some areas on the border of Thailand. He's thinking some of the explosives are coming from Burma. Just like Laos was a free zone to supply to VC in Viet Nam. We're going to buzz through and get our eyes on a couple sites."

Sean wasn't comfortable with flying by the seat of his pants, unless he was the one doing it on his own. "What are you saying is your reason to be flying into Myanmar?"

"We're not. We'll catch a ride on a C-146A Wolfhound that belongs to the 524th Air Force Special Operations squadron from Cannon Air Force Base in New Mexico. Then grab a civil Beechcraft King Air 350 to nudge closer in and, finally, a local helo and fly along Thailand and just nudge in a few clicks. They won't scramble up and we'll be in helos below radar and whatnot."

"Shit, Sir, are you sure we don't need to roll a bit heavier?"

Havens was starting to agree. "And you're not worried about the HIND gunships patrolling the area?"

A number of the team members looked around at each other. HINDs were clearly something they had not counted on.

"Nah, they're co-piloted by Russians and we'll have a Russian transport helo supplied by Delta's Echo squadron. They'll leave us alone. They look for ground smugglers and Karan rebels, not commercial overflight."

"Hope you're right."

"Hope isn't a plan," Danger 6 reminded him.

"I'm not sure if what you have is a plan."

Sean addressed the situation in passing with Rick in the hallway.

"Rick, I can tell you even before our after action report hotwash, this is already a goat-rope."

"We need to get eyes on, Sean. These guys will be fine. They've done it their whole careers."

"I still think they should wave off and put a little more time on the planning."

"Noted, Sean. Now go back and help them with what we've got. I've got enough to deal with. Four more intel leads were targeted in the last day. That makes twelve killings CONUS in the last week. We're getting blinded."

"Geez. News still says last ones were from terrorists. Anyone claiming?" Sean inquired.

Not having much to share, Rick gave a quick summation. "ISIS says they did it from Facebook and LinkedIn targeting as retaliation. But it's not their MO. Just their threat."

"Foreign nation?"

"I don't know. Bigger issue is getting the D.C. intel folks to show to work. They're completely freaked out and rightfully so. But so far, it looks like all the hits have been on Agency intel."

"It means someone doesn't want us to get smart on something," Sean suggested. "They're draining our institutional knowledge on things that take years to build insights on."

"What are the possibilities that the Pond could be doing that to prop up their own intelligence apparatus?"

"I hadn't even thought of that," Rick admitted, accepting the possibility.

"Maybe we should start."

Chapter 22

Draeger arrived at his hillside hideaway villa after nightfall. The stone structure had a dark, weathered wooden slat roof that blended into the hillside as he approached in the darkness. Headlights showed the heavy front door slightly ajar.

He had tried to reach Jason, to no avail. *Sorry, kid.*

The accounts were depleted. Draeger was certain they had killed Jason but still prayed that his minion was waiting at the safe house with good news.

Draeger's sidearm led the way, pushing the entrance with the barrel side.

Candles adorned the dark room. A glass of wine was poured and awaited his arrival on a modest table near the door. A woman's heeled shoe caught his eye on the planked floor. In succession were another shoe, stockings, undergarments. A shapely silhouette was visible even under the heavy blankets on the bed.

A gift from Kristoque? Desire was his guide.

Prescott was cautious, but his lust and insatiable appetite for a woman drew him closer. He paused, his wine in one hand and sidearm in the other. He regarded the white lace bra on the coarse rug. Classy, not slutty. Sophisticated. A woman's, not a young girl's. *Thank you. Finally.*

Draeger was aroused and gulped the wine, casting the glass aside like he was the guest of honor at a Viking feast. He lay the gun on a heavy wooden table and undressed without saying a word, then continued his stalking advance to his waiting conquest. Prescott could see the golden locks of the woman's hair as he approached the bed.

"Well, hello, my dear," he said, pulling the covers down slowly to reveal the candlelit flesh of the woman's back. Dark shadows and orange-yellow light rubbed her back in the wavering flame.

Draeger jumped back when he saw a black hole in her back. She rested on a dark pool of blood that soaked the bedsheets.

A deeply accented voice startled him further. "Welcome, Prescott Draeger, to your rebirth."

Draeger whipped around to see a man in a hooded black satin robe holding a wooden scepter topped with a golden cobra.

"Pagans wishing to enter must be willing to die to preserve the secrets of Propaganda Massonica Due."

The figure Tasered Draeger, who fell naked to the floor, pulsating under the current.

The electrocution paused so Draeger could listen. "We will see if you have contempt for danger, qualities of courage, and the willingness to fight to the death for your brothers. We need to know that you will destroy governments to form our clear way to anti-Communism and to reign over those who would defy the people of the Books."

The man adorned in the ceremonial robe shocked Prescott again with a series of high-voltage charges. "I hope that you enjoyed your wine. It will be your last for a while as we help you find yourself and find the path to the Pond. Or, as others would call us, Lodge P2, or P7. It matters not, as you will only know us as the Brotherhood."

He kicked Draeger in the abdomen. "Do I have your attention? I will tell you this once and never again."

"I am Agent Zero Six Five. I am a Wolf. And I will be your shepherd. Shall we begin?"

Two more figures emerged from the dark corners of the room and walked to the room's center.

"Tie him up," commanded the Masonic secret lodge agent.

Draeger popped up in a surprise assault against the two emerging men. They had anticipated the resistance. In a melee of kicks and blows, Draeger was quickly subdued.

Wolf Tasered Draeger again for good measure.

"Surely you don't take us for amateur businessmen, Mister Draeger. Why, we are one and the same. Trained warriors just like you. Sleep well while we prepare." Wolf kicked Draeger's head with the inside of his boot step.

Prescott Draeger was knocked unconscious. The rest would serve him well.

Chapter 23

While the team readied for their deployment, Havens decided it was a good time to check in on Lars and Maggie. He'd have to drive out of the compound to retrieve his phone. It could wait another ten to fifteen minutes. He reviewed the newly delivered travel arrangements and cover profiles.

Shit. I wanted the unofficial flight route. Dammit. I think they said that was being handled upstairs in G, or was it J? I'll handle it myself. Dammit.

Sean doubled back and cut through a wing he had yet to enter. He swiped his badge to see if he had access and the door clicked to open.

Finally, something works.

Havens knew the flight plan would be near another cover element and assumed it would be right on the other side of the wall if his bearings were true.

He looked at the door signs and team names to see if he could translate the compartmentalized coding.

Should be close, and if my guess is right, if I turn right here ....

Havens rounded the corner, picking up the pace so he could beat traffic once he left the base.

The brunette was looking down at her file and collided with Havens.

"Oh, gosh, sorry, I ..." Havens was dumbfounded. "I know you." He squinted his eyes, pulling from his mind something he had carefully tucked away years ago. He knew it to be true, but hoped he was mistaken.

She looked up at him with deep brown eyes that quickly returned to her file. She struggled to move around Havens.

It had been almost a decade, but her name came right back to him. "Jacqueline, right?" It might not be her real name, but it was the exact operational name. He would never forget it.

The woman moved to her right but was blocked by the hall wall. She said nothing.

"You remember, right? Turkey?"

Havens instinctively reached out and grabbed her arm, stopping her.

She stopped and, without looking back, responded, "It's Tanya. Jacqueline was my cover. You can't expect it to have been real. Any of it."

"Well yeah, I was …"

"I know who you were and are, Sean Havens." She turned, avoiding his gaze.

"How are you? I mean, how have you been? You're working here?"

"That's pretty observant of you. I'm fine. Things are fine. I am working on a flight pattern for your op. I need to get moving. Good to see you."

"Wait, I was coming down to get the plan. Can I see it?"

"You don't need to. It's not part of your tasking. No need to comment and you can't revise."

"I have a hunch on something and just wanted to see it."

"Sorry, Mr. Havens, I have to get this to our aviation support group."

"Wait, this isn't a JSOC op. It's Agency, which means ultimately it's for my eyes."

"You'll have to clear that with someone higher than me," she snapped.

"All these years, I never knew if you were OGA or Defense. That whole thing back then was pretty awkward."

"I have to go. Sorry to hear about your *wife*. I know how much she meant to you." Tanya paused for effect. "I'm sure we'll be seeing each other again."

"Sure," Sean replied, knowing he had no other response.

Tanya gave him a forced smile. As an afterthought, she added, "By the way, you know our old Turkish naval intelligence agency asset was found dead in Romania last year. So it *all* meant nothing, after all. Guess you were right."

Tanya turned and walked briskly away until she had cleared another corner. Her heart was pounding and she felt like she was suffocating.

"Thanks," Sean muttered. *That wasn't fair.* A new guilt resurfaced that had been stowed for years like the compartmented operation that it was. *That sucked.*

He was gob smacked. He remembered Tanya as an attractive, fragile woman. Smart, young, trusting, vulnerable. She had changed since Turkey. She was still eye-catching but in a different way. From what he could tell, she was more athletic. Her jawline more resolute. Fit, from the quick glance he got of her butt as she walked away. She was confident and gave off an air of being off-limits. Of built-up walls.

His mind wandered to Turkey.

I've got to check on Maggie. He tried to block Christina from his mind in shame. Turkey was off-limits. She was never allowed there. A spouse would never understand.

The voice in Sean Havens' head said to drive straight to the rehab center. A darker voice said to turn in to the little plaza where he spotted the black pickup truck in front of the boxing gym.

As Havens expected, the Marine was in the ring leering at Sean with a knowing grin.

"I came for that fight."

"You know it, old man. Get dressed and get some gloves."

Sean looked up to the ring at the Marine's opponent. "Mind stepping out and letting me borrow your mitts?"

The man shook his head willingly and pulled the gloves' Velcro straps. He tossed them down to Havens and offered him his wraps, which Sean passed on.

Havens was wearing rip-stop hiking pants, a pique polo shirt, and running shoes, but within a few seconds he and the

Marine were in the elevated ring. The younger man skipped around, shadow boxing in an impressive but overly done display of speed and high energy.

"C'mon, old fart. Let's see what you've got. Get those gloves up if those little arms can lift 'em." The young Marine was chiseled, with lean muscle upon muscle. "Get Some" was inked in indigo on his bare washboard stomach, with skulls to the sides and a bulldog underneath. His body art was a cornucopia of death metal symbols, American flags both waving and torn, and tribute scripts to his fallen brothers. The man danced all over the ring, swaying and popping in and out, shaking his head and flashing his arms all around.

Sean kept up his slow boxer hop, testing the balls of his feet and his composed rock and spring. Havens was still wearing his LALO Recon BUDS training shoes, one of the four pairs of LALO training shoes and boots he had liberated from one of the many JSOC supply cages. He held his ground and felt the balance and give of the floor.

"You didn't need to jack up my truck."

"Semper Fi, old man, I have no idea what you're talking about."

In an instant, the Marine leapt forward. He snapped off two quick jabs that caught Sean's jawline but failed to deliver significant impact.

Warning shots. Tracers testing reach.

A third jab had more zip. Havens absorbed the hard impact and noted that the solid pops were from the soldier's weaker left forward punch.

Shit, what's his right hand got? In the movies, this is where I get hit a few times then kick his ass, right? Fuck me.

"C'mon you old fart! Let's see it. Shake that dust off. What's that tattoo on your arm? Is that your wife's picture or some old girlfriend? Maybe a daughter. I'd fuck her. I like that mouth. Does she know you are a complete pussy?"

Havens stopped his hop for but a moment and lowered his gloves. The Marine capitalized on the distracted mental slip and Havens received another hard jab.

No, this is the part in the movie where I kill you.

"Ha! Fuckin' with your head, old man. Gotcha good."

Havens rocked back quickly and slipped to the right, just dodging an uppercut.

"Whoo-ey. You slip that or your knees crumblin', you old fart?" The Marine snapped another connected punch. It felt like a log hitting Havens straight to the forehead. "Hey, wake up, puss bag. At least make me sweat. My balls are still high and tight, they can't even bang against your wife's chin they're so cold."

The building wave surged over Sean. It swelled in his chest. It flowed through his arms and legs. Without letting his guard down, he glanced quickly at the two-day old fresh tattoo work on his forearm. It was an inked portrait of Christina. The template was made from one of his favorite selfie photographs of her that she had sent him while he traveled abroad to one of the many shitholes he frequented for advance intel or kinetic operations.

Enough of this! I'm done! You're done!

"Hey Pops, hit me or I'm going to destroy you," the Marine taunted, jumping in and out of Havens' reach.

Sean picked up his pace again and danced a bit to the left, drawing his young opponent toward a corner.

"'Old man' this, you shithead." Havens executed a series of jabs, propelling his left fist into the Marine's face. He gave his wrist twists before impact snapping his opponent back with the hard hits torqued by torso and hips.

His opponent tried to slip to the right and Havens threw a left hook with his entire body weight in transfer to his foe's chin. The Marine staggered back against the ropes and threw a sloppy hook.

Havens stepped in with another lead fist jab and a powerful right hand uppercut.

His opponent lowered his gloves and stumbled back to the left along the rope padding. He was met with Sean's heavy left hand, starting from his belly and coming up from the depths of a blindside, meeting his chin.

As the Marine's head sprung up, Havens threw a right elbow to the kid's ribs. Then a left elbow to the ribs. Havens smashed the side of his own head into the Marine's mouth and nose as he torqued his right arm back and launched it with a twist to his enemy's core.

Sean repeated the motion, crushing the tattooed laughing skulls with elbows that hammered bone against bone.

He kneed the young man's unpadded shorts, crushing his testicles with a driving lift.

Not laughing so much now, asshole. Now your balls are on your chin.

As his opponent crumbled, Havens balanced for a heavy kick to the torso.

"Whoa, whoa, whoa!" someone yelled from the rear. The shout was loud enough to catch Havens' attention. Sean blinked and in that moment watched the young man fall flat backwards into the ropes and fold to the ground, the Marine's face awash in blood.

"What in the hell are you doing, you madman?" The voice came from an older man, perhaps in his seventies. He directed to one of the gym staff, "Paul, get this kid a wet towel, some water, and maybe some salts. Rest of you pukes get away from the ring. No show here."

The old man climbed up into the ring and, after convincing himself the kid would be okay, turned on Havens. Four to five inches shorter than Sean, the old man gritted his teeth, his unruly, hairy brow bent over the tiny dark eyes that decorated the sides of a distorted bulbous boxer nose.

"Who the hell are you, Mickey from *Rocky*?"

Transfixed on the codger's face and the sight of the knocked-out sandbox warrior, Havens missed the bare fist punch just below his solar plexus.

Sean caved in, half bent over from shocking pain. He gasped for breath.

"Get outta my gym! You can't be in here like this!"

Though instincts said to hammer the man when he could catch his breath, Havens settled for "Fine." The sound was barely audible with no air to carry the word. Sean sucked wind and expelled, "Sorry."

"Who the hell are you?"

Sean pulled the Velcro from the gloves and dropped them on the mat. His knuckles were raw.

"You don't even have wraps?"

"Nope, just came in here to say hello to an old friend," Havens said matter-of-factly as he bounded down from the ring.

Another boxer stepped up to Havens. He went to pat Sean's shoulder.

Havens missed the intention but caught the movement with his right peripheral vision. Sean blocked the arm with the knife edge of his right hand and twisted in pivot, sending an open-hand blow to the man's sternum. The man was sent flying back and caught by another boxer who was still loitering around the scene.

Sean soon found himself surrounded by a small mob of angry soldiers.

"Let him go!" ordered the old boxer from the ring. "Let him walk out. Someone's going to get killed here."

Havens pretty much understood that this would be his last time in this gym. Time to go see Maggie.

The old man called out. "Get yourself some help, lad. You got a ticking time bomb in there."

Havens took a deep breath in and let it out. *Go to the car.* He turned back around and re-entered the gym. No one moved. No one challenged Havens.

Sean got in the face of the old man. "Since you have all the right answers, maybe you can tell me where to get that help. And before you get all Mister Miyagi on me or try to take me under your wing to get me out of my rut, know this. Nothing will help me. Nothing will stop me from wanting to come back in here and killing that fucking Marine."

Havens took another step forward and the men shuffled back, unsure of his intentions.

"I just wanted to be left alone. But he couldn't let up. I've done some pretty horrible things in my life, but I don't have night terrors; I sleep like a baby. I don't suck on a bottle drowning my sorrows, I head to the gym and I train. I train to deal with pain. But I don't talk to anyone and I don't mess with anyone. So if you want to push my buttons, push away. I'd be happy trying to take on everyone here, and not lose a wink of sleep or shed a tear if someone ended up dead. And guess what? That's what they pay me for. And they just hired me, again. Why? Because they like broken toys with nowhere to run." Havens reached up and flicked the old boxer in the head. "And I'm broken and running nowhere or from anyone."

Havens grabbed a forty-pound kettle bell off the rack and walked out to the parking lot. As he neared the black pickup truck he could see through the front window to a back window decal. Semper Fi, in red and yellow letters. *Enough vetting for me.* Sean swung the kettle bell into the driver's-side door, creating a huge dent. He then hefted it up and back down, smashing the windshield.

Sean Havens marched right back into the gym, set the bell down and headed off to see his daughter.

"We're even," he solidified. *Semper Fi, you asshole.*

Chapter 24

"I told you Americans would be here in your airspace," the pilot gloated to his client.

"How could you know?" The Myanmar co-pilot was trying to learn everything that he could sponge from the Russian military advisor.

"One, they don't practice proper OPSEC and they leave their unencrypted transponders on. We use real-time tracking of their aircraft. It captures their radio call-sign, GPS, altitude, and flight path. We know where the plane is going before they do."

"What exactly are you tracking?"

"Automatic dependent surveillance-broadcast. And we know the Wolfhound is for infiltration and exfiltration of the American special operations forces. Guide the head the body will follow."

When missions aren't recalled, they can move quickly. The two CIA-borrowed Turkish variant T-70 Sikorsky utility helicopters sped over Burma's lush landscape, cruising at 149 knots. They would be pushing their range from takeoff.

The pilots chose to fly well below the service ceiling to reduce their signature, which suited the men on board who took advantage of altitude for awareness and recce. Their lesser-known last-minute side mission included a slight diversion from the original plan.

Twenty kilometers before Thai airspace, they passed over the treetops, keeping watch for clearings along the border that were not marked on the maps they had studied for days.

Without warning, the giant HIND gunship popped up from the ridge, covered briefly by the dense jungle canopy. The helicopters hugged the trees. Their deep rotors beat and their turbines screamed as the swift armed fortresses prepared to engage the enemy.

Colonels Burkov and Akkhuratov, respectively, maneuvered their gunships. The Russian's military clients were wide-eyed in anticipation of the forthcoming helo kills.

The American crew members reacted to the HIND presence and shouted calm warnings to one another, which caused quite a stir in the back. The team peered from the windows in controlled desperation to identify the bogie problem.

Cooter was the first to see the flashes of red, orange, yellow, and white light as the gunship opened fire with its four-barrel rotary cannon and launched 57mm rockets.

The first helo banked at a sharp angle, tossing the men to one side. It leveled and attempted to climb.

The HIND spit rounds that tore the tail rotor to shreds, sending the ship spinning in forceful revolutions.

Amid the clamor, General Bain heard the pilot making a radio call of taking fire. To whom, he did not know. A veteran of helo crash survivability and an aviator in his own right, Bain mentally referenced the manufacturing model of the bird, evaluating the metal spine structure. *Keep the bird level, kid. If we go down, we need serious deceleration. Don't over-fly your machine.*

Bain and Chang locked eyes. Bain saw Chang looking around the ship, also assessing crash space. It had room to deform in the imminent crash sequence. Both men regarded the pilot and co-pilot. Not much crash space. If they survived, major blunt force trauma, broken limbs, brain damage. Another assured broken back.

The second helo shuddered from the impacts as the high-velocity rounds tore through the metal and composite body. It turned, then tumbled nose-down, winding in an acrobatic, uncontrolled descent. It screamed as it dropped in free fall to the canopy below.

Not seeing the other bird go down, Bain willed his own pilot and co-pilot to stop talking. No distress call was going to help. *Bet you did great in flight school, maybe the sandbox, but this is where the real stuff happens. Fucking aviate, don't communicate. Keep control!*

Another HIND gunship hovered above the tree hollow where the first aircraft went down.

Bain shouted to his men, "We're going down, sync your shit fast!" Bain bounced on his bench to get a feel. *Shit.* He had hoped for a seat equipped with hidden pistons to absorb the shock. Stupid. False hope. As he loaded in earlier, he remarked to himself that the rigidity would kill his back after an hour. He hoped it wouldn't kill him in the next minute. Bain looked to the back area. It was less cluttered with men and metal. The skeleton frame also spoke to him as being more reinforced. He regarded his men, then the open space. No time.

The bird began to drop and pitch. The aviators fought the machine. *I'm too old for this shit.* Bain unfastened his buckle and practically dove to the back, where he refastened.

Chang, too, was fast on the move and plugged himself in kitty-corner from Bain.

Bain tilted his head, curious.

"Hey, if you're going to survive, I need to be there to fix you. Your back's going to be fucked if we don't burn up."

Bain spread his pearly whites in a shit-eating grin. "You're saving your own ass. You're going to owe me one."

"Fine. I'll give you whatever you want."

The men chatted like they were enjoying tea and cakes while the rest of the crew panicked over the inevitable. The ship rocked as it fell but remained relatively level until the nose tipped upon impact with the foliage.

"Damn amateur," Bain cursed before everything went black.

Two large plumes of smoke rose above the wreckage, through the jungle foliage, and up to the heavens.

The heat below was extreme, withering leaves and brush around it.

Crackling sounds popped among the jungle sounds. The insides of the helo and the men snapped and sizzled. Plastic and wires coiled, liquefied, and crumpled.

A sole rotor bowed over the metal carcass that resembled a giant dead locust.

General Bain awoke. He raised his hands to his face in the first pre-check of life or death. He scanned his torso for any chest or stomach trauma. He lifted his shirt, looking for any major sources of blood aside from the visible scrapes. Pain shot through his core. Searing pain reverberated from his lower back. *Yep. Alive. Damn back jacked-up again.* He moved a knee and turned a shoulder. Both hurt, but they hurt before the accident. Par for the course.

"Stay still," a familiar voice said.

"Anyone else make it?"

"Nope."

"Cooter looked like a burnt marshmallow," Chang mused.

"Doc, did you pull me from the wreck?"

"Yep. We're even."

"Shit. I thought I had you."

"Maybe next time."

"Sir, we picked up a feed. Here's all we could salvage from the transmission."

MAYDAY, MAYDAY, MAYDAY. THIS IS P.C. TRANSPORT 109ER, PC ... 109ER, PC TRANSPORT ... BEARING ... 30 CLICKS FROM THAI ... RECEIVING INCOMING FROM ... HOSTILE ... GUNSHIP.

[END]

COPY, PC TRANSPORT 109, THIS IS TRANSPORT 110. WE HAVE VISUAL ...

[END]

"Get Havens in here for a huddle. We need a plan B *now* for Thailand."

Chapter 25

Rick leaned over the commo tech's shoulder for a better view of the screen.

His cologne was strong and the tech rolled her chair back, giving the spook full access to the terminal. She regained full access to fresh air.

The tech summarized what she couldn't see. "Sir, it's dark there now. We've caught a sighting of possible infrared light sticks from a satellite drone. Jungle is pretty thick where it went down. Looking now for an infrared strobe, but nothing so far in the area. Looks like the site is a complete terminal crash or it's now been abandoned. I'd say, given what I can make out, there could be possibility of survivors, but there would be heavy trauma and likely additional distress calls or signals, however obvious or discreet. On the other hand, whoever got them, if they were alive, got them fast. Can't see under the canopy and no heat signatures that would match."

"Why do you think someone got them?"

"We haven't seen the scan, but we received a verbal that unknown heat signature was heading to the site.

"Okay, keep looking."

"Roger that, Chief."

Tanya escorted Sean into the ops center, where he was informed that Rick needed him for the rest of the day. She passed a cube and turned her head to catch the eye of one of her friends, Commander Judith "Judy" Hannover.

The woman put her hand on her heart, pouting her lips at Tanya's pained expression. Years of margarita therapy hadn't helped Tanya put her operational contact back in a place of benign field-mandated relationships.

Tanya responded with a slight shrug, but her little facial tells revealed her true thoughts.

Sean stepped to Tanya's right and swiped his badge to open the door. The room was filled with bulging arms, flat screens, and testosterone-fueled attitude.

"Great, more assaulters and snipers. What *different* capabilities we're leveraging here," Tanya cracked.

Sean chuckled, relieved that she had broken the tension. As uncomfortable as their situation was, she was great at cutting the tension. He felt bad about how things went down in Turkey and looked forward to working with her on some analysis tasks.

"Hey, look, an Air Force combat controller's in here. At least we can relate better to him," Sean said in an attempt to keep the exchange going.

"Sean, I know what you've been doing. You don't have to play down your team work. I know you're one of them."

"I wouldn't say that." He hesitated to ask whether she had heard about it from someone else or was checking on him. He didn't want it to come off as flirtatious or accusatory. *Lose, lose.*

As they entered the room, only a few of the men looked up. They ignored Sean but sucked Tanya in from head to toe.

Tanya ignored the lustful gazes and moved a little closer to Sean.

Sean sensed her moving closer to him. He breathed in her flowery scent and seized the opportunity to engage her again.

"What've you been up to? I mean since … um … the last few years? I thought you were with the Agency at the time."

"I moved to Defense. Field work for a bit, then needed to mix things up. I took some time off. Had a family."

Sean felt a hint of disappointment. "Oh, nice. I never realized at the time that you were married. Congrats." *Sorry.*

"Thanks. I wasn't married then."

"Right. Well congratulations now."

"I'm still not married."

Sean knew it was time to shut up, but couldn't. "Oh, okay. I understand."

"No you don't."

She attempted her trademark smirky smile, trying to hold his eyes. Her hands were clammy and her chest tightened. With no windows and the stale, stagnant air, she felt claustrophobic. She wanted to run out of the building and into the sanctity of her car in the parking lot.

Hold your ground, sister. Do not give one inch to this bastard or the rest of these assholes in the room.

Sean regarded her as she twitched like a trapped squirrel. That was the Tanya he remembered. That was the Tanya he wanted to protect then ... and now. The thought surprised him.

"Hey, Tanya." Sean nudged her elbow with his own. "It's cool. You don't need to talk to me. I think you're a really great person and, you know, no hard feelings."

He regretted the words as soon as they passed his lips.

Tanya wasn't going that easy. He could see her struggling and decided to let her off the hook. "Miss Crowe, it was great to see you again. I'll take it from here." Sean extended his hand.

Crap. Operational or not, you can't always turn it off when you're under surveillance and Uncle Sam orders you to be naked with a partner while feigning a honeymoon to avoid arrest or worse.

"Thanks for dismissing me. I was supposed to be here, too." Tanya Crowe turned away and retreated in a quick gait, happy that she could make him feel like crap.

Sean watched her abrupt departure and recalled their conversations in Turkey. They had spoken intimately, knowing they were being listened to by surveillance ears. Sean knew that his operational profession of love to Tanya and the closeness of their cover activities had gone straight to her head. She interpreted his endearing words—and physical actions—as genuine.

She was new to field work at the time and the assignment had broken her heart. The man she had been searching for had been right there in her bed, in her arms. Problem was, he was married and in love with another woman and faking it all for his job. And now he was back. And worse ... potentially available.

Not giving Tanya another thought, Havens engaged those in the war room for a status. Back to business.

"Havens. Good, you're here. We have a situation with the team. Where's Ms. Crowe?"

"She had to leave. What's the SITREP?"

"They went down. No status. Situation is the team doesn't exist. It's even beyond typical special access programs since it's under Agency activities. We'll try to hire some locals and see if they can help out in seeing what their status is."

"They went down? Where? When?"

"Burma. Both ships. They gave a distress call."

"Burma?"

"Was it a collision or anti-aircraft?"

"Mayday stated hostile engagement."

Gunships, you idiots. I knew the HINDs would be out there. It stated in the reports that they made regular patrols and kept a close monitor of the airspace. "And do we know if there were survivors?"

"Not yet. We'll just have to wait it out."

"Wait for what?"

"I wanna see what we can learn in the next few days. Meanwhile, we need a Plan B to get someone in Thailand. I'll probably need to send you and Ms. Crowe. I saw in your file that you've worked together as a couple. She'll be the Agency support integration officer. You could do worse," Rick jeered.

"Wait. Two things. You're moving forward on the bombings and waiting for any call on search and rescue?"

"Our hands are tied. It was black. If it didn't exist, we don't know about it. If a tree falls in a forest, not sure it happened on my watch. If they survived, it will be unassisted evasion with no recovery plan on our side."

"I get that, but you can't task DoD or State to go after American businessmen?"

"How would we even know about them? You know how this works. So do they. Plus, the Thais know they weren't businessmen and are pissed that we were operating under the front."

"Thais knew?"

"They had a flight plan and have already tracked the copters. I suppose they were worried that someone might be sniffing out some of their activities along the border. Burma denies any crash, which either means they don't know or they are keeping it hush-hush until we fess up. The team didn't have Myanmar on the flight plan. We can't do much. Going in without an invite would be suspected, and we can't have any kinetic engagement at all."

"Can't we leak to the press or send in SOAR with a team for a quick PR search?"

"We talked it up with 160th, and the regiment thinks it's too high of a risk. Especially if they were brought down by the HIND. I've contacted Hank Hill from NRO's Mission Support Directorate to see what we can get from satellite. He's checking space-based infrared, getting some feeds from low and medium earth orbit."

"You can't just leave them out there. I'm surprised National Reconnaissance isn't contacting us."

"Why? It's not standard practice for them to cover clandestine ops, but it is standard practice for us to cut bait when we need to. If they're alive, they switch on the E&E skills get to a friendly border and then we figure things out. Half that crew has done it before in a real situation. If Bain is alive, that old dude has made it out of a lot of countries that he wasn't supposed to be in."

"We can't talk to our personnel recovery guys to assist in their evasion?"

"Sean. Anything we do would need to be unacknowledged, waived at this point, but would have too much of a bread-crumb trail. I have no authority for unassisted recovery or non-conventional native assisted recovery. It's up to them and whoever else might get tasked."

"I'll go."

"You can't go. You're not qualified."

"Qualified for what? That's never stopped anyone from sending me anywhere."

"Havens, I'm not sending in any of the Unit boys or Ground Branch types with someone who hasn't gone through formal selection and training and, frankly, I'm not willing to put them in danger for this situation either."

"Ah, so now there's a difference with my formal selection. Play all sides. This is messed up. It's our team."

"They are GRS contractors. They're not on permanent duty with the Agency. And those TDY are not PCS. There's a difference in protocol, liability, and insurance for non-blue badgers. That's how they won the bids. They aren't our team any more. They play by the same rules."

"They're Americans!"

"They're dead, and they don't exist to us. That's the game and we all know the stakes."

"You have a West Point General who went down! We always go after our own."

"Not today we don't. They were on their own."

"Rick, this is one hundred percent bullshit! I've spent time with your guys and SAS hostage rescue in Bosnia. Did it under General Bain with Draeger, too. I owe the general. Send me out, Rick. I'm going."

"It's not an option. Our priority is the IEDs and the Pond. Done. If they're alive, they can fight their way out. It's what they do. It's why they do the job for us. You're the only one who doesn't seem to remember the stakes and the acceptance of inherent dangers."

"Maybe I'm just tired of people being screwed in their service."

Jerry's phone rang. The old intel crow recognized the number immediately.

He said nothing when he opened the line.

"Hey, boy. Feelin' squeamish yet? You were warned. And don't say I wasn't clear. It's going to get darker before it gets lighter."

The phone line went dead.

Damn you, Robert. Another shoe shall fall.

Chapter 26

Sean knocked on Rick's office door, then immediately opened it and started right in.

"Rick, why can't we reach out to Special Operations Command-Pacific? Rear Admiral who commands Special Operations Command, Pacific commanded Naval Special Warfare Unit Three when I was in Bahrain. I can check it out."

"We're done, Sean. I need you in Thailand."

"Humor me, Rick."

Rick gave a heavy sigh, "No-go on SOCPAC or the JSOTF. Can't use the Air Force 353rd special ops group either. They're there to do survey and advisory work. If we use them as staging to support our ops, we have to partner with the locals. I don't need to tell you that we are dealing with dense single- to double-layer canopy, cross-compartmented dense terrain, and obscured lowlands. That degrades our commo and mobility for quick reaction and limits our effective aerial collection. Time needed to get to these men will be significant and there are too many intel gaps to just be able to drop in and have an effective plan."

Sean sat down in a burgundy-upholstered mahogany chair. None of the chairs matched in the small office.

"Sure, Sean, have a seat." Rick sat back, amused by the intensity but still annoyed with the audacity.

"I get that and still don't see what the hell Joint Task Forces are good for if we can't get theater support. This is in their charter. Prevent, counter, and respond? They failed all lines of effort in this mission. How about the Counter Narco-Terrorism Program at PACOM or JIATF-West? This is stupid soup."

"And I'll spell it out again. You're missing the big picture. Right now, those elements are focused on the partnership efforts to build capacity and capabilities. We're guests within JSOC and I can't tell them what to do for our missions."

"Are you kidding me? When did that happen?"

"Sean, don't push my buttons. As far as foreigners are concerned, they have to build relationships on trust. If we acknowledge that we did something outside of trust, we might not have them for something we really need. Same with our boys here."

"*Really* need? You have men down behind the wire who served. You don't need that?"

"They're contractors who left the military for more pay. That's what people see here. Those men took off their uniforms for a bigger paycheck. Even if I could, SOCPAC has a joint readiness combined exercise going on."

"What about all that bullshit of tightening the threat seams between TSOCs? That's an awful lot of daylight shining through that gap in my eyes."

"Sean, the PACOM AOR is bigger than you and your ranting fits of boo-hoo unfairness. You've done this long enough to know what has to be left alone. Right now SOF is focused on the warrior diplomat side. JSOC Operational Support Troops are stretched across the area and farther west running Jackal Cave JRX. And I can't get any ISA bodies. Bad timing. Even if I wanted it to go through, someone would shoot it down. Look at fuckin' Benghazi. And we acknowledged those were our people."

"Look, I just read that Thailand has had more than 350 IED events in the past eighteen months. That amount puts it up there with Somalia for casualties, nearing 1,200 people. You can send us in as a Counter-IED team, and give SOCPAC some radio-controlled IED jamming tech. Drop us off along the border. I know from our feeds that we have persistent surveillance on that area and within Burma. Call Eric Prince and have him give us a ride."

"It's not just about feeds, Sean. We need someone to catalog, manage, and access the data. And Echo Papa isn't an option."

"I can do the feeds and intel."

"You aren't accounting for rate of transmission, relevance, usability. It's not like we can just point a camera over that area."

"Are you joking? Can't or won't? Who do you think you're talking to? I know how this stuff works."

"We have a closed architecture for those feeds. It isn't open to their systems. We don't have instant interoperability and ubiquitous access to the applications. We don't have a targeted common operating baseline for you to use so we can discern patterns of life inside the data to know what is normal and what a threat is."

"You're being a rigid asshole."

"That's not part of this debate."

"He's right, you are an asshole." Tanya was peering into the office. She retracted a hair. "Well, you're being an asshole now."

"Ms. Crowe, I don't recall asking your opinion."

Sean turned around to see Tanya standing right behind his chair.

Rick sighed again. He moved around to the front of the desk and sat on it.

"Have a seat please, Tanya."

Sean, sensing Rick was trying, interjected, "What *is* within the realm of possibilities? I'd like to do something. Are there no foreign resources we can tap?"

Rick laughed out loud. "This is a perfect example of where our failure as a nation to properly support unconventional allies threatens our national security resources. We have nothing near there."

"And none of our own guys?"

"I'm willing to put two men in as recon. There are some standard RFI lists out there that maybe we can look at real quick. Chinese presence. Talk of an Iranian presence right in that area, and of course Russian."

"That's going to be a waste of time with no correlating unit destination, mission, tasks, and whatnot. In other words, you've got it backwards. We could do a thorough IPB and integrate the rest of the staff to include some special staff. Do an Intel Prep of the Battlespace in conjunction with Mission Analysis that will generate your initial list of RFIs. That and a few weeks will give us plenty of bureaucracy and lost time."

"You're unbelievable. You're running a million miles an hour in the wrong direction. And you missed my point, Havens, while you were trying to look smart in front of Ms. Crowe here. If I can attach someone to some intel requirements, maybe I can send someone out."

"Great. Send me in."

"I'm not sending in an Expendables Stallone team to go in and blow up the jungle."

"We're all expendable. You said it. I know the risk."

"You know what I mean. If we can get eyes on the target, maybe that's enough for me to take it to the next level. But this is going to take time. I have to find a couple guys with intel and jungle experience who are on contract."

"Rick. I'll go."

"What about the guy who was blubbering about never being through selection and needing to stay at a desk? You're not a soldier, remember?"

"I'm a man. And someone needs to man up to help these guys. I've selected myself. My kid would understand."

"I'm not sure you're right about Maggie. And you don't have jungle experience. Your records say you've never even been to Ft. Sherman's JOTC. Trust me, I actually checked. So give me some credit for not being an asshole."

"I've been sent to plenty of places I'd never visited before. Including Colombia and Venezuela."

"I know what you did there, and most of the time you were in vehicles. We still need a contractor who is more jungle experienced if we are going to do this."

"I've got someone. Special Forces, jungle, and he can be here in an hour."

Rick gave more than a courtesy inquiry. "Black hat stuff? You're not talking Billy, are you? He's still in Florida."

"No. But this guy has probably done some dark stuff over the years. How black hat, I don't know. I know he owns one," Havens smiled.

"Owns what?"

"A black hat."

"I don't know what that means. Anyway, you need to think about your daughter. What about dad stuff? It could be suicide for you if there is resistance out there. We won't have much of an escape and evasion plan for you guys. If I wasn't willing to go after one team, I'm certainly not going after two."

Sean paused, thinking about how Maggie would deal with him leaving again. She needed him. The team needed him. Maggie had Lars and her nurse for now. She would understand. She had to. "You had me in all this crazy training for this very thing." *I am such a horrible person raising my hand for this.*

"I have you training in case I need to send you somewhere with a team—in low-risk situations. Your training is a just in case. This is certainty of danger that we can't just pull you out of when things get hot."

"Sean, you don't have to do this," Tanya said nonchalantly. "You should stay for your daughter. The men probably didn't survive. We can see about infrared satellite and wait to see if there is any activity. NSA may be able to pick up some chatter about it."

"She's right, Sean. We have no backup. Wait it out. I still need to put someone with investigative experience in Thailand."

"They wouldn't wait it out for us. I'm going. I'm going to tell Maggie and then I have to go see my jungle guy. I might not be back this afternoon."

"Keep me posted. But that doesn't help what I need in Bangkok."

Tanya shook her head and handed Rick the documents he had requested earlier. Sean left the room but called back. "Get Lars!"

"He's not cleared."

"Then don't tell him anything. Just contract him to investigate the bombings as a case study for Sherman Kent Center or some site exploitation lessons learned."

Rick rolled his eyes, reviewed the documents, and switched the paper shredder to Security Level 6. He fed the contents through the cross-cut jaws and they gnashed the classified material into more than 15,000 particles.

When Sean was out of earshot, Tanya started in. "Sir, I thought Colonel MacIntyre said he had a team and even SOCOM was willing to lend a hand," she challenged. "You even said that you had a distress ping from the teams' ELT beacon. Sean can track off the 121 megahertz signal and locate them from the continuous homing transmission."

"Ms. Crowe, the emergency locator transmitters have false alerts. Russians are all over that area with their signal coverage. Those signals work off a Cospas-Sarsat system, which—and this is above your pay grade—has been compromised by other intel agencies. That's need to know, and he doesn't need to know anything else. That's why you're being assigned to this. Trust building starts now."

"But if you are just going to burn him..." she started before being abruptly cut off by Rick.

"I'm not burning him. I'm leveraging him. But if I had come up with the idea to send him, he would have bitched about it. If it's his idea, then he's all in. Thank you, Tanya, that'll be all."

Tanya took a hard swallow. The tightness in her chest was coming back. *Tanya, what are you doing? Sean is a good man and doesn't deserve this. But it could give us time together again.*

"Sir, then send me to Thailand to keep watch over him and to coordinate the ex-cop in Bangkok. I can work with embassy creds and work in a secure environment. There's no exposure. That way we can get equipment in through dip pouch too."

"I read your file, Ms. Crowe. I know why you're doing this."

"Don't play games. You knew that when you brought me in."

Indeed I did, thought Rick. *Thank you both for doing exactly what I wanted.*

Chapter 27

Sean was losing. He wanted to leave Maggie's room. They were both frustrated.

The conversation with his daughter had gone worse than anticipated. There were no tears, no pleading, no anger. Maggie simply responded with a single teenage, "Whatever."

He sat on the edge of her bed contemplating his next move. *Am I completely losing you, or is this what teens do?* Havens wasn't saying much to improve things and was not resonating with her psychological or physiological reasoning. He knew that he had lost his compass when Christina died, and now Sean realized how much his wife was the glue that bonded the family.

"Maggie, just let me know what you're thinking."

"Dad. It's fine. Really. Go."

"I can't tell if you are really fine or not. Are you? I won't go if you're not."

"If you are telling me that you have to go, then clearly you have to go. So go," Maggie encouraged, as she flipped a hand to dismiss him. "You always do anyway," she added.

Defeated, Sean walked away to avoid making matters worse. The bottom line was he wanted to go. He felt a duty to go. But he knew he should stay home. He was doing everything he could to follow the call of danger and adrenaline, and abandoning all that he had left of home in the process.

Standing outside of the rehabilitation center, Sean took refuge in the cool air and pine smells of North Carolina. Aimee was coming up the walkway, returning from a late lunch.

"You look like you've lost your best friend."

"I might have. I don't think we're friends anymore. We were so tight."

"Girls love their daddies, especially when they can deflect from battling with their moms."

"She was always good with Christina too."

"Did she bring up her mom and those questions?"

"No. What's she saying?"

"Well, you better go in for a round two before too long. What was the battle today?"

"I have to go away."

"Sean, they need to ease up on these trainings. I don't know where they keep sending you, but you have a little girl who needs you. I'm sure you're special, but Uncle Sam has plenty of other boys. Your girl only has one parent."

"I know. They changed my training tempo to be more local, but I have to do temporary duty somewhere. Someone needs help."

"I've heard that before. James Senior always needed to get somewhere where they needed his help." Aimee gave a motherly look at Sean, signaling that he knew what he should do, but if he wasn't going to do it, he best figure things out.

Havens just stood there, looking lost. He knew the hard answer and was looking for the easy way out.

"Well, if you are hardwired to get back in the field, that then takes a bit of compromise between you and Maggie. She needs to know that her dad isn't a store manager. You have to reassure her that she's secure in your absence. I don't have to rub it in, but she misses her mom something awful. She needs more than what you're giving. Even when you're with her, you're still not there."

"She won't talk about Christina with me."

"Well, she won't, probably. She holds you responsible and knows you have no answer for it. She's a young woman, so that communication will either come across in anger or indifference."

"I'd rather have the anger."

"Day isn't over yet, and it's not your choice. Give her some time. I'll subtly put my two cents in and see if I can help a bit. If she's doing better, and depending how long you'll be, maybe I can have her over to the house for a couple days. James Senior and I could use the company. She could use a change of scenery. That brother-in-law of yours, bless him, could probably use a break too."

"About that. About James. Think you'd let him stretch his legs for two to three weeks?"

Aimee's tone became more direct and frosty. If he couldn't confront his daughter, he sure as hell was going to be straight with Aimee. "Sean Havens, I don't like the sound of this at all. Now, you've gone and pissed *me* off."

Sean didn't convince Aimee.

Aimee dropped a few tears at first, then stuck out her chin. The thought that she could now lose her husband just when she was secure knowing that he had no more deployments was unsettling. On the other hand, she was afraid that she could lose him at home.

In the end, however, she was a patriot and her husband was a soldier who hungered to get back in the bush much like Sean Havens. To have her beloved husband die in the field would be better than letting him die at the homestead of depression and boredom. It was selfish, in her mind, to hold on, and ultimately she wanted the decision to be his with her blessing. She hoped James wouldn't make the decision lightly. She feared that he would.

"She said I can go?" exclaimed James with childlike enthusiasm. "Yes, yes. I'll go!"

"James, this isn't like we're going camping. We have to get you read into the situation back at the shop. I still have to jump through some hoops and paperwork. I just needed to sort out if you'd be willing to serve as a 'jungle consultant' contractor for us. You sure you're alright leaving Aimee? I don't mean to put you in a spot."

"Uh-huh. She's good. Sean, come in here," James motioned Sean into a room off the garage.

Within the windowless little wooden locked shanty, there were large impact-resistant storage bins, lockers, and wooden crates. "Welcome to my private loadout room. Look in this crate box, here, Sean. Let me see … I have a nice little DAGR."

James raised up the olive and black hand-held GPS receiver. "I've got a Stalker. OASYS-BAE Systems Thermal Monocular." He beamed. "Could come in handy wherever we are going." James pulled out more equipment like a boy rummaging through his toy box. "A Long Range Thermal Video, pocket laser range finder, ooh … SkeetIR Micro-thermal mono-sight, thermal binocs. They clip nicely on thermal night vision device, but I don't suppose we'll have helmets. Will we?" Not waiting for an answer, James continued sorting through his collection. "Sure wish I had this when I was doing LRRP ops in 'Nam."

"I take it you're in, regardless."

"I can bring my own weapons, if we need," said James, admiring more of his personal hardware. "What did you say? Am I in? Aimee said I was in, right?"

Sean questioned his own motives. He was doing the exact thing to Aimee that he was doing to Maggie. Or was he doing it to James Senior's only living son?

Chapter 28

Much to Sean's amazement, red tape issues were virtually nonexistent while getting James on-boarded and set up in the necessary systems. It was refreshing that procurement was such a breeze, but it still gave Sean pause as he walked down two flights of stairs and through the dim corridor to the training, evaluation, and operational research department, or TEOR. For something so verboten at first, it now seemed to be simpler in approvals than planning a two-day field training exercise. Havens put it to the back of his mind, as finding the general and the crew was priority.

Sean swiped his badge to access the TEOR department that resided deep within the bowels of the building. The access light switched from yellow to red. No go.

Dammit!

He swiped again. Then faster. Then in reverse. Nothing. Next option, the door pound.

While he waited for someone to answer, Havens continued scrutinizing the mental list of kit required for the mission. He hoped some of the latest and greatest technical low-profile gadgets would be available for their use. The wizards of TEOR were often composed of the old farts who disappeared from the battlefield due to their tenure, but still stayed in the game. They were sharp and proven, but on a decelerated ops tempo. They wanted to keep working and were willing to travel anywhere.

The door opened and a wiry old Delta plank holder instructed Havens to enter.

"Sean Havens?" the weathered man inquired.

"I am," Sean confirmed.

"Joe Johnson. Used to be squadron sergeant major back in the day."

"We've never met, but I've heard of you."

Joe stuffed both hands in his pockets. "Suppose I've heard of you too. I hear you're a good man. That goes plenty far. They said you'd be coming down here. Might as well c'mon in and we'll see what we can put together for you boys." As he walked, the man pulled up the worn grey Kühl outdoor pants that slipped from his waist, sagging lower with each step of his Vasque hiking boots on the concrete floor. He wore a faded olive drab Royal Robbins knit crew layered under a plaid long-sleeve flannel, both tucked in. A sheathed Leatherman multi-tool was attached to his nylon belt.

"Did they say what I was coming for?"

Joe picked a fingernail as he recited, "You're going in as a two-man reconnaissance team inserted into a dense area to gather intelligence on the area and crash. To confirm activity. This area is routinely patrolled by the Myanmar conscript army. After a short period of time, if you meet enemy resistance, you will not have backup, you will not have exfiltration options. There is no FOB monitoring your situation to assist with extraction. You are pretty much on your own, and you have little to no jungle experience. You will have no weapons or anything that affiliates you to a military entity. You're traveling with a retired long-tabber who had a solid reputation and solid jungle experience. That sum it up?"

"Pretty much."

"Well, sounds fun." Joe bit on the stubborn nail. "Don't sweat the jungle. I was never in Vietnam before I actually was." He chuckled as he opened another secured door into a large open tactical room. "You won't have radio, but if you need to get in contact via sat phones, these Blackphones will look like standard mobiles and work within standard tower zones in urban areas. Then we can give you standard Iridiums. Secure SIM card will encrypt your comms. You have a secure and a standard capability. Keep the secure where it can't be found, obviously. Do I need to remind you they will eat the battery pretty quickly?"

"Nope. Makes sense. I've dealt with that before."

"Good. Well, for that, I've got you boys a USB solar panel that you can unroll and plug in for a charge."

"Cool. Thanks. Looks like they looped you in well."

The older man gave Havens a dead look.

"I'm also setting you up with what looks like an Apple watch. Same capabilities, but this does have GPS, unlike the commercial brand. Also ties into your phone. Has some military apps behind other apps on the screen that you can just touch to access. Play around with it, get to understand how it works. I have it on a navy blue strap. Less operational looking, but still good at night. Non-reflective glass. I'm guessing you know the drill and can handle yourself or you wouldn't be here."

"Let's hope so."

The dead look returned.

"I served with Bain. Heard you went against the man to be part of the PR."

Havens wasn't sure what to say. *The personnel recovery op was supposed to be pretty compartmented. Isn't even a plan for recovery. Guy knows more than he should.*

"I'm not able to discuss details. You know how it is."

The man waved his hand. "Like all waters, there is the current you see and the one you don't. These walls have an undercurrent that exists to protect our own. But don't worry, I'm read in to Ice Snap or Ghost Hunter, you choose, and even to Primed Charge. Hell, I helped build the program back in the day before it was Ice Snap, or whatever the hell we call the damn thing." He cupped a hand over his mouth and pointed up. "So while the man does his cock blocking, we down here and elsewhere make things happen."

"Does that have anything to do with Primed Charge?"

"Sure, no matter who's running it, we know that any program designed with no oversight can go bad. Your program removes restrictions so you can go out and do deniable operations. We've been doing it for years. Hell, I was doing it with the Phoenix Program."

"So you all are just enabling it?"

"Son, things have a way of swinging back and hitting people in the ass. I'd like to think we remove the hinges. But keep in mind, we as a nation train a shit load of other governments and militaries. We use them for things like Primed Charge."

"Right, that's nothing new."

Joe held up a finger. "Well, let me ask you, Mr. Havens. Who's the analyst keeping a list of all those individuals and countries that we've trained so we can run them down as soon as we see something going to shit-—that looks like our own Primed Charge program?"

He had Sean's attention.

"No one. Performing high-value targeting missions that are deniable and using civilian clothes or cover and cloaking civilian deaths isn't our only playbook, but we sure as hell pass that playbook around to a lot of people. So watch your back and never forget that. You live by the sword, rest assured, you'll die by the sword."

"Comforting," Sean replied.

Joe gave Sean a friendly swat on the shoulder. "Just a reminder. Nothing to dwell on. And don't lose that watch. I have eyes on you. *We* have eyes on you. There is a game on that watch. You'll see a red dot float across the screen in game mode. You press that dot if you need something to get you out of a scrape and you don't want to run it through the chain of command. It has some preset responses. You can customize with a voice recording or a sync to your phone if you press the telephone icon."

"What will happen?"

"Don't know. We'll help however we can. No promises, just a promise we'll try."

"Does Rick know about this?"

"Why the fuck does he need to know about it? He's going to be *here*. You're the one heading downrange. He can't plan or direct a military op. This is our lane. Not his. Pope wants to make sure you have backup." The old soldier winked at Havens, then stuck a finger in Sean's chest. "Just don't fuck up. I owe Bain one. Don't go pushing the damn thing if you get the shits or miss your mommy."

"Will it work under the canopy?"

"Son. If you needed further instructions, I'd give them. But let me give you this bit of advice for your little trip. When you pack the rest of your gear, think about your feet. Keep 'em dry. Keep 'em light. A pound on your foot is about five pounds on your back. What are you wearing out there?"

"Can't speak for my partner, but I'll have some Lalo tactical that are darker brown so they look more recreational."

"Perfect. But make no mistake. You two going downrange in Burma isn't going to fool anyone that you're backpackers. All you need to worry about is not getting caught with shit that singles you out as military or intel. Got it?"

"Got it."

"Take one of these Geigerrig hydration system. Come back down and get 'em when you're ready. I'll have more kit set aside." Joe demonstrated the drinking system to Sean. "It has a purification filter and is pressurized so you can use it to flush wounds. Also, for your notes, a percent of your body weight in your kit's going to make you six seconds slower per mile. So do some math before you start humping off into the jungle. Which reminds me. The jungle is both your friend and foe. It is not a landscape. It's a system. A system of systems. For as much as it can hide the enemy, it can allow you to infiltrate with cloaking. But for that, you must learn to be part of it, not an observer. Don't fight it. Trust your instincts and take your time to listen and feel it."

"That's good advice. Thanks. I'll take what I can from your experience."

"Good to know. I'll give you one more."

"Shoot."

"You're more like us than those Agency boys. Watch your back, Sean Havens. We don't trust your boss. Neither should you."

Chapter 29

Back in the war room, Rick had Sean, James, and Tanya gathered.

"Your call sign is Mowgli 2 and your buddy will be Mountain 3. Sorry, no Fritter call sign for you, Havens," joked Rick with a wink to Sean.

"Who's Fritter?" questioned James while draining the rest of his coffee and handing it to Tanya for a refill. "No cream, just some sugar, Sugar."

Rick took the mug from Tanya with a disapproving look and handed it back to James. "Sir, coffee is just out the door to your right. Ms. Crowe has volunteered to monitor your whereabouts. She is a GS15. I assure you, she has presented qualifications suitable to the job."

"How so?" James crossed his arms with the coffee cup bobbing at the side, his eyebrows raised in genuine interest.

Tanya stepped in. "OGA out of Yale. Eight years as a political analyst, and two years abroad in operational support. I then supported SEAL Team 6 as a Joint Special Operations Task Force targeting liaison in the field for High Value Individuals throughout CENTCOM AOR and Iraq. I later moved to DIA to support Special Projects at TSOC level as a counterterror threat finance analyst. I've also been an intel instructor at SWCS, and have been an intelligence senior advisor here at JSOC since."

James looked around the room, unfazed. "So who's getting my coffee? Sounds like Ms. Crowe's underqualified to make a good cup of joe. Right, little girl?"

She wasn't amused.

"My bad. Did it again." He winked. "Here's my deal with women in ops. Let's just get this on the table, because your tours speak to me as light duty. The best females in intel are unrelenting patriots and devoted to a cause. But even better than that are ones who have skin in the game because they were blackmailed, lost a loved one, or they're hard-assed ladies attracted to the danger and glitz of covered lives. Frankly, you look like a smart young lady who wanted a change of scenery. I'm sorry, but I don't see hard knocks on your door. I see someone who could be unreliable and a tinge insecure. Now, if you had a moral or emotional issue, that could be interesting."

Tanya gave him the bird. "I don't owe you or anyone else my story. So keep your sexist remarks to yourself. I'll do my job, you do yours."

"Clearly we have an HR nightmare here. Sorry, Ms. Crowe. We'll show you where the coffee is, James, Ms. Crowe will be providing operational support in a manner in which she is well proven. If you need to make contact with her, she is Mother 4."

Rick cringed immediately from the call sign choice. "Guess I'm guilty too."

"Apology unaccepted," sighed Tanya, irritated by the incessant boy's club antics. Yale, and her enduring student loans, were supposed to bring her further than this in life.

"Noted," dismissed Rick, continuing, "If there are no further questions, let's get you on your way. There will be no need to contact me; go through Mother 4 for all comms. If you have to refer to me, I'm Mafia 6, but I want all channels direct to Tanya. She will be supporting you from the embassy in Thailand. We will have limited over-watch, so just get in, do your job, and get out. If you get into some shit, 'Boston' will be code for emergency."

"Boston?" James noodled on the significance.

"I hate Boston. That's all. Anyway, nothing fancy. That means *nothing* fancy, guys."

"Rick, what else do we need to cover to develop the situation once we're in-country? I reread the downed team's mission plans and all the intel I could pull. I take it James is all squared away with admin stuff and we can hit it?"

"You're a go, but there is nothing to develop. We just need to cover some more protocols before you all head out. No engagement. You will not be provided any arms from this end. There is no complexity, no need to be innovative, nothing to assess. Point...and shoot. The camera, that is."

"Understood," replied Sean.

James nodded.

"James, you understand?"

"Sure, I don't know what we'd be shooting at anyway. This is just a recon mission, right? I'm helping junior here along the way to make sure he doesn't get bit by mosquitoes, right?"

"That's it exactly, James."

Sean looked sheepishly at Tanya, who averted her eyes. "Thanks for making me look like I'm being babysat, guys."

Tanya reached out and tapped Sean lightly on the arm. "Sean, can I have a quick word?" It was friendly again. Like he remembered her in Turkey.

"Sure. Excuse me, Rick, one sec." Sean was curious but smiled in anticipation.

"This isn't something you can share with us, Ms. Crowe?"

She could have justified a reason, but instead simply stared at Rick in silence. After all, she was involuntarily reassigned here upon his request.

"Two minutes," Rick relented.

"What's up?"

"Sean, I hope you know that I'm just trying to help because I believe in what you're doing. That's all. I didn't insert myself because of anything else."

Like the fact that you developed feelings for me that almost disrupted our operation years ago, and then went MIA for four days? "Understood," Havens fibbed.

"It's just professional," Tanya said flatly.

"Tanya, Ms. Crowe, I'm not questioning anything. Thanks for having our backs. I've got a daughter to come back to. I trust you." Havens remained stoic to keep her at ease. He suspected, maybe hoped, that she was still interested. While he could certainly do worse, Sean Havens still deeply loved his late wife but needed all the allies he could muster in his fractured life. For a moment, regarding her outward strength and beauty, it crossed his mind that she could be a good mother to Maggie, and were he not married at the time, he would certainly have been interested in Tanya Crowe. Who was he kidding? He was enamored with her while on the mission, but he passed it off as duty tradecraft. Just duty.

"Roger that. Glad we go that all straight." Tanya smiled a crack for the first time. "Be safe." She reached out and touched his arm, snapping her hand immediately with wide eyes as Havens stiffened his torso as she entered his space.

He extended his hand for a shake. "Okay then, Tanya." Sean tumbled the back of his wedding ring as he turned away. He wondered if he really needed to take it off for this op. Deep within, Sean Havens was afraid that if he took it off it might not go back on.

Tanya was thinking she needed to call her mom and say she would be late. This day required margarita therapy with Judy.

Jason stared at his satellite phone. Another hour passed and he still couldn't bring himself to call Draeger. It had been more than a week since the two last talked. The money was gone. No trace. Jason had no idea if Draeger had taken it, but the fact that he didn't know before it happened meant that he wasn't included in the decision. He could be a dead man.

Jason's sister, Judy, would have been a good sounding board for such an issue, but that was off the table. Jason knew he was kidding himself about being able to cut all family ties. He wondered more than once if he could become a casualty if Draeger questioned his loyalty.

Why was he so frightened? This wasn't his fault. His other secret paralyzed him with fear. It was all Harrison Mann's doing. Harrison had used her as a bargaining chip, then lost her. Why didn't he tell Havens? And now Mann was dead thanks to Havens, at least according to Draeger. Unfortunately, this would likely rear its head as a distraction to Draeger. It wasn't Jason's fault, he was investigating accounts and probing some commo by order of Prescott.

Another thought crossed his mind. Sean Havens was always a decent guy, he deserved to know more than Draeger.

While wrestling with the right ethical and job security thing to do, one thing was certain to Jason. The fact that Christina Havens was alive and captive in a CIA safe house was inconvenient for a lot of people. The next question: how many people knew? And how safe was *he*?

Jason eyed his bug out bag in the corner of the small room.

Part II

"I come in peace.
I didn't bring artillery.
But I am pleading with you, with tears in my eyes.
If you fuck with me, I'll kill you all."

—General James N. Mattis, USMC,
Spring 2003

Chapter 30

On the flight, James shared how his buddy Colonel Hessberg had spent his life protecting natives in one of the last major sanctuaries of Eastern Burma, which they would be proximate to. The elite career military advisor, Hessberg, had become family to a Karen leader, General Kon, over the past decade. During this time, the two men had saved one another's lives as they dedicated themselves to pushing back a national army, superior in both size and strength, that threatened the Karen ethnic population. Hessberg would prove to be good support for logistics.

"Sean, the Karen villagers' noble and, at times, heroic efforts to secure this indigenous land against all odds have endured just as their grandfathers did in WWII fighting alongside the British and American OSS to stop the invading Japanese."

"You don't have to sell me. I take it that when you told Rick that you knew some local contacts that this was our plan, even though it wasn't our plan?"

"Who, me? Sandbagging sources and methods?"

"Won't our asking for their help just add to their feeling of being manipulated by Westerners, if we really have no real interest in helping them in *any* way while we are there?" Sean's question was phrased more as a statement to avoid future conflicts of interest.

"Skip the culture lesson, son. I'm not sure the Karens have a word for 'manipulated.' If we show them kindness and ask for help, they'll help. Colonel Hessberg wouldn't have agreed if it was an issue. Plus, they need a little help of their own. I figured a smart guy like you would know how."

"I guess my remark went over your head, unless you ignored it. I'm not sure we discussed another mission, James. I know Rick didn't."

"Quid pro quo, Sean. It's not another mission, it's our by, with, and through way for getting what we need. Rick knows all about Hessberg. Burmese military controls the central delta area and we're plopping down right on the outskirts of that in the surrounding ethnic area. You're going to love it out there, though. Really lush valleys, high cliffs, thick jungle."

Sean realized his too-good-to-be-true find would have some price. It would have been naïve to think otherwise. "When did you talk to Rick about this?"

Ignoring the question, James continued talking. "Sean, I'm sure our boys were taken down by one of the Hinds. Karen's threats have increased since the Burmese army started buying up a fleet of Hind Mi-24 and Mi-35 attack-helicopter gunships, white phosphorus chemical weapons, and forest-destroying bulldozers."

"So much for reform."

"Reform? You've got to be kidding."

"I was," said Sean, knowing James was climbing the soapbox anyway.

"News of a reformist government is bullshit. They're as corrupt as ever and they keep plundering deep into the frontier. They're using all this hardware and munitions to clear everything in their path and swipe the natural resources. Resources are valuable. So they pretty much enslave or conscript forced laborers from the jungle. Meanwhile, the bosses are securing lucrative Chinese hydraulic dam contracts. I'm guessing the Chinese won't be too happy to hear that Burma is holding Americans in the jungle. If the U.S. and allies get to sniffing around, they might get savvy to China's plans."

Sean's interest was piqued. "So it's possible that Chinese pressure would be directed to making any downed Americans go away. But wouldn't that also include ensuring no one came around searching?"

"I suppose you're right. But I don't have an answer for that, Sean. Meanwhile, this primitive Burmese culture is in silent struggle against a rogue military that's sustaining itself by preying on the desolate villages."

"So do you think they'll help us find our guys or will the Karen want it exploited for media attention?"

"Hmmm. That's a good question. And that's why we'll have to tee it up just right."

"How so?"

James was waiting for this capstone moment. "We share how pro-U.S. Karen people won't be alone when the Burmese military attacks them with the gunships. My guess is they will. So if we can get them to free our boys, we help them too."

"Free? Thought we were supposed to observe."

"Sean. Don't be a dipshit. Haven't you watched a single damn Chuck Norris movie?"

Sean chuckled. "Sure."

"Chuck Norris ain't never just snapped a photo and sent it back to the bosses to let them jerk it up and arrive a day after prisoners are moved."

"No. I guess not."

"So, the way I see it, if there is anything to find, we take some pictures, we commo in some intel, and whoa, shit, we found our boys walking around one morning in the jungle, so we just had to take them with us, right?"

"And you pretty much had this in your mind ever since we first chatted about it?"

"Boy, I've been dreaming of a moment like this since I hung up my uniform. Sean, we never really talked about this, but how much combat experience do you have? Figured we could get that out in the open now that we're going into combat."

"We aren't going into combat, James, we're doing recon. You heard Rick. It's not a free fire zone. It's a low vis op with no authority to engage." Sean smiled, reminding his elder of what ought not need be reminded.

"As you say, young Padawan. But you know, combat can really mess with your senses. Once we get into the jungle, your senses will heighten to a point of overload if you can't manage them," James warned. "And with more than 300,000 conscript armies running around the bush, I'd be surprised if we didn't have a run in."

"I get it. But I'm also not looking for it." Havens needed to assert his position better before he had a rogue situation on his hand. "You know, James, I used to deer hunt in Wisconsin."

"That right?"

"Yeah, and where they likely have 300,000-plus deer, I've been skunked before, never seeing one. I've also inserted enough to know the questions run amuck in the head and the mission plan, the job, the things left unsaid at home are all carried to the forefront of the mind by the little green mission demons."

"Well, on the one hand, I think you were probably too loud and scaring away deer. So that has me a tinge worried. But I'll amen you on your other statement. I can't tell you how many times I've quit the military in my mind and then can't wait for the next mission. It's like running a marathon after forty. Body hurts, too much to give up, but you can't skirt the challenge that just taunts the mind."

Havens chuckled in acknowledgement. "James, I'm pulling your leg about the mission. The Karen thing I'm not vested in. But one thing's for sure. If our guys are alive and being detained, we're going in."

"Atta boy." James was all juiced up now. "But Sean, jungle ground time is different from most other theaters. I never did drugs, but I have to imagine that jungle sensory overload is like ecstasy. Heightened sound, smells, and periphery movements are tweaked up real good. You just don't want to go bang a fattie chick," James giggled. "My boy told me that. Guess he musta experimented with a lil' a both."

"I think I know what you're talking about. The former," he corrected. "I spent a lot of time in the Middle East."

James dismissed Sean's comment with a wave. "That ol' dustbowl is nothin' like jungle. Shit, I spend so much time upcountry in Vietnam that I could smell a V.C. rice fart from a half mile away. I shit you not. Could tell if he had fish sauce on that rice or dog meat."

Sean just shook his head at the caricature that James was of an old Vietnam SOF warrior.

"You don't believe me. But when we get down there, you need to turn intuitive. All your soldiering training or that black arts voodoo you get from the Farm has to shift to muscle memory. If we're going to get out of there, you need to be constantly asking yourself questions while you are moving, stopping, listening, or taking a shit in the bushes. Control your senses, be aware of yourself, and if you need to kill someone or something to stay alive, forget your orders and get your hands bloody."

Sean kept his eyes engaged with James, a tried and true jungle combatant who looked to take on a mentoring role in this opportunity. But this wasn't Havens' first dance. Environments the world over had their nuances to become attuned to. Survival depended on it.

James reached into his backpack. "Here, I have a present for you." James pulled out a manila booklet and handed it to Sean. "You can throw it in the trash when we land. I'm going to catch some shuteye while you study up."

Sean accepted the manual and quietly read the cover, Special Forces Combat Recon Manual Republic of Vietnam. He grinned. "I read this in high school. This was prepared by Project Delta B-52."

A bit surprised, James inquired, "Why would a high schooler read a special forces manual?"

Sean retold a bit of the old story of Lieutenant Laughlin and the infamous green beret incident.

"Well I'll be. Di oppresso liber," James said with a smile while extending a fist bump to Sean. His face changed to a stoic resolve. "Read it over." James turned off his overhead cabin light.

Sean thumbed through the pages. Recon tips for movement formations, breaking encirclement, snatch and grabs. "Here we go again." *I hate the Army. But I love the fun.*

Within moments, James broke the silence. "And to answer your earlier question, Rick and I chatted about Hessberg over a year ago. So once I got involved, it stands to reason that the colonel is my go-to for a Burma friendly."

A year ago? Rick knew of James? Havens toyed with the watch face a bit. *Red button is probably a self-destruct mechanism. Why do I even try to trust people?*

Chapter 31

A full day later, another airplane, a bumpy drive, and the longtail motorboat buzzed and puttered as Sean and James progressed down the Moei River, mitigating the scrutiny of Thai-Burmese border checkpoints. An unexpected cough of the engine reminded both to crouch a bit lower and tighter to reduce their target signature.

James pointed to the longboat's shallow sidewalls. He mouthed, "No protection."

Sean nodded in understanding.

James stared at the sides. He was fit, but he was no longer quite as low and tight as he once was thirty years ago as a young soldier.

He leaned in to Sean to share some of his situational awareness advice. "We're exposed on this leg to surveillance and potential hostile engagement. Small arms fire." He pointed to the banks on either side. "Not more than fifty meters from our position, but this area is still pretty safe."

Sean knew that "safe" was a relative term. One just never knew when he might be an intended target in a region with ever-changing laws of the land.

James also knew that their intel was only as good as what Tom, their contact, could garner through conversations with locals and open source media outlets. James pondered on the fact that he and Sean were on their own as volunteer advisors, devoid of the intelligence community resources that he had in days not long past. Still, he grinned ear to ear as he sucked up the feeling of being home again up country.

Sean imagined who in the surrounding Thai jungle could be watching them and squinted to see if he could spot anyone within the tall grass and reeds along the narrow shoreline. He watched

James. The guy was beaming like he was taking his son on a first dad and lad Canadian fishing trip.

The two men constantly assessed where the threats could be at this moment or the next in the dense tropical vegetation. It was second nature to both.

The sun waned and their minds began to play tricks with the eyes as limited vision set in.

James leaned in again. "I can be somewhat paranoid, but that's how I have survived a life as a commando. I know that when it's my time, it's my time. But that doesn't mean I'm leaving everything to fate. Keep your eyes peeled and ears perked."

Then James sat back again with slightly dropped shoulders. He was relaxed and literally soaking in the aspects of this majestic land before time.

Despite the jungle-cloaking darkness as the sun dipped behind the mountains, James knew that the Thai billboards would have since passed and they were increasingly replaced by the dense lush forest. Here, between Thailand and Burma, it is nature in its entire splendor. And mosquitos that make Louisiana's look like amateurs.

Over the engine, Havens could sense the calm and tranquility before the nighttime critter sounds would emerge from the triple canopy.

A loud snap came from somewhere in the darkness. It echoed and both men tensed.

They were completely vulnerable in this semi-permissive operating environment. True symbiosis of the predator and prey relationship.

James lifted his head a bit. He pointed to the small cooking fires off the shore and, despite the motor's sounds, assumed that the crack and pop were the burning wood in open air.

"Ranger TV," James said, leaning in again as a tour host.

A few thin trails of camp smoke emanated from the dense canopy to a now moon-lit sky. Camps that the men couldn't quite make out beneath the shadowed foliage could be smelled when not seen.

Sean welcomed the light breeze across the water and the slight wind blowing from the boat's forward momentum. It was part of the cooling process from the day's oppressive heat.

Sean was conscious of the noise they were creating on the water, but James was comfortable knowing that night river travel was a common pattern of life here. It is the highway of the indigenous. They were fitting in to the jungle life's backdrop as long as they weren't stopped for the next 5-6 kilometers.

From the Thai border town of Mae Sot, or "little Burma," where Sean and James changed vehicles under the auspices of being on an adventure tour, they were easily tagged by a well-bribed shop owner. Clearly, as Westerners, they stood out. More importantly, any men looking like they could be trouble were reported.

Thai security had known that two travelers were in the area for days. Thai intelligence had likely known as soon as they passed through customs. The Burmese dictatorship and the State Peace and Development Council (SPDC) Army had no doubt been alerted as well. The SPDC junta's spies had potentially informed on the two men's whereabouts when they left the relative safety of Bangkok.

The civil war between the Karen and Burma had surpassed sixty years of fighting. Help continued to come and go. Despite cover legends, rough men couldn't feign the locals' common eyes. Newcomers with bird of prey eye movements were easily picked up by those attuned to such tells.

"Two men passed. They have entered the river by boat." The spy paused, then added into the handset, "Not Australian or English. These men, American." The spy paused again, listening. "Not big bags. They carry one each." He continued his report. "Not long bags. No. Old man and not so old, not so young. Old man smile a lot. Not so old man look around. He like bird. Watch everything. They comfortable in refugee camp. They not on tour or missionary. They trouble maybe for you."

The destination hooch in the valley was sandwiched between a couple of majestic mountain ranges and had been under watch by enemy snipers hoping to rid the area of foreign military advisors. On the other end of the handset was an SPDC military unit leader. He keyed a signal on his radio handset to his hunter tracker team.

The team leader signaled to his men and they started their move from deep within the forest to the water.

Despite the darkness, the moonlit reflection on the water and a visible open clearing told James and Sean that they had arrived. In moments, the motor slowed and they drew closer to the shore.

The guide signaled to the coastline.

A lit beacon reply was received and replied.

Time for the next leg.

Sean drew closer to James. "We walking or driving?"

James resettled his weight over his feet. He shuffled his boots a bit in the soil. He drew in a deep breath. "I don't think they have had more than the usual rain. Doesn't feel like it either. My guess is porters. No vehicles."

As they drew ashore, they were greeted by a Karen guide who welcomed them to his protection. He had four other kinsmen with him. All armed.

James and Sean fought to see in the darkness. Sean spotted movement as the shadows shifted.

James was trying to determine if there were other Karen walking out of their sight to ensure protection and to monitor against unwanted military outpost patrols.

Haven's hands felt swollen and clammy in the humidity. He was a bit on edge. *Maybe this wasn't such a great idea. I need a gun.*

The passage deeper into the territory was uneventful and the guides suggested taking a short break, encouraging the two Americans to doze off for a bit while the soldiers kept vigil. Not knowing how long of a hike awaited James and Sean, they didn't argue and agreed to close their eyes.

"Havens, put on your poncho liner."

"I'm okay, thanks."

"Havens, put on your poncho liner," James practically ordered, while pulling the plastic over his own head.

Sean did as he was told then re-secured and checked his water, a satellite phone, and light bag filled with first aid, some food, and a few other survival goodies should things go unexpectedly south in a hurry.

The rain fell just as Havens pulled the bag synch taut.

"You're welcome," James muttered as he let his body fall into sleep under the heavy drops falling from canopy openings and running off the liner. "When it stops raining, put the bug net on your face."

At about oh-dark thirty, there was another signal. The guides heard the signal, unwitting to their guests moments before. The party was here.

A deep American voice boomed in the intermittent shower of rain that was drawing to a close. "You didn't bring me much to work with if all you have are these two bags. Wake up, James."

"Do you really think I was asleep? I heard you dragging that gimp leg of yours a klick away."

"I'll bet that was the best sleep you have had in years."

"My friend, you know what? You're right. How's your hip?"

"Feels great, compared to my back." James reached out a hand that was met by the large meaty paws of Colonel Hessberg. The colonel pulled his old battle buddy up and they embraced in a warm bear hug.

"Let me introduce you to my boss, Tom. This is Sean Havens."

"Havens, huh? You friends with the old man?"

"I'd say that's fair. Good to meet you. Thanks for the hospitality."

"We aren't there yet, but I'm just wondering if we met once at Leavenworth. Did you ever teach at the Command General Staff College?"

"I did a few guest speaking engagements with SOF Studies and SAMS. Just some light IW content with the General and solo instruction a couple times."

"I'm thinking maybe that's where I've heard of you. Special forces?"

"No. Never in uniform. I worked with the dark side for a few paramilitary gigs and JSOC. Clan Asymmetric Solutions Force."

"Spook. Figures." Hessberg's disappointment was clear.

"Friendly spook," Havens clarified in an attempt to build trust.

"No such thing as a friendly intelligence service. I worked plenty of SOST missions for OGA. With military, you deploy when they have decent intel and when the brass has a willingness to sacrifice elite soldiers for a noble cause. You're greenlighted to go on the mission when the escape plan is as good as the ops plan. With OGA, you're on your own. Period. All men can be left behind. Thank you very little."

SOST. Spec Ops Support Team. This guy's been around the block too. Probably a tough old bird. Havens gave some slack in judgment, given the colonel was spot-on thus far.

"James, you can come with us. Afraid you'll have to send your spooky buddy back. I can't take any chances."

James followed the colonel while Sean stood dumbfounded, making sense of what was going on. "You heard the man, Sean, you best git yer ass out of here. Oh, Tom, did I mention that Sean had come up with a way to save your people here?"

"Nope. Best stay with us, Sean, don't want to miss chow this mornin'. Welcome."

Always a test. Always making a deal. There were times to question a situation, have a laugh, or keep your mouth shut. Sean chose to shut up and go with the flow.

Sounds of buzzing bugs and the occasional monkey howl were starting to become incessant white noise. Sean recognized the need to layer that noise as a background constant and use it as an alert to anything new in its midst if he was going to be able to pick out someone sneaking up in the foliage.

I wonder if they have bacon and coffee out here or if we'll be eating WWII MREs and dandelions. Not even going to think of pancakes. Havens smiled to himself. A consummate foodie at heart.

The Burmese sniper team heard the muffled voices. Killing the two travelers would ensure no additional assistance to the Karen. The sniper team leader, however, was sure that the big American was with them. He would be the primary target. If they could capture him, he might be able to lead them to General Kon. If they had to kill him, they would receive praise nonetheless.

The four men spread out along the hill slope with positional advantage over the narrow trail below.

"James, I do wish that you had brought us some more supplies. Your spook convince you not to?"

"Really, Tom? The way we came in-country, transporting commo equipment and military supplies across borders is a little more than just frowned upon. Besides, we're just here as observers. Karen have their ways of getting supplies by other intermediaries, mules, and fixers. I'm not one of them."

"It still would've helped."

James didn't give it another thought, as abiding by some rules and policies kept Thailand and the U.S. in passive support of the colonel's presence with the Karen. A violation would be a one-way ticket out of the jungle with no return permitted. Tom wouldn't take that chance and neither would James. Knowledge, however, knew no boundaries, nor can it be checked at borders. For that, these men would admit to smuggling mightily of their intellect, experience, and problem-framing abilities.

"Careful, Sean. We have to narrow our little column here. Feels like we are merging to a lesser-beaten foot trail. It'll also help us if we need to switch to countertracking to lose anyone pursuing us."

Sure enough, the trail eased to be wide enough for two men to easily walk side by side, but they would keep their line and spacing. The trail also allowed them to increase both speed and distance.

With no equipment-supported night vision, the men depended on their own retinal outfitting. Sean could tell that amidst the darkness, the bamboo surrounded them but they had ample room to find cover and return fire if attacked. Even though he was no jungle expert, he was concerned about slowing down or denying pursuers who could be tracking their route and intended destination. For that matter, Havens had no idea where they were going, and, for all he knew, the rebels were conducting proper route security.

The Karen rebels leading the party were armed with RPGs, M-16 and AK assault rifles, grenade launchers, and other assorted weapons provided from all corners of the world.

The fighters looked like a ragtag mishmosh of insurgents, but even Sean knew that they were among the finest combat-proven troops that he would ever come to know.

Alone with his thoughts, Sean reflected on the past year's events. Christina's murder. Maggie's near-death experience and now long road to full recovery. Leaving Chicago for yet another dangerous job. Killing Red. Killing Harrison Mann. Putting him through a wood chipper. What was he thinking? And Prescott Draeger, involved from the start. Havens continued to drift off in the walking rhythm along the trail and fell deeper into thought. What type of an organization was the Pond? Who led it? How would it be organized? How did it tie back to the intelligence and military communities?

Within Havens' musings, he tried not to step on anything he could walk over. Tried not to break anything and tested his footfalls in an attempt to stay on harder ground.

The snipers along the darkness-covered ridgeline remained motionless. They were waiting until the party was completely drawn in to the ambush. The lead sniper could still attack the Karen walking on point if they needed to let a few more into the trap.

A dog barked in the distance.

The team halted.

The point man scouted just forward on the trail.

Hold fire.

The jungle sounds were changing. Morning was coming. Cocks would soon welcome the sun. The villages would start to wake. The snipers were closer to the camp than they thought.

All clear, the signals were sent back to Havens, continuing the trek to the destination.

The snipers fingered their trigger guards. Wait until they drew closer to one another.

Something still wasn't right. Point stopped again and dropped just as the red flare thumped and exploded within the foliage.

Havens heard shouts and could make out motion on the top of the ridge. He dropped and watched as blue tracers laced the night. Weapons cracked and the bright lights added color to the white-hot lead with red illuminated jungle wallpaper.

Somebody give me a friggin' weapon!

The men in the small column remained low. Some crawled off trail but never fired a shot.

Silence.

A dog barked again.

The men around James and Havens were laughing. Tom crawled over and shared that their advance team had discovered the snipers and lit them up. It was the fourth time this month that they had encountered a kill team. Things were heating up. It was still funny to the Karen, who were regaling each other at how surprised the sniper team must have been. The Karen hadn't shot the snipers in the backs but instead surprised them with the flare and then attacked them face to face.

Havens felt a rush of adrenaline wash over him. He wanted to engage an adversary for the first time in months. His heart beat strong, blood surged through his body. He felt back in the game.

"How you doing, James?" asked Sean, doing a 180 head rotation to soak up the smoke sight and smells as daylight broke through the flora.

James' eyes were wide with excitement. "I about crapped my pants there for a bit. Someone give me a weapon. Observer my ass."

Tom laughed. "We're good for now. The team will begin the mountain ascent. You can have a weapon once we get to the camp. I don't want you slipping and shooting me in my bad leg."

"I thought they were both bad."

"Exactly. Plus, the leader in this village, General Pang, knowing him, he'll have his troops up for maneuvers and likely will not return until the mid-day heat drives them back to the village. I don't want you boys to go shooting up his team if they are sneakin' and creepin' around us. They aren't always too keen about *gullawa*. 'Whitey', that is."

"General Pang? I thought we were meeting someone else."

"We're not going to my village, we're heading to a different one. Change of plans."

"Then a change of plans here, too," Sean informed Tom.

"How's that?"

"Who's got an extra weapon for us?"

"Right, on," James lauded.

Chapter 32

Taking separate flights to Thailand, Tanya didn't formally meet Lars until they convened at the Royal Bangkok Sports Club.

Identifying Lars was easy given the description of his massive frame and oafish demeanor. The full spread of food before him added to the visual she had preconceived of him.

As she approached, Lars stood, gave a warm smile, and stretched out his wingspan in hospitable invitation.

"Welcome, to Thailand, Tanya." Lars offered the greeting like he was the ruler of the land. His outgoing demeanor immediately added to his likability.

Tanya's guard fell and she shook his hand with an equally warm smile.

"Well, Detective Bjorklund, thank you for inviting me to your country," she beamed.

Lars gave a hearty laugh and looked across his spread and well-positioned table on the patio. "Perhaps I've overdone it a bit." He raised his eyebrow, seeking approval. "You'll have to tell me how I submit expenses unless you just want to pick this one up. I can always put it on the Underhills' tab," he joked, making reference to an old Chevy Chase film.

You're just a big teddy bear aren't you? She caught the movie reference and added, "In that case, I'll have a steak sandwich and a … steak sandwich."

He chuckled. "Please sit." He pulled a chair for Tanya. "And just call me Lars. I'm retired, as you can see."

"Very well, Lars."

"I'd say I ordered for the two of us already, but you'd probably see right through that, wouldn't you?"

"I have no idea what you're talking about," she replied, reaching over for a batter-fried vegetable and dipping it in what was either a soy or fish sauce. She wasn't so adventurous in her food selection, but it was important to make a strong impression.

Soy. Thank god.

Normally much more aloof, Tanya sensed that Lars was much different from the cadre of rough men that she dealt with day by day. She suspected and hoped that, based on Lars' education, experience with the Chicago Police, and some other details in the file, he would be more collaborative in his work style. Admittedly, there was the intrigue of him being the brother of Sean Havens' late wife, Christina.

"Pretty amazing club here, right? Looks like our 'uncle' has been a member for some years. Pretty nice perk."

"Oh, its fine. A bit flashy for my taste," he said in full disclosure.

"I see you're completely out of your element," she joked, lifting a hand at the spread Lars had in front of him. "If you prefer, at some point we can go to the British Club. Pub food, beer, darts …"

Lars pointed to Tanya, taking aim with one eye open across his finger. "Now that's a deal. You look more like a darts and beers gal. That's a compliment, by the way."

"I may enjoy a ponytail through the ball cap and some jeans, but I'm not complaining about this one bit," she laughed genuinely—or so Lars surmised.

He smiled back. "So, while I'd like to go on with small talk and pleasantries, and getting to know you, I figure you have some news that Seanie is all safe?"

The balance of doing what was right and keeping classified secrets weighed towards sharing. "Lars, I don't know much and can share even less, but Sean is fine."

"You'll keep me posted, if you don't mind. Whatever you can. We don't have much in this Havens and Bjorklund family, but for now we have each other."

"I understand." Tanya took an uncomfortable gulp of ice water that had more sweat on the glass than liquid within. Clearly

Sean Havens' well-being was weighing heavily on both of their minds.

"Well, Lars, at the risk of pulling rank, let me share how I envision things going down here."

Chapter 33

"Hello, Jerry."

"What's the status of my boys in Myanmar, Robert?"

"I have no idea what you're talking about. Heard through my old Burma channels that there might have been a downed aircraft or two, but if a tree falls in the jungle and no one is there to see it on a trail or by satellite, did it really fall?"

"Why are you calling me on this line? How did you get it?"

"Oh, don't get your shorts all bunched up. You have bigger concerns than how I got your new number."

"And what might those be?"

"I wouldn't have cared if another department or DoD was sending those boys over to Thailand, but because it was directed from your son, it means you're sniffin' my shorts still. You changed your plans to take a peek in Burma. Naughty, naughty."

"They are evaluating the bombings."

"Jerry, there are bombings all over the globe."

"The mere fact that you are calling proved my hunches."

"You shouldn't have hunches about us if we are the last thing on your mind."

Jerry remained silent.

"I have no concern about you finding anything. My concern is you failed to heed warnings about backing off."

"My son has other priorities. This is a seventh floor Agency directorate matter that I have sanctioned and it has nothing to do with your organization."

"You forget, Jerry, we have space on the seventh floor, too. Equal distance from the director."

"There's greater distance between us than hallway proximity. Why in God's name they still allow the Pond a directorate presence in the building while trying to snuff your organization out remains the question of the century."

"Jerry, we were classmates. I know your tells even over the phone. You're lying. We are a necessary evil, and your efforts to stop us are only hurting our own people. I just want to let you know that I am watching. And know that I know you've sent your other puppet into Burma to find those mercenaries and to make mischief around our distribution site. I told you to trust me and just back off. Otherwise, these men will simply disappear just like the last ones you sent. You'll feel the fires of our hell throughout your organization. I will blind you. And I'd say you're to the point of needing a seeing eye dog pretty damn quick."

"You have militarized the Agency. I want it back. You are not conducting intelligence missions."

"Now, now, my little man. You have more traveler miles to Creech Air Force Base than I do. You and your little airplane toys are just as at fault. Once you started flying armed drones, Jerry, you went off the reservation of intel collection. My little Counterterrorist Center just took a little real estate while you played with toys. I'm no more or no less of a scalp hunter than you are. That 'gentleman intelligence' and 'don't read people's mail' went out long ago, and you were at the helm of it. Powder your wig and fluff your silk ascot but you're dark to the core. I'd venture darker than myself, and I take great pride in my abilities. We are one and the same. But I wear my true nature on my sleeve. You have yours like a friggin' suppository shoved far outta anyone's sight." Robert sighed. "And I know you're just pissed 'cuz I own the Discrete Capabilities Office too. You should've made a play long ago, but you figured they were just accountants covering our ops. Just took a little imagination to make them operational too, my friend."

The line disconnected before Jerry could respond or inquire.

It's our organization. As Director of Operations, it should be mine. They'll be coming for you, Sean. They'll be coming for all of us in one way or another. Our beloved CIA would rather man-hunt than spy. Indeed, I'm as much to blame. Well played, Robert. Well played.

Chapter 34

By late morning, the men arrived at camp. Tom was still reluctant to provide the men with weapons.

The small community was nestled in the forest of a steep mountain pass.

With the morning light and apparent eased tension of the guides as they drew closer to home, Tom began chatting.

"Sean, just to clue you in on a few things, as a career soldier with well over thirty years under my belt, most of it in special operations, I have met many fine warriors and many exceptional leaders. The Karen Major General, whom I believe you thought we were meeting, is among the few that I revere the most. Against the odds, he is protecting his people in the last major sanctuary in Eastern Burma. The man at this camp, however, is not."

"I'm not sure why we need to head here. Our exposure is supposed to be limited. Can't say I'm comfortable with the change. I understand the situation is pretty tense, but so are the sensitivities in our mission. As I'm sure you can appreciate." Sean pulled at his clothing. He felt as though he had sweat dripping from every pore in his body.

"Tense? Why, I'd say that's an understatement. The situation in Eastern Burma right now is this. There exists, for the time being, a last remaining liberated area, which is a jungle area wilderness region about 100 kilometers by 200 kilometers along the Thai border. That's where you are now."

"Okay. That I understand."

"This remote area is effectively being surrounded by all the different forces of globalization. For the Karen, not many of those forces are good. The Myanmar armed forces want access and control of the region, primarily because of the gold mines. The Karen, who are native inhabitants of this region, have one of the largest gold strata in all of South East Asia. This particular region has a couple of very prosperous-looking mines. That is just one threat to their existence."

Havens could tell that his operational concerns were not a priority to Tom, so he opted for rapport building before a change back to the issues at hand. "And what about the Chinese? James mentioned that they were a factor."

"Glad you asked. The Chinese are trying to build a series of thirteen dams along the length of the Salween River, and eventually they would like to continue down to the Indian Ocean. The Karen region has a couple of key dam sites that they want. As a major global power holder, the Chinese and their hydropower developers are in cahoots with both the Thai and the Burmese. They'd like to build roads and open waterways to facilitate the construction and logistical requirements. This, too, cuts right into Karen territories."

"So what's to stop them?"

"One of the few things stopping this from happening has to do with my friend. Major General Kon, the main Karen commander and the vice commanding general of the Karen National Liberation Army, is also the fifth brigade commander. This is his region. This area is where he grew up, it's where his mother lives, and it is where his father and grandfather lived. This very terrain is where his grandfather was a WWII veteran who fought alongside the British and the American OSS against the Japanese. As I think about it, generationally we have come full circle from the Special Forces roots in OSS with me there now and this grandson of an indigenous guerrilla still fighting for freedom, a defender of his people, and still being left behind by helping nations."

"Anything else that can stop the Chinese or Myanmar government?"

"Well, that's where things are getting interesting. We are seeing the Russians and Iranians more and more around here."

"Are they working together?"

"Sort of. Bit of a power play going on, but so far everyone's playing nice. That's what has us shittin' a bit. And a lot of folks at Bragg, as well."

"Think of this," Tom posed to Sean, "Could the Iranians close the Strait of Hurmuz all by themselves?"

"Probably not for long without killing their own oil reserves."

"Exactly. Could the Chinese close off water access and seize Taiwan?"

Sean rebounded, "Not likely without a U.S. confrontation."

"Could the Russians expand Westward after Crimea and Ukraine?"

"Current administration, hard to say. Not sure who would contest them."

"Could North Koreans come down and take South Korea?"

This time, James answered. "Shit, they could if the U.S. was too busy figuring what to do if they all joined up and exercised their conquests."

"Exactly," said Tom. "The new Axis is North Korea, China, Russia, and Iran. Who could contest it? They don't have to fire a single shot. Countries are collapsing from the pressure alone."

Sean was still having a hard time believing the scenario. "Why is this converging here?"

Tom slipped on the slick grass and momentarily lost his footing before recovering.

James and Sean looked down at the three-hundred-foot drop and both men moved a little closer to the other side of the trail.

Tom punched at his aching hip and answered, "Well, that mister spook is my question to you."

"How's that?" asked Havens.

"Your people have added something more into the mix of late. The CIA has taken an interest over the infrastructure, financing, and money movement of the methamphetamine trade. They are connecting the human trafficking, the opiates, marijuana, by backing off the supply and distribution angle and making ten to twenty percent in profits from the money movement. That's what's causing the gang wars out there in Thailand." Tom waved out to the horizon in the direction of Thailand. "The routes are getting pretty trafficky. That's why we're now seeing military outposts by the

Iranians, Chinese, and Russians. Well, the Russians pretty much use Myanmar's military as a surrogate."

"That's interesting, Tom," Sean endorsed. "See, we thought an insurgency was brewing and the bomb makers creating events in Southeast Asia might be getting their hands on whatever they could, even around here, sometimes using homemade explosives and other times military grade. But you're saying it's due to the factions of criminals that are likely getting it from their own nation, or those seconded to them."

"Bingo again. You're pretty smart. I'm surprised you want to hang around with James, here."

James turned around and gave Havens a wink. "Tom, Sean wanted me to help him with our friends who went down around here. I figured we could make this a combo approach and help you out just the same. But it sounds like you are about to get the crunch."

"That's exactly right. With all those countries looking to converge, Myanmar's junta is looking to profit as well. Plus, under slaves and conscripts, they can join the fun and make a move on Thailand. General Kon gets this. Under his care are somewhere between eighty to a hundred thousand villagers and third-wave rice farmers who are trying to protect a two-thousand-year-old Karen culture from all this encroachment. Frankly, it isn't easy. The Burmese military has thoroughly infiltrated the area with outposts and bases. Over the past decade they've developed a series of roughly sixteen outposts behind the village and the riverine border with all concrete reinforced helipads for the strategic use of Hind gunships to control the area."

"Shit, they can blast you and your Karens right out of the woods, Tom," James said, shaking his head.

"Well, that might be so. Tactically, the Burmese have borrowed from Sri Lankan counter-insurgency doctrine and maneuvers, which is a hammer and anvil approach using artillery, air, hind aerial gunships, and infantry to isolate resistance. Within this practice is the notion that killing the leaders is key. Like most resistance conflicts, if you kill the leaders, the forces fall into disarray and they can be herded into kill boxes for easy elimination. That's why I'm keeping an eye on Kon and have his back."

"How much time do you think you have?"

"Well, the rainy season is going to end and then they can get their vehicles through. We can already see what they've been doing and using in the Kachin state attacks. So far, they haven't been hesitant to use jets attack for bombing, plus hind attacks and chemical warfare. The extent has still to be determined. In the past, there has been use of mustard, CS, and then there is some use of white phosphorus too, which is a form of chem."

"Tom, isn't USASOC interested in this?"

"They were, but the intel that I'm getting is that the Burmese are now trumping up the charge that the general is a drug runner. The allegations against the Major General are false but they're intended as an information operation to garner political support, or at least passive resistance to the use of force to root out a bad actor. This is about as accurate as my little old grandma working for a Mexican cartel by selling crack on the street corner near her retirement home. It's ridiculous, but it's a way that they can justify the hunter killer teams and international support to assassinate this great warrior leader. Major General Kon is the farthest thing from a drug runner. He is one of the most virtuous general officer leaders that I have ever encountered. And that, Mr. Spook, is why I still am keeping an eye on you. And that's also why we are paying a visit to this fucker along the way. I think he may be involved in the setup."

Chapter 35

PASSPORT walked through the Charles de Gaulle Airport terminal and spotted one of his regional officers in the pre-arranged location reading a book titled *The Grey Man*. How fitting, PASSPORT observed.

"Steven, give us some space," he instructed his security element.

With a nod, Steven stepped to the side.

"Hello Warren. Catching up on some reading, I see. What brings you to Paris? Just a layover?"

"Business as usual, Thomas," he replied to PASSPORT, using an established cover name. Looking down at his novel, he added, "And this, one of my vices. I'm continuing on to Germany. No direct flight was available."

"I see."

"To what do I owe the pleasure?"

"By twist of fate, or Murphy's Law, it appears that Sean Havens has been sent to Burma."

"Burma? What the hell is in Burma?"

"We are in Burma. That's what the hell is in Burma."

"We are? How so?"

"Our interests are, and some of our affiliates. We have an outpost there that the Bonesmen have had an eye on since they lost control of it, but they haven't figured out a way to push us out. Probably up to your level, but we've gotten some wind from the ground through one of our doubles. I have no question that our site in Burma can handle themselves, but I see both an opportunity here and a threat."

"Continue."

"We were given a tip that allowed us to eliminate a team of contractors acting on behalf of the Agency that was going to sniff around Thailand by way of Burma, which gave us an opportunity to engage them. It worked out perfectly to further confound the intelligence community on what was transpiring around Bangkok, but it also plopped them down proximate to our activities."

"I'm listening."

"Further adding to the execution of our ruse, Sean Havens was sent to Southeast Asia to pick up the pieces."

PASSPORT inhaled through his nose, flaring the nostrils. "Havens is unpredictable. He has a tendency of getting out of scrapes and situations, and I am not one to bet that he can be outsmarted by some knuckle draggers. Certainly he can by someone, but I'm not going to spend time thinking of every permutation that he may find as an opportunity to survive or to discover what is not intended to be discovered. He's working directly for Langley's Bonesmen. They have their sights set on us. We have them running in circles as usual, but I don't want to take chances. Therefore, I want to redirect him to use his persistence in our favor."

"That's my point. We looked at the opportunity to shoot down the CIA team to keep them out of our hair. I'm now wondering if they didn't somehow sacrifice those men in attempt to make an excuse for Havens to get on the ground. I think they may be making a move on the outpost. There's a Special Forces colonel down there who used to do some black work for the Agency. They could use him as their man on the ground if our team vacated the area."

PASSPORT was growing impatient with the situation. "What do you have in mind?"

"Our organization through Silver Star renditioned Havens' wife from a crime scene, but Harrison Mann, the ops officer, had them save her life and replace the body. Neither Havens nor Mann knew that Christina was the Agency's Counterintelligence eyes on Havens. Our eyes. We had the Fed's Red Peterson ID the surrogate corpse that Mann had taken to the morgue. Clearly Mann wanted a bargaining chip in the community if folks learned he had killed an operator's family."

"This Mann fellow had a point. In the eyes of many within our circles, we killed Christina Havens, witting or not of her role. Those pieces of knowledge have a way of circulating in a rather inconvenient manner. If we allowed Draeger to free her, that could draw Havens back to the home front and put Draeger in some grace with men we may need in the future now that we have agreed to embrace him as one of our knights. Would Havens be a suitable candidate?" PASSPORT inquired.

"At one time we thought so, but he is anointed by the DO. Havens questions too much. I want people to do everything to win wars without being inconvenienced by moral justification. Best let him fade away and keep him at arm's length from us. His boss, a legacy, could be problematic, but we are negotiating that currently, and after we take office, that may no longer be an issue either. Many pieces, many players, but the time is almost nigh."

PASSPORT suppressed a smile. *Nigh. What a tool. That keeps a lot of options open to us for Mister Draeger, options to which he may be better suited. And maybe an opportunity to steer the Agency in ways we want through Havens.*

Chapter 36

The heat and humidity of the day sucked the energy from the Westerners making their trek up and down Burma's peaks and valleys.

"You boys done sucking wind yet? I've brought some of the toughest ex-Delta, SAS, and Special Forces through these mountain ranges to get to base. Having learned the hard way years back, I tell all these lone wolves that the mountain will bring them to their knees. I kid you not, it isn't for the faint of heart. I can't even imagine being on a stair climber in that gym adjusting it to the steepest slope of your life for over six hours. Never mind the added weight. They never listen and always assume it gets easier after we hit the summit."

Despite using a lock-step climb method to take periodic leg and muscle strain rest, Sean was puffing hard. "I thought we were on our way down."

"Almost, but little did you know, going down this last stretch is worse. My colleague learned that very quickly when he tumbled top-heavy. A good way down this double black diamond he'd avoided stepping on elephant dung and stepped right onto a big teak leaf the size of a placemat. Since I've been there and done that with the T-shirt, I can't say I thought it was funny and rushed down to see if he was dead."

They all gave nervous laughs.

"Oh, and if you all brought Lariam for the skeeters, it won't do you any good. You need Malarone for these provinces."

James turned to Havens and shrugged his shoulders. "Sorry, guess you were right, Sean."

Tom laughed. "We may be able to spare some, but the damage is probably done at this point. James, you know, this is similar to old trails we have tread as it pertains to the politics. The forces of intimidation, coercion, and terror through age-old ethnic rivals between non-Burmese ethnic minorities and the Burmese majority endures today. Well over half of Burma's military is focused on this region that we are trying to protect. Their scorched earth brutal policies leveraging rape and murder would be doled out to these tribal lands to seize everything from gold, gas, and uranium to oil and precious gems. The wrath is mighty as the ethnic resistance challenges the regime's power under a global spotlight."

"Silent genocide," James remarked.

"Indeed."

As they carefully traversed the downward sloping trail, Sean could make out the encampment of bamboo huts nestled in the hillside joined by narrow bamboo bridges that connected towers and ridgelines over the winding stream beds. He was near famished from the caloric spend and figured that James must be as well.

"So Tom, while I appreciate the ethnic diversity of cuisine around the world, I couldn't help hoping that we would not be dining on lizard this afternoon."

"You may not be so lucky, Mr. Havens. Quite frankly, it has never set well with my stomach, or should I say upper and lower GI tract, but when in Rome ..."

James pursed his lips. "I've got no problem with lizard. I kinda miss a good boa, too."

"Well, buddy, you just may get that but chances are we'll have some mélange of pork if we're lucky, but more likely chicken, goat, or other small game partnered with tasty greens and onions that'll be served raw or oil cooked in the large traditional woks. Fried egg jungle omelets tomorrow will probably be the morning delicacy if we don't have too bad a run-in with the leaders that I have to chat up. Just need to get them singing on the same sheet of music."

"Eggs, mmm," said James. As he turned back to smile at Havens, he stepped on a large, slick leaf that shot out underfoot. James tried to stop the fall, but his Bates boot couldn't find promise one the wet vegetation. Gravity and the slime sent James over the edge with his hand clawing at the ground to stop the descent into the jungle depth below. He caught a vine, which too started to follow in its slack.

Havens pounced on the makeshift rope and caught James's fall. Gaining some traction under his knees, then feet, Havens started pulling the vine hand over hand until he could see his buddy's face over the trail lip.

James's face was white as a ghost.

Sean stuck his boot in James's face. "Lalo. You should have gone with the Lalo," Haven's laughed as he then reached a hand down to pull James up.

"You pushed me just so you could make a point," James teased in return.

Neither of them noticed that Tom had stopped along the path and was just catching up. He stuffed a sat phone into one of his many pockets. "Okay, ladies, enough jungle antics. We're just about there," he scolded, squeezing past the Burma newbies and taking point.

Sean squinted over the chasm to see who was within eyesight. He scanned the area and noticed a couple more satellite dishes, solar panels, and a few large metal objects.

The Karen looked busy and, from his guess, quite resourceful. A number of the mountain lads from the village made their way up to greet the party. It was good to be at a place of rest for a bit, but they pressed on.

They continued the descent for another twenty minutes until Tom froze. Fist up, signaling to stop. He called out to the men behind. "Quick! Slide down the other slope side. Feet and knees together, arms crossed. Try to control your descent and get in the brush. Shit! They're here!"

James, who was still periodically wiping the foliage, soil, and his pride from his pants, didn't make out what Tom was saying. "What's he barking at?"

In the moment of pause that Sean took to absorb what was transpiring, he heard the faint beating drawing near.

"Sean! James! Move!" Tom shouted.

Before sliding down the mountainside, Sean Havens looked over his right shoulder to see the black dotted Mi-24 HIND gunships in echelon formation.

As the column slid, they were overwhelmed by rotor wash and the noise of two more gunships that popped up and launched 57mm unguided rockets into the camp and hillside. The flying armored tanks hovered over the village as 80mm smaller rockets shot from the wingtip triple rail missile racks toward the frail huts. The explosions were deafening.

One HIND nudged closer to the hillside in a controlled side shift. Though Havens was descending at a high speed, he could follow the 12.7mm Gatling gun that oriented to the evacuating villagers. The fire spit at the hillside, ripping the first of the Karen soldiers.

A distracting round impacted the HIND, pulling it away momentarily from its target.

On a small cliff rise, two young Karens fired .50 high-powered rifles at the gunship. They aimed at the rotor, tail, boom, and transmission, firing continuously at the highest rate of fire before the HIND responded with a door-mounted machine gun, forcing the boys to cover before releasing an Igla missile.

The ridge and those it sheltered exploded into oblivion.

Havens' rate of speed diminished slightly as vegetation and smaller saplings and bamboo slowed his descent. He caught a glimpse of Tom and James nestled in a small covered crevice. They called for him to join them.

The two gunships advanced and, with gaining speed, cut over the tree line and made a sharp turn outward away from the village. The beating rotors of the approaching formation were deafening.

"Did Tom say chemical weapons? Napalm?" he yelled to James.

Havens' eyes followed three young Karen children running toward the village. Whether they were off playing or doing chores, Havens didn't know, but their instincts to run home out of fear overrode the unperceived danger.

His clothes frayed and limbs bleeding from the deep foliage gashes, Havens bounded from the shelter and headed toward the children.

The first of the HINDs released more rockets directed toward the largest structure remaining in the camp. It exploded with an enormous fireball that rattled the ground.

The children stumbled, giving Havens enough time to move closer.

Burned and mutilated bodies littered the encampment, staining the bright green grass with blood.

Havens started sprinting once he reached the base of the slope. He scooped the children up with both arms and continued running. He was nearly through the exposed opening when the next two HIND gunships fired dozens of rockets that exploded all around the scene.

Havens stumbled and uncontrollably smashed down on the children as he fell. Between the deafening noises and his ringing ears, their shrieks of pain and fear were felt as vibrations but unheard.

Looking back, Havens saw the release of the fourth gunship. He regained his legs and collected the children in a mad sprint to the river now visible before him.

The roar of the flames was deafening. He flung himself into a dive with the children, not knowing or caring about the water's depth or contents below.

Chapter 37

To say that Robert was cross was an understatement. He pulled lint from his pants as he sat in the car, phone pressed to his ear. "You should have let her die."

"That was apparently the plan. Once Agency counterintelligence gained another asset that could keep better tabs on Havens, we no longer needed his wife. Plus, blackmailing her no longer worked once it was outed that her brother Lars was on the take. One of Draeger's men in Chicago decided to keep her for insurance. Guess he was okay smoking everyone but in hindsight thought there could be community blowback for killing the Havens family."

"That, boy, is why you don't use a 9mm round. Or at least tap the target in the head." Robert inadvertently tapped his own head with a finger.

"I'll remember to pass that on next time we use a surrogate agent who uses another surrogate agent who uses surrogate gang members. Did you want them in a two- or three-week training?"

"Love the sarcasm. Don't like the timing of it."

"I still think this plan is too complex. This is a loose end that just needs to be cut. We're getting too distracted with baggage. With games."

"Noted. But it presents an opportunity for us with the Agency. Is she in decent health? Meaning, are we saving a damned vegetable?"

"She's weak but mobile. She's in the Agency safe house under the watch of your men. We have an idea to use one of our new associates to get her out and regain some favor in the community. She was in a coma for some time, but our clinician induced it so she could recover. After the assault on the Havens home, ambulances took the wife and child. The child was barely alive but the wife was declared dead on the scene. Some overly ambitious paramedic thought he would try his hand at intracardiac injection. We had a monitor on the radio frequencies and learned of it. Mann had a team intercept the ambulance and found a quick surrogate. Since she was a CI asset, we interceded, had her operated on as a Jane Doe, then transported her to one of our facilities. We told Mann she died despite our best efforts. I think it rattled him knowing Havens would have his head. Havens had to have killed him and gotten rid of the body."

"Good god. That's too fuckin' risky. But, in the spirit of a little fun, I think this is something I can use." Robert smiled and envisioned himself pushing Jerry's head down in a tub of water.

Chapter 38

James came down the ridge to lay closer supporting fire against the HIND gunships. He had a second weapon for Sean and a belt with ammunition loosely strapped to his back.

Havens waded the children to safety and left them under the care of to two younger Karen rebel soldiers. Probably no more than twelve or thirteen years old, the young men hurried the crying children to safety with both compassion and confident authority. Seeing James fast approaching, Sean ran up the uneven terrain to meet his comrade. Taking a weapon, he focused his mind to be on offense as the first HIND took another pass.

"Guess they'll let us have toys now," James shouted, not missing a beat in preparing to attack.

Knees bent and weapons charged, they staggered their steps as they ran heel-toe to minimize the jarring, compensating for the bounce as they sped across the path while engaging their targets.

Another flying shooter tried to flank the two men.

James grabbed Sean's shoulder, pulling him back to back as they continued shooting, pushing back on the line of fire.

"The cockpit windshield is bulletproof!" Havens shouted. "There are a few soft spots, but we can't get to them from this angle."

In solid rhythm, the two men fired at the second HIND making a pass and replaced clips at intervals that never slowed their flying lead toward the gunship.

The colonel neared and shouted that the HINDs were breaking off and flying back to base.

Absence of helicopter and armament noises invited new sounds of crying and the crackling of fires that continued to feed on the village huts.

The men said nothing. Each broke off in different directions to aid the villagers.

Havens' heart was pounding. His vision blurred and his ears rang. He tripped over his own feet and stumbled to the ground. He closed his eyes and wished he were back home with his daughter. The screams, crying, and crackles of the fires were overwhelming. Getting back in the game was no longer as sexy as it had seemed hours ago. Sean started to curl. A darkness was passing over his mind. It felt warm, and he rested.

A lone cry pulled him out of his mental womb.

Havens opened his eyes and willed his body to move. Limb over limb, he crawled and elevated himself to heed the call. He was quickly back up on his feet and running to help.

Chapter 39

Lars Bjorklund scanned the cordoned-off destruction from the nightclub bombing. Prior to his departure to Thailand, he read a significant amount of global media reports on the bombing. A number of Thai news statements attributed responsibility to the Patani United Liberation Organization, or PULO, one of the active separatist movements in Thailand's Muslim south.

The PULO denied involvement. While PULO had been involved with car bombings, such as this incident, their targets had predominantly focused on public infrastructure buildings, police stations, and public officials.

The PULO-Thai amnesty program had also countered the theory, arguing that the collaboration was making headway between the government and the liberation group.

Others speculated an al-Qaeda or ISIS link. A charred and dismembered body was found in and around the backseat of a vehicle parked outside the club's wreckage that seemed to be the site of the charge. The apparent suicide bomber was identified as a local Islamic evangelist. U.S. media was conflicted in their reporting on involvement, but generally agreed it had been Islamic fundamentalists. BBC supported the logic, with other world reporters bowing to the assumptions. U.S. politicians soaked up hours of media coverage and pointed fingers at ISIS and administrative weakness in addressing the global threat.

Lars moseyed to the collapsed structure as cars and motorcycles whizzed around the debris removal workers and scrap metal trucks. *This place isn't third-world. Why haven't they cleaned it all up already?* The former Chicago detective removed a thin packet from his pocket and tore the foil wrapping. He pulled out an explosives detection technology wipe and firmly guided it across a shattered and blackened rear-view mirror amidst the rubble. Lars assumed that the part was from the suicide vehicle. The piece had deep black scorch pattern residue burned on the metal. An explosion from the vehicle-borne improvised explosive would have created a heat and fire trajectory outward and past the front of the car. He hoped the metal would contain explosive traces. Seconds later, the white cloth displayed bluish purple stain.

Lars nodded his head. *Ammonium nitrate and TNT.* He turned to his left and right to see if anyone was paying attention to his activities. Lars studied the location where the vehicle would have been pre-explosion. He examined the buildings across the street to visualize wreckage and blast pattern evidence. He studied the destroyed discotheque. There was more debris forced outside of the building than collapsed inward from the street.

Seeing no one paying attention to him, Lars moved closer to a blown-in wall of the building. He stepped over toppled masonry and charred wood beaming. His footing was unsteady on the rubble that gave away under his weight. Instinctively, he reached out and sliced his hand along a shredded metal bar also bent outward to the street.

This place is hosed. No way the car out front did all of this. Car would have had five hundred pounds of combined explosives max. My guess, from blast pattern across the street and associated wreckage, maybe 200 at best. This is a blast from within. Why cover it up unless the primary bomber did it from within?

From across the street, the watcher called Paulo. "The American is here. He's not a tourist."

The watcher paused, awaiting instructions.

"Yes. I will follow and contact you once I find out."

Steadied on the rubble and nursing a fairly deep gash on his hand, Lars opened brown, green, and purple foil packets. He took all three wipes in one hand while compressing the gash with his pinkie and ring fingers. He rubbed the cloths along the bar and what was left of an outward wall.

Lars stepped back to the street while examining the white testing material. Emerging color started to streak the sheets. *Curious.* While it darkened, Lars thought more about the scenario.

Media said that in 2005 militants in Thailand attacked military patrols using VBIEDs and IEDs, utilizing cell phone initiation systems and typically about a hundred to a hundred and fifty pounds of explosives. Four main active militant groups in Thailand couldn't have done this unless they were united or tied to another group. No one claimed responsibility that could be vetted. I'll have to check out the hotel too.

"Hello," Lars said to the evidence in his hand. Greenish-black ink spots continued to spread. *HME. Big-time explosives. Military grade. Blame extremists for the blast, but the real targeting was done from within. Blast range from the car was probably lethal to only fifty or sixty feet, judging by the window and structural damage around the area. The inside damage was predominantly contained to the building. That might rule out political outcry, demonstration of capabilities, and media attention as primary strategic objectives. I suppose this was an assassination or a max casualty way to scare the shit out of people with more AQ rag heads. Seanie, this is the hell fires of your world and I want nothing to do with it.*

Two young Thai ladies passed Lars. One noticed his bloody hand.

"You won help? We clean you up good. Massage too?"

Lars sheepishly looked down to the ground. He pursed his lips and raised his watch hand. *Hmm. I've got time.*

He smiled at the girls. "How old are you?"

The women glanced at one another, one raising her thinly shaped eyebrows. "How old you won? Virgin. You like?" She purred as she started to pose and touch her colleague, rubbing the other woman's back, shoulders, and gliding a finger to her friend's breast curvature that filled the tight top.

"I know you both aren't damn virgins. You at least twenty years old?"

"She eighteen, I twenty-five."

"Ladies, as long as you don't have balls under those little skirts, I'm in."

245

The woman giggled and extended a hand. She took his hand and drew it near her skirt. "No balls. You feel."

Lars snatched his hand back. He scoped the street for prying eyes. "I believe you. All good."

"You American?"

"Yes, I am. Shall we go?" Lars looked back to see if he had a tail. *All good.*

Chapter 40

Casualties in the village were relatively low, but the cries of those who lost loved ones continued to ring out in shrill wails and long, mourning moans.

Sean sat alongside James as Tom spoke to the surviving leadership.

Havens doodled in the dirt with a small stick. "We have to come up with a solution to their Hind gunship threats. If we could, it would be a devastating surprise to the attackers if they stage more helicopter assaults on the Karen positions. Part of me would love to see it happen all around here and watch the bedlam that unfolds upon the Myanmar air force if they keep attacking."

"Sean, the Burmese are basically using these tribes as surrogates or proxies to influence, corrupt, infiltrate, whatever, other neighboring tribes. Burmese have no interest in these ethnics. There hasn't been interest in nearly 100 years. There has always been animosity and warfare out here in the bush. But the Burmese are using these others to accomplish what they do not have access to do. Alliances are hidden. I'm guessing what Tom is dealing with is a lot of vetting, promise-making, and maybe some counterintelligence."

"I have some great counter helo tactics that could be very effective."

"Where'd you learn that stuff?" James asked, quite hopeful and surprised. He granted Sean a wry smile.

"It's theoretical. I never actually did it. Yet. But I think it could work. I'll check with Tom."

James nodded. "Well, as happy as I am that you're willing to help, I'm seeing another side to what Tom said. The Burmese have so many soldiers. Killing them doesn't make any difference to leadership. They simply conscript more."

"What are you saying?"

"Maybe Tom should tell them to let one or two dams be built. They could become stakeholders to get some profit. They have nothing now since the Burmese give them no recognition or rights as indigenous land holders. So that is a problem. A band of a thousand guys is not going to stop them. Me and you sure as shit can't make a difference." James lifted his head, squinted, and took in the ruin of the village. "It's like a Dark Ages, feudalistic setup where you have highly empowered generals who cut deals locally and then a central government that is trying to reform and say all kinds of things and make overtures to the west, and then the guys in the field don't give a rat's ass. They can't be touched. Say what you want, we're doing our thing. They can keep their armies in the field through a rape, pillage and plunder approach."

"They don't have very powerful weapons."

"Tom told me the village that he stays at bought an M-2 barrel and a U.S. Army .50 cal from the Thai. They knocked down a Burmese microwave relay dish at 1500 meters. Built in jungle engineering facilities. Bamboo hut with Chinese generator and a lathe. They buy .50 cal shells that are Vietnam era. Dry in the sun and make sure powder is good. Get all green corrosion off them. They have a Remington 700 with Leupold scope. They shoot bulldozers in the crank case and engine block to stop forestry clearing. They make mega claymores that can take out a whole platoon."

"With what?"

"Conduit pipe, napalm, and rice mixed with gas to thicken. Four-gallon can of that stuff can make the Burmese scamper back to the outpost."

A young girl approached the men with a small tray. It was filled with eggs and fried green bananas. Her face was long from the morning's horrific events.

Sean's eyes welled. *They killed your people and burned your huts and you're making food for guests.*

James was moved, as well. "We gotta do something, Sean."

"You heard Tom. If this has been going on for hundreds of years and Tom is bringing in a bunch of other advisors, we can't make a difference. James, I keep going back and forth. We need to focus on our mission and find our guys or the wreckage. This is a policy play."

"Tell that to those kids."

"You're right. Let me think of something."

Chapter 41

Lars spotted a hotel that would meet his immediate needs. It took some extra financial inducements to the hotel clerk to forgo any information sharing and passport validation.

The women were eager. Former detective Bjorklund could hardly contain himself either. The clerk, a young Thai man, gave Lars a wink as he dropped the room key in Lars' enormous palm.

"Hey buddy, if you want to come up too in a bit, I'll leave the door unlocked." Lars handed the man a small wad of bhat currency. "We'll be in the shower first, so just come in if we don't hear you."

The clerk giggled nervously, thinking it must be a joke, but clearly this American had money. "Ha ha. I have to work," he said by way of an excuse.

"No worries, my friend. I'm a policeman. You'll be safe. Unless I brought handcuffs." Lars smacked the girl closest to him on the bottom, then gave her a little pinch to seal the deal and guided them to the room elevator for a few-hour respite.

What are you getting yourself into? Lars thought to himself as he escorted the women into his room. The halls were empty. The hotel was quiet. Seedy. It felt sinful. He couldn't wait.

The watcher made a call outside the hotel entrance. "He is at a small private hotel. Near the second blast site. I'll text the address."

Less than thirty minutes later, Paulo handed the watcher a small handgun. "Do you know the room and floor?"

"Yes. The desk clerk said the big one is a very dirty man. An American policeman. Do you think he is dangerous?"

"We have to see what he is doing. Then kill him. I must leave the country tonight for other business." Paulo flashed a blade. "We'll make it a robbery. Don't shoot unless you must."

As they approached the room, the two men heard laughing and sounds of ecstasy. Testing the door, they found it unlocked, as the clerk had said it would be. The men quietly entered the room, weapons drawn.

The naked women bounced on the bed, paying no notice to the uninvited guests.

The shower was on, the bathroom door ajar.

Paulo signaled to the watcher to open the bathroom door before the prostitutes noticed. He paused for a second, thinking better of reacting based on the scene before him. The sounds were off. Water was falling straight down with no body to interrupt the streams. Paulo turned back to the shadows and ducked.

Lars Bjorklund hammered the broken chair leg down, just glancing Paulo's head and hitting his shoulder. On the upswing, Lars cracked the wood across the watcher's face.

Paulo instinctively kicked out but met Lars's solid thigh that did not budge. Paulo flipped himself back up and slashed out in front while regaining balance for his next move.

Lars was ready to put one over the Wrigley Field bleachers. His swing was in motion and made contact with Paulo. The wood caught Paulo right in the forehead and knocked him out cold. Both men lay unconscious on the floor. *And it's outta here!*

"Thank you, ladies, you can get dressed now," Lars said, nearly breathless. He twirled the wooden leg around, fancying himself as the Babe, before dialing Tanya Crowe. She answered almost immediately. "Hey, T-bone. Its Lars. Gonna need a little help. Seem to have found some trouble."

Chapter 42

James and Sean saw Tom heading toward them with two different Karen soldiers.

"They lost some key leaders here today. I'm going to need to stay here for a bit and help them get back on their feet. I've convinced them to strengthen their alliance with the Major General. These men shared how Myanmar armed forces have visited the village in the past months pressuring them … in a variety of ways."

James and Sean remained silent.

"These men know where your wreckage is. They said there were survivors taken to the Iranian encampment. Three, maybe four survivors."

"Holy shit." Sean smacked James on the arm in excitement.

James spit on the ground. "That's good news. How many men maintain that camp?"

Tom addressed the Karen warriors in local dialect.

Everyone saw the Karen show four fingers.

Sean's expression intensified. "I want to know about the Iranian base that the guys are being held in. What activities does that base support?"

Tom seemed quite familiar with the site. "Mostly, it's a small landing strip where drugs are shipped in and out. They do the same with money. What currency, I don't know. I suspect, or, shall I say, it is suspected, that the explosives in a few of the larger Thai blasts were Iranian. They smuggle any of that from one of the other trafficking routes. Chinese charge a pretty hefty tax now to the Iranians since the flow is heavy and it is encroaching on the mining areas where they are excavating and clearing for the roads to the dams they want to build. Name registered to the place is Khatam al-Anbiya. Supposedly a company for construction and engineering.

They also have a reputation for uranium enrichment, which is a possibility in this area but they don't have the right equipment."

"Do tensions ever run high?" Sean asked.

"Couple standoffs. Few Persians were found dead. Suspected that it was Chinese security, but no one did anything about it." Tom seemed to pause in thought after his remark.

Havens pushed for more. "How long ago was that?"

"Oh, let me think now, not more than three weeks." Tom's facial features seemed to intensify as he added, "Chinese and Iranians mind their p's and q's with some of the air patrols that swing by from the Russians. They send around one or two of the gunships pretty regularly. Myanmar forces also move through the area. Few sapper hunter killer teams and some officers who collect taxes. Matter of fact, couple of them recently went missing not too far from the area of the Iranian base. Our scouts have said there is increased military presence sniffing around looking for their men. They aren't letting up on these people."

The read on Tom's face was of dire frustration with the plight of the region. He had true concern for his mission but a look of resolution to see that *his* group of Karen were protected.

"How far is the Iranian base from here?"

"Few hours or so. Question is, Mister Spy-guy, what can you do about it?" Tom challenged.

Hank Hill of the National Reconnaissance Office's Mission Support Directorate entered Gadsby's Tavern in Alexandria. It was 12:30. His wife was less than approving of the midweek late-night rendezvous. Spotting Rick at the end of the bar, he sauntered down and pulled up a bar stool.

"Don't see you much anymore now that you're down there with the snake eaters."

Rick toasted his glass in recognition.

"What are you drinking?"

The bartender headed their way.

"Red Breast. Irish whisky. Do you want to try it first?"

"Thanks. I'll just get one." Hank made eye contact with the approaching bartender and pointed to Rick's glass. "I'll have the same."

Rick sat back and studied his old friend. "We're getting old. Good to see you. Thanks for coming out. I know Vicky probably wasn't pleased."

"She's fine. I told her we wanted to stay away from the McLean area."

Hank's drink arrived. He tilted his glass to toast. "Cheers."

"Cheers."

"So, what's up?"

"Well, you know how I asked you for some imagery on that crash site in Burma?"

"Sure. It's what you wanted, right?"

"Spot on. I'm going to send you another request. It'll be formal. It is going to be based on a sensor coordinate. My task order to you will be to capture still images of the area and some video. If the sensor is moving, will you have someone that can monitor the feeds live?"

"I can put someone on it."

"Thanks."

"What's the part that you needed a face-to-face for? We've been doing this a long time together. Tell me the footnote."

"I also need you to capture video and imagery on the signal source. It's one of my guys. But I need it zoomed in enough that it captures his activity and context could be lost. You may want to program the area to include Bravo Site 62. We've had the territory since the OSS was in Burma."

"One thing at a time. Relating to your guy, meaning, you may need something to wag a dog and have to single this individual out."

"I can't put that in message traffic, nor do I want you to bundle the feeds together. I'd like the special request items sent directly to me. I'd also like to know if anyone else is requesting information on the signal or the area."

J.T. PATTEN

"Rick, if its compartmented, you know I can't tell you who else might be interested."

Rick downed his drink and put forty dollars on the bar. "Hey, thanks for letting me borrow your windbreaker last month." He folded the light jacket and handed it to Hank with a meaningful look.

Not quite understanding, Hank accepted the coat he had never lent and felt an object about the size and weight of a hardcover book. His finger pressure indicated that the bulk was in a wrap or envelope. The character of his friend confirmed the hunch. "What?"

"You're daughter's tuition for the next two years." Rick clarified discreetly. "Have the feeds sent directly to me, and any inquiries emailed to me on secure. Make the subject ... Red Breast. Enjoy." He patted Hank on the shoulder, confident in a solidified deal.

Sean Havens was lost in thought. He was processing everything that Tom had said about the region, everything happening to the CIA analysts being targeted, and those who were killed in Thailand's blasts.

"Tom, let me run this past you. Chinese have been beefing up their military with highly sophisticated weaponry and forces while we reduce our budgets. America has lost its grip on the Pacific. If what you say is happening, there is no way that the U.S. would send in ships. The Chinese DF-21D anti-ship ballistic missile has sea boys shitting. Russia is making their moves, and China is making a move on Senkaku islands north of Taiwan. They are basically uncontested in claiming the chain of islands and increasing their patrol craft in the area." Sean paused a moment for any differing reaction.

"Go on," Tom encouraged.

James was struggling to keep up but remained tuned in.

"Then, here in Burma, it's a bit like what you and James may have experienced directly or in doctrine about Vietnam. Myanmar's leaders are exploiting the Chinese and Russians just like the North

256

Vietnamese did. Soviets gave billions in military assistance just like we're seeing here. They played off each other to increase aid."

James held up a hand. "Roger, Sean, I'm tracking but not exactly following what you are thinking. Break it down for this old country boy."

Tom was still nodding. "James, Sean is saying that there might be some competition going on here. That means tension could be high. If we were to push the envelope a bit we could cause friction between Russia and China. Iran, if they're here, would have to pick a side, or they would fill the gap in the country."

James' eyes lit up as the details came together.

"Exactly! And just like Vietnam, the U.S. will do anything to avoid direct intervention so we don't provoke them into a war. History repeats itself. We won't provoke them, so they know they have carte blanche to position themselves ..." Sean paused. "Holy shit!"

The men looked concerned as they asked, "What?" in unison.

"Thailand. The Pond. Those explosions. They were small, provocative approaches to elicit a response of some sort. What else could they be? The targeting of intel analysts in the U.S. is to ensure no one connects the dots. I'll bet the targets are Iranian, Russian, and Chinese SMEs. If they haven't hit them all, they're mixed in so no one figures that out too." Sean looked around him in the jungle as if searching for a white board.

Now Tom was lost. "What intel analyst targeting?"

James jumped in with a quick news brief on what was occurring in D.C. and other parts of late.

Tom got it. "So let me ask you a stumper for argument's sake, Sean. What if you're wrong?"

"If I'm wrong about Burma, then just like Vietnam, the Chinese and Russians are using the country and potentially region for transnational sanctuary to stage incursions. One way to validate this is to check the Chinese and Russian sites for supply caches. But I suspect that DIA and NRO would have picked up on this since major buildups would have to be outside of the jungle canopy for airlift and whatnot. Plus, Tom, the Karen would have picked up on this and relayed it to you, right?"

"I think you're right, Sean. So we're back to scenario one, which I'm not sure we can do anything about. Shit, look at this place. We can't even defend against the HIND gunships. With their night vision, we've even started to hear of sorties in the dark. We could expect one any time. They've been patrolling in the darkness pretty much every night over by the mountain base." Tom shook his head in futility. "We can't do shit with what we have."

James chimed in with squinted eyes. "Sean, I've not known you long, but I can see those wheels cranking in your noggin'. What's you got cookin' up there, son?"

Sean remained quiet.

"Sean! You in there, boy?" James playfully knocked on the younger man's head.

Sean Havens broke a smile. "I've got an idea. I need a few of these Karen soldiers. And point me to your fuel area and rice."

"James said that you have some old-man portable Stingers and RedEyes that are crated but don't work."

"Yeah, so what? Karen were robbed of almost two hundred grand for two pallets of anti-helo weapons that are all inert."

"Are they in good condition?"

"Sure. All crated, tarped, beautiful but worthless. We have two that do work, but we've been surprised each time there was an opportunity to defend with one. And they aren't here, they're at my camp."

"Have you recorded any regular pattern that you can count on?"

"The only thing that is regular is an evening pass between 2200 and 2300 in a clearing about three clicks away, and a weekly training run that happens pretty much every week about another seven clicks from here. We just never grabbed the tiger by the tail lest more come. Most that come this way are from the Meiktila base in the north central part of the country. Local basing a little closer to us could be staged with advance transport, but we have yet to hear of that happening. Really things are just ratcheting up now. What

SAFE HAVENS: PRIMED CHARGE

else do you want to know? If nothing else, we head out to the wreckage first light."

Kid, someone has your number. You're doing exactly what they said you would. This is too easy.

Chapter 43

Jason remained in the efficiency apartment. With no friends, no family, no country, he felt deeply alone. Paranoia was also setting in. This business was getting too dark. He knew too much and too few people knew what he was doing, save for Draeger, which was not very comforting. He feared that under Draeger's threats his sister would be in danger if someone learned of their communications. And then there was Sean Havens. Guilt ate away at Jason knowing the wife once thought dead was indeed alive.

Jason began typing on his laptop. The security token was activated. He searched through Draeger's bank accounts. The funds were gone!

Jason pulled up the general's cached Silver Star side account. He noticed a new physical address had been updated and the former P.O. Box address was erased. The general must be out of the business and getting sloppy. Probably greedy, siphoning discreet moneys that were not being monitored and moving them to his own accounts. There was money in the general's account.

Did Draeger take out his money? Shit. If he did, he doesn't need me. I'm of no value. If someone else took the money, I'm toast.

Within reach was Jason's unsecured iPad. He needed advice. He needed a clean conscience. He needed to talk to Sean Havens. No. Havens had little clout. Jason rushed to a spare bedroom that held his bags. In a side zippered pouch was a card. A card given to him at a random dinner. That was his play.

Jason sorted through his papers until he found what he was looking for. The red, white, and blue circled crest of the CIA lifted his spirits as he validated his recollection and confirmed the title. *Inspector General, Central Intelligence Agency*. It was time to make a call, grab some things, and disappear.

.

Chapter 44

After a high-protein breakfast of some animal neither Sean nor James could or wanted to identify, the small party moved out.

James patted his belly. "Gotta say, Sean, I'm full. I sure would have preferred some pancakes and coffee."

"You did *not* just say that."

Tom chatted with a couple locals then turned back to his Americans. "I'll go with you, but I'm lettin' you know our OPTEMPO movement to contact will be less than 500 meters per hour, even if I send some of my young guys ahead to scout. It's really thick over there."

The men came across the wreckage in the late afternoon. The first of the helicopters was reduced to forty feet of debris. Chunks of metal resembling smashed junkyard automobiles with jagged black and green chunks looked out of place in the pristine jungle.

The second Sikorsky rested on the jungle floor like a prehistoric dragonfly with broken wings, its glass eyes shattered and caved in. The front end was bent into a wry Cheshire Cat smile. A pilot door was open. Blood stained the interior. There were no bodies.

"I'm just going to throw this out there. Could animals have taken the bodies?" Havens wondered aloud.

The party shuffled about and Havens dialed up Tanya.

"Mother," she answered dryly.

"Mowgli, hear. How copy?"

"Good copy. What's the good word?"

"No joy at the site. No sightings. No human remains. Over."

"Roger that. Negative on any further transmission activity. Can you uplink the wreckage photos to the team here so we can further review? Over."

"Understood. We will continue to monitor. Over."

"Roger. We have confirmation that it was two HIND gunships that engaged our crew. Over."

"Copy that. Anything else? Over."

There was a long pause.

"Repeating Mother. Anything else? Over."

"Nothing more, Mowgli. Gangster is trying to get a wide-area airborne system in your area. He's trying to get a CorvusEye infrared and full-motion imagery video sensor and turret put on an aircraft that can be sent to your area and provide support from 15,000 feet. Infrared can help with the canopy issues."

"Roger that. Thank him. Over."

"Will do. Mowgli, Gangster has vetted a nearby encampment as hostile. Be safe."

"You have any force intel? Could use some numbers, visual, patterns and other details."

"Roger that."

"Thanks much, you keep safe too. Keep an eye on Baloo. Mowgli out."

One of the Karens found what he suspected to be track.

Havens and the team trekked through the jungle, tracking as best they could the likely location of any survivors. Two Karen rebels took turns as point and sign scouts. The lead tracker called for frequent listening halts. The team remained perfectly still and positioned themselves lower down in the terrain to minimize attraction.

Sean trudged through a murky brown brook littered with rocks and dead jungle foliage. Without much prior recon, James silently followed Tom and the Karen. He suggested the water path would semi-mask their travels if adversary scouts and other unknown dangers sought to hunt the search party. They could walk faster as well.

The Karen disagreed due to the size of the group. He cited tells such as footprints on the bank of entry, color changes in shallow river beds, rocks splashed with water, and disturbed foliage over the streams being disrupted. James was overruled but ecstatic.

A consummate student of warfare and the arts of manhunting and reconnaissance, James made mental notes for the future.

The team initially traveled at a close interval, gradually spreading out as they came closer to the destination.

James stumbled over a fallen bamboo tree as they moved from dense growth to open spaces. The brook they were forced to wade through at shin height spread to a wide pool of shallow water that trickled off into narrow streams in a path that no longer suited their course. Sean, just ahead, didn't catch the slip as he was again lost in thought about his responsibility as a father and their crumbling bond. He was also distracted thinking about Tanya, and questioning adding another woman to the mix when he couldn't even care for Maggie's emotional needs.

The path widened to an area about twenty feet across. High ridgelines surrounded the men and their heads spun for constant situational awareness and testing of senses.

The heat was oppressive despite the shade and periodic cool breeze. Havens' palms were equally damp from perspiration and anxious anticipation of the danger that potentially surrounded him.

A stalking hunter killer team could observe the group without notice and pick off any one of them at any time. Aware of this, each man observed the jungle in a manner that disregarded the general pattern of foliage directly in front and around and instead tried to look through it. Scouts periodically squatted lower to gain vantage through some of the undergrowth for additional signs and sightings.

Sean heard a loud snap in the forest. Whipping his head, James caught his reflexive response and gave a chuckle.

"Boy, you have a bad case of the spooks. That or you just woke up."

Havens ignored the comment as they approached another small clearing with yet another ravine cutting across the trail. Sean moved ahead of James to mix things up a bit.

A bridge had been constructed with four long, stripped tree trunks. Sunken bamboo had been used as long stakes to prevent the bridge's tree trunks from separating. Worn rope joined the wood and secured the bridge for foot traffic.

Sean looked back quizzically at James, who shrugged. Tom quietly informed them both, "Smuggler route."

Havens estimated that the team was about half a click away from the Iranian compound. He moved closer to James for a brief chat.

"James, if there were any survivors, they would have had to have been marched or carried through here. I don't see how we're going to find any disturbed state, given the lapse of time since they went down. With smugglers about, I'm guessing the Iranians wouldn't want hostages. Smugglers might want a ransom, but I don't believe there have been any demands. I can't see them being at the target site. I'm not so sure we want to stir the pot too much. Let's stick to observation when we get closer and make sure we don't engage without a firm plan."

James patted Havens on the shoulder. "We'll still be able to pick up aged sign beyond footprints, Sean. That's why we're traveling close to the trail. It'll give us a good track picture. Tom and his boys likely got a good mental picture from the incident site. Probably being careful not to lure us into a trap while still mapping any sequence of events. These locals will grasp the more subtle comparisons that we'll miss. And I've spent enough tours in Nam to know that if you think you have POW in a camp, you go in and get 'em out. You wait, they get moved. It's your op, but if we think our boys are in there, I'm not waiting around."

Tom had moved back to the men again. When Havens sensed his presence, his uneasiness doubled. He hadn't heard Tom move up on them at all.

"Whatta we have here? Second thoughts or something I need to know?"

"We're good. Sean was just rationalizing. Let's press on."

"Damn right, James. It's not much farther and I don't want our asses flying in the wind. We're already leaving enough depressions and breaks for anyone looking to sneak up on us to have a good estimate of our spacing and movements. We're running a pretty straight line with no deception tactics to save us from camping out. I don't have time for you intel guys to be second guessing every step of the way. Let's keep rolling. After the bridge it gets pretty tight again. We'll have limited vis until the next clearing, where the airstrip and a small plain open up to the compound. The road is just opposite, so we want to be real quiet in case they have extra company. I'll send some of the boys ahead as we get closer and the rest of us will phase from ghost walks down to cat and kitten walks and crawls. Havens, you may not have been taught this but once on patrol, switch on, stay on, and remember, there is always someone ready to switch you off. If we have to engage, shoot low—and to kill. If someone is following us, they will tune in and know our intentions by indicator pace and the distance between our tracks. We're making it easy because of you here. If this were my play, we would take a week to do this. They'll shoot first." James and Tom moved ahead, leaving Sean Havens behind with his thoughts and second guessing.

Sean nodded and followed along.

A small green snake with viper pits crossed his path, its lime and yellow hues blending perfectly with the surrounding colors save for the brown, sandy earth it slithered across. At less than eighteen inches and no thicker than a quarter, Havens was again reminded of the dangers that lurked in Burma, both seen and unseen. He wondered what his daughter was doing at that very moment. Bad thoughts continued to enter his mind about his derelict responsibilities as a father. Most men would have stayed at home. They would have left the business that tore apart their lives. *Am I addicted to this shit?* he wondered. Trees swayed at the tops, signifying a breeze unfelt at jungle depths.

A monkey howled.

Havens continued to listen to the jungle anthem of insects, rotten branches falling, and small bird chirps. Sweat ran down his neck and face. Incessant dampness clung to him. His feet felt hot and slick in his boots. Bites, stings, and scratches adorned his hands. He rubbed the grit staining his fingers in a subconscious act of self-loathing. *What's there to be addicted about in this? What made me think I was the right guy for this job? I'm nothing. I'm nobody. I'm not a member of anyone's team.* Sean inhaled and whiffed the indescribable warm, musty aroma. The stuffy rotting vegetation and natural plant smells were a cornucopia of fresh sweetness and stale musk … and body odor.

From the corner of Havens' left eye, he saw the green hand just before it crossed his face. Instinctively, he winced, pulling back his head. His right eye saw the blurred grey blade flash like lightning below his jaw. The open green hand slapped down and palmed Havens' face for but a moment. The blade never found flesh.

Sean heard the all-too-familiar expelled gasp and last breath that he had heard throughout his career as whoever was behind him expired and collapsed to the ground. Havens caught his balance and resisted gravity pulling him to the ground.

He flipped to see a would-be assassin whose neck was slit wide. From the dark deep crevice of skin, muscle and cartilage-filled crimson blood flowed in stark contrast to the man's olive camouflage face paint. Another form stood in the shadows, covered in mud and foliage. A bloodied knife was at his side, blood dripping from black matte steel. Dry earth cracked on the man's face as pink gums and white teeth greeted Sean with a friendly, "Hey, Fritter!"

"Chang?"

"Why else would a Chinese guy be running around in Burma?" Doc asked. "Unless I was one of those fucking Communist Chinese, frackin' or whatever they are doing by the big waters?" Doc Chang shrugged, shaking off camouflage leaves and bark peelings, yet Sean just stood frozen.

"I never even heard him." Sean stared down at the dead soldier.

"That's because you are a fritter and I am a damned warrior god who saves weenies like you," Doc taunted with a smile.

Havens heard another voice. "Funny, Havens, I didn't think they sold lattes in Myanmar's jungles. Are you lost?"

Havens turned to see General Bain sporting the same homemade ghillie suit as doc.

Sean smiled in relief. "You made it too. How many are left?"

General Bain shook his head solemnly. "We're it. I was thrown and came out okay. Doc here was pretty banged up, but I managed to pull him from the wreck and patch him up."

"You *so* lie. I saved him. General's back is broken again, but he insists we keep reconning the area instead of getting our asses out of here."

"I'm pretty sure I saved you even before we went down."

Chang suppressed a smile and looked at the ground, grasping for a comeback that didn't come.

Havens broke the silence. "Where are the bodies? What have you been monitoring?"

"It took me a while to recoup from the crash. There's been a bunch of hunters in the woods. Myanmar special forces, best we can tell. Scouts and hunter-killer types. They've been keeping an eye on what we thought were Iranians. Please tell me these guys you're with aren't the whole PR team."

"Wait, they aren't Iranians?"

Doc interrupted. "No. They're Americans, Fritter. Damn Americans. They came for the bodies. Danger 6 said they flew them right out of here."

Havens turned his attention to General Bain. "False flag?"

He nodded in confirmation. "Yeah. 'Fraid so. Smuggling. Probably some of our boys. I saw a few bodies that they loaded. Some that they didn't. Don't know where they all went, but the bodies that were left aren't there anymore."

"And they have a huge storage facility with explosives." Chang illustrated with his hands outstretched, still holding the knife.

Havens suddenly saw Chang fly backward, then near immediately heard the subsonic rapport crack.

Bain saw Havens' crew's arms at the ready. "Hold fire!" he yelled.

Sean dove to assess Chang.

"Holy shit, Fritter! Get me out of this damned jungle. Bad juju."

"Looks like it just clipped your shoulder. In and out. Lucked out."

"Really? Lucky? You think lucky? Do you know how long it takes to be able to dodge a bullet like that right when it makes impact? I completely spun to avoid it. Now who's the sonofabitch who shot me?"

Chapter 45

Lars did as Tanya instructed, securing the two men as best as he could. He used torn bedsheet strips and contained them in the bathroom until she and an embassy security team could make it across town to the room.

As Lars peered out the dingy hotel window at the dank alley below, he heard what sounded like a crash coming from the bathroom.

Lars charged the door.

Paulo exited the bathroom bloodied and unbound. He and Lars both paused for a moment, searching for the reason they recognized each other. Paulo broke the gaze and attacked. He slashed Lars across the face with razor-sharp porcelain.

Lars instinctively raised his arms, leaving a wide body target exposed.

Paulo capitalized on the movement and thrust the makeshift weapon into Lars' abdomen. He tore into the flesh and pulled the sharp object across Lars' gut before dashing out of the hotel room.

Preparing to give chase, Lars saw his dark blood pooling on the floor and the white porcelain piece sticking out of his gut. He fell to his knees, then dropped over to his side in pain. From the floor, he could see into the bathroom.

The watcher lay to his side, his throat torn. Broken porcelain lay around him, with a large, bloodied piece next to his head.

Shit. That wasn't so smart. But the man. I know that man.

Chapter 46

With news of the encampment and the fate of the dead contractors, the party, including Doc and General Bain, returned to the village before darkness set in.

The small Karen settlement was quiet. The sobs had died and it appeared to be business as usual for the war-torn people. Seeing that the Americans returned with more of their own created no disdain. The men were welcomed and a small feast was prepared. Doc received some medical supplies and worked on his own wounds.

Dusk crept into the camp, staining the dirt with heavy shadow. The muffled surrounding sounds retreated as the silent call to rouse creatures of the night stirred a new legion of jungle chatter.

The mood soon changed for the villagers. To Sean, it felt like gloom and uncertainty now hung heavy in the damp air. Fear gripped the villagers, who anticipated more war machines. Or was it something else? Sean couldn't put a finger on it. Was it Tom?

General Bain was explaining to the men around the campfire that he suspected that organized criminal syndicates were smuggling precursor chemicals into the Iranian site. From what he could tell, the land and air traffic was coming from a mix of Chinese, Laotian, Thai, and maybe even Indian resources. "I'm thinking the Americans are involved in the precursor chemicals business as the real profit mechanism. They can claim hands off once the chemicals are shipped to heroin refineries and amphetamine-type stimulant labs."

Sean listened intently, and thought it made sense. The picture was unfolding. "We used to be involved in that. I remember doing some old readings and seeing some old reports. Old CIA, around the time that you old farts were running around, the CIA was involved with the major pharmaceutical companies to make precursor chemicals. Agency folks would distribute them to Southeast Asia and the golden triangle for the heroin trade."

"This looks Agency to me," James cemented. "If they did something to our guys, though, I say we burn the place down."

General Bain added, "Pretty sure it's still going on. When I was doing long-range reconnaissance work in Vietnam, most of the Agency guys we linked up to were buying heroin and opium at inflated prices from Laotians and the various tribes. They did it to create economic dependence and good will. Just like Afghanistan. We, and I mean the U.S., partnered with the drug traffickers in the Golden Triangle as pretty effective anti-communist allies. They were good fighters, too. Tom, the Agency has been doing this in Burma since the 1950s, or thereabouts." Bain tilted his head with a knowing glare. "We both know that the CIA never gave up de facto immunity in an enforcement-free zone of operation right smack around this area where Thailand, Burma, and Laos provide safe haven. Meaning near us."

Tom jumped in. "Hang on, guys. This is my neighborhood. I'm not exactly sure what part of the Agency is involved, but I know that chemicals like acetic anhydride and ephedrine come through the rat lines from Thailand to clandestine labs here in Burma. From what we've learned working with the smugglers, the acetic anhydride is made in Indonesia while the other chems are brokered through chem houses and moved across Malaysia into Thailand. The big-ticket items like pseudoephedrine and ephedrine come through some of the same rat lines from couriers or by air and maritime to the region and then through Thailand to Burma. Big methamphetamine production centers here and in Laos and Cambodia. That outpost isn't American, and frankly I'd like to see it gone, but maybe instead of taking out the facilities we focus on the men on the ground."

Doc added, "Most of what the big cheese and I saw was the chemicals. We did some sneaking and peeking when we saw what looked to be Iranians but ended up being some Iranian-looking dudes who were all speaking English."

Tom interjected again. "It's not English. They're Iranian. We really need to take them out."

Sean questioned, "So wait, what part makes you think it's intel or government related?"

"The wires. Antennae and dishes. Same tools. I say ring up your boys and find out. But I'll tell you one thing. They didn't come across our crash site with litters and first aid. They were armed to the tooth. They took plenty of pictures and made some satellite calls that we couldn't hear, but it was more about confirming dead than seeing what more could be done and identifying our men."

"Fuckin' Iranians and smugglers," Tom said with disgust. "I know that's what it is. Okay, guys. Let's break up for the night and get some rest. No need to beat a dead horse."

Sean pushed for more validation. "Tom, why is Burma so key in the transport? Would the Agency set up camp here?"

"Havens, leave it alone. The Agency should be involved, but not like they are doing in the capital. The U.S. is negotiating with corrupt leadership. They just want to beat the Russians and Chinese in here. They want a cut of the gold rush too." Tom paused. "But you're right, Sean. Maybe if we could take out the Iranian outpost, that could be a good start for the Agency in the area." He lowered his voice. "Which is why we're still at this camp. There are some nefarious relationships going on with the leadership here and the junta. Drug trafficking as well."

Then why are we here? Havens felt the goal posts moving for the umpteenth time.

Tom further validated that, saying, "It goes to Shan State. Militia groups and porous locations with limited rule of law. Big money in their pseudoephedrine activities. Traffickers send it all up to India and then some back to China. I'm guessing they can send it to China through the mining companies. Mix it in with the resources they're pulling and sending back. Pay a levee on the gold they're stealing out of here, but big profit is in the drugs. They can probably comingle the two for instruction to the financial system."

Chang was hopped up on morphine. "Listen to you guys. You sound like Fritter." He giggled uncontrollably. "Bunch of dorks talking policy and analytical shit. Hey Fritter, I'm keeping that Geiger counter water pack of yours."

"Geigerrig. You can have it. It was going to be the prize for first guy shot, anyway."

Doc gave a big thumbs up and shit eating grin, as if he had actually won the prize.

Tom got up and kicked the fire apart. "Let's hit it, guys. I'm turning in. No more talk about that outpost. Some of the locals here may be listening."

General Bain agreed. "I could hit a rack. My back is swelling pretty bad. Sean, I did mean to ask about the HINDs that you said swept through here."

James said, "Sean may have an idea about how these folks could defeat the helos."

"It's just a concept," Sean explained. "The value of any weapon system is only realized through skillful employment on the battlefield. If we take what we know of the HIND, how we can actually use it tactically, and come up with a force design, we will have our solution."

"No shit, Sherlock. Did you make that PowerPoint on your own?" Tom stood.

"Sean, Tom's right. No time for fifty-pound head shit," said James, who had hoped Sean had something more concrete.

"Sorry, I'll rephrase. We know that we're screwed if the assault comes from cannon, rocket, napalm, bombs, or CBU if it's an Mig-24 or 35 HIND. From what I saw, there were about eight missiles mounted on four outer wing pylons. These guys, as Tom said, have been making evening sorties. Means they probably have the night attack version fitted with western sensors and avionics. My guess is they are using Russian 'Shovak' night vision goggles over flying with just electronics."

"Your guess?" Tom criticized. "Afraid these people need more than guesses. C'mon guys, its late."

"Given our location, they are coming from the Meiktila base. Given location and mission, they will probably keep with just two HIND at a time but could scramble a couple more if need be. They won't get here for a while. We know the HIND is pretty much immune to small arms fire. Pilot and co-pilot are armored from the titanium bathtub around them. All these enhancements make it harder to perform with the weight increase and new horsepower increase. In a perfect world, we would need a Redeye or Stinger to bring these down. With what we have, our best bet is to destroy the helo with .50 cal targeting rotor, tail boom or transmission area, blind or strike fear in the pilot, or cause a maneuver malfunction. Their formation tactic is come in together and each go right or left. That gives us a little time for them to both be close. Should be at a distance 75-90 meters with maybe a 30-degree angle, unless they do a surprise pop up and launch but we should hear them."

"Where did you dig this geek up?" Tom was clearly agitated.

"I think we can leverage the trees to virtually picket a flight patch with jungle IED mortars. I have a few of the soldiers testing out a prototype, hollowing just a bit of the trees toward the top."

"You what?" Tom stepped back into the fire ring. "Who the fuck do you think you are?"

"Just trying to help. When we first arrived, you said you wanted help. I'm helping. The Karen showed me after chows how they can climb up and add a bucket with some of the homemade napalm I made with rice and diesel. I'm trying to think of a way to get shape charges in buckets with a focal point of a foot or so. They are going to prime and wire them, lower a bag of projectiles too. They can wrap trees in rolls to keep explosions directed up. When helo is over the area, clack them off while the belly is reinforced. The blades should come apart. You can have secondary napalm that will jack up visibility and the heat change can affect lift. I gave the guys two of my remote detonators so we can test them out."

"You're dicking around with scarce resources, stranger. You don't just come in here and disrupt what I've been doing for years."

James came to Havens' defense. "Tom, Sean's just trying to help. You did ask for help."

Bain piled on. "He's pretty good at this kind of shit."

"Havens is the best donut alive," Doc giggled.

"Tom, I didn't mean any disrespect. *I don't trust you, asshole.* Since there appears to be a radio at the Iranian base, I speak enough Persian to make a distress call blaming the Chinese for an attack. The HINDs will check out both sites. If we even have one working Stinger and a couple .50 cals, we can make it look like it's coming from the Chinese. Take all those old dysfunctional weapons and leave the crates around the Chinese perimeter. Take the shots from that cover and they'll light up the boxes—ideally. They shouldn't hesitate to shoot them up. That should cool things a bit when it becomes more of an international issue between the groups. At the very least, it buys us time and creates more visibility to the HIND activity. And if we can commandeer one of the planes that lands at the Iranian base, General Bain can use that to get us back to Thailand."

The plan sounded dubious at best.

Havens' enthusiasm showed trying to garner support. "What do we have to lose?"

"And where do we get all of these explosives, MacGyver?"

"We can use more rice and diesel to make our own napalm paste. Do you have any hydrogen peroxide, ethanol, sulfuric acid, antifreeze, aluminum, fertilizer with ammonium nitrate? We can take the chemical components and precursors to come up with something useful for oxidizers and fuels that will create an explosive."

No one around the fire spoke.

One of the Karen warriors approached Tom, crouching low and whispering something inaudible to the group. Tom nodded, the lines over his brow coming together in resolved thought. He patted the young soldier's shoulder and addressed the group.

Tom's tone changed. "Fine. We'll take the Chinese location. The Chinese have been a problem for us with their mining and hydraulic efforts. They pay bribes and encroach on the Karen territories. We can take up positions near their heavy machinery to try and draw fire. There's a trafficking camp there too where they run captured Rohingya Muslims through. Burmese and Thai runners take the women and girls through Burma to Thailand and out to traffickers waiting at sea. Chinese have bought a number of the Rohingya men to work as slave labor there too. The distraction will also help us free those poor souls. We're in."

Sean Havens was bothered by the attitude shift. It sounded like appeasement.

General Bain sounded off on the matter. "I can pretty much fly anything that I have seen come in, but we won't have much room for four men."

James rustled in his seat and spoke up. "I'll stay back." As Sean started to protest, he raised a hand. "I'll get to my wife and let her know. I think there is a lot of good I can do out here as a missionary."

"A missionary?" Sean questioned.

"Well, I think Aimee could use a diversion and come out here as well. I can't say I'm going to do much preachin' or reading from the good book, but in Sundee school they keep tellin' me how I'm one of God's soldiers. That sounds like 'mission-ary' work to me. And I figure that if these people are the ones I'm helping, then they are subcontractors through me as one of God's soldiers. If the man upstairs has a problem with me doing his work by, with, and through these heathen people, then he can take it up with his Staff Sergeant St. Peter."

"Why would he ask St. Peter?" General Bain asked, knowing he was just playing the role of straight man.

"Well, I figure St. Peter is the gatekeeper, so he must be Heaven's procurement officer."

The party chuckled.

"I'll just call upon that Holy Spirit. Seems like He would be a good shadow warrior that I could lean on doing the work of God to kill these communists in the woods here." He gave Tom a wink. "Bet most of those folks in the congregation thought I was sleepin'."

James addressed one of the Karen men. "You hear that, amigo? I'm stayin' a bit, so get ready to sell me your hooch. I'll give you some Christian-anity for it."

"James, most of these men are already Christians," corrected Tom.

James spat some tobacco juice. "Well shit, hallelujah, my work is half done. Now we can focus on some killin'. Let me see what kinda gear you guys are playin' with. Besides," James took a long and serious pause, "Aimee and I discussed this. She knew that I might not come back. Whether I was dead at home or dead here, I need to be alive again. I'm alive here, and I'm staying."

Tom wasn't liking the news at all. "Get some shuteye, James, and think this through. It's not all it's cracked up to be. *You're going to want to leave, brother.*

Chapter 47

The next afternoon, James inspected the M-16 with sentimental admiration. He slapped Havens on the arm for attention. Sean was eyeballing the Karen fabricated lower receivers and a different tinted upper receiver.

"Sean, you see this?" James pointed to the serial numbers etched in the weapon. "Five serial numbers. Five. Can you believe that?"

Sean looked back down at the assault rifle he was inspecting. "I'm not sure what that means."

"Tom, you know, right?" James was smiling ear to ear. "Sean, these are vintage Vietnam stock from early '60's."

Sean craned his neck now with a bit more interest. He asked Tom, "Why are you guys working with M-16s over AKs? Availability?"

"The ammo," Tom responded. "Ammo is available. The 7.62 ammo is in shorter supply around here and costly. As you can see from the receiver you were inspecting, we have to fabricate some items here in the sticks."

Tom beckoned to a Karen soldier and instructed him to fetch some items from their arsenal.

The young soldier and two of his fellow tribesmen returned with heavy armfuls of long guns.

Tom assisted the men and passed the weapons over to James and Sean.

"Holy shit," exclaimed Sean as one in particular dropped to his lap.

The surrounding men chuckled. Tom explained, "That's our pig. Homemade .50 cal. Ugly but does the job. The rest is what it is, 308s and a few 7.62s. We have just a few Remington 700s. They're the best we can get. Even have some Garands." Tom handed over a worn but well-maintained M1.

Sean worked the bolt with ease. "They do a lot better keeping things clean and working than in the Middle East."

Like a proud father, Tom validated, "These men have a lot of pride and appreciation. It's a different culture. They also work well with a hierarchy that supports an NCO type role between foot soldier and leader. But since many leaders are tribal chiefs or the equivalent, respect and duty come pretty naturally."

Havens grew quiet and started fidgeting with his watch. James noticed. "Can't figure out what time it is?"

"I think I know what time it is. That's part of the problem."

"Come again?"

Havens remained transfixed on his watch. "This watch. I let my daughter hold on to mine. Had a custom one made by a SWAT guy at a training. He came up with his own based on the critique of tactical watches on the market. The lume hands and dial of the watch were often too bright and could compromise a position. I told my wife about it and she ended up surprising me with a gift."

"This one looks like a decent enough watch. What's really buggin' you?"

"That's just it. She wanted me to quit this work. I thought I wanted out too. And here I have this little girl at home and she doesn't have a mom or a dad. Yet, I still make decisions to leave. What eats me up is as soon as I'm away, I start wallowing in this self-pity about my decision. It's like I'm damned if I do, damned if I don't. I'm just never happy anymore. It's not like me. I can't shake it."

"You're a good dad, Sean. Aimee's told me as much."

"I'm a shit dad. Because I'm here, she's there, and for as much as I tell myself that I will never leave her side, I'm here, and I enjoy being here. I'm playing with these weapons with full knowledge that I'm heading into something I shouldn't. We aren't even working our mission now. And we're getting all spun up about these people like we're the Expendables or some mercenary team defending what's right. That's not our mission. We were supposed to get these guys, or get pictures and get out."

"Sometimes missions change. We're doing what's right."

"No, James. You're doing what's right because you know this should be done but our country isn't doing anything about it. There's a reason for that. What is it? I don't know. If these guys who came across our wreckage are really Iranians, CIA, drug traffickers, we aren't supposed to know. We could blow that place up and take those dud Stinger missiles and bring them near the Chinese camp and send off pictures that the Agency could exploit. We can shoot down a Russian or Ukranian HIND, but what is that going to do? We're fucking pawns trying to do what's right, but someone higher up the food chain has another agenda that could either be protecting or hurting us. Who the hell knows if whatever we do will screw that up? And if that's the case, I need to just do my job and man up and get home to my kid. I love this work, but if I don't get out of it, it'll eat me alive."

"Well kid, that's for you to decide. I can't let myself go there. I'm a soldier and I'll do what I was told and I'll do what I think is right—now that the man isn't giving me orders. My boys and a lot of other great men died for this country, and I have to believe that some of those powers in lofty place don't take that lightly."

Havens gave a dismissive grunt.

"Don't you disrespect those who gave all, Sean. I share the same cynicism at times, but I have to put it aside. This is the team we're on, and it's the team we root for. Right or wrong. It's our team and we don't question it. I'm leaving a grieving woman alone at home, too. She either works, cooks, or helps others to keep going. She worries too much about me and how I'm dealing with things. I don't have the heart to tell her I'm proud of my boy's sacrifices. I don't mourn them. I revere them. I'm in my own self-pity. I never saw myself going out on a porch swing waitin' for dinner."

"Maybe you're right. I've just been screwed before by believing."

"You've been through a lot. I get it. We all have. Wars leave wounds. Nothing's the same when you come back."

"I just think I need to make a choice and stick with it."

"Don't get rigid in your thinking. You'll force yourself into more self-loathing and one morning put a barrel to your head. I've done it dozens of times myself. Thing is, I haven't thought about that once since I got here."

Doc Chang emerged from behind one of the few standing hootches, startling Sean.

"Could have killed you, Havens."

"You about did, you asshole. How's your arm?"

Chang chuckled in delight. "Good. Glad I was shot by the AK. General wants to talk a bit."

"Let's go."

The general was still laying on the hard ground when Havens and Chang approached.

"I heard you, Chang." The general struggled to roll over and sit up. "Dammit!" he cursed the pain.

"Still bad, huh? You taking anything for it?"

"Nope, I need to keep the pain so I know where it is and don't screw it up more. Thanks for coming over."

"Sure. What's up?"

"We need to be on the same page here. Who's coming to get us, or are we on our own?"

"I called my point of contact a bit ago and we need to get back to Thailand. All of us. They can send someone to the border or, since I mentioned the plane potential, they said we can get coordinates for an airstrip."

"Well, we need to finish this mission. I like Tom, and I think these people need some help, but we need to complete our mission."

"I agree. I was just saying that to James."

"And what does he say?"

"He's inclined to help out here. You heard him around the fire."

"Okay. Well, he did his mission anyway, which was to get you to the crash site, from what I understand."

"That's correct."

"Okay. Now the only thing that isn't settin' well with me are those hostages or slaves by that Chinese camp. Can you take pictures at night with that camera they gave you?"

"Maybe. I've got an AstroScope, a low light and night vision system that converts my Nikon into a pretty powerful night-time image capture system. It transforms moonlit or starlit scenes into bright, but the canopy might neutralize that. I also have the Tactigram app on my phone so I can upload and mark up images from the camera and send everything back to headquarters. But bottom line, no guarantees."

"Okay, well, let's assume no. They give you any fancy apps on your phone that can help us get some honesty traces and real-time heat maps to see any enemy troops or critical masses of soldiers?"

"No."

"Well, shit. And nothing to locate radio messages sent?"

"Nope."

The party quieted as someone approached. It was Tom.

"Hey boys, all good?"

"All good, Tom," replied General Bain. "Care to join us? We were just envisioning having a virtual bourbon."

"Meet me by the fire after evening chows and I'll have some of the virtual good stuff. I'll be there in a while. Have to do a couple things."

"Deal."

As Tom passed and headed off into the jungle, the guys resumed their talk. Havens watched Tom for longer than he could see him and then continued. "To answer your question about apps, nope. There is a beacon application that relays my information and location back. Everything is encrypted and signal isn't anything that can get picked up by hostiles."

Chang chimed in. "Yeah, sure worked for our helo. Stealth. Total stealth. No one will be tracking you. 'Til *boom*."

As the darkness of the evening settled in, the concert of jungle sounds quieted and the rapid crescendo of machine engines entered. The scene erupted with the sounds of an explosion and uncontrolled cycles of screaming. Blood, organs, bone, and incendiary gel danced in the score, joined as one.

Chapter 48

Lars curled into the fetal position on the cheap hotel room floor with his abdominal trauma. He knew from years of forensics that he wasn't suffering from massive blood loss and the major vascular organs in his abdominal cavity were not likely ruptured. The pain, on the other hand, was excruciating and the jagged edge of the porcelain cut with every movement. Still, it could have been much worse. A sharp punch of the object would have caused him to bleed out. Best case, it would have been a hell of a wound to heal.

He contemplated removing the porcelain but was concerned about additional trauma. Lars rolled onto his back, putting some direct pressure on the wound while retrieving his cell phone from his pocket with a free hand.

Tanya Crowe answered.

"Hi honey, you still thinking of coming by here? I could use a paramedic. Seems a toilet knife has found its way into my stomach and the bad guy got away." Lars fought another wave of pain. "I could use an Advil or two and need to remove something big and white and sharp from my abdomen."

"We're on our way. Lars, even though you came into the country legitimately, I need you to trust us and not call for an ambulance. We don't need more questions about our activity here, and I don't think you'll want to see a story about you being in a seedy hotel."

"Works for me. But I think I might need a little more help than a hemostatic dressing and band-aid on top."

"We'll see you soon. Hang on. I'm reaching out to the Regional Medical Officer as soon as we disconnect."

Tanya hung up. In the car was the embassy Regional Security Officer and a political officer, who was actually a covered spook. "Lars was injured, but we can't get locals involved. Do you have any medical resources here that won't ask questions? This guy might have seen someone involved in the bombings. I'll call the RMO—as long as he will take direction."

Paulo's heart rate slowly calmed. He had succeeded in getting away but knew that he could be identified by the big oaf in the hotel room. He cursed himself for not finishing the job. The task now weighed upon him alongside his other priorities.

Chapter 49

A mechanical whining sounded from the distance. As the noise grew more resolute, so did the evidence that a military attack against the village was in order.

Flashes of white, orange, and yellow lit the surrounding camp as the machines passed overhead. The sounds faded briefly, then returned.

The HIND gunships made another napalm pass on the village. Fires raged and confusion abounded. The flames jumped quickly from hut to hut, engulfing all within.

Havens, General Bain, and Doc Chang tried to herd the villagers away from the flammable gelling agent that was massacring their families.

Another gunship passed and opened fire. Havens watched as the bodies were silhouetted by the flames engulfing the village behind them.

"*Move*, Havens!" the general ordered.

"I need to find James!"

"We're all going to get cooked if we don't get out of here!"

"There!" Doc shouted. James and Tom were running to cover, each carrying wounded children. James had wrapped a woobie poncho liner around the child. Sean couldn't tell if the youngster was wounded or not.

"You brought this!" Tom screamed towards Havens. "This happened when *you* came! Get off this land! *Don't come back!*"

Sean turned to James. "Best get going, Sean. You guys all go. We'll handle this," he shouted back as the men put the children down in a safer cover.

"But ..."

"*Go!*"

Another explosion erupted with the jelly-like substance plastering and burning everything it touched.

"Napalm. I hate napalm," muttered James as he turned his back and ran with Tom.

"Havens, you and Doc get a head start to the airfield. I'll follow behind and grab some of the weapons. We'll need them," directed General Bain.

"We'll all go together. One is none, two ... well, three, is one," Havens recommended.

"In that case, you and Doc get the weapons, I'll get a little start. I don't know how long my back can hold up."

"Just like old times, buddy." The situation dictated that a smile would be fully inappropriate, but in the fray, James was in his element. Life sparkled in his eyes. Duty called.

Tom was more solemn. "It's been an honor serving with you, James." He patted his old ODA team member firmly on the back. "Let's go get some more."

As they started off, Tom shouted, "I hear something over here. You head out that way back toward the main huts."

"You got it, buddy," James called back, heading into the thick. He turned taking in his old pal and gave a thumbs up. "Thanks," he mouthed.

The strip of infrared glint tape that Tom placed on the back of James' shirt alerted the HIND gunship pilot to the target.

The pilot leveled out readying the weapons. James in the electronic sights.

With a stern lip, Tom muttered, "Sorry, man. You can't stay here to do what I need to save these people. Thank you, too. Rest easy, brother. I'll get you back home. This tribe needs to be eradicated to save my village and to put our spooks back in business."

Chapter 50

The embassy RMO had a comprehensive aid and field surgical kit that sufficed to remove the porcelain from Lars' abdomen.

"Tanya, I know you were sizing up all of my manhood. You thought for a moment that I could lose a few pounds. But I'll have you know, this girth … I mean, the girth around my waist," he winked, "protects me from knife wounds."

"He'll be fine, but he needs rest to keep these sutures secure."

"Hear that, Tanya? You stay at your place tonight. I need to rest."

The RMO tried to suppress his smile. "I think the meds are working on him. You feeling any pain, Mr. Bjorklund?"

"I'm hungry. Where can I get a burrito around here? Tanya, can you have the embassy make me a burrito? You're cute, pull some strings. You might have to show some leg."

Tanya patted Lars on the arm in a gesture of kindness—or tolerance. "How about you tell me about the guy who stabbed you?"

"He's probably the bomber. Weirdo. I've seen guys all hyped up on drugs and crazy shit, but this guy is like that yet focused. He's not on drugs. He's evil."

"Let's not get ahead of ourselves, Lars."

"Nope. He's a bomber. I know it. You get me a burrito and a date with you and I'll tell you why." Lars waved his hand to erase his last statement. "Better yet. You go out with my brother-in-law. He's a good guy. He was good to my sister. The best!"

"Lars. Why do you think he's the bomber?"

"Steak burrito with guacamole and chorizo and a date with Sean."

291

At first, Tanya had blushed, but the urgency of the situation frustrated her. Or so she told herself. "Lars, why is he the fucking bomber? Cut this bullshit out!"

Lars raised his eyebrows and caught the eyes of the RSO and the covered agent. He started giggling. "If you are a lesbian and don't know any Mexicans in Thailand, you could have just said so." He closed his eyes and laughed out loud again. "Hey, guys, I have a drug sensitivity, so be careful what you give me, okay?"

The RSO took over. "Lars. I know a place that has a Thai version of an upright burrito. It's called gaeng hanglay. The best part of it is the women who serve it. They're some of the most beautiful in all of Thailand. You and I can go there while Tanya and your brother in-law go out for a date."

"What?" Tanya feigned protest.

A closed-mouth glare from the RSO told Tanya to keep quiet.

"Guys, I'm not holding out on you, I'm just having a little fun. He has bleaching and burns on his hands and wrists. The tips are really clean and then it looks to spread up the dermis. Classic chemical burns from a screw-up. Put that in context with everything else. The site that I examined told me that heavy-duty explosives were used and then masked with a jihadi IED. Someone is getting fingered and that mad bomber is involved. For surely."

"Who's Shirley?" Tanya was writing down notes.

Lars jabbed his thumb in her direction. "Is she a blonde wearing a wig?"

Chapter 51

Havens and Doc caught up to General Bain. As they were embarking down the trail, James was lying in a pool of his own blood, riddled with rounds from the HIND gunship's 12.7 mm Yakushev-Borzov Yak-B Gatling gun.

Tom shielded his Iridium satellite phone for better clarity of sound even though the noise from the attack helicopters had subsided. "We were attacked out here but all of the operators are dead. You guys are in the clear. Stall the air shipments until dusk. Nothing to worry about. Just may have some surveillance from high altitude. Don't show our hand. I also have some guys patrolling in your area, so don't go shooting at folks lurking around the perimeter."

"Roger that boss. WILCO."

Tom gave a heavy sigh. It was a dirty deal he had cut and the village had lost a significant amount of people he cared about, but ultimately it would give other Karen people better protection and more global exposure with the atrocity. He'd have to make a video in the morning and push it for viral exposure. The Chinese, of course, would be left alone. They paid a handsome price for secure rat lines to support non-traditional logistics. If you make a deal with the devil, you'll be forced to dance a sinner's swing or two. *Di oppresso liber.* He lied to himself, knowing he had sold his soul for the third time that year under the guise of helping the greater good. With any luck, Sean and team would kill the Pond members and Tom would be back in business under a new flag.

Despite his broken back, Gen Bain navigated the trail like an indigenous scout. Having cut his teeth in Vietnam as a long range reconnaissance soldier, he loved the bush and the dark. Similarly,

Doc Chang was a natural, while Havens acclimated with effort but surprising finesse.

Bain paused for a moment, assessing his surroundings. His fist closed, his arm at a ninety-degree angle that brought the small group to halt. The darkness swallowed the hand signs but their closeness assured mutual understanding of intentions. Their silent advances reduced chances of being detected by anyone in the jungle.

Havens fought against his wandering mind. Tanya constantly came into the picture. Christina had known something was wrong when he returned from the mission. She was his wife, his best friend. But at the time, she didn't know everything about his job. The trip was uneventful, he lied. In any woman's eyes, he cheated. Duty to Uncle Sam or not, he had made an oath to his wife, to God, and to their witnesses. The lovemaking had saved his and Tanya's lives and solidified their cover under watchful electronic eyes hidden in the walls.

Chang noticed Havens wasn't on full alert when they stopped and Sean took more steps. Doc closed the distance and used two fingers to point to his own eyes. He then cast his arm forward down the trail toward Bain to remind Sean to keep paying attention to the point man.

Bain looked back and lobbed a virtual baseball forward, silently telling Chang and Havens to move up. With adjusted eyes, they were all seeing better.

Sean felt his senses awaken as he cleared his mind and clicked on his operational awareness.

By sun-up, the three men were in their hides with Havens' head now in the game.

Havens was instructed to move around the perimeter of the so-called Iranian base.

The drab wooden buildings blended well with the surrounding jungle hues. A main structure had an attached storage facility that may have at one time doubled as a hanger, which made sense given the airstrip. Fuel drums and propane tanks were scattered on either side of the strip and buildings.

The plan was to wait until the plane landed and then, depending on the number of visible individuals, the team would seize the plane.

Havens moved slowly through the jungle overgrowth heading off to his assigned hide area. The others moved opposite to their designated spots. The rainforest's biodiversity was extensive. The jungle rot was over powering as Sean crawled along the forest floor. His hands clawed as he neared wet, claylike soil. He suddenly sunk down a foot and felt what he initially thought was a tree root.

Havens jerked his hand out of the thick goop. His breathing had nearly stopped. Havens closed his eyes. He had to reach back down. He forced his arm back into the muck. His hand crawled along the object, grasping it. He moved his hand along what he knew was a wrist, an arm, a torso. Sean started pulling the brown soup away. It filled in with every attempt to unbury the unknown dead. Havens knew what he had to do next. He probed back to the arm. He wanted a left arm and felt down from a forearm to the wrist. There is was. His fingers fumbled but were dexterous enough to unfasten the object. Once released, Havens pulled the watch from the mud. He rubbed the glass with his wet and muddy thumb. It was a Casio G-shock, the same watch that most of General Bain's crew sported. He couldn't be sure, yet he was. The dead weren't all flown out. They were buried. Tom was involved. The men at the camp were spooks, and this was another fucked-up cloaked operation with no regard for the innocent and committed men who died unwittingly in vain.

Dammit!

Havens fumbled to clean his sopping hand so he could activate his phone. He marked coordinates and forwarded them to Tanya. These men would not be MIA on his watch. Not even Cooter. Piece of shit he was, he was all in for his country and for the job. *I will not be a pawn and these lives will not be wasted.*

As Havens low-crawled to a good visual position, his mind raced.

How can I keep working for a government with no regard for its warriors? Fodder. We're just fodder. Use us up and let us kill each other.

Leave the veterans rotting in their homes. In the hospitals. On the streets. Hope they blow their brains out so you don't have to fix their heads and pay their benefits. I'm done. This time it has to be final.

The same thoughts played back constantly in Sean's head as he lay in concealment for hours breathing the musty jungle floor.

Havens first saw men exit the building before he heard the approaching buzz of an incoming propeller aircraft. Two men stood talking as they awaited the landing. They appeared to be unarmed. Their demeanor was casual. Sean couldn't make out what they were saying, but he watched their body language. One of the men was describing something using big arm motions. He waved his arms about and then lowered an arm quickly with a raised uppercut motion. The other man appeared to be laughing and tilted his head back. He shook his head. The other man was nodding his head. He raised his hand for a high-five. They fist bumped.

Fist bump? High-five? Big movements?

Havens sloughed his pack off and pulled out his camera. He zoomed in closer.

Yeah, these dudes are absolutely not Persians. Gotta be American. Maybe European. Nah, the gestures and how they're carrying themselves are totally American. We can't engage them. I'm not killing more Americans. No way.

Havens viewed the men through the lens. *Ah, shit. You guys are definitely strapped. Putting this useless thing away.* Havens pouched the camera and unslung the M-16 rifle. He took aim. Sean couldn't quite make out the firearms at one guy's side and the other guy's shoulder holster. *And you guys are definitely spooks or mercs. Shit. Now what? Can't just kill you and take your plane. Wait. What the hell are you doing disposing of fellow soldiers? Ah, this shit. Shit. Shit. Shit. Shit. We'd know if you're CIA, so probably Pond. Which means I could really give two shits, and we're back to where we were hours ago, just capping whoever is here and taking their ride.*

Havens leveled the rifle to get a better feel and tightened the stock to his shoulder. He was ready to fire as he thought about these guys even killing a piece of shit like Cooter. They needed to pay. His finger moved to the trigger.

Question is whether Rick knew this was here. He pulled his finger back and had another thought.

Still holding up the classic M-16, Havens pulled out his mobile device. *No range here at this spot. Last transmission not sent. Can't text Tanya. So what's going on here? Helo cuts through Burma on the way to Thailand. Stupid flight plan unless it's looking for something in Burma. Clearly why no one let me get involved or see the initial planning. So that's covered up. Check. Gets shot down by HIND. Just happens to be near some Iranian smuggling base, which is American. Not an accident. Another cover-up. Check. So why do the Russians care, and if it's CIA, wouldn't we warn our dudes about HIND presence? Just also happens to be near a Karen village with an ex-special forces Colonel, who just happens to not know that there are fellow Americans in his Area of Operations. That's bullshit. Tom would have to know what was going on here, especially if his smuggling networks are illicit. He would want to know everything going on within 100 kilometers. Shit. James! Wait. James knows Tom, so does James know what's going on? No, I picked James. I knew he was a jungle guy and bored. I picked him from my network. Well, Aimee's network. No, he said he met Rick before and spoke about Burma. I've been played again. Question is, why do they need me here? What's my value? What's my purpose?*

The satellite lens remained locked on to Sean Havens' position while also capturing surrounding activities.

The plane had landed amidst Havens' mulling. It taxied to the small warehouse. The pilot disembarked and gave a friendly but casual wave to the two men. He was smaller. Ethnic. Maybe Burmese. Maybe Thai. Havens couldn't tell. Didn't matter. Havens now knew that whatever operation was going down at this site, it had a foreign face to it with the business end back to the Americans.

General Bain was right. So, in all this mess, he and Doc are probably still clean. I'm guessing that their survival is somehow screwing up whatever plan someone had. Damn. Do I need to go back for James? Something smells like big time shit. We've gotta go back for James. No, I need to go back for Maggie and get out of this shit.

Havens had a visual of Bain and Chang.

Through the foliage, Havens could see Bain nodding to him.

Havens gave a thumbs up. *Friendly?*

Bain moved his head slightly for a better view.

Havens slid his hand in the visual opening, and Bain negated the signal with a thumbs down. *Enemy.*

Bain motioned with his right hand and pushed down with his right to Chang, who had a clear field of view.

Chang started slow, quiet movements to his right toward the plane.

Havens decided he would wave Bain and Chang off and try to disarm the men instead of killing them. They might have answers.

A stick snapped under Chang's movement but the on-going propeller noise muffled the noise. Chang wasn't looking at Havens. He was looking at the ground.

Bain lifted his rifle to the targets.

Crap. Havens followed suit and took aim. *These guys are Americans. I can't just kill them. How do you know they're enemy? That could be me out there. That could be any one of us doing shit we don't know about. I'm going in.*

As the men started unloading boxes from the plane's cargo hold, one man crumpled and the rifle rapport cracked the sound barrier. A second man then fell as another shot rang out. The pilot froze in fear for but a moment before his body spun and fell to the ground and the third rapport snapped in the jungle cover.

Sean's heart dropped as the men fell. Doc Chang rushed from the his hide site, engaging the men on the ground, pulling head shots to each of the fallen men. *Jesus, Chang.* Havens couldn't tell if they had been wounded or were already dead. Didn't matter. Dead was dead now.

Sean was on his feet, running. He carried the rifle passively low at waist level. As he approached, he inspected one of the boxes that was darkening at the corners.

He slung his weapon over his shoulder, cut the tape down the box seam and gently lifted a flap. A bottle was cracked and the liquid was bubbling as it touched other material in the box. *Acid.*

"What is it, Fritter?" inquired Doc.

"Acid, I think. Was in a brown bottle. There are five others still intact." Havens walked to the plane and inspected the cargo hold. He cut into more boxes and perused the contents. "Precursor chemicals. My guess, someone is refining drugs or making explosives. If we're tying your mission over here to Thailand, my guess is bombs. But could be drugs. Anyone's guess. Could be what Bain was saying about CIA involvement." Havens glared at Doc Chang, waiting for answers.

Chang held fast with a blank stare on his face.

Bain called out to the men. "Guys, let's get going."

"We can't leave this place. It's no good. What was your mission coming into this area, sir?"

"Sean, we need to leave."

"General, you guys were flown to Thailand via Burma. In a helo nonetheless, which doesn't have the range for where you were going and coming from. And you were shot out of the sky. For this?"

"Sean, we need to go."

"Yeah, I know, but aren't you going to tell me what the hell is going on here? I'm thinking Tom was involved, and I brought a man into this who could be in danger. I feel responsible."

"That guy came on his own, Fritter," interjected Chang, who had laid down his weapon and was rifling through the men's pockets.

"Chang, let's go. No souvenirs." The general boarded the plane without looking back. "Let's go, Havens!"

Havens pulled out his camera and started snapping photos of the area. He shot stills of the dead and entered the building.

"Havens, don't you take another photo of these men. This never happened."

The satellite recorded Havens' movements near the dead men and the boxes.

"I'm going in," said Sean, ignoring the requests.

Inside the structure, stacked from floor to ceiling, Sean saw a complete storage of chemicals, compounds, electronics, and mixing apparatuses. The next room was a radio room that led to another chamber. Havens did a quick site exploitation, grabbing handfuls of papers that were on the tables and snapping photos. He looked around for any computers or devices and spotted a closed laptop, which he first grabbed and then left on a table with the papers on top as he searched the rest of the quarters.

The next room was dark and appeared to be a kitchen or break area. He heard a creak and turned back to the sound.

Havens slung his camera over his neck with his left hand and retrieved the firearm from the small of his back. He brought the weapon up to high ready point with both hands and tried to make out anything in the darkness.

Another creak, and then a dark form rushed to Havens' left. Instinctively, as the form drew closer Havens removed a hand from his pistol grip and thrust out and up. His palmstrike found promise and he felt the flesh and bone of his attacker. An arm grabbed at Havens' shoulder while another tried to hammer his other gun-wielding arm.

Havens moved his left hand down and inside, trying to push off of his assailant to build a better close quarter fighting position.

A hand just met Havens' throat as Sean shoved his attacker. It wasn't enough and pain shot through Sean's wrist. He ignored it and sent a hook upwards. Strike. Bone to bone. He wanted to know if the man was American, but clearly neither of them was going to stop for a handshake and introduction. Havens popped another punch to the chest of his attacker to try and hit him off balance and press the trigger. The rifle sling dropped and the weight of the M-16 tugged at his firing arm. Havens opened the distance. Keeping muzzle down, he started firing, gradually raising the firearm as he stepped back and readjusted while keeping a blind eye out in the darkness for additional threats. The gunshot's flash lighting menaced his pupils. The attacker was not down and lunged again, digging his fingers into Havens' face. Havens thrust the muzzle into his attacker and fired additional shots on the target's abdomen.

A haunting grunt expelled spit and heat at Havens' face. Then pain shot through Havens' mouth and nose as a skull smashed down with incredible force.

Havens had the presence of mind to retain his weapon and lifted it out, high, and across, then blindly hammered it down.

The attacker dropped to the floor, grabbing the camera strap and pulling Havens down with him. Sean reached out and fired the last of his rounds directly into the dark heap as he dropped to his knees.

"Fritter!"

From behind, Havens recognized Chang's voice.

Despite the darkness, Havens tried to identify any more threats and built more shots in that direction. His recent training with different spectrums of trigger pulls in varied target areas was coming in handy. Havens was prepared to put more shots on target.

"Let's get the hell outta here, Chang."

"What happened?"

"I don't know, but we're torching this place."

"What?"

Under Chang's protest, Havens scoured the warehouse area while demanding that Doc keep ready for any other encounters.

"Hey! Let's go! I moved the bodies in. What are you doing?" the general shouted at Havens. "Havens, get in the damned plane or I'm leaving you!"

"No, sir, you are not! Your mission died when your helo went down and your crew was killed. Mine starts here. This is my target, and I'm targeting it. Get in that plane and we'll be right out. Go!"

Not my fault if this place accidently goes up in flames. Who's going to know I was even here?

Chang turned back to Havens to see what was going on. Havens used a small survival lighter and soon a flame was chasing down a narrow trail of liquid.

The men ran out of the building and sprinted another thirty feet to the aircraft.

"Shit, Havens, you could have bought us more time!"

"Bain, you were supposed to stay in the plane! Oh, shit!" shouted Havens.

"What now?

"I forgot the fucking computer. Shit! Let me out, quick!"

"If that shit, blows, we …"

"Let me out and move the plane!"

Havens sprinted to the warehouse, thankful that he had at least moved the intel close to the door before torching the place. Despite the whine of propeller engines, Havens felt the deep pounding and vibration of an all too familiar sound approaching from the air. He raced into the entryway and collected the laptop and papers. Havens halted as he contemplated looming scenarios while the boxes, crates, and cardboard vats became engulfed in flames. He felt the heat rising quickly.

The pulsating sound of blade slamming neared.

Havens tore through the rooms for one last pass and realized he had never reloaded. It was too late. He was in the dark room. He fumbled along the walls, hoping for a light switch. The hum of the generator told him the site had power from the onset of their assault.

An open switch illuminated the room, which was a congregating area with maps pinned to the walls. Flicking an eye to the ground, he saw that his attacker remained face down with a pool of blood outlining his torso. Havens started shooting images blindly at the walls while making his exit. He could feel the equalized air pressure smoothing out the sound of the helo. He knew that it was now hovering overhead.

Not taking any chances, he left the rifle in the building. The handgun he tucked back into place.

As Havens exited the building, he could see the HIND hovering, tilted, with the pilot looking straight at Sean.

Havens gave the pilot a friendly wave, then motioned him toward the back of the building with a series of concentrated yet haphazard gestures designed to project instruction and collaboration. *Glad we moved the bodies, douchebag,* he smiled.

When the HIND failed to move, Havens with one hand trying to diminish the blade wash, gestured furiously for the HIND to move away and to the rear of the building.

The ruse worked. Just as the gunship turned, Havens slightly angled his camera and fired off as many shots as he could before sprinting to the plane.

The satellite zoomed on Havens as he waved in partnership with the HIND, giving a thumbs up.

Havens hoped that the pilot would remain confused and potentially radio in an inquiry.

The first eruption within the structure burst doors and windows with a cascading series that thrust both flame and cloud into the air.

The HIND quickly maneuvered back, and Havens took more photos of the explosion with the HIND in the backdrop just to the side of the Iranian flag that remained hoisted on a narrow pole.

Sean rushed inside the plane. "Hit it! While they're figuring out what is going on!"

Bain sped down the dirt runway.

Havens shouted to Bain, "Don't look like you're trying to outrun him. Slow it up like you're flying with purpose."

"Fritter, it's going to blow us out of the sky!"

"I don't think so. If you saw the approach, it didn't come in as an attack. I could hear the changing Doppler sound of the rotors and how they shifted speed on their approach. It was sniffing around, not coming in for a kill. Give me a radio headset."

Next, kid, you're going to tell me you could feel the difference in your balls between the tail rotor and the main rotor blades. "Sean, there's nothing here. These are probably the same guys who blew our shit out of the sky. They don't give warning shots!"

"Then don't head right for the border. Make it look like you're staying in-country. Let's see what it does."

The general turned the plane slightly away from his preferred destination. "You better know what you are doing, Havens. I need my intel guy thinking this through. Not the guy doing stupid shit back there. He's still stalking us."

"Just keep on it. What's some international plane signal you can use to send him away? What is swaying your wings back and forth?"

"It sure as hell doesn't mean back the hell off and don't shoot us out of the sky!"

"Try it. And then take your turn out of Burma."

The general took a hand off of the control and wiped his palm on his pants. "Chang, you make sure we invoice the Agency for time and a half."

Chang smiled. "Screw that, I'm going back into medicine."

Bain smiled.

Chang stared at Havens. "You don't know what you are doing, do you?"

With an honest face, Havens replied, "I'm working on it."

Chang nodded. "If we don't get our asses shot off, I'll clean up those lacerations on you. You okay?"

"I just want to go home. One thing at a time."

"Me too." Chang leaned up to the cockpit. "Give this thing some gas! Havens said we're clear."

"Okay!" The plane picked up speed and Chang sat back.

Havens leaned forward and gave Chang a hairy eye-ball.

"What? You don't know, I don't know. So, let's speed things up one way or another."

Havens sat back and thumbed through the images on the camera's preview display. He pulled a connection cord from his kit and connected it to his mobile device.

Chang watched as Havens scrolled, selected, then typed. Doc nodded in approval. He didn't know what Sean Havens was doing, but he knew this was what Havens did best.

"Sean, the HIND is staying its course and seems to have closed in a bit with increased speed."

"We're fucked," Chang observed.

"Make that double. Another HIND up ahead. What else you have in that ass of yours, Havens?"

Havens remained silent.

"Havens!"

"I'm thinking!"

"We don't have time be thinking. I need something now!"

"Turn to the camp!"

"What camp?"

"The only camp we've been staying at!"

"Havens, what the hell will that do? I don't even know where it is!"

"General." Havens nudged up toward the cockpit. "Follow that line along the cliffs. Drop down slowly to near treetop level."

"What the fuck is that going to do?"

"I'm going to try out my prototypes."

"We never did anything. They don't have projectiles."

"I know. So we better not screw this up. Keep your speed. Trust me."

Doc Chang was less convinced. "We're going to die. Fritter killed us with a banana gun idea."

Chapter 52

The plane was flying just over the lush canopies. The majesty of the landscape would have been something to take in were it not for death closing in from behind.

Both HIND gunships had closed to a side-by-side formation at the rear of their aircraft. They vectored to intercept the small plane that was gradually speeding up while containing its movements. Cats playing with a mouse.

Havens considered the pre-established "Boston" mayday call, but it would be futile. Instead, he pulled out a small radio transmitter and dialed a specific channel. "I set this up as a best test with the Karens, despite Tom's protests. I need you to draw them in closer. They need to be tighter. "

"Did you want me to just call them up and ask, Havens?" The general was beyond soured but still held out for a miracle. "Untested, huh?"

"Start shifting to your left and your right. They will try to box you in closer and hopefully increase their speed. In about two klicks, I need you to give it everything you got. On my go."

"And what if your plan doesn't work?"

"Say a prayer."

"We're going to die," Chang repeated.

"Turn a little to the left. See the little clearing coming up? I need you to drop and go right between those two trees. See how they are a bit taller than the others?"

"Sean, it's a fucking jungle. Which two trees? The whole damned panorama is trees. Couldn't you have spray painted them at least?" The general smiled despite the gravity of the situation.

"Sir, if you make me go up there and fly this thing for you, I'll be pissed. Right there. When you get your back fixed, go see an optometrist. I know where we are."

"I got 'em. This better fucking work." He turned back to Havens. "This is getting fun."

Just as the plane passed the trees, Havens pressed the signal on his device. Without missing a beat, he changed channels and pressed the second. *C'mon, dominoes!*

In mere seconds, the treetop ignited with a large bursting flare-up just as the HIND approached.

"Yes!" Sean twisted back trying to see while hoping his plan continued to work.

Quickly the gunship banked to the left in a routine evasive maneuver. His counterpart experienced the same phenomena and was forced to bank right.

The two HIND gunships veered toward one another as each was focused on their own survival.

Immediately recognizing the danger, the HIND pilots tried to correct space, but the rotors met, drawing both ships in with additional momentum as the blades sheered. The HINDs were pulled into one another and collided, crumpling in their descent.

The small plane erupted in cheers. Bain turned toward the border in a confident maneuver towards freedom.

As he passed over the camp, the team could view the massacre below that had ensued with their departure to the Iranian site.

Bodies remained as they had fallen. Huts were burned out.

"Take it lower," said Havens in a somber tone, the victory dance pushed to the side.

At the low altitude, the men could make out the soldiers, the women and children. Chang craned his neck. He made out the light blue shirt that James was wearing when they departed the previous night. James lay alone about fifty yards from the rest of the villagers.

Chang was going to keep the observation to himself but thought better of withholding. "Fritter, I don't think your buddy made it."

Havens had been looking out the other side and tried to quickly reorient himself to see what Chang was talking about.

"Did you see him? What'd you see?"

"General, you may need to take another pass," Chang requested.

"Guys, we need to get out of here. We can't help from here. Stick to the mission."

"Yeah," said Chang. "Looks like gunship stitched him up."

"Shit. We need to retrieve his body."

"No go, Havens. Nowhere to land. No time."

Havens thumbed his watch and moved to the emergency app. He contemplated sending an alert and dropping the watch from the plane near James. Aimee was going to be heartbroken. Sean felt responsible.

Bain broke the silence. "Havens, I know what's going through your head. I'll make another pass. You grab coordinates and send them to HQ. James had a chance to go out like he would have wanted. In combat. Don't mourn him. 'Til Valhalla.'" The general sent a salute to the scene below. *"Di oppresso liber."*

"Roger that," Havens conceded. "He certainly would have wanted to go down in a fight." Sean pressed a hand to the window, his heart tight with remorse. He curled a lip and fought back the emotions. War was not his thing.

Chang, on the other hand, was reluctant to let go of something. "Tom said these guys were bowing down to the Burmese. Burma just wiped them out. We take out a base and were witnesses to an atrocity. No one wanted those people helped. Those people were wiped out. And it happened right when you got there, Fritter. That means you were tracked or reported."

"Not pointing a finger, Doc, but you guys also happened to be shot down just in that area, conveniently near a fake Iranian explosives site that correlates to our original tasking."

No one said a word.

"I think we all got played," Bain conceded. The general wiped his sweaty hands on his pants again. Maybe he did prefer fly fishing after all. He checked the speed, altitude, and direction. He lowered the plane to just above the tree tops. His back throbbed. *I'm going to buy that property in Wilmington. Hell with this.*

Havens interrupted the general's thoughts. He leaned in to the general. "Sir, how have you done this all these years? Managing a family with all the deployments?"

Keeping eyes ahead, "It's different for military guys than you, Sean. When we leave, even on sensitive missions, our families, friends, neighbors all know we're off to go kill people. So they pitch in and support the mission. Car pools, meal trains, emotional support. It's a support system. You spooks feel a need to compartmentalize everything. So everyone's in the dark. No one's baking a casserole for your wife if they think you're on a business trip. Logistically and from a support perspective, CIA and all the other alphabet agencies have really done their people and families a disservice. Your secrets are no deeper than ours. Matter of fact, I bet there is less gossiping in military families than with spooks about where a husband is deployed. Nothing to figure out with us soldiers. With you all, everyone is trying to guess what you do, where you go, or how you're involved. It's no secret. People know. They just play your game and leave your families alone to fend for themselves. Probably figure you aren't really good people if you lie all the time."

Sean said nothing and sat back. The words resonated. Lies had come too easily. His life was surrounded by them.

Chapter 53

Tanya Crowe repositioned herself in the uncomfortable faux leather chair. The American embassy in Thailand was decent enough, but all ambassadors seemed to put Agency folks in the closest thing to a broom closet.

"Did you send the pictures, Ms. Crowe?"

"Rick, you should have them by now. Anything?"

"Yep. Just popped up." Rick paused on the line. Tanya waited again.

After another couple minutes passed, she couldn't contain herself any longer. "Well? Seem like something we could pull off?"

Rick remained silent and Tanya waited.

"I'll take it from here, Ms. Crowe, but yes. I can use this. These pictures certainly demonstrate that Burma has attacked a village and an Iranian location, which could put pressure on Russia, given their HIND advisor presence in the area. I think we can get this to our propaganda folks and have them spin something up nicely. Humanitarian issue for sure." Rick flipped over the glossies on his desk. Sean Havens waving to a HIND with U.S. bodies dead around him. The General and Doc Chang armed. Rogue elements. Dead villagers. *That's a good insurance policy,* Rick thought. *Thank you, boys. Plausible deniability for me since your orders were to not engage.*

"Spin?"

"I'm sorry, create a proper narrative," Rick guided gently. *Careful. You need to let them do this but still keep your ass out of a sling. Tom came through giving us images of a village attack in progress. Don't get that on high resolution live feed every day.*

"And any luck with what Lars came up with? He is doing fine, by the way, since you haven't asked." Tanya held her breath, questioning her tone.

"I'm glad to hear that. Can't say that I completely understand how that all transpired, but obviously there is a connection and I've got a couple teams working on the description you gave, analysis of travelers, and any surveillance that we can get our hands on without tipping off the Thais. We have to access their systems surreptitiously."

"Thanks. I'm sorry if that sounded brash."

"How far out are your guys from getting Havens and the package? We contacted Thai Intelligence and they are ensuring safe passage of the plane in their air space."

"We won't get him back for about five hours. He said the others are going to require medical attention. We can likely get that taken care of with our resources and put them on a naval vessel until we decide the best way to extract them back CONUS."

"Okay. Make arrangements to have the general and his guy taken care of. I read the line about MIA potentially at the coordinates Havens passed on. We'll get a team of body snatchers in the country tonight."

Tanya said nothing. *You can do that now?*

"Ms. Crowe? You still there?" Rick asked into the silence.

"Yes, sir. I'm just doing a little thinking. I'm curious as to how there are men available to retrieve the bodies now, but there was no one available before when you allowed Mr. Havens to go."

Not missing a beat, Rick replied, "At the time there was no one available. People roll on and roll off all the time. Now I have assets available, and now I have solid intel that there may be missing Americans at a specific location. You've been doing this long enough to know that the people in lofty places like specifics and focused missions. They don't like exploratory operations with nebulous outcomes. Plus, different animals make different footprints. We can use a different animal at this point."

"I don't understand that, but whatever. So you're going to broadcast a message about an Iranian site being attacked by Russians, and at the same time you're sending in a team to that site, which will be converged upon by Iranians and Russians. Probably Burmese as well."

"I'm curious, Ms. Crowe, how long you are looking to stay in the intelligence business?"

"I'm curious too. Is that all?"

"I think that is more than enough of this conversation. Watch yourself, Ms. Crowe. Intelligence professionals answer other people's questions when they are asked. When they don't answer questions and ask them instead, they're just assholes. No one values assholes."

Rick disconnected the call. *You're a smart woman, Ms. Crowe. I wish the community had more tolerance for strong women. God knows we couldn't do worse with more of you. Hopefully I've motivated you properly now for the next steps.*

Tanya was furious. She couldn't wait until Havens landed. He would listen to her. That's all she needed, someone to vent to. Sean always listened. Well, he did in Turkey. *Dammit, men could be such assholes.*

Rick sat for a moment. He contemplated his place. He was an asshole. He was a pawn for his father. He likely was a pawn for some smokescreen investigation into the Pond. He worried more about managing the people below him than he did proactively trying to make a difference and carving out his own future. *Yes, Ms. Crowe, I really am an asshole. And what the hell do I even stand for?*

The flight was uneventful despite the pins and needles that each man was flying on. Havens received a response from Tanya regarding the arrangements. He couldn't wait to get on the ground to a place where he could call his daughter. He looked forward to seeing Tanya Crowe. She instilled a glimmer of hope within all this madness.

Chapter 54

Paulo lit a candle in Our Lady of Songshan Catholic Church in Taipei, proximate to the Taiwan Stock Exchange. He said a prayer and found the seventeenth pew was empty. Reaching under the wooden bench, he retrieved a paper. *Yes. That is him. Lars Bjorklund. Retired Chicago Police detective. Freemason. Lodge … Brother to CIA asset Sean Havens. This big man. He is policeman. Yes. I remember. Not intelligence. He is a Mason … I spared you, and now shall grant you life. I will not break my brotherhood vows. They should not order the termination. Peace be with you, my brother.*

As Paulo prepared to kneel, he retrieved four volcanic rocks from a small pouch. He placed two of the coarse rocks on the floor and knelt on top of each. The next two he placed tightly behind each knee. He balanced himself to create pain from the objects and closed his eyes to meditate.

Blessed is the pain. Blessed art thou. My savior, my god, my life. I am your servant, your knight, your protector. May you greet the innocent sacrifices who meet my creations, and bless them to be received into your kingdom. Like lambs to the slaughter, they are the righteous. May the stain of their blood please you, and may you welcome me to the warmth of your hell fires.

Paulo bent and drooled spittle to his left on the stone church floor. Then he quietly spat to the right. In the breast pocket of his traveler's sport coat, he retrieved a phone. He touched a button on the device and the countdown started. As he rose, leaving the stones on the floor, he was approached by a priest.

The priest, a small Taiwanese man, kept one hand within his frock, while the other waved a finger to indicate Paulo's phone. He then smiled and reached out to Paulo, touching his shoulder.

Paulo gasped. The touch sent a childhood flashback of a much weaker lad in a similar church. "Get your filthy child-touching hands from me." Paulo's eyes raged, protecting a self who no longer existed. The priest withdrew immediately. In that moment, an explosion resonated within the quiet confines. Shattered pieces of pink, blue and green stained glass gleamed as daylight shone into the dark church, the shards falling like fall leaves. The tremor shook the ground. Candelabras fell to the floor and the few people in the church shrieked in terror.

Paulo had stepped toward the priest, his razor-sharp black dragon's tooth blade finding the priest's loin. Paulo thrust in and out, twisting his wrist with every strike, eviscerating the man of god. The priest collapsed to the floor. Paulo wiped his knife on the priest's white silk garb. *As we attack external enemies, we must attack our internal enemies as well. May demons wrestle your soul and feast upon it for eternity as I drive off the true enemies of the cross of Christ. And if your faith was true and chaste, then I have granted you glory to be with the Lord. We may live, we may die, but we are the Lord's. How glorious are we who return from battle, how blessed are we to die for the Lord and invite our judgment.*

The small motorcade of Toyota SUVs met Havens and his crew at the remote Thai runway.

After looking out the windows of the plane to get a sense of the welcome party, Sean opened the door to see Tanya approaching. For a moment, he wondered just how inappropriate it would be to give her a big hug. Even though Tanya was rightfully standoffish, Havens couldn't deny that something about her was filling a void in his heart.

The grunt behind him from Doc Chang put the boyish daydream in its rightful place.

"Shit, Havens, you running out to get a snow cone before the rest of us? Help me get the general out!"

Havens gave a hand to steady Chang and General Bain.

"You okay?" Sean asked, reading the pain on the general's face.

Bain grimaced as he stepped down. "Spasms. Sat too long. Probably tensed up too much during flight, not knowing if someone was going to shoot us out of the sky. So yeah, my back hurts because of you," he smiled.

Tanya reached in to give additional support. A medic was close behind her.

Havens took a whiff of her hair and clean smell. Fresh. Like she hadn't been out of the shower for long.

She looked back at Sean and gave a warm smile. "How are you doing? You guys smell a little ripe. Sir, you and Doc Chang will go with the corpsman. Sean, you come with me, get cleaned up, and then we'll make plans for a return CONUS."

General Bain leaked a smile and a wink at Havens. "Let her get some of the dirt behind your ears," he quipped.

"Fuckin' Fritter gets the girl. We did all the hard stuff and had to save his life. I should at least get a happy ending."

Tanya turned to Havens. "If you would like to give Doc Chang a hand job first, I'll be in the car." Doc slapped himself on the head.

Boys. She shifted her attention to General Bain. "Sir, I'm glad to see you made it out okay. Sorry about your men. We'll be taking care of them."

"Thank you. I just wish I knew where they were taken."

Tanya shot a puzzled look at Havens.

"I've not talked to the General about it yet. Sir, before shit hit the fan back there, I may have stumbled across our guys in an unmarked grave. I sent HQ the coordinates."

The general remained stoic. He'd lost many men before and had to leave a number of bodies behind over the years. He understood. "Thanks, Havens. And thanks again, Ms. …"

"Crowe, sir. Tanya Crowe." She gave a nod of appreciation for the acknowledgement.

"Sean, give me a shout when things get settled," Bain grimaced.

"Will do, sir. I'll check in on you in a week or so."

The general gave a thumbs-up and welcomed the assistance walking to the vehicle. "Give me a sec to catch my breath."

Chang gave Havens a wink and a thumbs-up.

"See you around, Chang. And thanks!"

"You'll always be my favorite weenie, Fritter. Good job out there. Tell your lady friend about your confirmed kills."

While Tanya remained locked in on Chang, he mouthed *Badass*.

She ignored it like she was forced to ignore other not-so-subtle harassment on a near-daily basis.

"Knock it off, Chang," scolded the general. "Ms. Crowe saved your life. You owe her a thanks, a beer, and Jameson sidekick."

Chang waved again as he assisted the corpsman with getting Bain into the vehicle.

Havens opened the back passenger door for Tanya, then closed it and walked around to the other side of the vehicle. The driver remained motionless. Oakley sunglasses, a 5.11 plaid short-sleeved tactical shirt. He was a caricature of embassy security failing to at least try to step it up.

"Never mind, I got this," Sean called up sarcastically.

The driver said nothing. Did nothing.

"We're all in. Thanks."

Nothing.

When Sean was belted in, Tanya patted his leg and said, "Thanks."

"For what?"

"For not being a dick and, actually, being a pretty decent guy."

The driver gave a slight head turn back to his passengers.

"Sure," Sean acknowledged as he pulled out his phone. "Mind if I make a call?"

"Not at all," she smiled, hoping this man was going to call his daughter.

Havens switched his SIM card from secure to unsecure and sure enough dialed Maggie thousands of miles away. He smiled broadly in anticipation. He was nervous but knew that he was done with this kind of work. He was excited to tell Maggie the news when he got home. The travel downtime would give him an opportunity to figure out how he would make money. The sale of the Chicago house would buy some time, but he would need that for another home and Maggie's college. *Geez, in another few years, she could be going away to college. Yeah, definitely the right move. Let's get this girl out and about. Start living. Go down to Wilmington and take her to see the ocean. Do some movies and daddy-daughter date night. Bake some shit together. I can get my girly side on and tap into super dad. Lifelong mission. Operation Fix the Family ... where no one gets killed.*

He looked down at his leg. Tanya's hand remained on the seat close to his.

Maggie's recorded voice instructed that anyone with a good reason for calling her should leave a message as she was likely "hacking a government installation or learning to walk again."

Great message, kid. Sound like you need a parent again. You're getting too snarky.

Nonchalantly, he put his hand on his leg inches from hers. *Play cool, Sean. Help the daughter at home before you involve yourself with another woman you can't take care of.*

He realized the message prompt had signaled seconds ago. "Uh, hi, Maggie. It's Dad. I'm coming back soon. Sorry I couldn't get to a phone for a long time. Hope all is well. I'll see you soon. I love you. Hope you're okay. Love you. And call me when you get this message."

Tanya extended a pinkie finger up to Sean's. She kept looking straight ahead.

Havens stammered again while still on the phone. "Um. I'll talk to you later. Bye. I love you." Disappointed that Maggie wasn't there and simultaneously feeling like he was cheating on his daughter and his wife, he moved his finger away.

Tanya pulled her hand away.

You're not married anymore. Christina would want you to move on. Right? Havens put his hand down, but hers was already back on her lap. *Damn.*

"How are you getting along with Lars?" he asked in an effort to dissolve the awkwardness. "Pretty smart guy, huh? Probably solved a lot of the Thailand issues by now?"

Back to business. Tanya responded with an even tenor. "Very smart. I'll tell you more when we are more free to speak, but he has a couple leads on things that were very helpful. He did get slightly injured. Slight altercation with the suspect, but he's okay."

Sean's eyes widened with genuine concern. "What kind of altercation? How hurt is he?"

"He's going to be down for another few days. He was stabbed, but the blade was shallow. It didn't go deep enough for a significant injury."

"Shit. You should have told me."

"And tell you something that you couldn't take care of while in the field? I took care of him like he was my own family, thank you very much." Tanya turned to the window. *Asshole.*

"My bad. You're right, and thank you. So, not deep enough meaning that it's a good thing he keeps a layer of security tissue?" Havens tried desperately to draw her back in.

She didn't turn from the window. "That's pretty much how Lars would have put it as well."

"Glad he's okay. Can I see him?"

"We can go right now, or you can clean up at my place and then I can debrief you …" She stopped but turned and gave him a sheepish smile. "Sorry."

Havens chuckled. "You can fill me in, and then maybe I'll understand more of what Lars was involved with. I've got to clean some cuts and stuff too. I'm sure I smell like hell."

"You do," the driver called back, suddenly reminding Sean and Tanya that they were not alone and were being chaperoned like two young teens.

Tanya put her hand back between the two of them. *You've worked too hard to be playing these games. Do your job, take a chance, and be the strong woman you are.* Tanya looked out of the corner of her eye, hoping he was looking at her. Nope. She cast her eyes back to the Thai surroundings, trying to lose herself and push Sean Havens out of her mind for a bit. For the next hour neither one of them spoke and neither could think of anything but the other.

Sean crossed his thumb to his fourth finger to rub his ring. *Shit!* It was gone. The mud. His stomach sank. *Son of a bitch.* He swallowed hard and put his head against the window as the vehicle bumped along. *You're a real beauty, Havens.* The greater loss was that he no longer had a wife to explain losing his wedding ring to.

Chapter 55

Prescott Draeger wrestled with his bindings, swearing at the man sitting at his bedside. Wolf had removed his cloak days ago and was now placing electrodes on Draeger's head.

Prescott's detox was hell. The IV continued to push fluids and nutrients to his body.

"You know I'm going to kill you when I'm released."

Wolf laughed. "Good, you have regained your focus and clarity of mission. See, we are making progress."

"Screw you. What's this shit now, electroshock?"

"Hardly. But a man of your intellect will appreciate this."

"Fuck you!"

Wolf ignored the incessant cursing. They had a long road ahead of them, but they were making progress. He was confident that in the next few hours he could untie Draeger with minimal threat.

"Prescott, whether you want to admit it or not, your addictions and cravings derive from your battle fatigue. Your feelings of anxiety, fear and depression are rooted in the many war-related events that you have experienced."

"Oh great. Now I get to tell you about my mommy."

"The electrodes will do the work." Wolf plugged the wires into his laptop. "We are looking at a few key areas: hyper-agitation or arousal, memory intrusions, and avoidance. You also have associate physical stressors, such as the headaches or your heart racing. I had this too. We Italians fought with you in Iraq. I have spent much time in Libya. Very unpleasant work, at times."

"Great. Now I'm a victim of military testing."

"Not at all. In most humans, when a person relaxes and closes their eyes, they have a surge of alpha waves in the visual cortex. This is part of the brain's balancing of chemicals and energy.

Because of the traumatic visualizations we have experienced, our brains have trained themselves to avoid the alpha response. You have turned off your normal response."

Draeger listened without interrupting.

Wolf turned his screen. "In this neurofeedback assessment, I will be able to tell how your brain is reacting. I promise that I will not take you back to anyplace you don't want to go. The sensors will act like a heart monitor so we can see where adjustments can be made to correct abnormal disturbances."

"With drugs, or are you going to stick electrodes in my brain or cut something out?"

"This is silly. Don't think such things."

Wolf clicked on another screen. It was a graphical image with spheres, lines, colors, a timer, and scoring visual. "When I see the balance of your alpha, beta, theta, delta, and gamma waves, I'll know what goals we can set to achieve an improved state of mind. The pills, the rage, the paranoia. It can be gone."

Do it. Fix this shit. "And if I refuse?"

Wolf leveled an unseen Berretta at Draeger's temple. "Then you are worth nothing to the Order and we can save everyone a lot of time."

Careful not to build hope, Draeger was at least captivated enough to proceed. *Fine. Start flipping your switches, Dr. Frankenstein.*

"Now let me unbind you."

Chapter 56

Lars lay on the hospital bed looking like a grizzly bear sprawled on a swimming pool float.

Tanya next to him pecking away on a mobile device. Her hair was pulled back in a ponytail. Her face appeared freshly washed and makeup free. She could pass for a college student sitting in morning class.

Havens knocked respectfully before entering through the open door.

"Hey, bro. Heard you found some trouble again." Havens winced to show he accepted responsibility for putting his brother-in-law in harm's way yet again.

"Par for the course with you, Seany. Holy shit, you look like hell. I'm guessing it wasn't a bar fight."

"I'm all right. Just glad to see you doing well. Sorry I got you into this. Tanya said you had some luck on the bombings, though"

"Yeah, well, she could show her appreciation through a decent meal," he winked. "If I didn't think she was taken, I'd make a play for her. Fine woman there, even if she can't satisfy my culinary requirements."

"Don't get me started Lars. You're the only man in all of Thailand who has had burgers and shakes delivered to you," Tanya scolded.

Lars conceded with a smile. "So how did you fare on your little adventure?"

Cautiously, Sean threw him a few bones. "I think I know where some of the explosive compounds originated, but there's no way to know if it was coincidence or not. Some intel that I got from a map shows Bangkok as what may be a distro point. But with air transport, stuff could be flowing anywhere."

"A map, huh? Don't suppose the other sites from the news are showing up?"

"What other sites?"

"Well," Lars leaned over, reaching for a pad of paper on the bedside table. He waved the pad at Tanya. "Told you I'd put this to good use." Lars licked a finger and swept through the pages. "Here."

"Whatcha got?" Havens moved closer to Lars and peered at the notes.

Lars pulled it back and flipped it over on his chest. "I'll read it. Give me some space. This is how I get my four squares a day. You move over there."

Havens glanced at Tanya.

"He spoon feeds us his analysis in exchange for American food, which we have made in the embassy and brought to him. I haven't told him that I already made a full copy with my phone while he slept."

Ignoring the ruse, Lars continued, "I've been looking at bomb sites around the globe that have occurred over the past year or so. Post 9/11, Tokyo had one. Killed about twenty people. They blamed it on a free trade nut wad. London had a few bombings. Shanghai had one."

Sean interrupted "But wasn't Shanghai an inadvertent explosion?"

"Doesn't matter. It happened." Lars lifted a finger to signal his desire to continue uninterrupted. "Hong Kong, Sao Paulo, Sydney, and, just yesterday, Taiwan and Frankfurt."

"Frankfurt was bombed?"

Tanya nodded. "Yeah, we don't know much yet. Initial reports say it involved Syrian refugees. Threw the market for a whirl. So did Taiwan. Similar to Paris and Brussels."

"Bingo!" announced Lars.

"Bingo what?" Havens asked. Lars waited patiently for the lightbulb to go off. "Top world stock market exchange locations," Sean concluded.

"Yep," Lars confirmed with pride. "Give Shaggy over here a Scooby snack."

Havens pulled out his phone and searched a photo that he had taken of the map on the plane. He widened the screen with his fingers, swiped a finger across, and held fast while studying the image.

No one interrupted him.

"Those points match what I've got. Read them off again."

Lars started again. Halfway through he muttered, "Shame. These are nice places. I've had a chance to go to most of these locations."

"Why did you go to those places? I remember you going and you saying you could go pretty cheaply."

"Guys, let's stick to the ..." Tanya interrupted.

"Shush." Havens held up a hand to Tanya.

"You did not just shush me. We've talked about this before."

"Masons," Lars responded. "I stayed at a Mason lodge in each city. That's pretty much how I travel when I go to a big city if I'm not staying with a friend. It's either free or nominal for cleaning fees."

"See," Havens gloated a bit. "I wasn't shushing you for the hell of it."

Lars turned his head, watching them bicker. "You two know each other pretty well?"

In unison, Sean replied "no" while Tanya replied "yes."

Tanya's mouth opened and Sean immediately started retracting. "Well, kind of. Anyway, that doesn't matter here."

Lars held up his hands in protest. "Hey, I'm just sayin'. You two are like an old married couple. I see there's history. You should explore it." He winked at Sean.

Flustered, Tanya shifted back to the topic. "So why markets? Disrupt the economy? Russia seems to be the only one not on the list. You think they are paying proxies?"

Lars raised his eyebrows but waited for Sean to respond.

Havens looked at the floor, thinking. *Disrupt or profit? Russia disrupting doesn't do much good if they have a lot of their money in these markets. Most countries are spread out and would take a hit if something happened. Who would benefit?*

"Sean?"

"Excuse me one minute, please, Ms. Crowe ..."

Lars guffawed. "That means 'shush,' Tanya."

"You guys are assholes."

You would benefit if you knew when an event would disrupt a market and either invest or pull out. Do it once, you could make a mint. Do it a lot, you would make shit tons. Buy off governments, fund elections, bribe officials. Build war chests while weakening others. "Holy crap," Sean whispered in astonishment.

"Well that's pretty genius," Tanya dismissed with an eye roll. Then it hit her. She whirled to Sean. "Funding mechanism?"

Lars whistled.

An orderly slowed as he approached the room of Lars Bjorklund. He looked to his right, making eye contact with Lars, which the scrub-adorned man quickly averted and continued on his way.

Lars raised a hand to Tanya. "Second time that guy has passed since you two got here. May want to check it out."

Tanya moved to the door. "Who?"

"I dunno, orderly or something. Asian. You should take a peek."

Sean looked at Tanya, then looked to Lars.

While Tanya was craning her neck, Lars signaled Havens to come closer. He handed Sean a small folded piece of paper.

"Good to see you, Seany. We need to get back to Maggie. Have you heard from her?"

"I left a message but haven't heard back yet."

"Sean, this is murky stuff. Get out of here. Get back to Maggie. I know I have to stay here for a bit, but get away from here and all this shit. It's going to suck you in and get us all killed. If I choke on a fry or something, I have my personal information in a box of Christina's at the storage vault we share. It says 'Christina and Lars, Family Photos.'"

Havens looked to the door. Tanya was no longer there. "You bluffing about that guy?"

"No," Lars said firmly. "Get me the hell out of here. There are eyes on me here and I don't know whose."

"Okay. Let me see what I can do. What does the doctor say?"

"Says I run the risk of an infection. I'm guessing more from this hospital than the knife."

Havens patted his pocket. "This something I should read right away?"

"Sooner than later."

"Okay. Anything else on this whole bomb thing?"

Tanya entered the room. "No one that I could see. You say you've seen him before?"

"I've seen a few folks who just don't seem right."

"Why didn't you say anything?"

"'Cause I didn't have my boy here." Lars made a fist and gently punched Sean's leg.

"I got it, you don't trust me." The look of disappointment on Tanya's face was genuine. She started to chew on the inside of her cheek.

"Tanya, I trust you, but I don't trust the people you guys work for."

Sean agreed. "Tanya, let's get the hell out of here. He's a damn civilian casualty, we got what we came for and now we just need to get intel to the right folks so they can do some traveler pattern analysis with the big data boxes."

"I'll head back to the embassy. You come with and we can get your stuff back in dip pouches if they have to send us back commercially."

"Can you get someone posted outside Lars' door?"

"It'll draw some suspicion."

"Who cares? Handcuff him to the bed or something. If Lars thinks something stinks, he's probably right on the money. If he saw the bomber responsible for the Thai attacks, he should be in protective custody or something. Why not get him to a safe house at this point? I know we can get an IV drip set up for him. Probably doesn't need much physician care at this point that he can't get from someone on our payroll. Did you guys have a sketch artist?"

Lars gave Tanya a knowing look. "Told ya."

"As I told you, we don't have anyone here that can do that."

"Perfect," Sean interjected. "Then he is a priority government witness to get back CONUS on the first plane out. We can get on a military flight back home. Have JSOC or OGA reach out to a Bureau liaison if we need to."

"It's worth a try," Tanya settled.

"I should be okay while you guys are away, but I agree. Without sounding paranoid, I'd feel better outta here. This is where the bad guys or CIA come in and put a pillow over my head or fill my IV with something to kill me."

Havens wasn't sure if his brother-in law was serious or just wanting to get home.

Tanya headed for the door.

"Take this." Havens handed Lars a .45 auto. "Stick it under your pillow. That way if they try to put a pillow over your head you can smoke 'em."

"He can't have that," Tanya interjected.

"Why not?"

"Because he can't. He's not allowed to."

"If he was allowed to he wouldn't be in this situation. If he gets busted, we get him diplomatic immunity. Quit worrying. Operator up."

"Fuck you, Havens!" Tanya Crowe stormed out.

Havens watched her then turned back to Lars. "I'll see you in a bit. Keep that by your side and don't fall asleep. That's when they get you." Sean winked at Lars.

"Don't worry about me. She's a hot one."

"Nah, something I just said that I said before to her and it didn't turn out too well."

"Christina knew about it?"

"Shit, Lars, I didn't have an affair with her. I swear."

"I know that about you. She's good people. I'm guessing that, like you, she's gotten caught up in some shit. But she's sharp. I gave her a hard time, but she's pretty trust-worthy, I think. You came up in our conversations a few times. I think she's either interested in you or she's loyal and protective. She sure did me right. If I didn't know better, I'd say she wanted my approval."

"No time for that shit now, Lars. We need to get home and back to Maggie."

"And how. Now go chase that piece of ass and get Hillary Clinton to sign off on us getting out before things get hot."

Havens laughed. "I'll send her an email."

"Make sure it's a Yahoo account so she gets it. Write Top Secret."

"Allll right. See you soon."

"And read my note!"

Havens gave the hallways another check, but he really wasn't quite sure what he was looking for. He hoped for a feeling of something that seemed out of place. The feeling never came. *Where are you, Crowe? I don't need this drama shit.*

Tanya was outside of the hospital when Havens exited.

Havens was more than perturbed. "What the hell is wrong with you?"

She spun. "You are. You bring out my worst. You don't respect me as an equal. I'm like some, some arm candy aide to you and a sticking post when you needed cover. You never even saw me as a peer. You wouldn't treat a guy like you treated me. I'm like some piece of ass to you that you don't even want around."

"A piece of ass to me? I was married. What don't you get about that? I did a job. That's all!"

"So how were things between you and your wife? Did you ever tell her about us?"

"Where is this going? What 'us'? Don't pull this psycho-bitch stuff on me."

"*Excuse me?* I'm talking about what we did."

"Tanya, let me just get this out there. I like you. I like you a lot. What we did in Turkey was to save our lives. We were under surveillance. They would have killed us if they didn't think we were lovers."

"Sean, I know what we had to do, but you have to admit there was a connection. You can't deny that."

"Yeah, there was a connection. Maybe there still even is. But I'm married." Sean stopped. "At the time, I was married. I have to chalk it up to serving Uncle Sam."

"Nice."

Tanya started to walk away.

"Tanya. Wait. I used to disappear for weeks at a time without my wife asking me where I was or what I was doing. She knew that was the job. I had a wife and child. Under the circumstances, believe it or not she would have understood."

"She wouldn't have understood how you kissed me."

That's true. "What exactly is your point?"

"I just want to know if you two were happy. It's harder for spooks than it is for military wives. There's the same stress, but no support structure. There might even be more stress because of the secrets and uncertainty."

"Are you asking because you're curious, because you're still interested in me or because you're going to go campaign for military wives?"

"What makes you think I'm interested? I'm just doing my job! Just like you."

Sean extended his arms and gently held Tanya's frame. "Tanya, I care for you. I'm still having a hard time with Christina's death. I loved her. I loved her with everything. And I have a confused and troubled and wounded little girl to take care of. I'd like to have a relationship with you, but I want to be fair."

"'Fair' like I'll always be in third place?"

"'Fair' like you deserve to be loved in a way that you want to be loved. I'm far from even being able to love my child in the way that I'm supposed to. I don't want to exist like this. I don't want the baggage. But on the other hand, that's all I want. I want my kid, I want my wife, I want you. That's pretty complicated for a guy who can hardly keep his own head clear of a lot of shit."

A tear rolled down Tanya's cheek. Sean was just about to raise his hand to wipe the hurt from her face when Tanya forced Sean's arms down slowly to his sides. He leaned in as she lifted her chin. She longed for his kiss, yet she couldn't bring herself to succumb to it. As he neared her lips, she moved to the side.

"I can't, Sean."

"What? I thought we were ..."

"I have a Yale degree in Foreign Relations! I was recruited just like you. And for some reason, all I get sent out for is arm candy stuff. That's why I quit. That's why I took some sucky-ass Defense analysis job. So someone will just see what I write and analyze and know that I'm good, damn good at my job, and then they'll take me seriously. It's pretty shitty pay for what I bring to the table, but I feel like I'm making a difference. If no one else agrees, I'll just go back to D.C. and make two hundred grand as a consultant in a high-end think tank."

"Fine. I won't kiss you."

"What?"

"In the movies, the guy shuts the ranting chick up with a big kiss. Sexual tension, mutual interest, all that shit is brewing. I like you. I don't see you as my equal because I want to protect you. I tried to protect you in Turkey. Not my mission. But I also had feelings for you and I had to put that aside because I love my wife. I feel like I cheated on her, and really, I did."

"You really miss her, don't you?"

"Tanya, I'll always love my wife. But I have a huge void without her and you more than fill it. You want me to live my life differently. And if the time is ever right, I'd like to explore it with you. But not now. Shit, I've totally neglected my daughter and justified it by saying I had to do this financially. I could really give two shits about these bombings or this market manipulation. So if you have something to say to me, just say it and quit with this high-school shit. You're better than that."

Tanya stood dumbfounded. She was pissed, she was happy, she was relieved, and she was scared. "There's more."

"Then tell me more. Quit dicking around. I'm a little fucked in the head these days and don't really have a handle on my sensitive side that knows how to deal with chicks or anything else in life right now. Not that I ever did. Sorry."

"I would have preferred the kiss."

A quadrotor drone rose to the second story of the hospital, the vertically oriented propellers slowing as the craft neared the building's face. It continued to rise to the glass window. Its pilot created a tad more torque, thrusting the drone gently on the pane to make a tapping sound.

What the? Lars heard continued tapping to the right of his bed. With the drapes closed, he was unable to identify the sound. Curious, he held the bedrail and swung his large legs over the side using just enough momentum to elevate himself to a standing position without too much abdominal pain. The stitches pulled and he knew he had ripped a couple. Struggling, he reached for the drapes.

Havens heard the high-pitched whirring of the unmanned aerial vehicle. He turned his head to orient the sound.

Tanya squinted her eyes reflexively as she, too, picked up the noise. "Sounds like one of those model airplanes. I heard it a few minutes ago when I came out. It seemed to go around the building."

"There are no parks near the hospital. This isn't good." Recalling recent use of toy UAVs in Chicago, Sean bolted to the hospital entrance. "I know what this is."

Lars grasped the vinyl curtains and flung them open as the carbon fiber composite's tapping continued.

The unmanned aerial vehicle rose to eye level. The camera eye zoomed. The rotorcraft pitched back forty-five degrees, exposing its underbelly, a grey taped clay block with a metal covering.

"Shit." Lars closed his eyes.

Havens and Tanya Crowe heard the explosion as they entered the building. Burning debris arched through the air and fell to the ground.

"Lars!" Sean screamed as he increased his pace.

Staff and visitors were already panicking, charging toward Sean as he ran against them. Havens squeezed past, knocking some to the ground as he led with strong shoulders and elbowed his way to the elevator bank. He chose the stairway to the left and leapt up the stairs three at a time, bounding up toward his brother-in-law's floor.

The doors burst open as more staff evacuated the level. Havens held fast to the rail as he fought the surge of people trying to force him back down. He swatted and pushed against them as he ascended and flung himself through the doorway.

Sean could smell burning and see debris in the hallway. It was coming from Lars' room.

The acrid stench of burnt hair, flesh and plastic was overpowering. "Aw shit, Lars."

The room was a wreck. A few flames lingered. A heat flash mark was on the ceiling. Lars lay in a heap. His limp arm, twisted by the foot of the bed, was now feet from where it was positioned minutes earlier. Glass fragments littered the linoleum floor.

Chapter 57

It was weird meeting his father at a hotel in Virginia Beach. Not exactly a halfway point.

"Son, thanks for meeting me. We need to have a little chat. I'm afraid that I have been less than forthcoming about something concerning Sean Havens."

Jerry had both the television and radio on to create white noise. He had driven on his own to the hotel, foregoing the black warwagon or towncar with armed chauffeur.

"I think there's a lot that you have been holding back. Just don't tell me he's my brother."

"As fond as I am of the boy, I assure you that he isn't. Although you could do worse for a sibling."

"Cut to the chase, Jerry."

"Please. Sit." Jerry chose an armchair and loosened the laces on his black wingtip shoes. "I don't know why you are so defensive about him. In our business, I shouldn't have to reinforce that he has always been simply a means to an end. It's what we do. It's what I have always done. That said, it would be a lie if I told you I didn't have a bit of a place in my heart for the man. Well, at least that piston of a kid that I recruited. Golly, has it been that long?" Jerry took a deep breath and flitted his eyelids, reminiscing for a moment of years gone by all too quickly.

"Spill it, Pop."

"His wife, Christina. She never perished."

"Bullshit." Rick's boredom had turned on a dime to full attention and astonishment. His expression hung in the air for want of immediate validation.

"It was a blindspot, of sorts."

"You call that a blindspot? Where the hell is she? Is it Havens? What did he do with her?"

Jerry waved his hand, dismissing his son's conspiracy theory. The reality was much more absurd.

"We don't have all the details. In short, she was evidently taken by the Pond as a sort of bargaining chip but then moved to a sort of mutual interest. No, neutral ground is a better way to phrase it."

Rick let out a whistle, put his hands on his hips and started walking in a small circle. "You fucking knew, didn't you? This isn't *new* news. You knew." Rick stared hard at his father.

"Yes, I am afraid I did. I should have told you."

"Really? You think you *should* have told me? And aren't you forgetting someone? Maybe, oh, I don't know ..." Rick stopped walking and in disgust with his father shouted, "Sean Havens?"

"It was complicated."

"*Complicated?*" Rick repeated incredulously.

"Please," Jerry sighed. He needed patience from his son so he could continue.

Rick threw up his hands while still reeling with the news.

"There has been a storm brewing. I'm trying to protect you and ensure your rightful place in the Agency."

"The Agency? What does my future with the Agency have to do with anything? Certainly nothing with Havens or his wife. I'm not even sure how much longer I want to stay. I can retire."

"Don't say that," Jerry spat. "You come from a lineage of family members who have served in the silent shadows. You could be DDO. A seventh-floor man. We have paved the way and can't let the changing of the guards allow our enemies to gain power within the Agency. The Pond will take over. They will take over everything."

"Dad. Do you hear yourself? How are they any different from your directorate? How are the men serving the Pond any different than Company men? Or do you mean Bonesmen?" Rick's voice was dripping with contempt all too familiar to his father. To say it was a disappointment that Rick refused to be a Yale Man was an understatement. Before Jerry could comment, Rick continued. "They all are doing a mission that they believe is patriotic and securing our nation's place in the world while securing power for their own ilk."

"Son, you have no idea. The President has a few candidates to choose from to run the Agency. They are all linked to the Pond. If we were to assassinate the president, the vice president would still select from that pool."

"What did you just say?"

"Don't have me say it again. You know full well what I said. It isn't the first time we have had to take matters into our own hands. Now, we need to eliminate the candidates. It pales in comparison to what they have done to our rank and file—or how they have attempted to blind us now."

"You're mad!" Rick turned from his father. "We've got to tell Havens. Someone owes him that much. Where is his wife?"

"Rick, you mustn't. The repercussions are too great. There are trade-offs. A pawn for a pawn. A queen for a queen. We have encouraged the Pond to terminate her as soon as possible. It's a game you wouldn't understand. A battle of gentlemen that has to be played by certain … rules. Understood by, well, no offense, but elites."

"Are you completely out of it? You think you are elite? You are a federal employee."

"There's history."

"History authorizes you to kill a woman who is already supposed to be dead, and who was innocent the whole time? Where is she?"

"About two and a half hours from here as the crow flies but I can't let you go. And regardless, she won't be the same. They broke her down and never rebuilt her."

"And what are you going to do to stop me?" Rick asked as he walked toward the door.

"I will reason with you first. Then the choice is yours."

Rick flipped the locked door latch. "Screw that! I'm not sure what I stand for these days, but it sure has to be more than this."

Rick heard Jerry chamber a round as he turned the knob.

Chapter 58

Lars lay in his own crime scene at his brother in-law's feet. His bare torso was riddled with jutting shrapnel and lacerations. Shards of glass were everywhere.

The detective's head was not visible under the bed, where his shoulders met the frame. The giant of a man lay still amidst the chaos in the hallways.

Havens paced the room like a zoo animal crazed by containment. Wails and pleads for help emanated from the halls into the room. *What are you possibly screaming for? This was a contained kill. You have no right to cry. Oh, geez, Lars. What did I just do? What did I just do?*

Sean moved to fully assess Lars as his cell phone rang. The call gave him a startle as his mind was worlds away. *Of all times, who the fuck is calling?* Havens grabbed the mobile device. *Maggie. Oh, no, no, no. Maggie. Not now. I have to answer.*

"Hello?"

Tanya interrupted. "Sean …"

"Not now!"

Tanya backed away, understanding, and assessed the scene. She was not quite sure whether she and Sean should pitch in or flee.

"Dad?"

"Yes!" Havens shouted above the noises while plugging an ear and muffling the phone.

"Dad?"

"Yes! It's me!" Sean moved around the room. Lars long legs limp before him.

"Um, is this a bad time?"

"Yes! I mean no. What's up? I can barely hear you. Speak up, Maggie!"

"Dad, what's going on? What's that noise? Are you okay?"

"Yes. Yes. Everything is fine," he lied to his daughter.

Silence.

"Maggie?"

The line went dead.

"Dammit!"

Tanya, kept her distance at the room entrance. She was watching Sean curse his phone and redial. "Sean, I think maybe we shouldn't be here. At the very least, you shouldn't be here."

Havens ignored Tanya as he reached a busy signal. "Busy? How are you busy?" he muttered to himself and refingered the keys. Again he reached no one.

"Sean?"

"Can't you just shut the hell up for a second?" He screamed. "If you want to go, go! I've got my fucking brother-in law all blown to shit around this room, so, no, I really don't give two shits about our status here or being an embarrassment right now to this fucking country of ours that is doing absolutely *shit* right now about me and my family that keeps getting wasted wherever I go!"

Tanya stood her ground in understanding.

A ring sounded in the corner of the room. Havens looked left and right, but Tanya had already tracked it and was heading toward the sound. By the third ring, she had Lars' phone in her hand.

She handed it to Havens. "It says 'Mags.'"

"Thank god!"

Chapter 59

"Shoot me, Dad. Go ahead. Show me where you place family over cloak and dagger. Might as well, it'll never be the same after this. And you thought last Christmas sucked," Rick chuckled bitterly.

"I'm not going to shoot you, son. I just need your undivided attention and to understand the seriousness of what I have to say," Jerry replied, exasperated.

"Well, you have my attention. You've lost my loyalty, but I'm sure as shit not moving, you crazy old turd." Rick folded his arms in the futility of the situation.

"I'll show my hand, Rick. In truth, the Pond is fully within the Agency. Most of the new guard are involved. Upper echelons are further crossed into a very influential element called P2. It's compartmented away from the Pond, yet they task one another. P2, or Propaganda Due in Italian, was a nineteenth century Mason lodge. It was originally composed of Armed Forces members—generals and admirals—and grew to be the core power structures of Italy."

"Dad, I've heard of P2. Degenerate Freemasons. Linked to the Mafia. What does that have to do with us and taking down the Pond? That should make it easier. First things first, no matter who they are aligned to."

"I don't think you understand." Jerry closed his eyes for but a second, as if contemplating a great reveal. "The National Security Act of 1947 allowed us certain liberties in the name of defense. My old Agency pals Cline, Casey, Shackley, and others got their fingers in the darker circles that opened a number of exotic routes and means for the CIA to wage shadow wars. The Pond, through P2, is coagulated across clandestine communities globally. They were both a tool against Communism, so they moved to inner circles of power."

"What inner circles. How far? The Presidency?"

"The Presidency. If that were only the case. It goes beyond this. It spans markets, governments, the Vatican. They have power in institutions and throughout society."

"You said the Mafia was involved. Who is the major family?"

"Son, in New York alone, it spans Colombo, Bonanno, Gambino, Lucchese, and Genovese. Forgive me. Scratch Lucchese. They are trying to go more legitimate, which is another problem. But these were spawned in part from Italy by the Inzerillo and the Spatolas from Sicily."

"This is absurd." Rick flung his hands out and away denying any plausibility to the words of his father. "There is no way an intelligence or splinter society can rein in all these players. There is no way they should stand for the Pond's violence."

"It's what unites them. Attacks are used to direct public outrage at governments or illicit groups. The crime groups are considered strategic affiliates and drugs, trafficking, and smuggling are all interlocked."

"Who leads this?"

"It's layered, Rick. The Pond and P2 intersect through my old schoolmate, Robert. The Pond is run by PASSPORT. P2 is run by the Rose of Twenty. Their chancellor goes by the name or code of LUCIANI. The overwhelming majority are Roman Catholics."

"So how do they influence other global players? Duffel bags of cash and opportunity don't spawn loyalty."

"Rick, we have had presidents who were part of the Rose of Twenty. The Yakuza, Chinese Triads have not been penetrated, to our knowledge. As you may know, they are our closest allies in the drug trade. But we have conceded ground in Burma."

"Burma?"

"Yes."

"You're the one, aren't you? You approved the mission to Thailand by saying you were doing something with drugs in

Burma. You had no intention of those men making it to Thailand. That's why you approved short-range helos. They were never going to make it to another base camp for refueling. You knew about Colonel Hessberg. You knew Tom would give me a show that we could use for leverage later in the international community."

"There was a greater strategy, I'm afraid. We did need an asset in Burma with abilities to bring in profits from Thailand. We lost Afghanistan. We needed our routes back but couldn't take them by force. Our golden triangle routes became a Pond possession of from within the Agency. They siphoned off profits, access, and distribution while we were powerless to stop them."

"Stop them? You mean you were powerless to take their profits, which you just got back." A look of disappointment crossed Rick's face. "Havens. That's why you saved Havens. You knew he would want to save his old crew and then he could be pushed next to Thailand."

"He's a noble man but, I am afraid, just a man. He paved the way for Hessberg. He's been our other man on the ground working with the Karen. Havens had to disrupt a few things first. We didn't know what exactly he would do, but we knew that he would shake things up somehow. Most other men would require a plan. Havens was more secure as we knew he would create an appropriate plan as he shaped the environment analytically."

"Jeezus. I played Havens and you played me. Who is protecting this conglomeration? Why are they untouchable? Don't you all have people in Washington at equally high levels?"

"We don't know who is involved. That is why I needed you to do this as a program office out and away from the Beltway. We don't know who to trust, or to what levels from within. A monster like that must devour itself or be devoured virally. I didn't play you, I knew and expected what you would do, just as you did with Sean Havens. Its knowing ourselves and trusting our own to do what needs to be done without explicitly asking. Its trust."

"Trust." Rick still felt betrayed but couldn't play the hand and be the hypocrite. "I suppose I understand. But you guys are just pissed that someone is benefiting more from it than your Yale buddies. Or am I wrong?"

"Open your damn mind! It's not about Yale. It's about circles of trust!" Jerry shouted. "Why can't you see that?"

"It's about greed," Rick spat. "Greed for power and wealth. Defenders of free will and democracy. All bullshit. Screwing our own. Screwing me. Screwing your golden boy Sean Havens. So what's the deal with Havens' wife? Explain the purpose of that. Whacking a guy's family, or sorry, at least *allowing* it to happen by the forces of trust and predictability."

Jerry looked down to the floor in indignity. "*We* have her."

"You've got to be kidding me."

Chapter 60

Warrior second, dad first at the moment, Havens answered Lars' phone.

"Hey."

"Dad? What's going on? Why did you answer Uncle Lars' phone?" *I knew you were together. I can't even trust him anymore.*

Lie. Now isn't the time. "Hey Mags. Can you hang on? I want to talk to you, but there's a lot going on. I have to run downstairs, so hang with me. I'm putting you on mute. It may take me a minute or two but please don't hang up, okay?"

"Okay," Maggie agreed, unsure. Nothing was ever easy with her dad. Its why she called her uncle as backup. Uncle Lars had always been straight with her. Or so she had thought until now.

Havens nodded to Tanya, conceding his need to exit pronto.

He held Lars' phone to his chest despite the phone being set to mute as he raced down the stairs, Tanya close behind him.

Outside the hospital and a hundred yards from the chaos, it was time to try again.

"Hi, Mags. You still there?"

"Dad? Where are you? Why do you have Uncle Lars' phone?" Not waiting for an answer, she continued, "When are you coming home?"

Truth for a change. Havens sighed. Tanya signaled with her hands that she was willing to stay or go, as he preferred.

"Dad?"

Havens indicated to Tanya that it was fine for her to stay but turned and shielded himself while he spoke to his daughter a continent away.

"I'm here, kiddo. I'm coming home soon. You okay? How's your walking coming along?"

"Dad, what was all that in the background?"

"An explosion." *Half lie.* "I'm okay. Your uncle was badly hurt. It has to do with that conversation that you and I had. Your uncle was helping me."

"Oh my god. Is he okay?"

"Why is the CIA holding Havens' wife? Really, how much worse can this get?" Rick pressed.

"We have little insight to what the Pond affiliates within the CIA used Havens for. We don't know where he went, what he did, or who he met with. We are compartmented out of their systems, and of course his travel and personae were covered."

"What does that have to do with his wife?" Rick persisted.

"Our acquiring her from the Pond gave us...an opportunity."

"For what?"

"To see if she knew where he was going. It was just a hunch, but we thought Havens might have shared some tidbits of his travels with her from time to time. Anything was better than nothing to help us piece together some clues."

"Let me guess. You got nothing."

Jerry was abashed. He nodded in agreement. "I'm afraid that we have been unsuccessful. There was some lost time during her recovery, and there might have been some issues with the stress trauma she went through in the shooting incident. But we are fairly certain that she knows nothing."

"What makes you think she would have talked anyway? This is ridiculous."

"Counterintelligence."

"Meaning what?"

"Meaning that was our leverage. Mrs. Havens' brother has always been on our radar for an exploit risk. He was less than clean, shall we say."

"And she knew this?"

"It became known to her at a point in time when we needed her to keep details of her own husband. It was at a time that she questioned her husband. She questioned his fidelity. She started nosing around in areas she shouldn't. We leveraged that distrust for exploratory purposes on our end."

"We were using her as an asset against our own?"

"The situation warranted it, I'm afraid."

"No, you had to give up her husband to the Pond, and like a bunch of fucking spoiled babies, you smeared her brother and basically forced her into being your mole by letting her think her husband was cheating on her!"

"CI informant. And it was by the book."

"By the book because you didn't think at the time you lost CI to the Pond. But you did. And maybe that's why they whacked her in the first place."

"It's a possibility."

Rick sat down. He raised his hands to his face. Jerry remained silent. After a minute, Rick put his hands down and took a deep breath. He looked up at his father in broken disappointment. "What are you going to do with her?"

Jerry looked away.

"Pops? Really. You can't. Havens isn't my favorite person, but he and his kid deserve better."

"Son, she has no information. She would be a liability now. She's already dead to her family."

Rick closed his eyes for a moment. "What's next?"

.

Chapter 61

"I'm coming home, Maggie. Next flight I can get, I'm outta here. You've been left alone for too long." Havens added, "I've screwed up. And I'm sorry."

"It's okay, Dad." Maggie smiled at Perkins. It was nice sitting outside with him and getting out of the rehab confines.

A small bit of relief passed through Sean. While the loss of Lars haunted him, he knew that he was finally making the right choice. Enough of this. Time to be a family man again.

"I'll call you with the details."

"Okay, Dad. I can't wait to tell Aimee." The momentary elation flipped to dread.

James.

In the conversation lull, Maggie spotted the old man approaching. She smiled. He was here again. Maggie waved and he waved back with a genial grin. The man was grandfatherly. Sweet. He was nice to spend time just watching and chatting with Maggie and Perkins. The man with the big blue ring.

"Okay, Mags. I'll be in touch soon. Love you."

"I love you, too, Dad."

He could sense her smiling as she parted. At least *she* was safe.

"And Dad?"

"Yeah?"

"Thanks."

"Bye, Mags. I'll see you soon."

Troubled, but knowing her timing was bad, Tanya approached. "Sean, we need to get to the embassy."

"You go. I've got to go back in. Call Rick, get me on a flight, and find out what we need to do to get my brother-in-law back to the States."

"What about the mission?"

"Mission? That's done. We found Bain, the rest of the crew was toast. Lars was supposed to help here, and now he's dead. There's some bullshit going on both here in Thailand and Burma that I'm not privy to that probably killed James. So fuck the mission. I'm done. I quit." Havens walked away into the sea of calamity at the hospital entrance.

Not knowing whether she should follow or head to the embassy, Tanya stood alone with her racing thoughts.

As Sean walked into the building, he remembered the note from Lars. Withdrawing it and unfolding the paper, he saw a sketch and writing: *Sean, this is the guy. Looks like my sketch work paid off. I know this man. Violardo. Italian Freemason Master. I think he is or was a military officer. Remembered because I stayed as a reciprocal guest in Italy at a Mason lodge where he spoke a number of years ago. Talked about how Masons helped save his boy with Swiss doctors. He's aged some, but I know it's the same guy. Shook his hand there. Same burns. BTW. I like this girl. She's interested in you. You have my blessing. -Lars*

The note toyed with Sean's mind and he stopped at the edge of the stairwell. Was this the bomber?

"Sean?"

He turned to find Tanya.

"I'm going to the embassy, but just wanted to make sure you were okay first." She looked at him hesitantly.

Havens pulled Tanya in and gave her a gentle but passionate kiss on the lips. He could feel her go rigid in surprise then relax into the moment. Breaking off, he caressed her arm. "I'm figuring it all out. Take this to the embassy and see what you can find out. If you can find his name anywhere, see if he is on any flights. Try all targets with bombings. Then…" Havens' mind was running at warp speed as thoughts were falling into place. "Then see if there are Mason lodges within a mile or two of the bombings."

His eyes tilted upward as he thought. "Also map Mason lodges to any other big cities where there have been bomb or terrorist attacks in the past, but not yet this year. Narrow that down by locations with major stock exchanges."

Tanya understood where he was going with this but she was still processing the kiss. Her instincts kicked in to absorb everything he was saying. She knew he cared for her but had to push her elation to the back of her mind. For now, she was being treated as a professional partner.

Not waiting for a reply, Havens darted up the stairs. He called back, "And then get us both out of here."

Chapter 62

Lars Bjorklund stirred. "Sean…Sean…Sean?" he moaned.

"Lars?"

"Seany?"

Havens ran to the bed and dropped, paying no attention to the glass pieces littering the floor. He felt like an idiot for not assessing vitals prior. "Lars, you alive?"

"I'm still working on that one. Pretty sure I'm blown up, though."

"Can you move? I'm sorry, I just assumed…" A glass shard was pressing into Havens' knees, but he remained attentive.

"I hurt real bad. I'm not sure if I'm stuck or if I can't move. It hurts, so that's good. I can wiggle my fingers and feet some."

"Okay, Lars. Don't move. I'm gonna get you out. And then we are all getting out of this shit."

Part III

"There are hunters and there are victims. By your discipline, cunning, obedience, and alertness, you will decide if you are a hunter or a victim. It's really a hell of a lot of fun. You're going to have a blast out here!"

—General James N. Mattis, USMC, 2003-2004

Chapter 63

"Comms all good now?" Rick inquired from the Tanberg video conference system back CONUS, and, for Rick, back in Fayetteville.

Sean and Tanya simultaneously confirmed. Tanya added, "All personnel are out of the SCIF, too. It's just us, sir. No Agency or embassy personnel have inquired about our use of the SCIF. RSO said it was swept yesterday."

Rick knew the Thai embassy's Regional Security Officer personally and was certain that he did a thorough job keeping any foreign bugs out of the sovereign building. "Same on my end," Rick confirmed. "Sean, are you comfortable with the arrangements for Lars? I understand he's going to be okay in due time."

"Yeah, thanks. They have him over at the naval base now and are looking to transport him back in a few days after he recovers from the surgeries. He's pretty screwed up. Can't really be on his back or front. I'm not sure how they're mobilizing him."

"Sounds like that was a pretty close call."

"I wouldn't say he's too agile, but I guess he had enough presence of mind to slam those drapes and dive. Blast was focused at standing level and without tamping it went outward in a 360. Wasn't a real sophisticated VBIED. Concrete wall shielded a lot of the direct blast and the hospital bed saved him from head trauma. Still, the force and concussion blew out a ton of glass and other things."

"Well, that's good news. I understand that you two are wrapping everything up but wanted to run something past me?"

"Yes, sir," Tanya affirmed as she spread out printed copies of search content. "But it's just a hypothesis. You didn't need to go through all the trouble of clearing a room. Nothing we have goes outside of TS/SCI levels."

"That's okay. Just wanted to make sure we could all speak freely. Whaddaya have?"

Havens started. "Well, I see you're sitting, so just open your mind for a bit. We think it actually might be coming out of, well, an irregular Freemason lodge."

Havens paused, waiting for Rick to shoot down his statement as ridiculous.

"I'm listening."

"Oh, all right. So, this isn't recognized by mainstream Freemasonary. There is an offshoot of the organization and there are individuals who have used it as a front. It seems that this one in particular, P2, has links to the Pond. It also seems that the lodge, this one from Italy, has been frequented by politicians, government officials, and a variety of dissidents over the years. It seems that they have united under a common purpose and formed a secret collective."

Tanya nodded along with Havens' narrative. She added, "This is beyond masonic mischief. It's a society that has a number of power player linkages that seem to go back to the Agency and a number of U.S. politicians and corporate elites."

Rick fidgeted in his chair. It appeared that they were losing him. The reality was that he couldn't believe they were putting something together that he had missed for years.

"We think this is where the bomber came from. His name is Paulo Violardo. Italian military intel."

Rick held up his hands. "Let's back this out. We have bombings across the globe, we have analysts from Langley being killed …"

"And some bullshit in Burma …" Havens piled on.

"Exactly, Sean. This is all a stretch. Who are the targets of an Italian mad bomber and why would the Pond be involved?"

"The people killed were all vulnerable and the objective was for targeted people or locations. The secret society provides the OPSEC. They have the built-in security measures needed and the means to do target collection while keeping a plot hidden from outsiders. Through the Mason lodges, they would have to be able to do recon and surveillance for the plot."

"Okay, Sean, now you lost me. I think this is thin. You jumped from secret lodges to Freemasons. Who's driving them around, Shriners in their go-carts and fez caps?"

"I think the Pond helped fund this and P2 provided the expertise for devices and resources. Or vice versa. That's how our bomber, or bombers, could get commercial and military-grade power sources, switches, initiators, precursors. Lars gave a report to Tanya that was pretty substantial. Talking to General Bain, I'm guessing that if the Pond, or the Agency with guys supporting the Pond, was set up in Burma, the stuff they are running around the golden triangle is either logistically supportive or it's used to curry favor or bribes. I don't know exactly. Rick, do you know anyone at the Agency running Southeast Asian drug ops?"

Sure. We still control the heroin trade. "Back up. We have a diverse set of command, time, victim operated devices. Some precursors, from what I understand, were dual use improvised. Main charges are blends of homemade, commercial, military. I agree it could be a network, but it could be more loose. Honestly, it sounds more realistic to be ISIS and extremist ideology. I'm not buying the Mason stuff, guys. Sorry. Let's table this until you get back."

Before Rick could get up from his chair and sign off, Havens kept at it. "Rick, Tanya was able to access a Homeland Security database, TripWire. She did some research and studied their OSINT IED Report. The bombings over the past year all coincide with previous bombings, down to the very compounds and MO used." Havens gestured to Tanya to continue.

"Sir, Sean's right," Tanya confirmed. "Lars took some samples of the hotel area that had an explosion. They did some clean-up, but he still found trace. Same thing with the club where the D-boys were killed. Lars got indicators from a number of compounds. Whoever is doing the bombing is fronting the blasts with local patterns but putting extra kick in for greater explosive stability and effect. It's not ISIS or apartment-based bomb-making terrorists."

"Okay, let's just say this is some other group. Table the Masons for now."

"Not Masons, P2," Sean corrected.

"Whatever. My next question is about what has yet to be targeted from the prior incident list. We know of France and Spain in the past weeks."

"That's right. France, Spain. So UK, and the U.S. if we don't count the analysts as prime targets. In the U.S., I would guess New York City would be likely."

Rick gave a deep sigh. "Sean, NYC is always likely. You guys have to give me something to work with."

"Rick, one of the oddities is that there has been a combination of white and black smoke that was reported to have emanated from the blasts. The white indicates this was likely a smokeless or black-powder explosion and the black smoke would have come from a military-type explosive like C-4 or plastic explosives. Obviously, the explosions happening in rapid succession indicates these were likely terrorist attacks. They're moving west. I'll bet they've been smoking the intel community members so they can fly under the radar. We all know who would have equal capabilities and both foreign and domestic access."

Rick pursed his lips. His mouth was dry and his tongue felt heavy. With a lick and a swallow, he managed to get out, "Okay. Sounds like the Pond. What next?"

Tanya stood up. She placed her palms on the table and leaned in toward the camera. "Sir, we need three avenues of approach: identify the bombers, identify the targets, and identify the leadership. If we knew more about the organization, we would know if they have leadership succession. It's violent, clandestine, and ideologically based, like a terrorist organization, but this group might be more resilient since it's composed largely of former military leaders, correct?"

"Um, yeah. It looks that way. Sean, would you agree?"

"Actually, sir, that is what Sean told me, I just wanted to see how you would react if it came from me," Tanya smirked.

Sean interjected, "Rick, given the fact that from the military side, these guys may have been involved in Pakistan, Syria, Yemen … have you noticed any crime increases in Ecuador, political protests in Belgium, demonstrations in Chile that could have been construed as Pond-related? Those are just off the top of my head right now."

"Hard to say, Sean," Rick acknowledged. "With the others being political transitions, armed conflict, and I'm guessing Thailand, France, and some of the other bombings being made to look like religious extremism, whoever is running this has a hierarchy and multiple layers. We may not be able to cut off the head of the snake."

"So start with one. Start with the Pond."

"No shit, Sean. That's why we brought you in. I'm not sure that what you're saying brings us any closer. I'm just getting a data dump."

Tanya sat back down. Sean looked frustrated.

Rick looked around the room, which was still empty. He didn't know what he was looking for, but he knew he was about to put his ass, and potentially his life, on the line.

He lowered his voice. "Look, guys, you're on the right track."

Sean and Tanya perked up.

"Here's what we know about the Pond. We know the Pond is run by a current Agency deputy director, Robert Johnsen. He has an ops officer named PASSPORT who handles global operations. Based on Robert's background, he would not give explicit orders, he would only demand that end-state objectives be met. We can't touch Robert and don't know PASSPORT's identity. If we could reach both of them, we could at least take out some of the Agency threat, but not all of it. If they have any lists, then we would be able to identify other insider threats. But we don't have access to that either. This shit is going to keep going and, hell, I can hardly keep my investments afloat. If we can't get our arms around this, I'm going to sell off my holdings and keep them in cash reserves because the shit is really going to hit the fan."

Havens looked at Tanya, who drilled a stare right back into him.

Sean was having an a-ha moment. "Rick, not only can they put people in office, they can manipulate the markets. Who can we get in touch with who is a trusted asset within DOJ, FINRA, or the SEC?"

"I'm not sure, but I know who to ask. Is this another rabbit hole, Sean?"

"Rick, how long have you been tracking the Pond?"

"I suppose about five to seven years."

"Who was covering them before that?"

"I know my dad had some guys on it, but I'm not sure who was assigned. The project had been out of the Agency for a while and evidently there wasn't any documentation that was passed on. We had to pick up from scratch."

"Who said you had to pick up from scratch?" Sean pressed.

"I don't see how it's any of your damn business. We have bigger problems than the history of the Pond investigation."

"Maybe not. Rick, is it possible that the Pond is nothing more than a big agent of influence? A provocateur that arises to make chaos out of things? To shift opinions and stir up trouble?"

Rick remained silent and attentive.

"I've been told that I was seconded to the Pond, seconded to the CIA, seconded to JSOC, when all along it was Title 50 work under the CIA. I don't believe that the Pond is a separate organization. I think the Pond exists as an ideology. Like Klansmen. Like ISIS."

"Bullshit."

"I honestly think that the Pond exists across the community as a conservative underground OSS type collective. Think starfish and the spider."

"Wait a second. Project Starfish." Rick snapped his fingers. "Years ago, there was a DoD start-up project that grew from a small Pentagon program office. The focus was on a leaderless organization of patriots who believed in the old OSS ways. Once it started to grow, people started carving it up and making it a conventional organization.

The combatant commands got involved and Starfish became part of JFCOM."

"Where did it go from there?"

"Nowhere. The members all quit and it sort of fizzled out. But there were a lot of Beltway bandits at senior levels, and then it spread to DC social elites and well-to-dos."

"So, not too unlike the OSS?"

"I was on an email listserv and a few IC guys wanted to meet up and discuss Starfish. They said it would be better to be 'a big starfish in small pond.' I didn't have much time for it and the guy who was taking the ball was a guy that Jerry didn't much like."

"Is it worth checking out?"

"Yeah, but let me check something first." Rick thumbed his mobile device frantically.

"Whatcha doing?" inquired Sean, puzzled and worried that his hunch was taking a strange course.

"Sean, I had an old email account that I was using." Rick paused. His fingers spread and typed and scrolled. "Damn. It's on my unsecured phone in the car."

"And?"

"Hold on." Rick's brow pulled into a frown while he searched his memory. He keyed in something on his device. "Holy shit," Rick cursed dryly. "I think some of them are here. Generals. SES members. Ex-Agency warlords. All the grey beards and white hairs that were Vietnam SOG, spooks, senators, business leads. There was a whole community of interest that has morphed into a community of purpose. A network. The old Pond was real and I suspect someone was able to start it up again somehow for funding, or maybe, as you suggest, it just became an ideological movement with control questions for access or close member links that could break off. Just like what we are seeing in the Pond's intel."

"So it grew slowly, or through scalp hunters who keep an eye out for uniquely qualified and disenfranchised people."

"Precisely, but from what I see here, Sean, there are old Pond members in the Agency with Directorate authority. Seventh-floor types."

"Rick, you said senators. Any of them listed there who are viable new CIA Directors?"

"Yeah, Milton Greenway. He's on the Senate Select Committee for Intel."

"He's a hawk. Wants to invade Iran. Rick, all this shit over the last year isn't about global politics. It's national politics between the power players. All that crap in Thailand, Europe, and here is a smoke screen to embarrass the current administration and Agency leads. I'm guessing the analysts that were killed are those who would be SMEs for what is really happening in those areas. I'll bet you lost Iranian, Russian, Chinese, and similar Intel leads. People who could contradict what power players may be saying. They've blinded the intel community by taking out those in the know. A conservative shift in views, reactions, and politically motivated responses just moves the power to your Starfish boys. That's great!" Sean exclaimed.

"Why the hell is that great?"

"Because now we have a hit list!" Havens pointed a finger gun at the screen and shot.

And you, Havens, have figured it out. I'm staying out of this. "I'll forward you the mail list from my unsecure line to yours. See if you recognize any names. Keep in mind, not everyone is involved. Just because someone's on the list doesn't make them a bad actor."

"Kill 'em all, let God sort them out."

"Not funny, Sean. Not funny."

I'm not exactly joking. "Chat with you later, Rick."

Chapter 64

"What time is our flight?" Havens asked.

Tanya checked her mobile device. "We have four hours until we need to leave for the airport. We need to swing by the COS office and get your passport. They got you an entry stamp."

"Okay, great. Thanks." Havens flipped through more of the papers and reached into Tanya's stack.

"Sean, why didn't you give Rick more info about Paulo being a potential hard hit I think the JSOC analysts that I sent stuff to will get some intel soon. From the note that Lars gave you." She blushed. "The part about the bomber and the sketch."

"Ha, ha, spill it," he coaxed.

She tightened her smile. "We know he's our guy."

"Yeah, and when we confirm it and give it to Rick, what do you think will happen?"

"He'll send it up the chain."

"Exactly."

"So what are you thinking?"

Sean reached out and put his hand on Tanya's. "Tanya. These guys are causing global mayhem. That's bad. But frankly, that's not my lane. I can't change it. Here's what I *can* do. These people killed my wife. They nearly killed my daughter and my brother-in-law. I was ready to quit today. I called my daughter and said I was coming home. Now I have to call her and tell her that I'm not."

"You're not?" Tanya contained her shock from his change of plans.

"Nope." Havens stacked up the papers and stood. "I'm going to tell her that I have to keep a promise to her that I made earlier this month."

"Which is?"

"I'm going to kill these motherfuckers."

"Sean, wait. You need to think this out. You can't just go killing people off. Certainly not in the U.S. You'll get yourself killed. Are you insane?"

"Probably."

She bit her lip and shook her head. "That's not the way," she rebuked.

"Tanya, I know what's going on here with this Pond, P2, the whole lot. I built this shit myself. They have a bunch of nominee directors of off-the-books companies conducting thousands of illicit transactions all over the world. It works hand in hand with their shell companies. They use those companies to buy legitimate companies. Once due diligence is performed by legitimate banks, they burn them. Meanwhile, they make investments. Since they know what they are going to attack, they can play the markets and make billions. For a cut, the owners of those companies have to pay a levy, probably in the form of campaign contributions to elect and keep politicians that will support their interests. So, our Italian guy? He's not traveling by his true name. He's not traveling by an Italian passport. You need to look for a British Virgin Islands passport. Ireland or New Zealand. Matter of fact, try checking into Omar Hodge Building Torotola British Virgin Islands. You did this before in threat finance work. Find one of those passports that is traveling all over the world to our hotspots. If you get a big hit on that, see where the next flight is booked. Wherever he's going, there is going to be a big boom. I need to run before our flight. I just put in another SIM card and missed a bunch of calls from a friend in D.C. Anything else?"

Tanya cleared her throat. "Well, we should probably talk about your son."

Chapter 65

"When were you going to tell me?" Havens finally managed to stammer during their flight.

Tanya put down the paper she was reading. "You haven't said a word for hours and now you want to talk on the plane?"

"I had a right to know."

"You had no right. You weren't a father. You were 'operational.' Isn't that the word you used?"

"That's not fair. This is someone's *life*. I had a right to know."

"You don't think I tried to find you? Tell me," Tanya lowered her voice more. "How the hell am I supposed to find a covered person in a project that is compartmented and an entity that doesn't officially exist? I knew you weren't CIA after I checked everything I could, but anything aside from that was a closed door and I couldn't ask anyone."

Havens remained silent.

"I wasn't going to not have the baby, despite the fact that it completely destroyed my career at the Agency. I had to get a job through Defense after I took leave. So don't go lecturing me."

"I'm surprised." Sean paused. "That's not even the word. I'm completely blown away. It only happened the once and it wasn't even supposed to happen."

"Well, blame yourself, Quickdraw." Tanya eked out a small smile.

"You should have told me as soon as you saw me again."

"Oh, right. 'Hey, stranger. Remember me? You said we needed to have sex so we wouldn't get killed in Turkey. Then you disappeared. Here's a child support bill.'"

"Child support. Shit, Tanya. I hadn't even thought of that. I … I'm sure I owe you a lot. But you know it wasn't like that in Turkey. You make it sound like I was a senior and you were a freshman on spring break."

"Stick to the issue, Sean. You don't exist. You're not a father to him. Uncle Sam might as well be his biological father." Her voice rose. Tanya looked around. Her fellow passengers seemed to be minding their own business.

"What's his name? Do you have a picture?"

"I don't carry a picture of him when I do work travel overseas. I guess he is a pretty good blend of both of us. Dark hair. Darker complexion. His name is Sam."

Havens grinned at the correlation. "That's funny."

She gave him a stern look. "He's proud that his father was a soldier, but sad that he died in the war."

Sean's slowly mounting happiness was quickly doused by the news that the boy thought his dad was dead. He swallowed.

"I see."

Tanya could tell Sean was hurt, but she couldn't ever have imagined that Havens would be part of their life. At least, not like Tanya wanted him to be. Sean was available now, but he had baggage. The kind that neither she, nor her son, were ready for. Her mom, the boy's secondary caregiver, would not be pleased that she shared the news with Havens. Or her bestie. Or her shrink.

"Tanya. Who else knows?"

Friggin' mind reader? "A few people. No one you would know, or who would know you."

"Why would we be put together for this mission?"

"We weren't. I was assign …" *Jerry.*

"And you said to James that you were recruited from Yale." *Jerry.* "Did you tell an Agency or DOD shrink?"

"Yes," she admitted sheepishly.

"They read our files. They put us together."

"Matchmakers?" She looked in Havens' eyes for some softness.

His eyes were dark and cold. "No. Puppet masters."

"What do you mean?"

"It means that they are counting on you to be a softie headcase who is going to get all clingy on me. Which I by no means am saying you are. It's just what they are expecting. And they expect me to need a family and direction. Right now I'm a wild card. Unstable."

"What are you going to do?"

"Same thing I said I was going to do. I'm heading north when we land. Right after I get some things."

"I see." Tanya tilted her head down and cast her eyes on her small carry on. She thought of her son's photo in the zippered inside pocket of the satchel. "I might be a little bit of a head case. I shared with my therapist that I saw you and hoped you might be interested in me."

Sean heaved a big breath in and out, then put his hand on Tanya's leg. He patted it gently and looked over, giving her a smile and a wink. He kept his hand on her leg. She put her hand over his.

Chapter 66

Sean Havens hopped the fence and crossed the fifty yards of meticulously groomed lawn. Key on the Starfish list was an individual he had worked for in the past. General Frye. The man was now a retired general officer who was involved with Silver Star, the entity that set Havens up and orchestrated the attack on his family.

Rick approved Havens' request for two days off to see his daughter. Sean had spent three hours with Maggie and two long hours with Aimee sharing the news of James. He then drove from Fort Bragg to the National Capital Region, where he identified one of the targets and performed some quick recce both physically and in cyber. While she was not cleared, and not permitted, Havens had indulged his daughter with some basic hacking questions that would now come in handy.

Aimee accepted the news with strength knowing that James would want to go out that way—still serving his country. Some deeply buried part of her had known that James wouldn't be coming back. She came to terms with that when he left, and subconsciously prepared for it each day that he was gone. She would miss him dearly, but frequent deployments had turned their marriage to one of friendship and respect. It was his last dance. Aimee was happy that he could have the final deployment that he felt so desperately robbed of. Sean shared how James was killed saving Karen villagers. Rick had provided a civilian citation, which she accepted with great pride. News that the military would likely recover the body for a funeral also helped. The Army chaplain, a family friend, showed up just before they parted ways. Aimee had lost so much, but she was a Pineland woman. Heart of gold forged from iron.

Sean hoped the mission now would fare better. Without some technical expertise from X, he'd have to wing it a bit.

The drug-laced steaks were a failure. Plan B fixed the situation and silenced the guard dogs before it happened. As a dog lover, shooting the dogs was unpleasant for Sean. The two dead Rottweilers now laying along the fence line would agree.

Havens thumbed his iPhone to check Wi-Fi connection points. He knew the alarm would have a Wi-Fi or radio backup if the line was cut. He scrolled the IP and MAC addresses and finally saw the vendor name he was searching for. It showed as being inactive. Havens refreshed his mobile application. Inactive. He could use some technical advice. *Where the hell did X disappear to, anyway?*

Worst case scenario, he entered the house, the alarm went off, and he smashed the speaker to silence the noise. Then he would have three to four minutes, minimum, to get what he needed. That was plenty of time. Sean Havens had enough ammo to take out any first responders, but that would be out of the question, even if the tables were turned on him by some fluke event.

From a zippered pocket, Havens pulled out his lock-pick and attempted to first breach what appeared to be a utility door. The deadbolt was accommodating. So too was the lower lock.

Thank you.

Havens cracked the door slightly. With less than a quarter inch open, he pulled a dental mirror out and shone a small light to find an alarm sensor. *Bingo.*

Havens switched one set of tools for another, retrieving a small metal magnetic strip with adhesive on its back. He lifted the little white bar up to the crack, gently opening the door and placing the plastic-coated metal strip on the alarm sensor.

Silence.

Havens waited in the darkness to see if his eyes would adjust to the lack of light well enough to guide his way. There was a dim light shining a few rooms away. Best go with the NVGs. Better safe than sorry.

Sean worked his way through the lower level of the McMansion, keeping as close to the walls as he could. At times the hardwood floors creaked. Havens tried to estimate where joists would be to minimize the give and maximize nailed support on the flooring.

Shit! Another creak.

Havens mounted the staircase, feet spread to climb the steps using the same theory of noise reduction.

Creak. *Shit!*

Judging by the exterior architecture from the front and rear of the house, Sean's hypothesis was that the master suite would be to the left. As a backup plan, he had reviewed the builder's house plan samples, which seemed to correlate to his hunch.

He depressed the latch handle that emitted a glowing white green visual from his eyewear. Cracking the door open inch by inch, he could hear snoring.

The general's wife had passed more than a year ago. The sleeping man was alone.

Approaching the bed, Havens covered the general's mouth with a gloved hand and rapped him on the head with the black silencer.

Quick to wake, the general's eyes flashed wide with terror. *Havens!*

"Hello again, sir. Here's the drill. You are not going to make a sound until we clear some things up. You are alone in this home, correct? Shake up yes, side no."

The general shook no.

"Is the other person in the home armed? Same drill."

General Frye closed his eyes and shook his head no.

"Is it a man?"

The general shook no.

"A woman?"

He nodded yes.

"Family?"

Frye confirmed again.

"Then you best be real quiet." *And then I'm going to kill you anyway for my little girl.*

The general nodded.

"You know you took everything from me," Havens said dryly. "You played me like a pawn. Used friends against me. Turned brothers against brothers. I'm going to take my hand from your mouth and you are going to tell me who gave you your orders. Do you understand?"

The general closed his eyes. Havens gave the older man a solid rap on the forehead again with the pistol. The eyes widened again in fear, but with a sense of purpose to withhold information. "Do you understand?" Havens asked again, more aggressively this time. Sean put the handgun barrel opening between the man's eyes. "I have no reason to let you live if you aren't going to help me. I have no reason to let anyone in the house live, for that matter."

The man just stared up at Havens, processing his limited options.

"Papa?"

Havens spun on heel and toe to engage the unexpected third party. He pointed his sidearm at the noise.

A young girl was visible through the limited lighting. The general struggled to speak. Havens could tell the man's fear was earnest for the child's well-being. Sean slowly lifted his hand, his gun still trained on his target.

"Sweetie, go back to bed. You go to your mama's room if you need something. Go, now," General Frye instructed in soft voice.

The girl remained still. Havens knew that she could see him despite the relative darkness of the room.

Sean thought it best to speak. "It's okay, honey. I'm a friend of your grandpa. He called me about something for work."

"How did you get in the house? Papa said it's safe in the house."

The general sat up for the first time. Havens moved his firearm cross body to his left so the barrel was again felt by the general. "Go on. Go to your mommy's room," he encouraged, a bit more forcefully this time.

Havens worried she might call out or alert her mommy of the strange man in Papa's dark room. *Not going to work. Shit. How am I going to kill you now? And you know that I can't. I need leverage.*

"Honey, why don't you crawl in bed with Papa. You can snuggle up next to him and I'll be leaving in just a minute. Can you do that for me?"

"You're a burglar."

"No, I'm not a burglar. Burglars are bad guys. I used to work for your papa with the military soldiers."

"My papa's a general. He has a fancy uniform," the girl informed Havens both enthusiastically and loudly.

"Shhh," Havens said in a small voice. "We don't want to wake up Mommy."

"She's already awake. I heard her when I left my room. She is calling someone. She said on the phone she thinks someone is in the house. I did good not bothering her when I could tell she was on her phone, so I came to your room. I did good, right, Papa? Oh, hi, Mommy!"

Sean whipped around to see the woman in the shadows. He saw something long protruding waist level from her. Havens was certain it wasn't a broom.

"*Who are you?* The police are on their way. Margie, run downstairs to your spot. I have a shotgun, mister, and I will blow your ass straight to Hell. *Go, Margie! Now!*"

Havens grabbed the general and put the gun to his head.

"No one is moving! Margie, you stay right there. Ma'am, I'm not planning on hurting anyone unless someone does something stupid. You are on the verge of real stupidity. Turn on a light. My name is Sean Havens. I work for the government. My family was attacked on orders from your father. My wife was killed. You probably saw it on the news. The Chicago family killed. The Chicago train wreck. The Acela line. Minneapolis. They are all linked. I just needed a name from your father. That's all I want. I knew your brother, Robbie, who died in Enduring Freedom. I mean you no harm."

"Dad?"

Havens heard her voice shake. She was listening. She didn't see Sean's story as beyond the realm of possible. Robbie Frye, the general's son, was a man Havens had once known. He was a good man who served honorably and gave his all for his brothers in combat.

Havens pressed the gun more forcibly on the general.

"Dianna, don't do anything foolish. But don't move the gun. I know this man. Right now, you are a threat to him. Don't become a target. Sean, your wife isn't dead. She's very much alive."

Sean's arm dropped.

Dianna flipped on the lights.

Still processing the news, Sean turned to Dianna. Blinded by the light change, he squinted his eyes and pulled slightly away.

The general ordered, "Shoot, Dianna, shoot! Run, Margie!"

Havens dove to the side. His finger, never on the pistol trigger, moved down on the grip as he used his right wrist and slightly bent arm to guide his fall to a momentum tuck and roll Aikido move that sprung him up to Dianna's position.

The loud shotgun pop in the bedroom caused Margie to stop in her flight and scream.

Dianna screamed next, seeing the bloodied gore oozing from her father and realizing she was responsible for it.

"Stupid woman, I was telling the truth!"

Havens ripped the shotgun from her hands. Resisting striking Dianna in front of Margie, he threw the shotgun across the bedroom.

The little girl howled in terror, holding her ears and stomping up and down in a rapid panic march but moving nowhere.

Havens blocked her view. He commanded Dianna, "Get her outta here and take her to your room!"

"You bastard, you killed him! You killed him!"

I was going to, but … "You shot him, woman! Get your kid out of here! She shouldn't see this!"

Havens heard the general wheezing. The sucking chest wound was causing his body to shut down.

He grabbed the general's pajama shirt at the lapels, drawing the man up. "Tell me about my wife! I swear I'll butcher your family like you did mine!"

Dianna screamed. She grabbed Margie by the arm and hauled her from the room.

"Don't test me, general, I've got nothing to lose."

The dying man took no chances with his own kin. Havens heard sirens nearing in the distance.

"Alive." Blood frothed at the general's lips. He gurgled and swallowed hard, gasping for air.

"Where?" Havens shook the dying man. "Who has her?"

"She is safe. CIA took her from us." The old man sputtered and seized. Blood melted from his slack jaw. His eyes started rolling back in his head.

"Where, you old bastard?" Sean shook the general. He resisted slapping the old man.

The general swallowed hard. He grabbed Havens' arms. Squeezing and gasping, he expelled "Middleburg."

"Middleburg?"

Havens pushed the man's arms down and shifted immediate attention to a window at the rear of the room. Fearing drawing more attention with noise, Sean opened the window as fast as he could, tangling the sheers and curtains. Looking down, he saw that the landscaping along the brick exterior was soft-limb evergreen bushes of some sort. No matter. In the next instant, Havens was dropping, feet and knees together, just to the side of the bushes. He drew his knees up and rolled to the side to absorb the impact.

That's gonna hurt tomorrow.

Havens bounded across the lawn. He heard tires screeching, and then voices. Doors opened and slammed and feet pounded against concrete.

Breaking and entering. That's all they have me on. Killing dogs. They can't hold me for killing dogs if there are no dogs.

When Havens was upon the canine carcasses, he tossed them over the fence and followed after. He grabbed their collars, dragging them behind him in a low crouch as he fled the area. Still under cover of darkness as he reached his vehicle, he popped the trunk, hid his weapon under the spare tire, and piled the dead dogs over the tire cover.

Sorry, pups.

Miles down the road, Havens pulled off on a tucked-away gravel road. He knew of an abandoned small quarry that was deep with water from an accidental spring leak. Sean remorsefully tossed the dogs into the deep pool and headed off for answers. His mind never letting go of the possibility of Christina being alive, but his heart was filled with dread that it could be a fruitless lie.

The CIA? Best call Rick.

He felt sick. A wave of nausea passed through his body and he tightened his sphincter. A headache was setting in.

Chapter 67

Havens was ready to dial Rick when his phone vibrated.

Tanya. He answered reluctantly.

"Sean? Where are you?"

"Tanya, I can't talk. Something's come up."

"Well, you might want to hear this. Paulo is heading to New York City. The target has been identified. He has another flight in two days to London. That means tomorrow or the next NYC is going to get hit."

"Tanya, I can't deal with this now. Get the intel to Rick and let him figure it out."

"Sean! You said yourself they wouldn't do anything about it in time. If anything goes wrong, Paulo will get tipped off and disappear."

Sean rubbed his aching head with his free hand. "Tanya, one of the targets just said Christina is still alive."

A rush of panic washed over Tanya. "Oh my God, Sean. Do you believe him?"

"I don't know. He's dead now. I don't know what to do."

She felt as though an elephant just copped a squat on her chest. "Do you know where she is?" Tanya prodded not sure she wanted to know.

"Not completely. Just a town. He said the CIA has her. I know of an old Agency safe house out there. We used to bring vetted assets there for polygraphs. It's too far-fetched, but nothing has made sense over the last year."

"Okay. You go there. I'll go to New York."

"And search the whole city?"

"No, Sean. I know where he's staying."

"I need to call Rick. Let me call you back."

Chapter 68

"Hello, Jerry," came a familiar and unwelcome voice on the phone.

Slow to wake from his sleep, Jerry slurred, "What do you want now, Robert? Good god, does your harassment know no hours?" Jerry blindly groped the nightstand for his glasses.

"I figured your prostate is so enlarged at your age that you might be up taking a piss. I saw you at the garden today. Find what you were looking for?"

"It's almost planting season. That's a foolish observation."

"Yeah? Well that's funny."

"Why is that funny?"

"'Cause I know a Jew boy was digging out there the night before. Matter of fact, I know it was one of Meir Dagan's Jew boys. So, I sez to myself, *Why would the former director of Seyeret Matkal, now retired, have one of his old boys out by your garden plot at night?*"

Jerry remained silent, his hands growing clammy.

"Cat got your tongue?"

Jerry hit speaker on the device so he could simultaneously check for any priority emails. Everything was status quo. "If I had a dead drop there, you would know it by now and certainly wouldn't tell me."

"I would if I could read *Jew*."

"Playing an ignorant and racist hillbilly doesn't suit you. You would cipher or translate any note you found and relish your access to my sources. And further, I might add, tradecraft would not have me associated with a drop and pickup in a place I frequented. So, Robert, what do you want?" Jerry was up and out of bed. He pulled the sheets taught across the mattress. The call required an early trip to the office.

"One of my boys died tonight. Guessing by the intel that I have, that Havens boy did it. That's called sniffin'. Matter of fact, that's now snuffin'. I'm going to need some assurances now. Frankly, I don't know what my boy told your boy. Given it was General Frye, he likely pissed off Havens with the wife and kid thing. I'm guessing your boy was pretty motivated. Can't imagine what intel he collected before killing the general in cold blood."

"Maybe you should kill yourself and ask him in Hell." Jerry decided on the oxblood loafers over the black wingtips. He closed the closet door and headed to the bathroom.

"You know, you never were really good at articulating threats, or whatever you want to call that pussy remark. I'm guessing one of two things. He shared about Havens' wife, whom you have, so that doesn't bother me much. Or he shared about my organization. That could wreck some planning."

"Isn't that a shame?" Jerry muted the phone and turned the shower handle to hot. He left the bathroom and sat at the foot of the bed on a Victorian upholstered tufted bench.

"Well, it will be for you. This is about America. This is about once again becoming a dominant superpower. And if you put your dick in it and fuck it up, I will personally see to it that your Bonesmen and all their generational linkages are wiped from this planet. See, my target is in New York." Robert waited for a reaction.

"You wouldn't dare," Jerry braved. He was now engaged again in the dialogue.

Now sell him. Robert softened his tone. "Hear me out. Chinese and Russian oligarchs are laundering their dirty rubles in high-end Manhattan apartments. Got some in the Time Warner Center, 200 block of West 25th Street in Midtown. Some even on Wall Street across from the stock exchange. I'm looking to disrupt that a bit. I'd like my man to remain unmolested. In turn, we make it look like a domestic terror act. FBI takes the blame and you all get more power to work domestically. I can assure that with the upcoming elections. We already have our man."

"Lies. If you are hitting New York City, I'd bet anything that your network will be buying up U.S. Treasuries as safe havens for assets. Right now, most brokerage houses are operating at a risk off position, so they're buying equities. After the bombing, they will go to only secure investments. You'll start playing derivative markets and buy cheap calls for option trading. Bottom line, if you are planning this, your network knows what the markets will do and when and can play both sides of buying and selling in our market just as you have been doing globally."

Robert gave a loud whistle. "Boy, someone has been doing his homework. But here is the catch."

"Always a catch, Robert."

"You let this go, and I have a way for your Bonesmen to get a payoff too. One, you invest the same way that we would invest. Two, we are placing the explosives in high-rent areas where there is this shameful foreign investment. Nothing too big in the way of explosives. We don't want to hurt anyone. There will be some structural and cosmetic damage, but those investors haven't bought insurance due to the 'know your customer' provisions. You with me, smart guy? Uninsured, they will have to pay cash for repairs or dump the place for another."

"Meaning?"

"Don't be a dimwit. You and your boys prepare to purchase the real estate in cash. The price will be well below what the Chinese or Russians paid. Then, as a political act of goodwill, you can sell it back to those same buyers later for much higher prices. It'll be our way of giving back from 9/11. Regulators never checked the market sell offs then, and it certainly won't cause a blip on our radar now, especially since we have more regulators in our pocket. Everyone will come out a winner."

The phone went silent.

"Think about it, Jerry. New York City will get to rebuild and modernize."

"Is the President on board?"

"Frankly, I don't think we'll bother to ask him. He's gone rogue on us, thinking nothing will happen to us on a big scale. Dumb liberal pussy. I'm still not sure that we'll let him serve it out. That's not my call. That's up to the Order. We like the V.P."

"And what do we have planned for their markets? I know you won't stop with New York."

"We do the same as we have been doing. We'll create an event in their territory, buy up the equity market shares using bogus trade receipts. When they call them, they'll be of no value. The Bank of England has a large investment portfolio on this area, so we would have you instruct them to sell off now and jump in on real estate investments just outside the blast zone. My boys win, your boys win, American diplomacy wins, the population remains fearful, and we keep spending on defense. Winner, winner, chicken dinner."

Jerry processed the scheme, silently looking for a trap.

Robert seemed to read his mind. "You can't stop this."

"I can try."

"For what? Your people would crucify you if they learned what they had in their grasp."

"Even if we save one person, it's worth the effort to try."

"Jer-itol, I told you. Minimal casualties. If you think it's about the people, you're an idiot. Want to know the real casualty? They're already dropping. The markets. It's not about bodies. It's about public trust. Market response. We're tanking. What purpose could that serve? We need people to make money, to reinvest money and get this country back on its feet. We make money because we are the ones putting it up. We build the infrastructure, we create jobs. We should make the rules."

"I'm not sure why you're telling me all this."

"Who would you tell? You don't know who's in your camp these days. You and your boys don't need to come to the Order. We just need to be better aligned. It's better for the country and better for individuals. Ultimately, it's better for the world."

"What do you need from me?"

"That's the spirit!" Robert hooted. "Well, I have a score to settle with Sean Havens."

"You have no score. You don't even know the man."

"Feels like a score. He happened to be the guy who got propped up before you took him off. I don't like to lose. Can't let that go. I'd like him dead. I'd also like a counterintelligence blemish at the Agency. Tom Walkins, up in counterintelligence, isn't playing with either of us. Let's kill Havens. We'll save his wife and the Agency CI takes the blame for detaining her. Mother and daughter are reunited. You give them some cash to make their lives better. Least we can do being good Christian men. Well, I'm just speaking for myself here. And we both win by having someone of mutual interest replace Walkins in the CI department."

"And what do my people and I get out of it?"

"Well, riches to start. Golden Triangle trade routes. I'll give you back the Agency. I'm retiring and we'd rather take over DoD under this new administration. We'll prop up Milton Greenway as CIA Director. Senate Select Committee for Intel. He's one of yours." *As far as you know*, Robert thought.

"Done."

"Oh, and hands off PASSPORT. You just let us be. Find something else for your son. Give him any of our former posts at the Agency. Clear our guys out. And keep away from Panama for the time being. Clear all funds out. No questions asked."

"Agreed."

"And Jerry?"

"Yes, Robert?"

"Don't you fuck me!"

Don't count me out just yet.

"I have a different proposal." Jerry gave a heavy sigh. He walked back to the closet and exchanged the loafers for the black wing-tips. "You'll like this better. And then we're even."

"I'm listening."

Havens dialed Rick's secure mobile. While it rang, he wiped his forehead. He felt hot. Dizzy. Rick answered the phone just before the call went to voicemail.

"Did you get caught? Do I need to bail you out?"

"Whaddya mean?" Sean searched around himself for a bottle of water. He felt feverish.

"Havens, I can't force you to be a team player. That would mean you would communicate to me your intentions and plans. I knew you were going straight to the target list."

Sean pulled his car over to the side of the road. He needed to walk this unsettled feeling off.

"Rick, one of the reasons I don't go to you, or anyone else, is the fact that I don't know who I can trust. I just learned my wife may be alive and in CIA custody. The only reason I'm not jumping through this line and tearing your throat out is I can't let myself believe it's true."

"It's not true. Not to my knowledge. There would be no reason for the Agency to be holding your wife. Think about it." Rick cast his eyes to his own bed. Large enough for two, but only used for the occasional hook-up. Fewer and farther between these days. Rick wasn't the marrying type. He lied to himself that what Havens was now going through was validation to being a bachelor.

"The general said she was at a safe house in Middleburg," Havens countered.

"Well, there *is* a safe house there, but I can guarantee your wife isn't there, nor is she anywhere else. I'm sorry, Sean. I wish it was true."

"Yeah. Me too. Hope is an evil emotion." Sean had walked about a hundred yards from his car. He wanted to sit back down and groaned at the thought of walking back. The nausea persisted. It had to be the emotional roller coaster of hope that he was stuck on.

Rick cleared his throat. "Did you find anything else of use?"

Sean released a deep exhale. Sparkles swirled before his eyes. "Tanya thinks there could be a link in … let me rephrase. She believes the bomber suspect is heading to New York. His pattern matches our hypothesis and analysis. We know where he is heading and I would like your permission to investigate further."

"Holy shit, Havens. Did you just ask for my *permission*?"

"Cut me some slack, Rick, I'm trying."

"Go to New York. And Sean, I don't want to rub salt in a wound, but you have a tendency of getting people around you hurt.

I'm not saying it's your fault. You might want to keep Tanya occupied with something else if you think you may endanger her."

"She's pretty sharp, Rick."

"Sean, she's real sharp. She's an analyst. Not a shooter. There was a reason she was pulled from the field at OGA."

"I know the reason behind that."

"I doubt it. She had a hellatious time getting out of the op you were on and then had a pretty hairy experience supporting SEAL MLEs afterward. She had the tickets and got the T-shirts, but she isn't as field-savvy as she should be."

"Then why attach her to me and send her to Thailand?" Back in the car, Sean let his head fall back on the rest. The phone felt heavy.

"Because she was staying in the embassy and she is the only person I could think of in your file that you would trust. Not my first rodeo with you, cowboy."

"Thanks, Rick," Sean moaned.

"Better get going, Havens. I might start thinking you're trained."

"I'm trying."

"I know, buddy. Hey, you alright? You sound a little out of it."

"I'm alright. Just wiped. Think its catching up to me. Then this thing with Christina. Just took the wind out of my sails. Not that you're my therapist, but just feel a bit alone all of a sudden. Speaking of which, any backup that you can send?"

"Three for three. I'm impressed you're opening your trust to me, but no. You're on your own. Just the way you like it, right? You going to be able to handle it? I'm sorry for the letdown."

"Yeah, and to your last point, I'm thinking I can almost start trusting you, too."

Rick paused for a moment of transparency. "Don't." He hung up.

"Well. Good talk, Rick." *In that case, I need to call some friends.* Havens looked at his watch. 2:45 AM. He was sweating profusely. *Still time to call the Bad Monkey bar in Tampa. Someone who could rally the band will be still finishing a can of PBR. Could always try Mad Dogs and Blue Iguana, too.* "Somehow, I need to close my eyes for a minute," Havens said out loud and put the car back in drive. Sean swatted at a buzzing mosquito. It hit him. *You little shits. Malaria. We had the wrong meds for the strain. Lovely.*

Chapter 69

The United Airlines pilot came on the loudspeaker and announced advanced landing preparations for New York City's LaGuardia airport. Sitting in his window seat, Paulo marvelled at the city on approach. The Statue of Liberty caught his eye.

Isis, Isira, Lebertus. Liberty now they call you. You whore of Babylon. You will bow and submit for your vile ways.

Fatigue was consuming Havens by the time he arrived in New York City. His muscles and joints ached. The plan was to reconnect with Tanya when he arrived. She was going to handle logistics and provide a SITREP.

"Tanya, Sean here."

"Where are you now, Sean?"

"Just coming out of Queens Midtown Tunnel," he yawned.

"Why'd you go that way?"

"Tanya. I'm here, okay? Never mind my directions. You weren't exactly explicit about where I needed to go."

"Sheesh. I thought you would have figured it out. I'm across from the Grand Masonic Lodge. Cut over and get to 23rd Street. I have two adjoining hotel rooms. One is overlooking the lodge front entrance and the other is a corner. It overlooks a vacant building, but from the window you can access a rooftop with a fire escape. Should be good for stakeout."

"Shit!" Sean spun his head and watched the exit pass by.

"What? I thought it was great!"

"No, not you. Missed the turn. Okay, I'm going to ditch my ride a couple blocks away. Is there a back or side entrance to the hotel? I'm guessing our friend doesn't know who we are, but I don't want to take a chance."

"It's New York. Not Chicago. No alleys."

"Just answer the fucking question, Tanya!"

"Hey! If we're working together, don't be a prick! I know you were dealt a shit blow of hope, but don't fucking take it out on me by being a complete asshole."

"That pretty well sums it up." His remorse showed.

"Hurry up. And change your attitude. Shit, Sean, you're as high maintenance as I am. Crazy bitch-boy."

Havens smiled. Frankly, he was looking forward to seeing her. "What room? I'm dressed low vis. I have kit with me."

"Go to the corner room, 523."

"Roger that. Need anything while I'm free to grab things?"

"Nope. I think we're good. Thanks."

"Well, let's hope he's here."

"He is. I got on a flight that landed before his. I went a couple gates over from his arrival and watched him get off the plane."

"Holy shit. Please tell me you're joking."

"Not at all. I did good, right?"

"Were you seen?"

"No," she replied flatly. "I was completely discreet. No way he saw me. Think I'm getting better at the field work stuff," she replied with pride.

"Tanya! I'm not talking about him! A guy like that is going to have watchers. People watching people watching him!"

Tanya didn't say a word.

"Did you follow him?"

"No. I knew he was going to the lodge, so I stayed back. I took a cab to the hotel."

"Did you go straight? Please tell me you had the cabbie drive you around for a while so you could run an SDR."

"I didn't think of surveillance detection routes." Tanya was crestfallen. Espionage 101. Failed.

"Get out of the room."

"Sean, I'm sure its fine."

"Tanya! Get out of the damned room now!"

"Sean. Don't talk to me like I am a kid."

"Get out of the fucking room now! Don't make me lose you, too!"

Havens dropped his phone on the passenger seat and floored the gas pedal.

Tanya used the bathroom, collected her things, and headed for the door.

A knock came from the adjoining room entrance.

That was fast. Prick.

"You know Havens heard about his wife," Rick told Jerry on the phone.

"I suspected. I received a call quite early this morning. About 2 AM. It was Robert." The support staff member cleared the bone china and serving dishes from Jerry's office, parting with a nod, rolling the cart out of the room and closing the door behind.

"Don't suppose it was anything you could have shared with me right after? Same team, right Jerry?"

Rick had endured a lifetime of secrets with his old man, and despite being in the same secret organization, Rick was still out of the loop.

"It's interesting how and when you address me as your father and when you address me by my first name."

"Too bad that's not what I called you to discuss," Rick said flatly.

"I didn't tell you, as I don't tell you many things. As long as it won't hurt you, I allow your reactions to be genuine. One less thing to hide in this bloody profession of ours. You assuaged him of the notion of his wife, no doubt."

"I lied. When will you ever just say it like it is?"

"And I made a deal." Jerry reviewed the images of Burma on his 24-inch desktop monitor.

"You sold him out. I thought we had an understanding."

"Son, it will save lives. You, yourself, said that Havens can't be relied upon. That his utility will be more costly than his value at this point in his life."

395

"He deserves better. He has heart. The guy has lost nearly everything and he should be with his kid and yet he's still trying to save the world, running off to ..." *Shit!*

"Where is he, son?" Jerry keyed in text to pull a map of Manhattan.

"Screw you."

"He's going to New York, isn't he, Rick?" Jerry zoomed in on the map. He switched the view to see actual buildings and street imagery in 3D.

"Leave it alone."

"Rick, they are going to let his wife live. She will be reunited with Sean's daughter. His wife and child will be much better off together than his daughter will be with a father running all over the world. Let him go."

Jerry typed across the keyboard. He retrieved a display of presidential candidates, double clicking on one in particular.

"No. I won't. No more. No more, Dad."

"If you don't give him up, they'll kill his wife, kill his child, hunt him down anyway, and it will spoil our ... détente."

"You are bowing to the Pond."

"I am being forced to bow to much more than the Pond for the good of our family, the CIA, and our nation. Your future. Your safety, Rick."

"I know what I need to do."

"Their blood will be on your hands, Rick." Jerry stood from his desk and walked to the window overlooking the dense woods surrounding the Langley complex.

"I won't stand by and watch this happen. And shame on you." Rick thumbed the End Call button. *I can be in Virginia before nightfall. I'll get her for you, Sean. It takes more than just you to make a team.*

Chapter 70

While Tanya was rushed and recognized the urgency in Sean's voice, in a moment of déjà vu, she remembered once opening the hotel room door for Sean so many years ago in Turkey. How she had anticipated his arrival that day. How she anticipated him now. He pissed her off, and yet, she never felt safer than when he was around.

As she unlatched the lock, the door flung inward, knocking her head and slamming her against the wall. Two large men burst through the door, one flinging her like a rag doll into the room.

Tanya fell backward but had the presence of mind not to fight the momentum. She rolled out while reaching for her concealed carry from the small of her back.

The man closest to her had already holstered his firearm, confident that he had control of the situation. He floundered with a suitcoat that covered his weapon.

Tanya unloaded on him with her Beretta Nano 9mm pistol. She stitched the man center-mass, working the rounds up to his forehead as he tumbled forward. She moved to her left but was blocked by a low ottoman just out of sight.

Her pistol hand was knocked down by the assaulter's dead fall.

The second assaulter cracked down across her forehead with the black polymer of a Glock 26 handgun.

Exiting the elevator, Havens oriented himself to the door numbers, spun and sprinted down the hall. He pounded on the first of the two hotel room doors.

No response.

Havens pounded again with one hand and redialed Tanya's number with the other.

Nothing.

Looking to his left and right, he eyed the door and frame. Metal. *Fuck it.*

Havens unholstered a concealed HK45. He shot twice at the lock and shouldered through the door.

"Tanya! Tanya!" He tore through the entryway missing subtle signs of the scuffle. He was hit with another wave of nausea and lightheadedness.

Okay, maybe she left for a bit. He looked for any evidence of items she might have left behind. *Cleared out. Maybe she listened and left. No. She would have called or answered.* Havens checked his watch. It had been just over fifteen minutes since they spoke last. *You have maybe two minutes here, tops. Okay. Assumption. They have her. Would she have fought? Yes. She would have tried to buy time. Would she have screamed? Yes, unless they surprised her and muffled the sound. Or threatened her at gun point. Assume she's abducted since she's not dead here. They would want to know what she wants. Interrogate her here.*

Shit! He spotted two cups of coffee. In a few leaps to the mugs, he saw one was half empty. He felt both. One warm. The second hot. *She made me coffee. They knew someone else was coming.* The aroma of the coffee made him wretch. *Get it together, Havens. Power through.*

He scanned the room high and low, frantically searched for a clue. The door to the adjoining room was closed. *Give me something, anything, Tanya!*

The door was unlocked. He entered the next room.

Big, dead man is a good clue. Shit!

Havens went straight for the other room door and saw a few small, dark circles on the grey carpet. He pressed down on the mark. The blood was fresh.

His phone rang while he was trying to find a trail.

Tanya! No.

"Hey, brother," Sean answered hopefully.

"S'up Frittah! Heard you were looking for me."

"Reilly, I'm up to my ass in a situation."

Conor O'Reilly, or Reilly, was a former Navy SEAL with a specialty in hostage rescue. The two men had known each other for years collaborating on asymmetric warfare applications down in Tampa. Havens continued, "I don't know if I can pay anything, but I just lost my partner in an abduction in New York City. I need your bloodhound skills. And I suspect we might have another terror event in the city in the next day or two."

"Well, fuck! I want in on that. I'm just pulling my dick at CENTCOM …"

"Reilly, man, I don't mean to cut you off, but it might be too late. I'd need you and some of the guys here now. A few hours, max."

"Well, shit. If it's credible, can't the powers that be help?"

"It's credible, but more involvement could blow it. We don't have time to plan. I need dudes who have already planned. This is perfect for you since it's a K&R situation now too. Fuck. I'm at a loss."

"Well, good news is some of the guys are in NYC now."

"For what?"

"There's still fighting over by Ground Zero to get the statute moved. There's a ceremony. Tommy, Puck, Cheeto, and 8-Ball are still there. They drove up, so I know they have heat in their rigs. Shit, they were even demoing some stuff and had a shooting event in Jersey on the way. They may be well charged with toys. I could be there with some more cats too, but I need a ride. What's the latest you could still use us?"

Havens checked his watch as if he had an answer. "I dunno, maybe …" *The button.* "Reilly, let me call you back. I have an idea but I have to see if I can find her right now. She took out one guy and is either escaping and evading or they have her. See if you can get in touch with the other dudes. Put them on standby and tell them I have a national security situation."

"You got it, brother. Out."

Havens thumbed his watch to the app where the distress button was hidden. He pressed the red dot. *Here goes nothing.*

Sean Havens continued scanning the carpet for any clues. He headed toward the stairwell.

The Masonic Hall glowed in the darkness of the side street. Its crest was displayed with two beaming lights over the double door. Gold leaf adorned the stone carvings in ornate trim, decorative sculpturing, and framing. The first two floors had varying palettes of stained glass with shades of pink, green, orange, and purple. The dark blue flag of the grand lodge of New York flapped in the breeze. Havens noted the wind blowing to the west at ten to fifteen miles per hour. The entryway was well lit with four stairs leading up to the main hall. The place still looked deserted. No one came or went.

Havens had a perfect view from the vacant building. The nausea ripped through him again, tearing his insides. He was torn between the sudden urge to vomit and explode in the toilet.

"Why are you men here?"
"She's still not talking," the Pond regular informed.
"Push her more. And stay in the hotel. You are like children." *Like my beautiful boy. I pray you can forgive me. Enough!* "Do I need to assist?" inquired Paulo, his mood beyond soured.

The Pond operator searched his partner's expression for how to answer. The second operative simply shrugged. "Um, she's unconscious. We might have struck her too hard."

"But she was regaining consciousness when you first reported to me. Do you perhaps see a problem coming here and leaving the woman?"

"She was." The two operators had complicated things. Best intentions meant nothing. The more senior of the two added, "We used enhanced techniques."

"You Americans and your waterboarding." Paulo was used to dealing with less competent men, but wondered where he could find a more elite class.

"We should probably wait," the younger operator closed.

Paulo buzzed his lips unwilling to deal further. "This is no problem. We are nearly finished. Be vigilant. Do you have men posted as security? Our assets will start to arrive soon. Do you have the instructions?"

"Yes. Just have them put the bags in the solar trash compactors down Wall Street and the other locations before the markets open in the morning." The Pond operator checked a map and compared it to a list. "We have ten sites total."

The less seasoned operator continued to watch Paulo intently.

"Do you make the picture yet? Do you see how we will please the Order?" Paulo smiled.

The young operator shook his head. "I'm just assigned to this duty. That sounds above my pay grade, and this whole thing is a little weird."

"Yes. Yes. This is most apparent, and unfortunate. I will teach you. We have three jars. This one to contain the magnesium and potassium metal filings. This, liquid bromine, and this, the HELIX compounds. High Energy Liquid Explosive. You all have brought my shopping goods perfectly."

"How is it going to work?"

Paulo smiled patiently. "The …"

A third operator interrupted. "That's the problem with general purpose guys. No explosives training. The assets will put the bags in the solar trash compactors lining the streets around the city. Compactors can activate when the electronic eye sees the trash is full or through wireless remote—or through remote with a timer. It compacts, breaks the glasses, they violently react to ignite the HELIX."

"Yes. Yes. Very good. These compactors have been timed by friends to compact after the market opening and during rush hour."

The other operator got it. "And then the compaction tamps the charge. The compactor becomes the shrapnel and encasement and with the pressure of compact gases can't escape. Fuck! That's awesome. How big of a blast?" He grinned.

Paulo waited for a response from anyone in the room.

"I will tell you," Paulo said proudly. Ready to launch another technical diatribe, he assessed his audience. "Big." Paulo continued to fill the jars.

"Wait a second. Who's our target? Civilians?" the young operator questioned.

Paulo gave a hard look at the Pond point of contact leading the operation. The man shrugged his shoulders, not quite understanding why his team member wasn't quite with the program.

Paulo circled the room. "Young man. When a civilian becomes a target, the assassin need not be a sadist. Nor..." Paulo waved a finger of instruction to make his point, "Nor to be a psychopath. To inflict pain or harm without grievance, yes, this could be sadist. We should feel the pain. But it is our obedience to authority to the group where we belong. This. This is where we identify more with our own groups than with those outside of our group. We are not desensitized. We are detached. Some of us may be motivated. I am motivated to conduct my deeds, regrettable, but necessary due to a pressure point on my soul."

Paulo walked behind the young man who was trancelike in the scholarly lecture.

"Our targets, my young man, are those who have not yet seen the light of the new order. I am sad to say that they are men and woman like yourself." Paulo Violardo flicked the dragon's claw open as he reached around the man's throat. He sunk the point deep and drew the dark blade across the man's neck, ripping life from left to right. Paulo yanked the soldier's chair backward, sending the man gurgling to the floor.

"Excuse me. I must wash my hands."

Havens watched through the digital Nikonos Kodak DCS 425 camera as two men crossed Avenue of the Americas together and headed his way up 23rd. He blinked his eyes, hoping to clear them as he snapped away, capturing individuals and features as best as he could under the conditions of light and blind spots. Sean fought the overwhelming fatigue that was catching up to him.

Heads on swivels, the men tried to downplay their scanning for tails or other threats. They entered the lodge. Minutes later more pairs entered.

As the sixth pair of men approached, Sean noticed something different. One man pulled luggage and a satchel behind him. He wore a pilot's uniform. Zooming, it looked to Havens like a large United logo on the bags. Oddly, his counterpart did the scanning. The security element, or whatever he was, wore dark glasses. He had just a slight hitch to his gait. The pilot walked with purpose. Normal. Absent his counterpart, Sean would have dismissed him entirely. As the pilot passed through the heavy doors and walked up the marble stairs, he slowly turned and looked up toward Havens' window. Just a regular dude.

You're not Paulo. Who the hell are you?

Havens demanded more of his mind. The situation. The operating tradecraft. The guy was a grey man. The counterpart was not. *The tell. Rick mentioned a tell in our brief. Maybe one guy looks normal, the other one still an operator. Do you travel in pairs when you're high ranked? Security? Yes. A spook and a heavy. Could this be PASSPORT?*

Sean Havens vomited uncontrollably. *Shitty time to be catching malaria or the flu, Sean.*

Chapter 71

The contract operators gathered at the abandoned farm a mile from Christina's captors. The interior lights from the helo cockpit glowed, creating an spooky outline of the pilot finalizing last-minute checks.

Draeger stood in front of the two SUVs and addressed the assault team one last time. The team leader requested any final instructions before loading up in the helo.

"So you think this will be a pretty quick and easy take-down, huh?"

Draeger suppressed a smile. "It'll be a piece of cake. Lightly armed. This is a low-security site, but the powers that be don't want to take any chances with the hostage being held." *Tell the story, sell the story.*

"Roger that. Happy to help on any kidnap and rescue when we can get one out alive."

"John, make sure that you are FBI when your team is communicating their identification." Draeger scanned the group, which was illuminated by the truck headlights. He saw the flag shoulder patches and FBI chest patches on the men's assault smocks. "When you clear the building, all elements in the house except the woman need to be terminated. "

"Roger that, Prescott. We'll conduct the initial strike and lock down with surgical shoots like we sketched. To confirm, I will call the red, yellow, and green for action. I command the shoot, no shoot but you are not expecting any adverse action to the hostage, correct?"

Draeger was slightly lost in thought anticipating the outcome. He suppressed his enthusiasm. He felt great. Fresh. Healthy. Driven.

"Prescott. You understand?"

Draeger regained focus. "Yes. Yes. All good."

"So, once again, my team will give me a SITREP. We will do the takedown quarterbacked from the helo TOC. Each team is on different channels."

"Yes. Yes. I think this is overkill, but you know best. You guys mount up and I will head off to the target with the other team to get into their positions. John, when you extract, I need you to take this diplomatic pouch with you and have your man bring it directly to the Hoover building. It's locked and sealed. Someone will meet your guy in the lobby. That will clear you guys and provide the additional evidence that my directorate needs to get the Feds."

"You got it, Prescott. Thanks for thinking of us."

"No worries, John. We bled together in Mogadishu." *Better fist-bump this fucking numb-nuts Ranger.* "I knew I could trust you and wanted to get your new company in the game. If this goes off without a hitch, you can expect plenty of contract work from the CIA."

"I won't argue with that." John returned the fist-bump with a grin.

"All right. I'm heading out. See you at the objective. Just signal me when you are all clear and I'll take over the hostage. Then you guys bug out to the next point."

"Just like we planned."

"I'll wire you the last twenty-five percent of payment by sun-up."

"You've already been more than fair, Prescott. Good to reconnect."

Draeger drove with the advance team and parked just outside of view and ear of any sentries. Recon had shown only one to two lookouts at any point, and that was only in the form of sporadic window peeks and cursory walks around the house. It was a low-risk safe house and typically there were no more than a couple individuals present. Prescott Draeger had withheld most of that information from the contractors. This was more about show than firepower.

The ground team moved into their positions, awaiting the aerial assault team that was fast approaching.

John, a former Delta operator who had worked the same battlefields as Draeger a few times in the past, would call the assault.

As soon as Draeger heard the audibles from his headset, he smiled. *Stupid knuckle dragger. You save the day, I save the prom queen.*

"This is India 1 to Gandhi, how copy?"

"Copy, India 1, this is Gandhi, over."

"Gandhi. Looks like we can move to position, over."

"Roger that, India one. We are in the air on the move."

"India 2, this is Gandhi, how copy?"

"Copy. Gandhi, this is India 2."

"India 3, do you copy?"

"Copy, copy, copy, Gandhi. India 3 all good. I'm sitting right next to you."

The helo banked for the approach.

"Give it one more far pass, I can't see the stack yet," John ordered the pilot.

"Roger that, heading out before approach. Let me know if you don't have visual."

"Assault team, Indias 1, 2. You are now Phase line yellow. Move into your positions."

"India 1, Hold on your stack. I still want you about 20 meters from breech point."

"Copy that, Gandhi. Await your command."

"Gandhi, this is India 2. We are in position."

"Copy, India 2. SITREP.

"Target just stepped out on porch. Clear shot from here."

"Copy that India 2, hold 'til my command."

"India 3, unload on touchdown."

"Copy that Gandhi. India 3 in position."

The helo pulled in and flared a bit overdramatically, given the situation. John called out the final authorization.

"All teams, you are phase line green. On my count. Five, four, three, two, one. Go!"

"Phase line, you are now red. Prepare move to positions to take house. You are authorized for shots on target."

The man standing outside the safe house was more curious than alarmed. *What's all the fanfare?*

His chest cavity exploded, the round finding its mark right at the breast bone. The approaching team point double-tapped the lifeless body in the head. The second man in the team stack fired a shotgun with breeching round at the lock and kicked the door in. The stack rushed in to clear.

The second team smashed through the rear door effortlessly and engaged a target sitting at the kitchen table, unarmed save for a spoon and a late-night snack bowl of cereal.

Christina Havens screamed as the assault team kicked in her bedroom door. She trembled, crouched in the furthest corner of the room. Her body rocked back and forth in a trancelike state.

"We have objective," she heard over the shouts of "Clear!" and "FBI!"

Christina responded to the voices with exaggerated twitches and spastic movements.

John signaled to Draeger that all was clear and the objective was secured.

He and the teams all folded into the helo and lifted off. Draeger watched the rotary winged aircraft gain altitude and shift direction for extraction. *Yep. Too easy. But that's what happens when you raid a bunch of shrinks and grass-eating Intel weenies.* Prescott armed the device and sent a signal.

Nothing.

The helo started to speed off as planned. *Fucking better not have a damn signal jammer. Shit, shit, shit!* Draeger lifted the device, turning it in all directions. He hammered on the back of the plastic.

Chill. Relax. Think. Reset. Close your eyes for a second. You have time. Now calm, Draeger re-examined the device. *How did Havens teach me to troubleshoot these things?* On the bottom, the signal set was switched to the wrong band. Draeger changed the setting and pressed the button again.

The night sky lit up with a flash.

I like this. His heartrate continued to slow.

The helicopter exploded, sending flaming wreckage through the blackness before falling to the ground with all its passengers.

Draeger exhaled in relief as he marched up the walkway to find Christina Havens. He stepped over the corpse at the door with complete indifference.

Chapter 72

Havens jumped down the flights of stairs, preparing for pursuit.

"Hey, dickhead!"

Sean froze in his tracks on the landing. The main floor was dark. He identified nine silhouettes.

"Guys, this is not a bachelor party. Someone lied."

"Fritter, I wanna know how come you called Reilly first and not us? You loyal to frogs now?" one of the shadows asked.

"Man, am I glad to see you guys!" Sean exclaimed to the assorted lot of bearded men. The men he had known in his thirties were now in their forties or fifties. No less fit and no less dedicated to the greater SOF family.

"S'up dog?" Cheeto stepped up and embraced Havens. The rest of the men crowded in for bro-hugs, back pats and head smacks. Reilly, Tommy, Puck, 8-Ball. Havens stood in the midst of a career's worth of bubbas and beer buddies hailing from Special Forces 10th group and 5th group, Delta, Naval Special Warfare, and … Air Force.

"Sir?" Havens squinted.

"Guess you talked to CAG boys at Bragg and told them you needed a ride for us. Echo let me use a plane that was at MacDill. So I drove it. Sounded like we could have some fun. I figured it'd be a slow night in Tampa anyway."

"But I thought …"

"Don't think. We're here."

"Appreciate you coming, Major General. All you guys."

"That does bring us to a question, though, Fritter." Reilly was taking on the looming question from the group on his shoulders. "Whose dime is this on? Clearly, we didn't get orders on this. If its for you, we're all happy to help. If its for Uncle Sam, we're there too. But if you've gone rogue and get us killed, some of us have to know who's paying our survivor benefits. All of us need to know if we are outside of the law."

"Right man," Cheeto stuck his hands in his suit pants pocket.

Sean recognized that Cheeto was clearly uncomfortable in the attire. It further demonstrated his willingness to help. Sean couldn't remember seeing the man without a faded ball-cap of some sort.

Cheeto continued, "We'll help regardless, but its just one of those back of the mind things we just need to have in front of us."

"Yeah," Puck chimed in, "And we know you didn't have us wearing suits for office party stand-ins. Are we impersonating Feds? I don't give a shit, but dude, don't get us thrown in the pokey for twenty years."

"Oh, I got a question." Tommy had raised his hand slightly with a finger raised, "Since we're probably not rolling in heavy and we just have our sidearms or concealed carry, who springs us if we get pinched? Florida doesn't have reciprocity with New York for concealed carry."

"Dude, don't worry." Reilly dismissed with a grin, "Robert Hantman, the attorney who helps SEALs is right here in the city. We're already lawyered up."

"Bub, you're the only SEAL." Puck frowned still not catching whether this was banter or a legit backup plan.

"True," Reilly admitted with a somber expression, "You guys are probably fucked. But if you need to use my New York SEAL lawyer, add ten percent for the pass-through fee." He grinned through his thick beard.

"Dude, I know Hantman." Tommy added. "Anyone can call him. He helped some guys at Bragg too with their stripper divorces. Solid dude."

Havens let them get it all out, but he was freaking out, questioning Tanya's safety and any surveillance misses. The general picked up on this and was tiring from the bitching and chatting. "Guys, you'll all be taken care of if anything goes south. We wouldn't have been called if it wasn't of national importance. The fact that we were given an aircraft, comms, and the like should give you a tip as to who's got us covered, right, Fritter? Sean?"

"Sort of."

The general gave Havens a slight scowl.

"I work for a joint program office. I can't deputize you and give you an umbrella insurance policy," Havens confessed. "If something gets fucked up and someone gets arrested or sued, I don't have an answer for that. But what I do have is this. Many of you know General Bain. His consulting firm has a contract with my outfit. I reached out to him and, in the very worst case, we will roll you guys up under his contract and backdate everything. Not too different from black SOF. Regarding more specifics of why you are here, here's what I know. There is a highly credible national security threat here in this city that will take lives and weaken the economy and strength of this country. I know of one badass bomber who is responsible for nearly a dozen acts of terror. He's likely across the street. I also know that one of the best team partners I have ever had has been taken hostage, maybe worse, because of this mission. I don't have a lot of people I can call professionally. You guys are among the best I have ever worked with and the closest I have ever gotten as friends. I just need help and I don't know what that could mean."

8-Ball nodded in humility, "But you're buying us all beer and steak, right?"

"Sure," Sean laughed.

"Why didn't you say so?" Puck grinned.

"Fuggit." 8-Ball concluded, "Let's roll Havens."

"But we can still call that Hantman guy, right?" Tommy last-checked for assurances.

Sean's watch vibrated. A message scrolled.

Reilly's eyebrow raised, "That your Twitter feed going off? Tell us what you need us to do."

Havens scrolled through the text. "It's addresses. All around the city. There are five of them and then it just says Wall Street. Shit, I need to sit down."

"Intel on what's going down or Zagat restaurant ratings? You all right?" Reilly persisted.

"Dude, I'm starving," Cheeto complained.

Puck laughed at the big man whose tattoo sleeves spread to fingertips, "We ate a few hours ago."

"Still hungry. Think it was that last beer," Cheeto said wistfully.

Puck patted his buddy on the shoulder, "We're getting steaks later. On Havens."

"We might be dead by then," Cheeto countered.

"Guys, I think it might be the sites. Let me check." Havens switched to his mobile phone. He fought the urge to vomit again.

"Who's sending you this?"

"I don't know. And that's scaring the shit out of me right now." His head was throbbing. Confusion, frustration, and fever were converging at the expense of clear thought.

Chapter 73

Christina Havens was paralyzed with fear. The fact that they identified themselves as FBI meant nothing to her. Hearing the footfalls coming from the hallway toward her room, she shrunk her body closer to her corner sanctuary.

"Christina?" the voice called to her. It was familiar. Her head cocked to the left, her right ear processing the voice, her mind searching its synapse database of memories.

The voice called out again. Closer. "Christina? Is that you?"

He knows my husband. He knows Sean. Maybe he did those terrible things with Sean. Prescott? Prescott Draeger. Is that Prescott Draeger? He was at our house. He was quiet. Nice. Safe? She opened herself toward the voice, to the man in the room. Her head hurt.

"Christina, you okay?"

"Prescott?" Still unsure of whether he meant her harm, she melted back into the corner, her withered arms circling her body for security and a first line of defense.

Prescott was fixated on the small pool of wetness on the wood flooring under Christina. *You pissed yourself. Filthy skank.* Despite the mental fantasy buildup, Draeger felt less than no interest toward the woman now before him.

She was nothing like he remembered. She was bony. Frail. Draeger inhaled subconsciously as he tried to recall her fresh fragrance. He smelled lingering close quarters assault smells, he thought he smelled urine. Perhaps a light waft of body odor.

"Prescott, are you here to help me? Can you help me?" she pleaded and began sobbing again. Her nose ran. She wiped the mucus with her hand. Draeger winced as he caught the gleam of fluid on nearly translucent pale skin. He was disgusted.

"Christina, we have to get you out of here. Looks like you can walk. Do you have any clothes or just your gown?" *What am I saying? Fuck this. Fuck her. What a fucking waste. Calm. Move your mind.*

Prescott's finger danced at his side as he imagined toying with a pistol trigger guard. He sighed in disappointment. Part of him felt empty with the falling buildup of anticipation in seeing Christina. She was broken. Havens could have her.

"Prescott, where's Sean? Is he here?" She rose cautiously, testing the strength and balance of her legs as she moved closer to Draeger.

Her movements were creepy. As she reached out to him for support and an embrace, he smelled her rancid breath that had a slight hint of medicine. Her eyes were sunken and greyed circles rode her bulging cheekbones. Her skin looked thin and a bit yellow.

"Prescott, where's Sean? Is he here?" she pleaded again, clenching Draeger's jacket with bony fists. "Don't let him come here to kill me!"

That settled it. For Prescott Draeger, fantasy was far from reality. Grass was not greener on the other side. Draeger fought for clarity. He fought for purpose. He no longer coveted this woman, nor did he covet Sean Havens' life.

"Prescott!"

In his mind, he grabbed Christina by her frail arms, squeezing with all his might. *I fucking hear you! Shut the hell up!* He visualized yelling while thrusting her backwards. Away from him and his frustration. He watched in his mind's eye as her withered form skidded along the floor and he was repulsed by this shell of a woman. He stared at the bony impressions of her spine that protruded under the thin cloth gown.

I wonder if I can break her back with my boot? No. Stick to the plan. Fuck that therapy. Fuck sunshine and roses and rainbows and all that shit. No, you need to gain her trust to regain Havens.

"Prescott Draeger, can you hear me?" Christina's voice was the melody he remembered when she spoke his name.

Chill.

"Christina, go clean yourself up." *You smell like shit.* "I'll get you back to Sean." Draeger checked his firearm and was excited about the next phase.

Chapter 74

With a plan established and commo gear passed out, half of the men headed out to the addresses that Havens provided. The rest stayed with Sean to find Tanya and Paulo.

"Good call on commo, sir," Reilly acknowledged to the general. He patted the SEAL on the back.

"Someone's got to look after you kids," the general replied. "I can't take all the credit. These tactical throat microphones and radios were in the bird. All charged. Fresh batteries. We lucked out."

Havens gave a nod. "Still, my bad not to think of this in the scramble. These Wavebands and Motorolas will be fine. Reilly, you go to the hotel next door. See if I missed anything that could be tracked. Next challenge: finding the suspect and any crew he may have. I have no idea if he is working alone or if he has watchers. Our intel has only tracked the individual and show nothing of others in his party. That means they use local resources or others are flying below our radar. In Thailand, we know he was with at least another guy when my brother-in law was attacked."

Tommy held up his iPad. "Guys, I have a layout of the Masonic lodge. These places are usually pretty quiet if there aren't meetings going on. I got into the member section and checked schedules. Nothing is going on today."

"You hack the site?"

"No, I put in my member ID. I'm a fucking Mason," Tommy informed Sean.

"These secret squirrel Masons are as good a representation of Masons in general as mafia dudes are of Italian Americans." Sean felt unfair accusing the Masons, in general. "Chances are, Masons here in NYC have no clue about this P2 shit."

"We've met a shit-ton of cops here with the Ground Zero work we did. I know two guys working tonight who said they couldn't meet up with us for drinks. I can call them and have them pave our entry to the building so we can check out the guest list."

"Make it happen," Havens said. "Quick, guys, I have no idea how much time we have. If Tanya is still alive, it's only because they still need her, or she's just being detained until the event. I don't see that as realistic."

Reilly was leaving, but called over his shoulder, "She's probably toast, but I'll have a look. If these guys are serious, they probably went heavy on her to see who else knew of their op. After that, she's a liability."

Puck could tell this was not sitting well with Havens. "All right, Reilly, head on over. Havens, let's assume we get NYPD here to assist. They will want to do things by the book unless we have a solid understanding with them from the start. Let's assume we can command that teaming, given this is a CT issue. In that case, I'll take lead. Reminder, since we have not executed together, some of us in a while, some of us ever—control the distance. Like it or not, we may be clearing the building. If we have active shooters, we need to dominate. Interlock fields of fire to overwhelm. Cover blind spots. 8-Ball, you cover rear scans. Eliminate immediate threats, control and clear. Sir, I know you want to be in the mix, but we could use command and control here. I wrote out the guys, their radio call signs, and their intended locations. This may be ad hoc, but we really need a quarterback."

"My pleasure. If you find some, just send them my way. I'll start roll call to see who is in position," the general said.

"Roger that, sir."

"Tommy, do you have a Mason card?"

"Yeah. I have a membership dues card. Shows I'm valid and paid up. Have it in my wallet."

"If there is anything going on, I'm wondering if it would be best for you to go in first as a legit Mason," Sean mused. "See if there are any room blocks or special guests, in particular an Italian that is staying for one or two nights. His name is Paulo, but I'm guessing he is using a different name. See what type of a ruse you can create."

"Sure, but that's more of your wheelhouse." Tommy pulled out the card from his wallet. "It doesn't have my picture on it." He handed it to Havens. "You know what you're looking for anyway. Maybe you should do the advance force recce and call us in."

The team all supported the idea as best.

"All right. But I need a suit. Cheeto, hand it over. Let's swap," Sean held out his hands.

"Bro, that's my new Jos A. Banks." Cheeto kept bitching as he and Sean disrobed. Cheeto looked up at Sean as he fought with a pants leg.

"Sorry, bud," Sean apologized.

"No! No way!" he protested.

Havens stood in a T-shirt but no underwear.

"You don't want Havens commando in your new pants?" joked Puck.

That's for sure with the bout of stomach problems I've been having.

The team was brought to tears at the scene.

"C'mon," Havens urged, "We gotta go!" Sean wobbled a bit and hoped no one saw.

Havens slipped out the vacant building door. Darkness shrouded his exit. Sean casually checked left to right and across the street at the temple. He strained to focus. There was no pedestrian traffic, and Havens could see down scant amounts of walkers toward Broadway. None were headed his way.

He crossed the street and heaved open the majestic doors. To his far left, he noticed movement about thirty feet away. In the shadows stood a man. Havens continued into the building as if it didn't matter. In the enclave, Sean quickly lifted the throat mic that was stashed in the suit jacket pocket. Happy that he was wearing a borrowed shirt with a larger neck size, he lifted the earpiece tucked down in his collar.

"Charlie 6, this is Bravo 1. Possible bogie 10 yards to my 9 in the street shadows."

"Copy Bravo 1, Charlie 6 will confirm visual with Bravo 3 and send out Bravo 2 to mind your 6."

"Tango Mike Charlie 6. Bravo 1 going radio dark."

"Roger that Bravo 1. Dial us when ready. Over."

"Bravo 1 out."

To any passersby or watchers, Havens looked like a tired businessman as he rubbed his ear, touched his throat, and replaced the microphone in his pocket.

Beholding the ornate décor as he approached the night attendant, he spotted a man casually sitting about twenty feet away and reading something on a mobile device. The man sized up Havens, but did not appear to change his demeanor.

"May I help you?" the attendant inquired. His voice echoed in the great entry and lounge areas.

Damn. Havens was hoping he could make his inquiry out of earshot. He was also now caught in a crossfire of verbal and visual communications. He broke contact with the sitting man to focus on the assistant. Havens prayed that the older man was a minimum-wage employee who would have little knowledge of the Freemasonry affairs.

"Hi. I'm from a lodge in Tampa. I'm staying down the street at the Marriott. Knew the lodge was here but forgot to check and see if you all had any rooms available or if I could look around."

"We request advance notice from lodge guests and all other visitors."

Recalling some names from the Grand Lodge's website, he started to improvise. "I completely understand. I spoke to Nikole, who said the same. I didn't know if I could make it over here after work, so I figured I'd just try to swing by. I know I missed the tour time." Havens gave his best scatterbrained impression.

In the pause of conversation, he pulled out his phone and touched a camera app. "Hey, I can take pictures in here, right?" Sean took a selfie in the entryway before he got an answer. "So, are you a trustee?"

As the attendant started to answer, Havens continued. "Can you take one of me? I want to message this right over to one of my brothers back in Tampa. He told me not to miss the Grand Lodge Room. Pretty amazing, I hear."

"Sir …"

"Oh, here. Just push this button." Havens struck a pose, arms outstretched with a cheesy "look at me!" face.

The attendant was compelled to take the photo. "What was the other room, the Renaissance Room?"

"Yes," the attendant replied, his face still stoic as he figured out this tourist. "I will have to see some identification."

"Sure!" Havens boomed. "Let me see if you got a good one." Sean's camera was set to "live." Looking at the photo, he could see a few moments before and after the shot were taken. The bystander in the back who Sean was trying to capture had blocked his face and lifted the phone to his other side.

Havens moved closer. "So what about the rooms, too? I met a guy on the plane over here. Italian guy. Said he was staying here too. Is he in here? Paulo or Pauli? That ring a bell?"

"Sir, I am afraid that those guests are in meetings and have requested not to be disturbed."

"Oh, no problem. I was just going to say hi. Meeting rooms are on the second floor, right? I won't go there. But I'd just like to see the sixth floor, oh, and the woodwork on the, ah, what's the one that's like a knight's room? Oh, here's my dues card." Havens flashed it as he moved toward the room's center.

"Sir, I'll need to see additional identification. The lodge is closed to visitors this evening."

"Yeah, but I'm not going to sleep here tonight. I'll just go up to the other floor and take a peek as long as I'm here. I'm not even sure if I can check out of my hotel at this point. My wife would shit if I got charged for two hotel rooms in New York City."

The watcher stood up and approached Havens. "Hey, the guy said no visitors. You best go back to your other hotel and come back tomorrow morning."

Havens continued walking as the watcher closed in to intercept him.

"I said …" he reached out for Havens' upper arm.

Havens threw his arm straight up, blocking the grab forearm to forearm, which he parried down and thrust back to the watcher's throat.

Caught by surprise, the watcher flowed with Havens' maneuvers then received Sean's open left palm heel to his temple. Havens pulled out a concealed carry with his right hand and spun it to the attendant. He pointed it with menacing authority.

"I just wanted to see a fucking room. Put the phone down. What floor is the Italian on? And how many people are up there with him?"

Unfazed, the Mason replied, "They are on the twelfth floor. There are eight guests in the Concord room. May I ask what this is about? We have other guests."

Havens tried to read the man's face. It was blank. Sean put his earpiece back in and attached the throat mic.

"Charlie 6, this is Bravo 1 …"

Havens heard commotion on the channel. A loud crack and thud resonated from the heavy front door. Havens and the Mason jumped as they saw a man collapse at the entry.

"Charlie 6, this is Bravo 2. Tango down. I have visual. Tango is down."

"All Bravo elements, this is Bravo 1 SITREP!"

"Bravo 1, Charlie 6. Bogie was headed your way. He was armed. All clear from our position. Over."

"Roger, Charlie 6. We have confirmed Tangos at the site. My level clear. Site is hot, send Bravos over. Any friendlies visible?"

"Bravo 2 in crow's nest, nothing vis. Best scoop this guy up pronto and make this happen. That was not suppressed fire on my end. Over."

"Roger, Bravo 2. Stay in your position as overwatch to mind our 6. Bravo 1, Charlie 6 switching out at Bravo 2 now. Bravo 2, you are now Charlie 6 command. We're coming to you, Bravo 1."

"Copy, copy, good call. All Alphas stand by."

Cheeto was the first to the lodge. "You guys go in. I'll bring him back to our hiding spot and dump him in the doorway. If we bring him in, he'll make a big smear. Best keep it outside in case someone comes by."

The others all scanned the street before entering the building. It remained clear.

"Feds?" the Mason inquired, now looking more cooperative.

"What else?" Havens validated. "You have a number of dangerous suspects in here using your facility. Are they all in the meeting room?"

"They are on eight. The Italian is checked in to room 423 in the attached building."

"Is it connected?"

The Mason nodded, "Yes, on the main floor. Just past the elevators, to your left."

"Have you seen a woman dragged in here? Also, a pilot, do you know who the pilot was?"

"I don't know of any woman, and I've been here all day. The pilot ..."

"You guys head up to 8, I'll be right behind," Sean interrupted.

The watcher knocked out on the floor was starting to rouse. "Havens, what about this guy?" asked Tommy, who fully appreciated the growing intensity of their involvement in Havens shit.

"Quick search, then knock him back out." Sean re-engaged the Mason, "Sorry, you were saying something about the pilot?"

"I've seen him a number of times here before. Spoke to him once. He's a good man. Colonel Casey. Former Air Force. No threat there."

"Did you say Colonel Casey?" the major general inquired through Havens earpiece.

Sean waited for anything more from the general. He turned away from the Mason and whispered, "You know him?"

"Yeah. He used to work CENTCOM J3X, was at SOCOM J3 as my deputy for a bit, and then he moved on to Task Force Grey. I thought he was still active duty. You know, he was William Casey's nephew. He's very much one of us."

425

PASSPORT. We know who PASSPORT is. He's gotta mean CIA Bill Casey's nephew. Part of the legacy system. Sean readdressed the Mason. "Who was the guy with him?"

"Sean, I'm coming over. We can't take out Casey," the general ordered.

Sean was trying to keep track of both conversations and didn't have time to tell the general to stand down and stay at his position.

The Mason pressed on curious as to whether he had Havens attention, "I don't know that he had an associate. There was another man who entered at the same time, but he was part of the party you're interested in. The colonel never spoke to the other gentleman."

"Do you have the name of the other gentleman?"

"No, they use a meeting reservation passphrase: Liberty. Wait," the Mason racked his brain for a nugget. "I may have heard him say Steven. Not sure."

"Uh, Sean?" Tommy interrupted.

"Yeah?"

"This isn't good."

"What's that, T?

"This dude's armed, but he has a State Department ID." Tommy re-read it to make sure, "Says DSS. Diplomatic Security Service. He's a federal employee."

"Not good. But doesn't change things," insisted Havens.

Havens gave the man a swift kick in the head, rendering him unconscious again.

Chapter 75

Prescott Draeger dialed the last mobile number that he had for Sean Havens. It went straight to voicemail. "Well, looks like you don't want to learn about your wife. That's inconvenient."

Draeger peered from the curtains and watched the incoming vehicle.

Alrighty then. Let's see if you are who I think you are. I'll wager that you turn your lights off in ... one ... two ... three. Bingo.

Sean's personal mobile number forwarded to his operational line. He glanced at his phone as it rang in case it was Maggie. She was one of the few who called that phone. The number was blocked.

Havens looked to his crew. "We have a couple options. We all hit the floor and work in a stack, or we let two guys split up to take the seventh and ninth floor stairwells."

Cheeto didn't like the idea, "We don't have maps of the place to know if they would take other stairwells. We're running tight on time, buddy. Let's hit this floor, see what's there, and get the hell out of here. Call it a day."

8-Ball agreed. The team was now questioning the mission's consequences, "Yeah, I say we go to ninth floor, split up the staircases and come down. That way we don't go up to eight, find them waiting for us and they whack us all in this elevator car."

"Can't split up. If we engage from two different sides, just don't shoot each other," Cheeto warned.

"Yeah, with just pistolays I don't see anyone spraying each other."

"Okay. When we get up there, I'll lead. Not sure if we will engage or not." Havens recognized the apprehension of the men.

They weren't used to Sean leading an assault team. He was usually "back of the bus" with them.

Cheeto patted Havens on the back. "Bro, just wanted to say this is *sooo* fucked up."

"Yeah, thanks for inviting us, Fritter." Puck smiled.

Step up and lead these men. "Let's go," Havens commanded with confidence.

As the men exited the ninth floor elevator and descended down the stairwell, they met no resistance.

Sean Havens deftly opened the door to the hall that led to the meeting rooms. As he peered out from behind the doorframe, he caught a glimpse of Paulo Violardo waiting for the elevator.

"Shit!" Havens pulled back. "Our guy is waiting for the elevator. You guys head to the room while I go after him. Tommy, you ring up the other guys on the radio. Shit. I can't lose him."

Havens had no choice but to make room for his guys to slip by and make a dash for Paulo without alerting the room.

The other team members were just emerging from the opposite side.

Paulo caught their movement and sought to evade, but he saw Havens charging at him. He froze for a moment and the elevator doors opened. Paulo jumped in and Havens dove after him.

Sean was surprised by Paulo, who had cached himself on the inside corner of the elevator.

Paulo checked Havens into the wall as the doors closed. Violardo made a snake strike to Havens' back with his dragon's claw knife. A ripping tool, it penetrated only an inch with Sean's pulling in of his back. Still, it caused extensive pain. Havens spun to his right.

The blade lost hold as Sean unwittingly moved with the curvature as he elbow-smashed Paulo into the other wall.

Paulo swung his arm and the hooked his blade back to Havens in another attempt to claw into Sean's vital organs.

Havens blocked the movement and Paulo dropped his own arm, slashing Havens across the forearm.

Sean screeched in pain. His eyes snapped wide with panic as he saw Paulo coming back up to his groin with the knife targeting a femoral artery.

Havens twisted and dropped his center of gravity. He slammed into Paulo's thigh and core.

Both men let out a yelp of pain as Paulo's hidden spiked cilis bore into the men's thighs.

Wild-eyed, Paulo snapped at Havens with a gnashing bite.

Havens tossed his head back quickly. As Paulo turned to the missed mark, Sean crashed down with a side head-butt to Paulo's cheek, breaking the orbital bone.

Sean's second wave attack was a flying left hand with fingers extended into Paulo's eyes. Havens' fingers went knuckle-deep in soft tissue and muscle and extended outward, causing Paulo to flail back into the elevator wall. Sean fought the blackness that was entering his vision. His body was shutting down.

The elevator started its descent.

Chapter 76

"What in the hell?"

Rick saw flaming wreckage not far from his destination. He continued on, unsure of what was going down at the safe house.

The scene was off as Rick approached the discreet CIA hideaway, from the vehicle to the overall feel.

Rick turned off the headlights and slowed the car to a crawl, then continued on foot.

His car's trunk light had been disabled for situations like this. Working quickly and silently, Rick retrieved an assault-style shotgun and chambered a shell.

He approached the perimeter quietly. It was eerily noiseless, save for sirens far off in the background. No doubt a response to the accident in the field that he passed.

Draeger watched from a darkened room's window. He was giddy with anticipation.

Rick crouched low. He scanned the house. *Havens deserves to know.* Rick lowered his phone to the ground and dimmed the screen light with one finger. With another, he dialed Havens. Then he thought better, disconnected, and silenced the device.

Rick was on the move again. Slowly, he squat-walked, shotgun at the ready. He headed to an unlit area where he would try to recce as well as possible and make his next move.

Draeger's eyes squinted in anticipation, a viper preparing to strike as its prey drew closer.

Rick came closer to the window. Draeger moistened his lower lip and raised his own weapon.

Chapter 77

As the two small teams of operators converged on the meeting room, the door opened.

An armed man peeked out to assess the ruckus. Seeing the assaulters rushing toward the room, he fired three shots. His panicked rounds were met with two center-mass shots to his forehead. Cheeto caught the door with a quick foot and shot his way toward the occupants, who scrambled to their feet and unholstered weapons. Tommy was next through the door, also now firing well-directed shots but heading to his right so the others could pour in.

The remaining crew pounced through.

"Cover up," Cheeto yelled with two live flashbangs. He flung them into the back corner of the room.

Every man in the room watched as the canisters soared through the air.

The shooting stopped and mouths dropped as the hurled metal headed toward glass bottles filled with chemical compounds.

Havens punched the elevator buttons as the light indicators passed five, then four. Desperate to stop the elevator from opening for authorities or other unwelcome parties, Havens hit the second floor button and readied to hit STOP.

As the metal broke, glass and flash charges ignited the HELIX and an explosive rush consumed the room, blowing out all windows and six floors above and below.

The elevator door opened on the second floor.

The colossal explosion rocked the building, knocking Havens to the floor and damaging the car pulley and counterweight. Darkness took over where light had been in the floor's hall and the elevator car plummeted to the lower level. Havens quickly rolled on top of Paulo.

The speed-sensing governor braked in the short fall but damaged the car doors. A variety of impaling, lacerating and crushing debris rained down on the men.

Jarred by the impact of the car against his body and head, Paulo moved slowly as he regained consciousness and tried to reorient himself. His eyes were blurred from the attack to their soft tissue. He closed them again, hoping the pain would subside.

The elevator lights flickered and hummed with an unnerving utility light luminescence.

Feeling a presence and sharp pain, Paulo opened his eyes to see Havens bent over him, the dragon's claw pushing into the skin above his carotid artery.

"Kill me."

"Where's the girl?"

"I failed."

"The girl!"

"Kill me."

Havens pressed the claw and drew blood. The sickness ran through him again. Sean willed it away. He was burning up.

Paulo laughed aloud. In a broken voice, he taunted, "When war's enemy's defeat is death, and your enemy's greater victory is death, how can you make threats? Put away the knife or run me through. It matters not, I think."

Havens pushed the claw deeper into Paulo's neck and pulled the blade into the tendons. Paulo remained motionless. Havens stomped down on the barbed area of Paulo's thigh.

Paulo sucked air. The sharpness of the pain surged through his body as the cilis tore beyond flesh to bone.

"Where is the girl?"

"Kill me, do not kill me, it matters not to me. Give me pain, it fuels my soul with righteousness."

"I'll find your son!"

"No!"

Ha! That did it. Where was the son? "I know all about his doctors, Switzerland …" He waited for a reaction. His only source of intelligence was from a man who was glad to suffer pain and was begging for death. He hoped there was a human. A father.

"You seek truth, but you would first have to understand the Truth. I'd like to know how you have come to find me and about my son. I try to be careful, but not so careful that it stands out. Clearly, you have access to know of me. Perhaps we can discuss this like enlightened men."

Havens grunted. "Enlightened men. You've been killing people all over the world. You kill for men who seek more money than they know what to do with. For power to manipulate. You're a pawn, just like me."

"I am no pawn. I am a servant. The servant is obedient by choice. A pawn has little choice and little enlightenment. Put the knife away. You are not a threat to me. I am no threat to you. The weapon serves only as false comfort. I am prepared for my sacrifice for the good of the Order. Your trust is a weapon to me. That is what we must overcome."

"Bullshit," Havens spat. "You're a shithead like all the other fanatics out there. God love you or damn you for having passion and faith in your cause, but you're being manipulated like a fucking ten-year-old Iraqi kid told to blow himself up to score some virgins. You're weak. You prey on others. I wish my brother-in-law had killed you in Thailand."

Paulo dismissed the venom with a shake of his head until Sean's last statement, when he paused and gave full attention. "Brother in Thailand?"

"Brother-in-law."

"When a man is joined to another man in family, he is a brother."

"Whatever." Havens sat back in the elevator. "Fuck," he snapped, lifting his hand quickly from a shard of the broken elevator mirror. He was running out of options and was completely exhausted. Part of him wished he had died in the explosion too. His mental and physical fortitude were waning from the non-stop mission over endless weeks.

"You trust me now, no?"

"No, I just realized I don't give a shit either."

"The big man. I did not try to kill him. I waged my escape. He is *gordo*. Fat. I did not strike his vital … organs. I did not make the decision to kill him. Even in battle. I cut fat and muscle wall. You see, he is my brother, too."

"Don't fucking say that. Don't you fucking say that at all," Havens threatened and pointed his pistol at Paulo. "You flew that UAV right up to the hospital window and tried to kill him because he could make a description of you."

"No. This is not so. I have met your brother." In a moment of his own clarity, Paulo put another piece together and radiated. "This is how you know of my son. From your brother in Italy. I spoke for a time of how the Freemason generosity paid for my child's needs. Soon I learned of the price I must pay. Servitude. I never saw my family again but know they are well as long as I remain loyal, it is my price. It is my curse. I seek always to find the strength. Your brother, he is a very smart man. I respect him. I gave the command that he should remain unharmed. He is a Mason. I am a Mason." Still, Paulo returned to looking perplexed. *Was this a trap? He, too, must trust again.* His face softened. "I would not kill him."

"Right. Okay, Paulo. You'll spare my *brother* because he carries the club card, prances around some hidden chamber in a robe with horns, and puts wax on his nipples or some shit with all you guys." Havens rose to his feet. "Time for me to see what the hell is going on and how to get the hell out of here. Time to give you your wish."

"No. I will tell you. The girl remains at the hotel. You let me go, I will tell you how to find her. I will make this trade to you. Your brother was not to be harmed. It comes as such a surprise to you? We are not so different."

"Seriously?"

"We are Westerners. We believe power is to be maintained for the betterment of lives. The strong must lead. The cost of sacrifices strengthens the souls of the righteous."

"You're fucked in the head."

"You are very vulgar man."

"Sorry, forgot my manners. You've killed hundreds. Maybe thousands. But I need to watch my mouth. *Fuck you.* How's that?"

Paulo raised a finger to Sean. "You are government or military. So am I. My organization has Americans. Great Americans. I work with your CIA too. Please. I am to give you proof. Give me trust." Paulo reached into a side pocket and withdrew a small metal cylinder that looked like a small cigar tube. "Please. She is on the fifth floor of the hotel." Paulo twisted the tube open, revealing that it held a smaller plastic tube.

"What Americans?" Havens felt uneasy. "What is that? What are you doing?" He lifted the gun again at Paulo, not knowing what else to do.

"Please. You are safe. Room 536. I will show you I am apologizing for your brother. For letting you find me and to have destroyed this beautiful temple. My people will know that I have spoken if I survive. Blessed are the meek. Blessed are the righteous. I ask only this of you. Marco and Lucinda Violardo. It is my son and my wife. I leave them in your hands. The Order will kill them. But you and your brother are good men. Please. You must trust as I must trust you. Please."

"Stop!" Havens commanded. "What are you doing?"

"*Non nobis Domine, non nobis, sed nomini tuo da glorium.*" Paulo snapped the tube.

J.T. PATTEN

Chapter 78

As Rick crept parallel to the window, Draeger unloaded on his target. The first trigger pull dropped Rick. The second, third, fourth, fifth, and sixth followed Draeger's arm movement, which chased where he hoped a body was. The flash of light in the darkness of the room and outside made it difficult to see.

Hit across the inside shoulder cuff, Rick fell and was struck again multiple times. He leveled the shotgun at the window and pulled the trigger.

The shotgun popped in the calm of the night and open yard.

Silence returned.

Christina Havens remained in the room, quaking from the noise. She cried out, "Stop it, stop it, stop it." She beat her fists into her forehead until the shooting ceased.

Draeger lay on the floor, regaining his breath. He reached across his body armor and felt the bleeding from his arm. "You dirty little fucker."

Rick dropped the shotgun and wheezed in the cool grass.

A black silhouette approached and stood over him. "Congratulations. You got me. I'll live. Doesn't look like you will."

"Prescott Draeger."

"Pretty much."

"Let her go."

"I am. That was the deal. Question is, what will I do with you?"

"Just leave her alone," Rick pleaded.

"Give me your phone, but call your dad."

Confused, Rick mustered from his failing body, "Why my dad?"

439

"Give me the phone after you have dialed or so help me I will go back in the house and break that little whore's bones one by one *with a fucking hammer!*"

Rick struggled for his phone.

Impatiently, Draeger kicked away Rick's shotgun, held his pistol to Rick's head, and retrieved the device. "Now it's your turn again. And please do as I say. I'm struggling a bit with a new approach on how to deal with things, and I'm not really wanting any setbacks." Draeger thumped Rick on the head with the magazine secured in the pistol grip.

Rick did as he was instructed.

"Hello?"

"Hello, sir."

"Who is this?"

"I was instructed to contact my superior once the act was done, but I wanted to talk to you first," Draeger drawled.

"Where is my son?"

"He's here. I'll pass the phone in a minute."

"Damn you!" Jerry cursed.

"Sir, I'm simply an errand boy. I'm a soldier, and I work for guys like you. So, with that out of the way, I'd like to work for the good guys again. I think I deserve the opportunity to not have to hide in shadows."

"Preposterous. I know who this is and what you've done."

"I can bring down the Pond. I can help you target the Order."

Jerry said nothing.

"Bring it right down from the inside. See, I've got some of these little paranoia tendencies still. If I could minimize them, that would work best for me and for you and your organization. I'd like to sleep better at night, and I don't think that's asking too much, given what I have done for this country."

"Let me talk to my son."

"Sure. Where are my manners? Here he is, all bleeding out. Here's how this will play. He'll be dead soon. I'll keep his phone. Keep the device certificates on his credentials updated for security, and you can call me anytime. I, in turn, will be your double. Sean Havens can be my handler."

"You know that will never work."

"Sure it will, old man. Because I'm going to give him his wife back, a big apology, and some assurances of his family's safety. I'll find a nice spot and just drop her off so he can get her and figure out what he's going to do next. Then I'll give him some time, and you will have a little chat with him about what a great guy I am. Technically, he shouldn't be mad at me. His daughter's alive, his wife's alive. The real bad guys are dead. I was just doing my job, like he does his. My coming around and saving his wife should buy some leverage. Here's your son. And remember, we keep this conversation going between us girls. I'll draft up a contract. Then you can poly me and we get on with the show."

Rick was expiring quickly. Draeger gave a swift, forceful kick to Rick's side. "Hey, sport, it's your dad. He wants to say goodbye."

Rick tried to reach for the phone and failed.

Draeger bent down giving Rick a hard series of slaps on the forehead. "I'll help you, pal."

He put the phone on speaker and held it close to Rick. "Okay, sir. He's on speaker now."

Rick tried to lift his head, but failed. "I know what you did. I know what you're doing," he wheezed. He sucked wind irregularly through his mouth and nose.

"Son?"

"Rot in hell, Dad."

Chapter 79

Havens saw a small white flash that burst into orange light within the tube.

"The gift of giving our lives justifies us at once in His eyes." Paulo placed the tube in his mouth. He gave Sean a little wave and closed his eyes.

Paulo's head exploded in a confined burst, emitting sound Havens had never heard before now would never forget.

Teeth, plastic, and gore burst from Paulo's mouth while his eyes and ears sprayed red. His broken head snapped back and made a soft splat like a ripe melon being dropped.

"Jeezus!" Havens cried out. His emotions manically ping-ponged between panic, horror, and relief.

Taking a breath, and knowing it was now or never to forge ahead, Sean searched Paulo's pockets and stuffed everything he found into his borrowed, and now trashed, suit jacket.

There were two more metal cartridges, cash, a billfold, a passport, and a mobile device on Paulo. All to be checked later.

My phone. Sean fumbled for his own device amidst the distractions. The radio was long since ripped away.

No bars. Seven missed calls. Unknown, Reilly, Reilly, Lars, Maggie, Unknown, and Reilly.

Maggie. All right, kid, let's get out of here. See if I can be a dad for once. He willed energy to his body and mind.

Havens tried to pry the doors open, to no avail. They were dented and lodged in the bent elevator frame.

Havens jumped and pulled at the crimped and buckling metal plates framing the elevator car ceiling. Concrete pieces and other debris fell through the opening. He braced himself against the waist-high hand rails and tore away loose sheets, letting the rubble fall to the side of the car.

Debris continued to fall through the hole, gradually filling the bottom of the car. With each of Sean's efforts, more powder fell, saturating the car with fine smoky dust. Havens hacked and his eyes watered, but he continued to dig and release chunks of concrete, pull wires, and yank on the metal cables.

A large piece shifted and blocked the opening. Havens clawed at the metal, his hands bloodied and raw. He hammered with his pistol, using the barrel as a pry. To widen the opening, he'd have to break the only work source of still flickering light.

He who dares wins. Havens tore at the assembly and frame. The chunk finally released, fell, and gave way to another flow of destroyed building material. The light suddenly extinguished.

Havens groped through the opening and felt a breeze. Struggling to pull himself up, he gashed his hands on the sharp metal. He felt the blood trickle.

Well, Paulo, here's your sacrifice.

"Hello!" Havens shouted. "Hello!" He retrieved his phone again. With the flashlight app, Havens could see that he only needed to climb about ten feet up. He could now hear shouts and sirens.

This oughta be interesting.

Chapter 80

Rick drew his last breath. He died knowing his father had made a choice. It was for Havens, Skull and Bones, or the CIA over his own flesh and blood.

Draeger took the phone off speaker. "Sorry about your son, sir. It was just business. Business that you arranged. Now. About my proposal. I double for you. Havens is my conduit. You give me my life back after we bring down the Pond, or at least after I help you take out the key players. Deal?"

"I'll have to think about it."

"What's to think about? See, I know you had your own son killed. I know you know about Christina Havens. I'm not sure where Sean is, but I promise you, if I save her and tell her that you knew all along … *whoooeeey*. He's going to fucking *killll* you. Think about it. You can't take out the Pond because you don't know where it exists. I'm an inside man. I'll get you whatever you need. Or I kill her and blame it on you. Sean will kill you. So, deal? Tick, tick."

"Under one condition," Jerry relented. "Please bring my boy's body in the house undesecrated. That's all."

"Not sure what kind of monster you think I am, but we can work that out later. Deal."

"Then you have my word. And we will proceed accordingly."

"I'll draft you some content in good faith and bring your son in." Draeger examined the device. "I'll reach out via his number and we can make arrangements."

"Prescott Draeger."

"Yes?"

"I know you. I know what you've done, and what you are capable of. I also know that you have been used. I know that you have not been leveraged or recognized for your intelligence and full abilities. If you indeed are veritably looking for an olive branch, I will help you. But young man, if I get so much as a fart's wind that I'm being played, I will kill you. I will hunt down any of your family and kill them as well. I ..."

"Yeah, you made your point. You'll be glad to know I don't have any family that I give a shit about, so it's just *mano a mano, hombre*. And you'll get your Pond and Order. Draeger out."

Jerry sighed deeply, then smiled. *Touché, Robert. Touché.*

Chapter 81

Havens was able to pry the elevator door farther open and was greeted with a crack of light. The shouts were instantly louder. A voice was close.

"Hello?" Sean signaled.

"Hey, I got one!"

Havens saw gloved fingers in the door crack. Sean reached for a hand hold along the shaft before the door opening stole his grip in exchange of freedom.

New York's finest were reaching in to grab Havens. Two firemen braced themselves with one hand while grabbing Sean with the others. Feeling weightless, he was lifted up and out to new chaos.

The floor was filled with fire and rescue, law enforcement, and flashes of media.

The rescue workers patted Havens on the back. Seeing an opportunity, he took advantage of the situation. "Oh my god," he wailed. "What happened? What happened?" His hands throbbed and he wiped his bloodied palms on his face like a victim in complete shock and disorientation.

"Is there anyone else down there?"

"No. I was coming down and the elevator just dropped. Oh my god!" Havens let his legs buckle a bit.

"Whoa, buddy, you're good now. Hey! Need to get this guy checked out."

An EMT rushed over and wove his arms under and around Havens. "You're real lucky, buddy. I gotcha."

A police officer called out to the EMT. "Hey, where did he come from?"

"He was in the elevator," the EMT replied.

"Holy shit. We'll be out there in a few. What a mess."

Once outside, Havens looked up for his eye in the sky overwatch. Windows were blown out as far as the eye could see. Debris littered the street.

The EMT escorted Havens past the hotel and their hide site.

"Hey, I think I got it. Let me just catch my breath. I just need a minute."

"We need to get you looked at," the EMT replied.

"Hey, I'm alive. Go back and see if you can help someone else. Really. Thank you. I can't thank you enough."

The EMT couldn't argue. "Okay, buddy. You go straight to the bus over there and they'll get you fixed up. Good luck," he said as he patted Sean's back and jogged back to the building.

Havens fast walked to the hotel. A police officer was directing hotel guests out of the building and preventing anyone from coming in.

"Hey buddy, go get yourself looked at down there. No one's to come back in the building. We're getting everyone out."

Havens struggled to pull his wallet from his swollen and bleeding hands. "I'm government counterterror. Fort Bragg. I need to get in."

"Terror. No shit. Fuckin' Mason hall."

"Thanks." Havens passed by, cutting any conversation short. *Better not be lying, Paulo, you sonofabitch.*

Havens again fought through the crowd of the hotel lobby. A sea of departing panic-stricken civilians. It was cookie cutter of the Thai hospital evacuation.

Every man for himself.

The hotel elevators were bringing guests down. He found the staircase and willed himself up the flights to the fifth floor and down the vacant hall to the room number.

It was locked. Havens was unsure who might still be behind the door. His pistol was long gone and damaged beyond repair, resting amidst the debris.

Reilly.

Havens moved from the door and found the small ice alcove, where he made the call.

"Dude, where the fuck are you? What happened? Holy shit. We're all back in the building camped out higher up. Cops found the dead guy but assumed it was from the blast. Who made it out?"

"I don't know. I just got out."

"Where the fuck are you? Holy shit, Havens. This is a clusterfuck shit show."

"Man, I know. I'm back at the hotel."

"The hotel? I searched high and low. I got nothing, Sean. Dead end."

"She's here. I know what room. I need a gun."

"Havens, if she's there, she's not going anywhere. Some of the other guys are across the street trying to help. They told cops they were military and wanted to chip in. We should be there, man. You should be there."

"You're right. I'll be right down."

"Sean, you're still going after her, aren't you?" Reilly pressed.

"He said she was alive. I know she's alive. There's no way the others got out."

"You did."

"I'll call you back."

On autopilot, Havens crossed the hall and pulled the fire alarm. He grabbed a Do Not Disturb sign, folded it in half, stuffed it into the door crease and fished for one of Paulo's devices in his pocket.

Sean inserted an end of the small explosive into the door. He bent the visible plastic until it snapped and stepped aside.

The explosive blew the handle. Havens kicked the door, armed only with resolve.

The room was lit. The alarm drowned out all sounds, save for voices on the television that could be heard in short intervals.

The bathroom door was locked. He leaned an ear to the door and heard nothing. Sean took a few more steps and peered around a wall that led to the bed chamber. It was clear.

Havens tried to turn the door handle. Locked. He took a step back, relieved to validate wooden door and a cheap lever component. Kicking the door, it flung open with a loud bang and bounced back.

He could see Tanya in the tub.

Her feet were bound with torn sheets. Another sheet was used to lift her feet up to a towel rack. Her hands were underneath her body, which was surrounded by inches of water. Her shirt was torn open, breasts exposed, and her mouth was also bound by sheet strips. Her head was near the tub faucet and the metal shower head was wrapped around her neck. Tanya's face was lacerated and bruised, her eyes red and blackened.

Her eyes watered as she gazed up at Sean Havens, helpless.

Sean untied her legs, gently lowering them to the side of the tub. He covered her breasts with the mass of sheet strips. His chest heaved and tears of his own rolled down his face.

Tanya closed her eyes. She did her best to assist Sean by moving her body or lifting her head so he could free her. She lifted her arms and, as he bent to lift her, Tanya embraced Sean deeply and let her emotions free.

"I knew you'd come," she whispered. "I knew it."

"I'm here, baby." Overcome with emotion, Sean broke down.

"You look like shit, Havens," she croaked while stroking his hair and holding him tight.

Sean gave a little laugh and pulled away. "Let's get you out of here."

"Take me anywhere, as long as I'm with you." She kissed his cheek. And did it again. And moved to his mouth."

He felt her swollen lips on his. "Does it hurt?"

She pulled back. "My lips? Or everything?" She smiled and reached for his bloodied hands. "We should probably get these taken care of." She looked into his eyes and at his face. "My god, Sean, you're white." She put her hand on his face and forehead. "You're burning up."

"I'm fighting a jungle bug, or probably just over tired."

"Can't say waterboard training helped me too much," Tanya said ruefully. "I said I was alone, and they somehow knew I was expecting someone."

"The coffee. Two cups."

"Ah. Way to go, Tanya," she scolded herself. "I did say I was DoD. They had my CAC ID card. I took a few pretty good hits then blacked out. Guess I screwed this up. Not fit for field again, Ms. Crowe." Tanya shrugged, then perked up a bit. "I got one of those goons."

Havens lifted her chin with the back of his hand. "Hey, you saved the day, girl. I saw you stitched up the guy pretty well. It went bad, but we got the bad guy and wrecked their plans."

"Paulo?"

"Yeah. Dead."

"You got him? That's why you look like shit." She reached for a cut on Sean's face, touching it gently with the pads of her fingertips. White, powdery dust enhanced Havens' ghostlike complexion.

"There was an explosion. I don't know exactly what happened yet. I had called in some friends for help. Next thing I know, I'm tussling with Paulo, they're still upstairs, and there was a huge explosion. Guessing a trip wire or something. Maybe something else went bad."

Tanya took in his tumble of words.

"Oof." Sean fought a wave of nausea that came over him. The frequency was growing. "So, Tanya, your analysis was spot-on. Not only did you find Paulo, his link to another HVT was established. A U.S. military colonel. He may be flying or covered as a United pilot. Not sure. Shit, I have to call Rick to tell him the guy's name."

"What high value target? Who is he?"

"A Colonel Casey. Christopher Casey. Goes back to a U.S. group that tasked Paulo, or who was working with his organization. High power structure, political elites. This whole Mason, Illuminati mumbo jumbo."

"But you said he was a pilot."

"Yeah. Probably why Rick and I couldn't fit him into any pattern. He isn't on fly lists because he does the flying. It was there the whole time. PASSPORT. Stupid miss."

"So where is he now?"

"No clue. He was in the Mason building across the street. Could have been killed, but my guess is no. I didn't have time to discuss it with Paulo."

"Yeah, better call Rick," Tanya said. "He can start tracking the guy and block travel. I need to call my mom and check in. She's gotta be worried sick."

"Yeah, I need to make calls too."

"Well, back to reality."

They both struggled to get up, moaning and groaning. Standing they gazed at one another knowingly.

"Thanks, hero." Tanya leaned in for another brief kiss. "You make your call in the bedroom, I can call by the door."

Chapter 82

"Hello? Rick?"

"Hello, old chum."

"Prescott?"

"Hey, we're on a first-name basis again. I like it."

Havens was silent.

"Need you to hear me out, Sean. You're going to want to hear this."

"I only need to hear the gurgle of blood coming from your mouth when I kill you."

"Eww. What a vision," Draeger cackled. "I was thinking we could square up and put this all behind us. I have your wife here for you. I just saved her life."

"What kind of game is this? Where are you?" Havens demanded.

"I'm in Virginia. So is she. Would you like to talk to her?"

"What the fuck are you talking about? I'm not playing games with you."

"Here, I have you on speaker. Say hello to your wife, Sean. She's back from the dead."

"Sean? Are you there?" It was the voice of a ghost.

"Christina?" Sean stammered. "I … I can't believe this. Are you okay?" The emotions burst from his eyes. "Is it really you?" Sean squeezed his wet eyelids with his fingers as he struggled to find his breath.

"I'm fine," she whispered.

"Thank god." His words escaped as frail whispers. His chest lurched repeatedly. Sean was without words. He drew his hand to his mouth. His head shook in sheer disbelief.

"Prescott came here. They were keeping me here. Somewhere. The FBI killed them. Prescott says he's bringing me to you. He said a man named Rick was coming to kill me. Are you at home? Where are you now?"

Prescott interrupted. "Excuse me." He pulled the phone away and took it off speaker. "Okay, old home days are over."

In the state of shock, words were failing Sean.

"Prescott, where are you?" he finally demanded. "Is she really all right? Please, I have to know. No games, buddy." He choked back his vulnerability in the situation.

"Buddy? See how far we've come in a matter of minutes? This is going to be so great."

"Prescott, I never had a problem with you. If you deliver Christina to me safely, I will walk away with no issue."

"No issue? Bullshit."

"Prescott, I'm pleading with you," Sean begged. "Please. Tell me where she is. Is she at the safe house? Where can I get her? What do you want?"

"What makes you think I want anything from you? Why would I need anything of yours? What makes you so fucking special, Sean Havens? We were the same!" *Chill. The mission.*

"What's going on? What's this about Rick?"

"Look, Sean. I'm sorry. This whole thing has been a goatrope. Rick was running me as a double and it all went bad. He's been manipulating us both for quite some time. Seems like he had his fingers in your shit from the beginning. I had no idea of half the things that had occurred with Harrison Mann, that whole Silver Star shit. Hey, I'm still not all right in the head, but I've certainly had time to do some thinking and I know there is no way to make things right. Seemed like the least I could do when I learned she was alive and later that your own boss was going to off her. They had leverage over my family. I've done horrible things, and I'm taking ownership of it. I can't believe I was so stupid. So used."

"Prescott, don't fuck with me. This is my wife and kid. You, or someone, took them once from me. It can't happen again."

The door slammed, startling Havens. "What the ..." *Tanya. Crap. She overheard. Not good. What have you gotten yourself into, you idiot?* Sean moved to check the hallway. *Gone. Oh, God. And she has my son.* His mind raced and his heart pulled in multiple directions.

"What?" Draeger demanded from the other end of the phone.

"Nothing. What were you saying?" Sean was growing impatient. Panic was building.

Havens' hands were sticky with blood. He shouldered the phone and washed his hands and gritted through soaping them. He rubbed furiously from the anxiety.

"We can meet you at a halfway point. I've got her, man. You, your wife, your daughter. You can all be a family again."

"This better not be a fucking trap, Prescott."

Havens wrapped his hands with the ripped sheets still on the bathroom floor.

"Let's figure out a spot, and I'll accommodate you so you feel safe. No tricks on my end. Let me find a spot and I'll call you back. Sean, I get how you feel. I'll drop her in a safe place of your choosing if that works better. Let me call back with some suggestions. Draeger, out."

Draeger chambered a round. "This is sooo fun," he said. "You should have seen me a few weeks ago." He whistled. "I was not doing so well."

Christina remained in silent shock. She was devoid of emotion. Flat. Dead.

"Well that went well," he said, winking at Christina.

Chapter 83

Havens rushed from the room, hoping Tanya would still be in the hallway. He called her line. Nothing.

His cell phone battery was near dead.

He needed a toilet again. Instead, he just cursed as he ran down hall. He checked the elevator area and then decided to go down the flight of stairs.

The lobby was near clear. Police were still maintained at the entrance.

"Hey. Did you just see a dark-haired woman leave?" he asked a uniform.

"Shit. Are you okay?" the cop asked, taking him in. "She looked about as messed up as you. She left a few minutes ago. I didn't pay much attention to where she went."

Havens called Tanya again. No luck.

Police were calling to him to get away from the cordoned-off zone.

He called Reilly.

"Dude. Where the fuck are you?" Reilly demanded.

"I found the girl. She was in pretty bad shape."

"Well, good for you. They're all gone, man."

"Who?"

"Everyone who was with you. Cheeto, 8-Ball, the general, Tommy. Gone, man. Fuck!"

"I'm sorry, man. I had no idea it would go down like this."

"Dude, Tommy just had a kid. He was done with this shit. And for what?"

"Man, they stopped the bombing of Wall Street. I don't know what happened up on that floor, but we got the guy who was responsible of the attacks across Asia, Europe. He's dead."

"How did you make it out?"

457

"Long story, but I was wrapped up with the bomber."

"Fuck, man. The losses never end."

"Where are you now?"

"We're in a back area in the Mason hall with the search and rescue team. We can't get up any stairs. Dammit. I can't believe this happened. You coming over to help?"

"I ... um, just got word that my wife is still alive. I'm supposed to go meet the rescue party in Virginia. I'm waiting for a call now."

The line was silent.

"Reilly?"

"Yeah, I'm here, man. Just turned out to be a pretty happy ending for you. Save the world, save yourself, go home to see your wife and kids. We'll clean up your shit."

Havens held his tongue.

"Man, that was outta line. I'm sorry. This whole shit. It just. Fuck. You know. There's just so few of us all left that get it. If we don't get killed over there, we get killed over here, or we kill ourselves. If the current administration doesn't want to listen to us or give a fuck about us, we deserve to have our fuck-off payday money, you know? Not to be millionaires, just to pay our bills, go travel to some places where we're not getting killed, and we can buy some drinks now and then for friends, and shit like that. But not to keep dying for things that don't even matter to most Americans."

"But we chose it."

"That's the thing, Havens. And I don't want this to sound harsh, because you've taken more lumps than the rest of us. But ... you're just not one of us. And that's on you. Not us."

It was a tough pill to swallow, but not the first time Havens had heard it.

Reilly laid in, "You always seem to pack up and go home. For all the years I've known you. Man, these fuckin' guys came for you. Just for you. Only because you asked them to. They didn't ask if it was a national security issue. All I had to say was you needed their help and it was going to require some pipehitters. That was all. You know why else?"

"Not sure at this point," Sean said wearily.

"Cause we all miss the call of a righteous war. But not for the man, for each other. For something that matters. These guys paid the ultimate price. For fuckin' *you*, man. And while there are a bunch of your brothers somewhere in that building, you go after a fucking chick. Forget about you weakening our combat lethality at the time, you turned your back on the guys to the left and right of you. Total unit cohesion disruption of our tuned machine. I don't want to get personal, but ten to one odds says you banged her or have feelings for her."

"She was my partner. She was working the mission. She needed help."

"Preach it to the Secretary of Defense. If that doesn't solidify the woman warrior debate, I don't know what does. Your brothers were working the mission, too. More than one of them. You just don't seem as committed to us as we are to you. That's the brotherhood. Man, I love you, but you treat us like … like fucking cousins sometimes. I'm fuckin' sorry, but that's just how I feel right now."

"I get it," Sean said, his voice dripping with regret.

"You know, we all get fucked up when we come back home and shit's all normal around us. It's too quiet. The shit that normal people chase is the stuff that we know doesn't matter once you've seen war. That's what *does* make you one of us. But the fact that you can always walk away like you're better than us or have more important shit to do, that's what I don't get. Dude, I gotta go. I'll take care of the guys. Who should I call about arrangements?"

"Um, I'll have to let you know."

"Fuck, Havens. Fuck. That's the shit I'm talking about, man." Reilly hung up. *Fucking used us, Brother. Fuck you.*

459

Havens stood alone.

The pandemonium all around him seemed distant. Muffled voices, high-pitched sirens, flashing lights. It was a world away.

Sean Havens just stared at the building, reflecting on a success that cost all those around him—again. Was it a success? What did he stop? Reilly was right. He lost friends who only stopped a single tactical event. It was an event that could be replicated tomorrow with another committed adversary and a new target and resources. The key was in finding and killing whomever was pulling the strings and discovering why those people were willing to take innocent lives, disrupt nations, rig elections.

All the enemies that Havens and his friends could kill by sacrificing their own lives didn't matter if the power players weren't willing to pay the ultimate price as well.

This is why I run. The sacrifices never matter. No matter how much I hope they will. Am I weak? Stupid?

Havens looked down at his watch. He resented that it wasn't the Smith & Bradley Rogue that his wife gave him. He resented that he took it off for the shackle of the government again.

It was a moment of clarity. Sean Havens knew two things for sure in that instant. One, he was addicted to the rush that dangerous conflict fed his soul. That's why he left all things normal. That's why he left his family. But he knew another thing. He loved his wife. He loved his daughter. And that was why he always came back, and for them he was willing to get clean from war.

But Tanya. Do I love her or did I miss Christina? I was OK putting Christina behind after a year. I can't think about not seeing Tanya again. Or my son ... God, I have a son.

Tanya was a woman who cared about Sean amongst the morass of backstabbing, conspiracy shit, and, above all, she gave him a reprieve from the feeling of loneliness and flat emotion that he felt as he sought a pleasure he once felt in his life but couldn't get back.

Was it war or love that he loved most?

I owe it to Christina. Not many people get second chances. I can do things better. I know I can. I have to. And if Prescott Draeger, the CIA, who the fuck ever, are playing a trick, god help them. I'll kill them all. I'm coming and I'm leaving this all behind for you and Maggie. But I can't just forget about Tanya. And I owe it to my son to be there.

The light-headedness was crawling down to his limbs, numbing along the course. He tried in vain to remember where his car was. Where star-like sparkles once were in his eyes, blackness overcame the light. Havens folded to the ground.

The former Mossad officer stood in the shadows watching Sean Havens claw desperately at the brick wall for leverage. "It's him."

Epilogue

"It looks like the derivative settlements are all deposited in the accounts. Futures options from our global portfolios are there, too. Start moving the funds to the proper campaign account donations. This administration is toast. We can take it all in full force."

"Any blow back from the Panama Papers? Your timing was brilliant."

"None. Our interests were compartmented and the disclosure to media sent a message to the various power players that was received loud and clear. Russia and China, in particular. I can't say they are all too pleased, but recognize our reach and power isn't a bluff. Putin's friends, the Pakistanis, and the Mubarak affiliates are scrambling."

"Fine. Fine job. And for the election, where are our majorities?"

"Senate. House. Agencies. Defense. Regulatory entities. DOJ. We got it all. Anything we missed?"

"None. Even if the current candidates shift and go independent, we have it covered with delegates. The Yale boys will soon realize they're surrounded. Powerless. It could put them in a spot where they push back with nothing to lose. They could try to pass things through before the election. The Commander in Chief isn't playing ball. It could be a loophole, so, with your permission, we are prepared to take the next step to better position the vice president for the election."

"Do you have what you need?"

"We have made an arrangement for one of our assets to go inside the Agency. We also have an understanding with a man they call 'X' who will be integral to our issue with the President."

"And how did you achieve such an understanding? Or do I want to know?"

"Classic offers they couldn't refuse. Although, at first he resisted and had sent some inflammatory information to another individual electronically."

"Did you obtain that information and eliminate the link?"

"We were able to elicit the information about the person it was sent to. Movements are in place to intercede."

"Will that be a problem?"

"No problem. A man called Sean Havens," PASSPORT confirmed. "We have a solution and it will be taken care of."

Tanya pulled up to her home. She looked in the rearview mirror and tried blinking and wiping away the redness of her eyes. The abrasions and muscle ache were nothing compared to the pain she was feeling now. As she turned off the rumbling Chevy Camaro in the driveway, she noticed the outdoor entry lights were out.

The house was dark except for the bright light emanating from the living room that faced the front of the house.

Tanya Crowe exited the vehicle, popped the trunk and retrieved her bags.

Heavy cloud cover hid the moon and stars. It trapped the cool humidity below. The dampness sent a chill through her body. She shuddered as she came up the walkway.

Sean Havens, you did it to me again.

The neighborhood was quiet. No dogs were barking and the next door neighbors, with all their constant extended houseguests, couldn't be heard shouting as was customary for this time of night. There was the couple, their siblings, and permutations of boyfriends, girlfriends, and others who shacked up. But they had each other. It must feel like a big family.

Tanya heard a deep thump as her son peered through the curtains from the grand picture window and slapped at the glass. He beamed with excitement and ran to the front door to greet his mom.

Tanya always said that her heart was divided. One side empty, and the other that was so full of love for Sam that it worked overtime to fill the other side.

Sam opened the door, smiling from ear to ear. He fumbled with the screen door lock, ready for a big hug.

Tanya's mom walked from the kitchen down the hall to help and wiped her hand on an apron.

"Sam, let me help you with that before you rip the dang door off the hinges," Grandma Crowe chided while greeting her daughter with a smile and a warm sparkle in her eyes. "You're much later than I expected, but welcome home."

"I had to swing by the shop for a few hours and finalize some things from my trip."

Grandma Crowe's smile faded and her eyebrows rose in a flash. She put her hand on Sam, quickly drawing him near.

Tanya froze as she heard the footfalls behind her.

"Hello, Tanya Crowe. And I presume this is Grandma Crowe?"

Tanya twisted to the sound.

In the darkness, she was unable to make out the figure until he stepped closer to the light, spilling across the porch from the house entryway.

"Prescott Draeger," leaked from her mouth in a whispered gasp.

"I'm so glad you remember me. It's been a while since our little romp in Turkey."

END

J.T. PATTEN

Acknowledgments

I choose to publish independently for personal and professional reasons. Doing this "alone" is hardly accurate, however. First and foremost, my wife is extremely supportive of my writing and publication even when the timing is less than ideal, or when my stories are less than ideal, and she is a great sounding board for crazy plot ideas and cover design improvements.

I'm also just figuring this writing thing out. It requires a lot of help for improvement. Thanks to the small military thriller community that takes care of its own authors. Namely, Mark Greaney, Josh Hood, Jack Murphy, Dalton Fury, Brad Taylor, and a number of others who are happy to provide each other, periodic assistance, advice, encouragement, and social media plugs. The thriller sub-genres have more to offer than guns, bullets, and blood. Ryan Steck, The Real Book Spy, does a lot to evangelize the more robust messages79 in these thrillers. Thanks to the posse of Beta readers and fans (of note: Bodo Pfündl, Amy Leavelle, Dylan Simon, and Brian O'Dowd) who provided suggestions and some ideas, edits, or who just asked the right questions. Thanks also to my editor, Laura Underhile; I greatly appreciate your time and assistance, and suggestions of voice improvements. I also appreciate the technical military help to ensure accuracy of helos, ops, and hardware. For this, thanks to Don Bently, Tim, Dave, Dan, the other Dave, the other Dan, and then the other other Dave. And thanks to my old spooky buddies, including author Joe Goldberg, a longtime buddy who still hashes ideas out with me over tacos, brisket, and Diet Cokes.

Oh, and thanks to the vendors who let me beat up their goods before I put them to operational book use: Lalo Tactical footwear, Smith & Bradley watches, and Geigerrig pressurized hydration systems.

If I missed anyone, sorry, I'll catch you next go 'round. More of Sean Havens to come.

Made in the USA
San Bernardino, CA
25 April 2016